THOUGHTS FOR A PORTAL

JEFFREY POOLE

Jeffrey Poole's Epic Fantasy Books
Bakkian Chronicles:
The Prophecy
Insurrection
Amulet of Aria
Disneyland Debacle (short story)
Winter Wonderland (short story)

Tales of Lentari
Lost City
Something Wyverian This Way Comes
A Portal For Your Thoughts
Thoughts For A Portal
Wizard in the Woods
Close Encounters of the Magical Kind
The Hunt for Red Oskorlisk (short story)
May the Fang be With You (Pirates trilogy #1)
The Hammer is Strong with This One (Pirates #2)
These are Not the Stones You're Looking For (Pirates #3)
Blast from the Past

Dragons of Andela
Harness the Fire
Strike the Spark
Clear the Water

Mysteries by J.M. Poole
The Corgi Case Files Series
18 delightful cozy mystery novels featuring corgi
sleuths, Sherlock and Watson

Thoughts For A Portal

Tales of Lentari, Book 4

Jeffrey Poole

Secret Staircase Books

Thoughts For A Portal
Published by Secret Staircase Books, an imprint of
Columbine Publishing Group, LLC
PO Box 416, Angel Fire, NM 87710

Book layout and design by Secret Staircase Books
First Secret Staircase paperback edition: July, 2023
First Secret Staircase e-book edition: July, 2023

* * *

Publisher's Cataloging-in-Publication Data

Poole, Jeffrey
Thoughts For A Portal / by Jeffrey Poole.
p. cm.
ISBN 978-1649141422 (paperback)
ISBN 978-1649141439 (e-book)

1. Lentari (Fictitious location)—Fiction. 2. Epic fantasy fiction
3. Dragons and mythical creatures—Fiction. 4. Time travel—Fiction.
I. Title

Tales of Lentari : Book 4.
Thoughts For A Portal
Poole, Jeffrey, Bakkian Chronicles epic fantasy series.

BISAC : FICTION / Fantasy/Epic.

813/.54

For Giliane —

You're my life, my love, and my inspiration. Every day I thank my lucky stars to have you by my side. Love you always & forever!

Acknowledgments

A small group of people were directly responsible for helping me create this book, and I hereby offer them my eternal thanks.

First and foremost, I need to thank my wife, Giliane. Thanks to her this book was written in only a few months. Many people may not think that writing a book in a few months is an accomplishment, but those who know me will attest to the fact that being able to release more than one book a year is simply amazing.

Next up are my beta readers. They sacrificed time out of their busy schedules to help me polish the story and catch those elusive typos and grammatical problems that always seem to creep into a story no matter how many times you proofread it. Caroline Thaung, Cher Lashley, Caroline Craven, Scott Poe, Jason Harvill, Deb Shapiro, Elizabeth Davis, and Sharon Bobbitt. I'd also like to mention my Secret Staircase readers: Susan Gross, Paula Webb, and Sandra Anderson. Thank you very much, guys! And I must also thank Jamie (Lia) and my mother for also taking a look for me. You guys are the best!

Last, and certainly not least, I have to thank you. The readers. Without you guys Lentari would have stopped with Amulet of Aria (Bakkian Chronicles #3). You guys have kept the series alive and have inspired me to write all kinds of adventures. Thank you from the bottom of my heart!

Table of Contents

Chapter 1 – Up a Creek

Great clouds of mist drifted high into the air, from the nearby waterfall. Standing before the base of the falls were three people, unmoving, not speaking: two men and one girl. After a few moments, Steve sank to the ground and let out a heavy sigh.

"I'm sure she's alright," the second man consoled the first.

Cecil was in his late twenties, had short, neatly combed brown hair, and was impeccably dressed in a long sleeve, albeit dirty, button-down white shirt with black trousers and matching black leather shoes. A banker by trade, he always dressed the part, whether he was behind the counter assisting patrons or relaxing with a book by the fire. This was someone who was more comfortable being inside and certainly didn't belong outdoors, let alone traipsing around outdoors in nineteenth century Lentari.

Steve surveyed his own messy clothing as he tried to

think. This whole thing had started with a request from the Lentarian king to investigate how several villagers had disappeared. With the discovery of a concealed portal, it seemed the answer was found. Except that his wife, Sarah, had vanished into the portal and Steve had jumped in after her. Finding themselves in the American West, more than a hundred years before their own time, was shocking enough (and a little bit cool). And then he met his own great-great-grandfather. Luther was one of the missing Lentarians whose disappearance was under investigation. Both time and place had become vastly distorted.

The bad news was that the portal that brought them together was one-way. There was no way back to Lentari unless someone could obtain a special crystal with which to create the two-way portal known in Steve and Sarah's present-day world. To solve the problem, Sarah teleported Steve to this very waterfall site two days ago. Tracking down a certain dwarf, riding a dragon named Pryllan, exchanging favors for the crystal … Steve was ready to go back and now he and Sarah were separated. And all Steve knew was that he and a banker from the nineteenth century were waiting here with another of the missing villagers, a teen girl with a love of herbs.

"What do you think happened to her?" Lissa timidly asked.

Steve's bloodshot eyes swung over to the teenager. He really could use a few hours of sleep but until he knew what had happened to Sarah, he didn't think he'd be able to.

"I'm not sure. We can't think about that right now."

Cecil's eyebrows shot up. "You're taking this a lot better than I thought you would."

"Oh, trust me, I really am not. I'm panicking inside, okay? Seeing how I can't do anything about that right now, we should instead focus on that which we can."

"And that is?" Cecil pressed.

"Getting out of here and getting our tails back to Idaho."

"How?"

"Let's go talk to Zevern. He's the present-day wizard in R'Tal. He's the one who created the portal that caused this whole mess. Maybe he can create another one for us."

"Zevern? As in Zevern the Magnificent?" Lissa cooed. "I've read about him. He's supposed to be one of the most powerful wizards who ever lived. Are we really going to meet him?"

"*I'm* going to meet him," Steve clarified with a scowl. "You'll get your chance, provided I don't throttle him first."

"Throttle him?" The girl looked over at Cecil. "What does that mean?"

"While I don't know what 'throttle' means, I'm sure we can speculate about its definition. You see, this wizard —"

"Enough, Cecil," Steve cut in. He looked at the young future healer and gave her a fleeting smile. "It means I'll do my best to prevent myself from knocking out his two front teeth."

"Oh. You don't like him?"

"Not one bit."

"Do you know him?"

Steve shook his head. "Not personally, no."

"Then how can you say you don't like someone if you haven't met them yet?"

"It's a long story."

Lissa batted her eyes at him. "Well, it's a long way to the castle."

Steve gave a sidelong glance over at Cecil, who was silently doubled over with laughter. He pointed at a nearby tree, and when Lissa turned to look, Steve reached behind the girl and smacked Cecil on the back of the head.

"Uh, sure. Where shall I start?"

"From the beginning, of course."

Steve swallowed nervously. Where was Pryllan when he needed her? "Mm-hmm. Well, it's like this…"

* * *

"What do you mean you're stuck here?" Kri'Calin demanded the instant they were brought before the Lentarian king in the Great Hall. "Did you not claim your wife was a teleporter?"

"Yes, but —"

"And was she not capable of jumping between worlds?"

"Yes, she can, but —"

"But what? What has happened? And who is this girl?"

Steve hooked an arm through Lissa's and pulled her up to his side. "This is Lissa. She's one of the missing villagers from my time."

"And you found her here? In Lentari? Shouldn't she have been found in your world?"

"You would think, and I would think, but apparently not."

"This makes no sense whatsoever. Zevern assured me his plan was foolproof. That portal, he assured me, would drop whoever used it in another world. It wasn't supposed to drop anyone here in Lentari."

Steve bit his tongue and tried to keep his voice as neutral as possible. "Why don't we ask him? I'd love to run a few things by him."

"Ooooo, I've *so* been looking forward to this!" Lissa squealed excitedly in his ear.

"You're gonna be sorely disappointed," Steve whispered back. "History books have a way of only focusing on a person's strong points. Flaws and weaknesses are seldom recorded for posterity."

"Flaws?" Kri'Calin repeated, overhearing Steve and Lissa's hushed conversation. "Weaknesses? With Zevern you'll find none."

"Then could you please call Mr. Perfect out here? It's high time we got him involved with this mess."

Kri'Calin motioned a young page over. "Inform Zevern his presence is requested in the Great Hall."

The young boy of ten or eleven bowed. "At once, Your Majesty."

After the boy scurried off, the king rose from his seat on the throne and approached Steve. He laid a fatherly hand on his shoulder.

"You fear for your wife. I can see it in your face."

Steve nodded glumly. "She wouldn't miss a rendezvous. She knew the only way we could return home was by her jhorun. Something has happened to her and I can only assume it's bad. I have to get back. That's why we came to you. I can only hope that your faith in your wizard isn't as misplaced as I think it is."

"Do you have a particular aversion to wizards?"

"Lately I do," Steve admitted. "The wizard from my time is powerful, but he's a little unorthodox at times. Then there's this other wizard that gets his kicks out of messing with people. He once put my mind in a dragon's body and my wife's in mine."

The king managed to hide his smile. "You don't say? That must have been an experience."

"While it was fun to be a dragon for a little while, I wouldn't recommend trying it anytime soon."

Kri'Calin nodded. "Acknowledged."

Ten minutes later, a loud fanfare of trumpets caused both Steve and the king to jump.

"I really need to speak with Zevern about that," the king muttered. "His arrival into a room should not be more grandiose than my own."

Steve turned to see two trumpeters, three serving boys, and a half dozen men ranging in age from early twenties to mid-sixties sweep into the room and flutter about. The two trumpeters raised their horns to their lips and prepared to let out another blast. Thankfully the king was quicker.

"That will be quite enough, thank you."

The trumpets were lowered and tucked back under the players' left arms.

"Why don't I hear anything?" a pompous voice called out. "Where are my trumpets?"

"Zevern, enough."

The king's voice was sharp and commanding. The gaggle of assistants parted and Steve got his first look at the resident wizard.

Zevern was in his early fifties, almost completely bald except for a thin tuft of flaming red hair under each ear, and was as wide as he was tall. The wizard was wearing the most garish orange robes Steve had ever seen, complete with tufted orange slippers that curved up at the toes.

"Why don't they just carry him in on a litter?" Steve grumbled under his breath, unimpressed.

The king leaned close. "I doubt his assistants could lift him. Besides, I wouldn't let him."

Steve snorted.

Zevern waddled up to Kri'Calin's throne and managed a small bow. His small, beady eyes gave Steve a quick once over and, seeing nothing worth his attention in the tall stranger, turned back to the king.

"You sent for me, Your Majesty? How may I serve you today?"

"Perhaps you can explain something for me, Zevern."

The wizard gave another deep bow, almost tipping over in the process. "I would be delighted, Your Majesty."

The king glanced around at the many people standing stiffly at attention and dismissed them all with a wave of his hand. Once the Great Hall was empty, save a few soldiers quietly standing guard nearby, Kri'Calin continued. "The portal you created for me. In Capily. Do you remember it?"

A wide grin split the wizard's rotund face. "Of course, I do, Your Majesty. It was some of my finest work."

"Yes, you told me that then. Now, I'm not so sure."

Zevern's smile faltered. "Your Majesty, you doubt my work? It sent that soldier off to another world, did it not?"

The king eyed Steve and nodded his head. Steve sent the wizard a scathing stare and stepped up next to him. Zevern didn't bother acknowledging his presence.

"What world?" Steve asked in the most mocking tone he could come up with. "What time? Do you even know what happened to the people that went through it?"

"Your Majesty, who is this peasant? I would prefer if he waits outside, like the other commoners."

The king glanced around the room again. There were nearly a dozen soldiers standing guard, spaced evenly all around the perimeter of the Great Hall. "We will continue this in the Antechamber."

Zevern's smug smile returned. "An excellent idea, Your Majesty."

Steve motioned for Cecil and Lissa to follow him into

the nearby room. Zevern scowled as he noticed he was being followed.

"Wait outside, peasant."

"No," Kri'Calin contradicted. "Those three people will be joining us."

"Whatever for, Your Majesty?"

"All in due time. Guards, you are dismissed. See to it we are not disturbed."

Once the door was closed, the king briskly rubbed his hands together and looked over at the cold hearth. He looked up at Steve and inclined his head toward the fireplace. "Would you?"

"Fear not," Zevern cut in. "I can light it in just a few moments."

Still glaring at the arrogant wizard, Steve lifted his left arm and released a jet of fire. The fireball slammed into the stacked logs and a few seconds later a blazing fire was crackling merrily away. The look of surprise on Zevern's face was priceless.

"How did you do that? The Antechamber prevents all but the strongest from using their jhorun in here. Who are you?"

Steve ignited both hands and took a few menacing steps toward the portly wizard. "I'm someone who doesn't like you very much."

Cecil and Lissa put a hand on each of Steve's shoulders and pulled him away from Zevern, who had started trembling. The king looked at the burning logs in the fireplace and nodded. "Well, that answers that. I do hope you'll forgive me for testing you, Steve."

Steve shrugged. "It's not the first time I've done that in here."

The king took a seat behind his desk and indicated the others should sit, too.

"You know this man?" Zevern sputtered, as he sank down on the chair closest to the king. He turned and pretended to notice Cecil and Lissa for the first time. "Who are these two? What are they doing here?"

"They're with me," Steve coldly informed him. "Eyes

over here, sport. You're dealing with me now."

Zevern nervously cleared his throat. After a few moments, his courage returned and his nose lifted. His mouth opened, ready to spew an angry retort, but he was cut off before he could get a single word out.

"My name is Steve. That's Cecil over there and the girl is Lissa. Lissa, like me, is not from this time. Our time is more than a hundred twenty years from now. She, and several other villagers, fell through your damn portal and were transported here. My own wife fell through and I went in after her. With me so far?"

"What are you talking about, 'my portal'? That's absurd. I haven't created any public portals."

"The king asked you to create a portal so that a soldier by the name of Luther could travel to another world and link it to here. It was all in the name of a prophecy the king had learned about." Steve turned to look at the king. "Am I right?"

Kri'Calin nodded. "You are correct."

"If you're referring to my one-of-a-kind *interdimensional* portal," Zevern haughtily told him, "then you're too late. That portal no longer exists. Portals of that magnitude require great skill and power to be called into being. I won't bore you with the specifics, dear boy, but believe me when I say that it is impossible for anyone else to use that particular portal."

Anger flared. The flames on Steve's hands, already burning hotter than normal, snaked up his arms and engulfed his chest.

"Listen to me carefully, pal. That portal is still active in my time. People have been falling through it for years. It's northeast of Capily, just inside the forest, within sight of the ocean. The anomaly, as the people from my time call it, is floating several inches off the ground and is lying horizontally. It's three, maybe four feet in diameter. Is any of this ringing a bell?"

Zevern's eyes had widened. His shocked eyes found the king's. Searching for sympathy, and not finding a single bit, the wizard turned back to Steve. "I, er, that's…"

"I'm not done. Not only is your portal responsible for the

disappearance of Lentari's own villagers, it also takes them back through time. What's worse, the time isn't consistent. The amount of time between my wife falling through the portal and when I followed her through had to be no more than thirty seconds, yet she arrived a full six months before I did. Did you catch that? My wife had to live in my home world for six months before I arrived. I should also tell you that in my world, over a hundred years ago, it was a very dangerous place to live. It still is."

Zevern's mouth kept opening and closing, all without him uttering a single syllable. Steve still wasn't finished.

"That soldier? The one you so carelessly sent through without knowing what was on the other side? That's my great-great-grandfather. He's been there now for over three years."

Zevern's face drained of color. "You are a descendant of Luther's?"

"Yes, I am."

"Then it worked!"

"Just a second there, pal. It hasn't worked yet. Something happened to Luther's athe crystal. The portal is powerless. Cecil and I came here to get another."

Zevern suddenly smiled. He took a breath and opened his mouth.

"Before you say it's impossible," Steve interrupted, "and ask me how we got here if Luther's portal isn't working, I'll add that my wife is a teleporter. She can jump between worlds. And no, don't tell me it's impossible. It clearly isn't. She brought Cecil and me over here to get Luther another athe crystal so his mission can be completed and I'll be able to use the portal in the future. Until that happens, then my own future is in jeopardy."

"Your wife ... she's a teleporter who can teleport between your world and Lentari? That's how you arrived here?"

Steve nodded. "Yes."

"And she will return you to your world?"

"I wish she could, but she hasn't. We were supposed to meet up with her last night, only she never showed. Something has happened to her."

Zevern nervously cleared his throat. "That's, ahh, a fine

predicament, if you ask me."

Steve crossed his arms over his chest. "I wasn't."

"What would you have me do?"

"You created the portal that caused this whole mess. You can create another one, only this time do it right. Get us back to my world. As long as you're at it, you can start working on creating a portal which will return us to our own time. Did you get all that? Perhaps you ought to write it down."

Zevern looked helplessly at the king.

"He's not like anything I had pictured," Steve heard Lissa whisper to Cecil.

"They never are," Cecil whispered back.

The king rose from his throne. "Well, Zevern? You heard him. We have to return him to his home. Create another portal. A stable one this time."

Zevern's round face fell as he stared at the floor. He mumbled something but it was so soft no one heard him.

"Speak up," the king commanded.

"I can't," Zevern whispered. Beads of sweat were trickling down his pudgy face. "I didn't have any idea how to create a portal which would link to another world, so I, er, I … I guessed."

The king's face darkened with rage. "You guessed? Are you jesting? You sent one of our men through a portal that you haphazardly created? This pleases me not, wizard."

"Didn't you take notes?" Steve asked, frowning. "Can't you recreate what you did the first time?"

Zevern sadly shook his head. "No, I cannot. Nothing I tried worked. I grew desperate. I used every potion at my disposal. I even tried brewing a few new ones. When it became apparent that I could not alter the portal's destination from Lentari then…"

"Then what?" the king snapped, after Zevern trailed off.

"Then I tried casting some spells."

"Which ones?" Kri'Calin asked. He slid a bottle of ink over to the wizard and then offered him a quill. "Write them down."

Zevern shied away from the ink bottle as though it was poisonous. Steve shook his head and scowled at the wizard.

"You're either unable or unwilling to write down which spells you used. I'm guessing it's the former, isn't it?"

When Zevern didn't respond, the king groaned aloud. "You can't remember which spells you've cast? I've known you to be quirky, Zevern, but never inept. Wizards be damned! I've boasted about you to the king of Ylani, you imbecile."

Zevern sat up straight in his chair. "I am no imbecile, Your Majesty. It shames me to think this is what you believe."

"Prove me wrong. Return these three home."

Zevern sadly shook his head. "I can do many things, Your Majesty. However, it became quite clear to me that I am no gatekeeper. That was Luther's job. It shames me to say this, but I used everything at my disposal to link a portal to another world. While I agree it wasn't very professional, I feel obligated to point out that I did succeed."

"Aye, you did," the king agreed. Then he frowned. "But not well. When this is all over, you and I are going to sit down and have a private discussion. And before you ask, no, you will not enjoy it."

Zevern's face fell.

"What do we do now?" Cecil asked. "It certainly doesn't sound like we will be able to return home after all."

Steve cast a final scowl in Zevern's direction before he turned back to Cecil. "Sarah and I haven't come this far to fail now. There's a way, we have to find it. I say we hold a brainstorming session. Let's hear some ideas, no matter how preposterous you think they might sound. Agreed?"

Kri'Calin nodded. "Agreed."

Cecil and Lissa both nodded. Zevern remained motionless. The only thing missing, Steve wryly noted, was the chirp of a cricket. He leaned forward and rested his elbows on the king's desk, eliciting a frown from the king.

"Okay, so creating another portal is out. What about teleporting? Sarah can do it. Maybe there's someone else who can?"

"There are five known teleporters in the kingdom," the king informed him. "All five can barely teleport themselves from one village to another without completely exhausting them."

"What about using a jorii?" Steve asked.

"What's a jorii?" Cecil wanted to know.

Steve curled his index finger against his thumb and held it up so Cecil could see. "It's a smoke-colored marble, about this big. It'll take a person's jhorun and amplify it to incredibly high levels. It should have the power to make a weak teleporter much stronger. Come to think of it, I should have mentioned that Luther has requested another jorii as well. I told him we'd pass along his request."

Cecil nodded enthusiastically. "I don't care what kind of marble it is. If it'll get us home then I'm all for it. Can you give us several of those marbles?"

Kri'Calin frowned. "I gave our last one to Luther."

It was Steve's turn to groan aloud. "You're out of joriis? Can't you get some more? Where do you get them, anyway?"

The king kept his face neutral as he stared at the fire thrower. "Do you mean to tell me that the king from your time has never told you where the joriis come from?"

Steve stared suspiciously at Kri'Calin. "No. I'll bite. Where do you get them?"

"You are apparently trusted by the royal family in your time."

Steve nodded eagerly. "You could say that."

"And they could clearly keep a secret."

Steve shrugged. "They obviously did."

"Good. Then so can I."

"What? Excuse me? You can't just tease me like that and then not tell me."

"I can and I just did."

"Fine. You're out of joriis. So that won't work. Who else has a suggestion? Lissa, got any ideas?"

The teenager shook her head, sending her brown tresses flying about. "About how to get back home? No, I'm sorry. Besides, I don't want to go to your world."

"You can't stay here," Steve told the stubborn girl. "This isn't your time. You want to get home? You're going to have to go to ours first so we can figure out how to jump back, er, forward to our correct time. If you stay here, that isn't going to happen."

Cecil hesitantly raised a hand into the air. Steve noticed it first.

"Dude, I told you we're not in school. You don't have to keep doing that. What's on your mind?"

Cecil pointed at the leather satchel still strapped securely in place across Steve's chest. "That's the crystal Luther needs, correct?"

Everyone seated around the desk turned to look down at the leather bag Steve was carrying. "That's right. Why do you ask?"

"If Luther gets that, could he not get the portal working by himself?"

Steve sighed. "That's what we're trying to figure out, Cecil. We need to get this in Luther's hands; however, as you can see, we have no idea how."

"We know there isn't a way to create a portal big enough for us to return home, correct? What about a little one? Could there be a way to get only that bag to him?"

The king opened his mouth to give the foreigner a negative answer, when he hesitated. He looked at Steve, who had also paused in mid-sentence. Together they turned to look at Zevern. The wizard had returned his gaze to the marble floor inside the Antechamber and kept it there.

"Is that possible?" Kri'Calin asked.

Zevern mumbled something, but again it was so soft that no one heard him.

"I grow tired of this, wizard," the king grumbled. "If you have anything to say, then please do so at a volume the rest of us can hear. It strikes me as odd that you've suddenly become so soft-spoken when you enjoy that damnable trumpeting as much as you do."

"I am not familiar with any method to get that crystal to another world," Zevern finally admitted. "I may have, uh, over exaggerated my talents a little when it comes to traveling between worlds."

"Be that as it may," Steve said in a loud voice, "I do like Cecil's suggestion."

Cecil beamed. "You do?"

"Yes. You're right. You suggested a very plausible

scenario. If we can get the crystal to Luther, he should be able to activate his portal and link it to the castle's, thereby completing his mission. He personally won't be able to use it but at least we can."

"Why won't he be able to use it?" the king inquired.

"It was something I learned a long time ago," Steve explained. "It was part of the prophecy. To make certain Luther was properly motivated, the portal was specifically programmed to not allow Luther home. Now, I don't know if he'll be able to activate it from his end, but we should at least be able to use it to return home."

Lissa suddenly fidgeted in her chair and tapped Steve on his arm, drawing his attention.

"What is it, Lissa? Do you have something to add?"

The girl nodded. She gave the king a shy smile before turning back to Steve. "Could we use a dennai?"

Steve blinked a few times. "Could we use a what? A deny? What's that?"

The king nodded thoughtfully as he sat back in his chair. "A dennai is a small portal used to transfer emergency communiqués between villages in times of crisis. They are for militia use only. Exactly how do you know about that, young lady?"

Lissa's cheeks flushed bright red. "I dated a boy whose brother is a soldier. He told me about them."

Steve looked over at the king. "A small portal? I didn't know those existed."

"How does a small portal help us?" Cecil wanted to know.

Growing more animated, Lissa began gesturing with her hands as she spoke. "A dennai uses much less power than a full-size portal. It would be far easier to change the destination on something no bigger than this," Lissa held up her hands and touched her fingertips together to form a circle.

Steve ran his fingers along the leather pouch he was wearing and felt the shape of the portal power crystal concealed within. Yes, it was small enough to fit through an opening that tiny. However, that didn't resolve the original problem.

"How would we change the dennai's destination?" Steve

asked. "Wouldn't we run into the same problem? There's no way to link it to another world."

"A gatekeeper could do it," the teenager insisted.

"If we had a gatekeeper, we could just use them to modify an existing portal and presto: problem solved. We wouldn't need this dennai thingamajig. However, we don't, so that puts us back in the same boat as we were before."

"Are there any other gatekeepers?" Cecil asked, as he turned to the king.

"A gatekeeper has some of the rarest jhorun ever recorded," the king acknowledged. "We have only known about a select few of them. Luther was the only one I have ever met."

Steve's face lit up and he whooped aloud. He turned to Lissa and gave her a hug. "That's it! Lissa, you're a genius!"

"I am?"

Steve turned to Kri'Calin. "We have to find Luther's family. He told me a few days ago that his jhorun was exceedingly rare, but it ran in his family. If we can find a family member, they might have the same jhorun and could be strong enough to tweak a teeny tiny portal to drop this crystal on my world."

The king had kept his expression blank as he listened to Steve's suggestion. "That is a good idea," Kri'Calin admitted.

Steve frowned. "Then why aren't you smiling?"

"Because Luther doesn't have any family. That's why he volunteered for the mission."

"No family? None at all?"

The king motioned for one of the guards. "Send for Captain Sauer."

The guard nodded and left the room.

"The captain knows every detail about the men serving under him. If Luther has any living relatives, he would know of it."

Five minutes later, the door to the Antechamber opened to admit the captain of the guards. Sauer moved with the assurance of someone confident in his abilities and comfortable with his place in life. His uniform was spotless, his boots polished, and his medals lined up in two neat rows on the upper left portion of his chest. He came to a stop before the king and bowed.

"You sent for me, Your Majesty?" Sauer finally glanced at the people sitting before the king's desk, noticed Steve staring back at him, and raised an eyebrow. "Shouldn't you be back in your own world by now?"

Steve shook his head. "Don't get me started, man."

The king coughed. "Captain, we need some information about Luther."

"What can I tell you, Your Majesty?"

"Luther's family. Does he have any living members left?"

Captain Sauer thought a moment. "His parents died before his fifth birthday. He was raised by his paternal uncle."

"Does the uncle live nearby?" Steve hopefully asked. "We need his help."

"Luther's uncle passed away three years ago."

"Does he have any cousins? Aunts? Grandparents?"

"No cousins, no aunts," Sauer answered, shaking his head. "No grandparents."

"No one at all?"

Captain Sauer shrugged. "That's why he volunteered for this mission. He had no other ties in Lentari to keep him here."

"So, he truly has no family," Cecil remarked. He ran a hand through his short hair. "I thought he was just trying to distance himself from them, like there had been some type of disagreement or something."

"Now you know," Sauer told him. He looked at the others. "Why do you want to know, if I may ask?"

"We were hoping he'd have a family member or two who might be willing to help us out. Sounds like my idea is a bust."

The captain nodded. "Indeed, unless you're adept at tracking down missing people."

The room fell silent.

"There *is* someone else?" the king asked, genuinely curious. "Who?"

"Luther's sister. She disappeared at the beginning of the year, never to be heard from again."

Steve let out the breath he hadn't realized he'd been holding. "That's just great. Let me guess. She fell through that damn portal, didn't she? Did she live in Capily?"

"The portal hadn't been created then," Zevern reminded everyone. "If the girl is missing, then it wasn't due to my portal."

"This time, anyway," Steve muttered as he shot another dark look at the wizard. Zevern promptly fell silent and returned his gaze to the marbled floor.

"It was the loss of his sister," Sauer explained, "that prompted him to reconsider the mission to another world. You see, I was about to promote him to lieutenant, but after his sister disappeared, he became despondent and unmotivated. Then one day he approached me and asked if anyone had volunteered for the mission to the other world. I said there hadn't. He volunteered. It was the first time in months that I saw him regain the spark of life that I had seen and admired in him so many times before."

"How long did he search?" Lissa's soft voice asked. "How long did he look for his sister?"

"I gave him an extended leave of absence," the captain explained. "He spent every waking second of those two months looking for some signs of her whereabouts. I had to dispatch several troops to bring him back."

Kri'Calin pulled several stacks of papers from one of the desk drawers. He started flipping through them. "When was this?" he demanded. "Which village did she live in?"

"Avin. This would have been early spring."

The king started skimming through the constable reports for the designated time.

"Here we are. Let's see. Avin's constable reported the disappearance of a young woman by the name of Mina. Nineteen years old, unmarried, and working as a bookbinder for the local scribe. No prior criminal history. Her employer said she didn't show for work one day. According to the employer, Mina had never missed a day. An investigation was launched but unable to turn up any evidence of foul play. Surviving family member is listed as Luther, currently enlisted in the king's army."

"Is there any mention about Luther searching for his sister for two months?" Steve asked. "Was he able to turn anything up?"

The king skimmed through another two pages before looking up. "No."

"You're suggesting we try and find a girl that's been missing for nearly six months now?" Cecil asked, incredulous. "That's our only option?"

"It's a long shot," Steve admitted, "but what choice do we have? The longer we stall here, the longer it's going to take to get home. Unless Zevern can create another portal, which by his own admission he can't, then this is our best option."

Kri'Calin motioned another guard over. He whispered something to the guard before returning his attention to the situation at hand. A door opened and closed somewhere behind them.

Steve hooked a thumb behind him. "Where's he off to?"

Almost immediately the guard returned and handed the king something concealed in a canvas drawstring bag. The guard bowed and returned to his station. The king held the bag out to Steve.

"What's this?"

"A dennai. I thought it prudent to give you one should your search be successful."

"How do I work it?"

"There's no point in answering," Captain Sauer told him. "This will eventually be linked to another world so there's no point in trying to explain its present function. The gatekeeper will know what to do."

Steve untied the bag's drawstring and peered inside. What he saw resembled a small pewter version of Sarah's handheld mirror. It had a three-inch handle with a slightly squashed spherical surface that was four inches long at its widest point. Steve pulled the small mirror out of the bag and looked at his reflection.

"Let me get this straight. I get to carry this, which looks like it belongs in a purse, while looking for yet another girl?"

Grinning, Kri'Calin held up another crystal portal key. "And we wish you the best of luck."

Chapter 2 – Directionally Impaired

Do you really think this will work?" Cecil asked, as they trudged through the forest. "Do you think Luther's sister will be able to make that mirror transport the crystal you're carrying all the way to Luther in our world?"

"The question you should be asking," Steve promptly answered, "is, 'do you really think we'll find her?' followed by, 'do you think the sister will have the same jhorun as Luther?'. I don't know, Cecil. We can only hope."

"Avin looks so different!"

Steve and Cecil turned to look back at Lissa, who was lagging behind as they passed dark streets lined with small quiet thatched cottages. Steve shrugged.

"Of course, it's different. Look at the style of the houses. I see simple construction with no more than two windows. The roof of that one looks as though it will collapse at any moment. I felt the same thing when I was walking through my city earlier, Lissa. The buildings were all small wooden structures that looked like they'd collapse if the slightest breeze were to blow on them. Many of them appeared to be held together by spit and glue."

Lissa made a face. "That's disgusting."

"It's a saying. Clearly the people who built those houses were not too worried about building to code."

"To code?" Cecil repeated. "I do not understand."

"Let's just say we weren't too worried about safety concerns back then."

"Ah."

"Are you sure you don't want to head back to the castle?" Steve asked the girl again. "Things could get dangerous out here. I don't want you to get hurt. Either of you."

"What about you?" Lissa countered. "What happens if you get hurt? You'll need me. I'm a healer. Well, I hope to be. One day. Besides, I don't want to stay there. I don't know anyone. You, on the other hand, I know."

"You do? Have we met before?"

"Only by reputation. That's why I think I'd be safer with you."

"You must be very well known in the Lentari of your time," Cecil softly murmured.

Steve nodded. "It's only because of the prophecy. Trust me. It's not as fun as it sounds, Lissa."

"Why not?" the girl inquired. She turned to look back at the eerily quiet village that was slowly being swallowed up by the surrounding trees.

"Everywhere I go people stop me to say hello, or to ask an opinion about something or other. Don't get me wrong, I think it's really nice that the people are so friendly, but I do miss being able to walk outside without getting mobbed. Sometimes I miss my anonymity." Steve offered Lissa a friendly smile. "How are you holding up?"

"It's just a shock," the teenager confided. "I never thought I'd walk through Avin at a time before my grandfather was born."

"Oh, yeah? Imagine meeting your great-great-grandfather in person and having a conversation with him."

Lissa giggled. "That must've been strange, meeting one's

own ancestor. What was he like?"

"He's nice. I think I'm a little more outgoing than he is."

"He has more hair than Steve," Cecil added with a chuckle.

Steve frowned at Cecil. "I keep it this short on purpose. And it's not because my hair is thinning or falling out. It's my own personal preference."

"Then why style it so short?" Cecil asked. "Even the militia at Fort Sherman has longer hair than yours."

"Perhaps it is stylish on his world in his time?" Lissa suggested, rallying to Steve's defense.

Steve smiled at her. "Yes. Exactly. Besides, if I let my hair grow out it becomes curly. I don't like curly hair."

Lissa's hands automatically moved up to run her fingers through her own long curly locks. "You don't?"

Steve cleared his throat. "That's not what I mean. My *wife* has long curly hair, and I love it. I love everything about her. She, uh…"

Lissa flashed him a smile and then wandered off so she could give the plant life further scrutiny.

"I think she likes you," Cecil whispered to him, coming up to walk by his side.

Steve grunted, but didn't say anything. A few minutes later, after walking together in total silence, Cecil cleared his throat. "Avin's constable sure didn't have any additional information for us about Mina's disappearance, did he?"

Steve shook his head. "His report was almost identical to the king's. The constable did say that since there was a living relative, namely Luther, then the house would be left alone."

"What does that tell us?" Cecil asked.

"It tells us that there shouldn't be anyone living in it. We can poke around without bothering anyone. We'll just have to be careful. They live nearly thirty minutes away from town. Chances are there won't be any neighbors nearby, so if a squatter were to break in then they'd have complete privacy to do whatever they wanted."

"Ah. A very good point. I wonder why his family chose to live so far away from town."

"Who knows? Perhaps they liked their privacy? It's hard to say."

"A thirty-minute walk from town is too far, if you ask me. What would happen if AnnaBelle fell ill? What if someone broke into our house? No, there will be no country living for us, thank you very much. Civilized people should live amongst civilized people, that's my motto."

An hour later found them all staring at three sets of footprints that were clearly visible in the soft dirt. Steve groaned. "Whose idea was it to put me in charge of navigation?"

Cecil gave a feeble attempt at a chuckle. "I thought you were joking about your sense of direction."

"Does anyone know which way is south?" Steve asked his two companions. "Perhaps we were angling too far to the west."

The three of them stood up and resumed walking. Lissa looked up to gauge the position of the sun. Then she twisted to her right and pointed back the way they had come. "North is that way."

"Good," Steve nodded, pleased. "We are heading in the right direction."

Cecil pulled Steve to a stop. "Those were our footprints. We're going in circles. We should go back to Avin and try again."

Steve stared at the evergreens completely surrounding them and then up at the distant treetops. He couldn't tell where the sun was, so how could the girl?

"Do you think you could find your way back to Avin?" Steve asked her.

"I'm not going back there just because you think it's too dangerous out here," Lissa promptly informed him. "I'm staying right here."

"I wasn't suggesting you leave. I was going to suggest that you lead the way back to the village and we can try again, this time with someone else calling the shots."

"Calling the shots?"

"Sorry. I'm suggesting we return to Avin and then let someone else try to find Luther's house besides me."

"Oh." Lissa's face brightened. "That sounds good to me. Come on, it should be this way."

She pushed her way past several saplings and headed north. Steve and Cecil were right on her heels. For a quarter of an hour, the two men followed the sprightly girl through the forest, navigating through thick clumps of bushes, listening to descriptions of various plants, and which treatments she'd successfully administered back in Capily. She talked about poultices made from the herb garden she tended behind her father's house. She regaled them about her many adventures exploring the woods while searching for more herbs for her growing pharmacopeia.

One of the village bakers had inadvertently caught a finger in a millstone and had broken it in several places. Not only had Lissa correctly set the fractured bones back into place, but the poultice she had wrapped around the baker's injured hand took the pain away and accelerated the healing process.

"He broke his finger almost three weeks ago," she happily informed them, "and has already started getting some feeling back into it. In a few more weeks, maybe a month or two, he should have full use of his hand."

"You'd give one of our doctors a run for his money," Steve murmured under his breath.

"Simply remarkable," Cecil exclaimed. "You did this all with herbal medicines?"

"What else would I use?" Lissa quizzically asked him.

Cecil and Steve shared a look. "Ah. Your point is taken, miss. You're going to make a fine healer some day."

Lissa beamed her pleasure at him.

"What do you mean *going to*?" Steve asked. "She's already there, as far as I'm concerned."

Lissa threw her arms around him, hugging him tightly. Suddenly, it looked and felt as though a large cloud passed over them, but a quick check skyward revealed the sky was clear. The forest went eerily quiet. No noise, no rustling insects, not a breath of wind. Steve noticed they were standing before a section of the woods that he was absolutely certain they hadn't passed before. The trees had darkened, almost as if scorched by dragon fire. They stood so close together that only scattered sunbeams made it through the canopy. The three companions nervously looked at each other.

"I don't like the look of this," Steve said to no one in particular. "I do believe we made another wrong turn somewhere."

"I'll second that," Cecil added.

"I'm certain Avin is not too far from the other side," Lissa told them, pointing at the dark woods. "Hopefully it isn't too bad. I might find some rare herbs in there."

"If you do, then you'll have to leave them be," Steve informed her, with a frown.

Lissa's young face showed her disapproval. "Why?"

"You don't want to do anything that could interfere with the future. What if you find a rare plant and you harvest it, not knowing that perhaps it was the last of its kind?"

"That's all the more reason to harvest it," Lissa answered. "We would need to preserve it."

"What if by preserving it you prevent the plant from being pollinated? What if it was going to spread its seeds and was due to repopulate itself, only now it can't? We must think of the repercussions."

Lissa's confident smile faded. "That makes sense. Very well. I won't harvest anything."

"Good. Now, everyone stick close. I don't trust this area."

Steve stepped up to the edge of the black trees and ignited both hands. He signaled the others to keep quiet and to follow his lead, only to have Lissa promptly push by him to resume walking out in front.

"What are you doing?" Steve hissed. "Get back here!"

"If we follow you, we'll get lost again," Lissa told him as she picked her way around several fallen trees.

"Like you're doing any better," Steve grumbled as he moved to follow the girl.

Lissa had just pushed her way past some dense moss-covered shrubs and disappeared from sight when they heard her let out a yelp of surprise.

"Lissa!" Steve called out. He eyed the surrounding vegetation and let both hands snuff out. Darkness threatened to envelope them. He nudged Cecil. "We need to move. Hurry!"

"Why did you extinguish your hands?"

Steve shoved Cecil through the brush. "Because I don't want to accidentally light anything on fire. Now quit talking and hurry up!"

"Hang on, Lissa!" Cecil shouted, as he tried to protect his face from the brambles. "We're coming!"

There was no answer. Mimicking Lissa, Cecil covered his face and barreled through the thick foliage, with Steve right on his heels.

Prickly thorns and briars scratched at their clothes and skin as they forged a path through the thick shrubs, anxious to see what had befallen Lissa. Steve heard Cecil give an alarmed shout and then fall silent. Cursing, Steve practically leapt forward and prepared to ignite his hands, expecting the worst.

The ground disappeared. He flailed his arms as he plunged straight down into a dark hole. A detached part of his brain wondered if a spell had conjured the pit. He gasped with alarm, then something collided with his head and the world winked out.

* * *

He didn't know how long he had been unconscious. He was dizzy, nauseated, and had a monster of a headache. He couldn't see a thing. Was it pitch black? Was he wearing some kind of blindfold? He tried to rise to his knees but cracked the top of his head on something directly above him. He began swaying harder.

The pain from the blow helped clear his head. He waited a few moments then tried again. He opened his eyes.

Nothing.

Then, however, he felt the pressure of something covering his eyes. So, he was blindfolded after all. He tried to remove the blindfold but discovered his wrists were bound tightly behind his back. His knees were hurting, pinned beneath him, like he was sitting on them. He shifted his weight to his right hip to slide his legs out from under him.

His legs were bound, too.

I am not going through this again, Steve thought crossly, remembering, years ago, when he had been taken prisoner by a band of thugs. He focused on his blindfold and ordered his jhorun to burn it off his head. After a few seconds he could smell something foul. He jerked his head to the right and felt the blindfold fall away. He slowly opened his eyes and took stock of his surroundings.

He was in an underground cavern. Jagged stalactites hung across the slightly domed ceiling. The red glow of a fire shone to his right. He was suspended six or seven feet from the ground in a small, square cage. No wonder he felt dizzy.

Steve turned to his right and saw another hanging cage. Cecil. His friend wasn't moving.

What about Lissa?

Steve craned his neck and checked the area. There were no more cages on his left, but on his right, he could see a long line of the hanging pens on a direct path toward the red glow of the fire. From his vantage point he couldn't tell if anyone, other than Cecil, was in the other cages.

Steve flexed his arms and felt the leather cord dig into his wrists. A quick blast of fire incinerated his bonds. His hands were free! He reached behind his back to reach the ropes around his ankles. Moments later he was completely free-- except for the fact he was still in a cage.

Steve squinted at the bars of his cell. They were dull white and covered with gouges, as though someone had attacked them with a chisel. He frowned. The bars weren't metal. The cages were made of bones. How gross! What was holding them together? Steve leaned forward for a closer look. Thick cord held the bones together, perhaps the tendons of whoever contributed the bones. Steve shuddered, realizing the cage stank of rotten meat and feces.

He pulled his shirt up over his nose and got to work, burning through the tendons. As strong as the cords were, they were no match for jets of fire. Thirty seconds later Steve had burned through the tendons holding one of his cage's walls together. The bone wall toppled forward, and he lurched forward and caught the grisly cell wall before it could crash to the floor.

Steve gingerly pulled himself out of his cage and dropped quietly to the ground. He set the bone wall down and carefully picked his way over to Cecil's cage.

"Cecil! Hey man, are you okay?"

There was a groan as the cell shook with Cecil's movements.

"Come on, man, wake up. It's time to leave."

Cecil groaned several more times but didn't awaken. Steve reached up and grabbed the cell with both hands, giving it a stern shake.

"Wake the hell up, dude. We gotta get out of here."

Cecil opened his eyes. "What happened?"

"We fell into some trap. We're getting out of here."

Steve freed his companion as he had freed himself. While Cecil stretched, Steve took the time to look around. They seemed to be in a smaller sub cavern of something much larger. The fire he had noted earlier was coming from the main cavern. Whatever had captured them must be there. Would it/they be waiting for them? They had to be quiet.

"Please help me."

The voice was barely a whisper. It had come from the cell next to Cecil's. However, it wasn't Lissa who had spoken. This voice belonged to a male.

"Who's there?" Steve softly called. He ignited his hands and instructed his jhorun to keep his flames as low as possible.

The third cage wobbled somewhat as the occupant tried to reach a hand through the bars. Only a few fingers made it through.

"Please help me, friend. I don't want to die. I'm next. Please," the voice urged, becoming more desperate, "you have to help me!"

"You're next for what?" Steve wanted to know.

"To be eaten," the soft voice answered.

"Then this is your lucky day, pal," Steve informed him. "No one is getting eaten today."

Steve started working on the bars. Even before he had a suitable opening, the stranger tried squeezing his way through in a frantic attempt to free himself from the cage.

"Hang on," Steve scolded. "You're gonna get burned if

you get too close. Let me…"

The stranger finally succeeded in pushing through the bars and would have taken a nasty fall if Steve and Cecil hadn't caught him. Steve's face wrinkled with disgust, as did Cecil's. The prisoner was filthy. Filthy and smelly, and if he didn't know any better, those stains on his arms were…

"Thank you!" the prisoner cried, as Steve and Cecil hurriedly lowered him to the rocky ground. From his crouched position on the ground, he latched on to Steve's legs and held him in a tight death grip. "You saved my life!"

Steve pried the stranger's hands off his legs and stared in horror at what had transferred to his own hands. The prisoner tried to stand, but his limbs were extremely weakened from his long stay in the cage. He could barely rise to his knees, and even then, he resembled little more than the most pathetic excuse of a human Steve had ever seen. The man groaned miserably.

"Your body is going to take some time to recover its mobility," Cecil told him.

Bright light briefly illuminated the cavern. Cecil turned to see Steve burn off the excrement that had been transferred to his arms, legs, and chest. Cecil approached and spread his arms and legs, reminiscent of Da Vinci's Vitruvian Man.

"Here. Do me, too."

"That's wrong on so many levels," Steve muttered. He doused his flames, satisfied he had burned off all traces of the stranger's feces. He laid a hand on Cecil's shoulder and repeated the order, but this time to focus on his companion. His jhorun complied.

"That is so weird," Cecil remarked, amazed, as he stared at the dancing flames twisting about his body as it searched for more things to burn.

Once Cecil was clean, Steve turned his attention to the stranger, who was still unsuccessfully trying to stand up straight.

"Who are you?" Steve asked him. "How long have you been here?"

"My name is Quinn," the man told them. "By my estimation I have been held prisoner for at least two weeks.

Two of the longest, most miserable weeks of my entire life. I never thought I would get out of that cage."

"And you were to be eaten?" Steve asked, incredulously.

"Look around you," Quinn told them. "There are bones everywhere. Even the cages are made from the remains of their victims."

"Who is responsible for this?" Steve demanded, growing angry.

Quinn slowly sank to the ground and whimpered. Steve cast a worried look around the small cavern.

"That's what I don't understand. They are supposed to be extinct!"

"What is?" Cecil asked, alarmed. "What's supposed to be extinct?"

"Griskis! We've been captured by a tribe of griskis!"

Cecil turned to Steve. "What's a griski?"

"Not a clue."

Quinn stared at the two of them. "How can you not know of the griskis? They were vicious, cannibalistic cousins of the therons that plagued the kingdom for centuries! They were wiped out over a hundred years ago. How can you not know this?"

Steve shrugged. "Well, for starters, I'm not Lentarian."

That one statement silenced their new companion. Quinn stared at Steve, as if noticing him for the first time.

"You don't know who I am? Sorry. Based on that comment about those little demon things, I thought you might have been from my time, too." Steve made a point of looking at his flaming hands and then back down at Quinn. "My name is Steve Miller."

Quinn finally noticed his rescuer's burning appendages. "You're the fire thrower! I know who you are!"

"Then you *are* from his time!" Cecil exclaimed.

Steve risked a glance at Cecil. "That explains these griski things. He doesn't know."

"What don't I know?" Quinn asked. "I've been a schoolmaster for years. I would test my knowledge against anyone's."

"What I mean," Steve corrected, "is that you don't

know about our present predicament. We aren't in our time anymore."

Quinn's eyes blinked with surprise. "What's that supposed to mean?"

"You're one of the villagers who fell through that portal, aren't you?"

"Is that what happened to me? I fell through a portal? I thought I had fallen into a pit and cracked my head. I woke up later and discovered myself surrounded by griskis. I've been in a cage ever since."

"So, you arrived here about two weeks ago, is that it?"

Quinn nodded. He managed to stand another inch or so higher. "That's right. Why? What has happened?"

"You fell through that portal and it transported you a hundred twenty years into the past."

Quinn was silent as he digested Steve's statement. "That does explain the griskis," Quinn decided. "I'm in the past? We are in the past?"

"Yes."

"What are you doing here? Did you fall in, too?"

"No, but my wife did. I followed Sarah in."

"That was noble of you."

"You'd do the same if you were married."

"How did you know I'm not?"

Steve shrugged. "Lucky guess."

"All pleasantries aside," Cecil began, looking off at the distant illuminated cavern, "do you think we can get out of here now? I really don't want to meet these griski creatures in person."

"You don't want to," Quinn agreed.

"I'm not leaving until I find Lissa," Steve vowed. "She's gotta be down here somewhere. I have to find her."

"Who's Lissa?" Quinn wanted to know. He managed to rise a few more inches.

"She's a girl from our time who also fell in."

"Wait. Lissa. Isn't that the name of the constable's daughter?"

"I don't know who her father is. I can tell you that she's from Capily."

"That's where I'm from. She must be the student I'm thinking of. Very gifted with herbs and medicines?"

"That's her," Steve confirmed.

"We cannot allow those infernal creatures to have their way with her."

"What will they do with her?" Cecil asked, confident he knew he wouldn't like the answer.

"They usually will keep any females they like for menial labor. Less chance of being overpowered, I suppose. I've seen one woman tending the cages on several occasions. I've tried talking to her but she won't even look at me. Lissa cannot be allowed to remain in their clutches. We have to find her. We will help you search."

"What happens if they don't like a female?" Steve asked, worriedly.

Quinn's gaze dropped to the ground. Cecil paled.

"I should have known better than to ask that," Steve sighed. He looked at his two companions. "You can help me better if you both get out of here."

"The more eyes we have searching, the more ground we can cover," Quinn argued. "Give me another hour or two and I should be able to get my limbs to fully cooperate with me again."

"Lissa may not have that much time," Steve argued. "If these things are as mean as you say they are, then I need to find her as soon as possible. I can cover more ground and better defend myself if I know I don't have to worry about you two. So, with that being said, do you think you can find the way out?"

Quinn looked around the decrepit cavern and the bone strewn floor. He painfully hobbled, with Cecil's help, over to the closest cavern wall and pointed to several different colored striations in the rock.

"Do you see this? Do you see this layer of rock? This is siltstone. It is a clastic sedimentary rock that forms from silt-sized weathered debris."

Steve nodded. "This helps us how?"

"Siltstone is prevalent all around Capily. We must be close to the surface."

"You're not close to Capily anymore," Steve informed him. "You're about thirty minutes south of Avin."

"Oh. Pah. It's the same for Avin."

"If you say so. You're telling me that you can find your way out by looking at these rocks?"

Quinn eagerly nodded. "Aye. We follow this layer of stone. If it becomes darker then we'll know we're going deeper. We don't want that."

Steve looked at Cecil and pointed at Quinn. "Help him. Get yourselves out of here."

"What if we're pursued?" Cecil asked, alarmed. "What if we're caught?"

"Don't worry," Steve assured his friend. "I'm going to create a diversion that is sure to get their attention. They'll be too preoccupied with me to worry about you. Get going."

Quinn draped an arm around Cecil's shoulder, much to his disgust. They both turned to look at Steve.

"Wait a few minutes then start looking for a way out," Steve instructed, as he pumped jhorun into his hands. The faint flames that had been flickering through his fingers blazed brightly. "I'll draw them off. Be ready."

"We will," Cecil assured him.

Steve turned on his heel and strode toward the opposite end of the cavern, toward the distant fire. He eyed his burning hands and hoped that whatever was about to happen wouldn't deplete his jhorun. Mythrin, his special green-bladed broadsword, was back in the Lentari of the future. It also meant that the special 'recharge' mimet discs were still attached to Mythrin's scabbard. There'd be no recharging his jhorun if it became exhausted. He'd have to be careful.

A loud shriek sounded directly in front of him. There was something there, something small. It was short, no taller than his knee, and walked around on two legs. It hunched over as it walked, appeared to be bowlegged, and had pointed ears. Its skin was a light gray color with dark discolorations visible on its arms, legs, and chest. The only clothing it wore was a simple loin cloth made of what Steve hoped was animal skins. He snorted with amusement. This was a griski? It looked like a miniature version of Igor, servant to Frankenstein.

The griski looked straight at Steve and opened its mouth, displaying row after row of sharp needle-like teeth. It let out a tremendous screech. It waited a few seconds and then let out another. And another.

A second griski appeared next to the first, dressed just as shabbily, only this one had dark brown skin. Then a third appeared, and then a fourth. Within moments over fifty of the little creatures had gathered at the mouth of the main cavern and were staring maliciously at Steve. Several, Steve noted with disgust, had begun salivating. The first griski let out another loud shriek and they all rushed forward, eager to be the first to sink their teeth into his flesh.

Steve brought up both arms and blasted a huge wall of flames directly at the mass of griskis. Over a hundred tiny legs scampered in all directions, with the vast majority reversing course and fleeing back toward the main cavern. Steve followed them, occasionally blasting out a jet of fire when one of the horrid little beings ventured too close.

They fled, screeching shrilly, into their main cavern. Stretching nearly two hundred feet in length and maybe a hundred feet at its widest point, the cavern was decorated much like the smaller one: bones and remnants of prior meals were everywhere.

Steve's eyes started watering from the foul, rotten odor. The closer he moved toward the large fire the stronger the stench became. He'd be lucky to keep his lunch down. A quick glance around this larger cavern revealed the existence of more tunnels, leading in every direction. Three of the openings were closed off by more of the bone bars. Holding pens for the women? Was that where Lissa was being held?

Steve angled off toward the closest sealed tunnel when he saw that the griskis were trying another attempt at overwhelming him with sheer numbers. He blasted several more jets of fire and watched, satisfied, as they fled. Then his smile faded. The little monsters were only retreating far enough to be safely out of range of his fire jets. Every time he turned his back the griskis pressed forward, eager to claim another meal.

"Get back, you ugly little boogers!"

He fired a blast at a small group of griskis who had broken away from the main bunch and were trying to quietly cut him off from the opposite direction. They screeched their indignation and rejoined the others.

He made it to the first of the holding pens and nearly vomited all over the crude bone bars. The smell nearly made him gag.

"Anyone in there?" he hesitantly asked. He generated a small chaser and had it fly into the cell.

He could see bits of broken bone, clumps of matted fur, and several other things he wished he could unsee. Thankfully, there were no signs of Lissa.

"Steve?"

Steve shot several more jets of fire at several bold griskis. They easily jumped out of the way and skittered into the darkness. The griski tribe was out there. It was waiting. Waiting for him to make a mistake.

"Lissa? Is that you?"

"Aye! Thank the wizards! I thought I was done for. Please! Please get me out of here!"

Steve peered inside the second holding pen and thankfully saw Lissa's young tear-stained face peering anxiously back at him. She made a move to grip the bars of her cell but refrained from doing so.

"Yeah, I wouldn't touch that, either," Steve confided as he began burning through the cell door. "I can't begin to tell you how nasty it is."

"Look out!" Lissa shouted. One griski had managed to circle the cavern, undetected, and was silently approaching on Steve's right.

He instantly blasted a jet from his right hand, but the griski had already moved to a safer distance. Steve glared at the noisy little creatures and eyed the one leering at him from the safety of a stalagmite much larger than it was. Steve's eyes narrowed. He had just the thing to wipe that smug grin off the monster's creepy face.

He held out his right hand, palm facing up, and generated a chaser. Instead of throwing it he allowed it to sit in his hand, burning merrily away. Steve quickly squatted and struck the floor of the cavern with the hand holding the chaser. The burning fireball melted into the ground and instantly streaked off, heading straight toward the pompous monster still grinning lecherously at him.

"Let's see you dodge that, Igor," Steve muttered. He watched his ground chaser leave a burning trail of fire as it chased down the now-panicking griski. A few seconds later they heard a shriek of pure agony. "I know I shouldn't gloat, but damn, that felt good," Steve told the girl.

"If you want to do that some more, I'll gladly look the other way," Lissa promised.

Steve finished burning through the last cord and yanked open the door. Lissa threw her arms around him and hugged him tight.

"Thankyouthankyouthankyou," the teenager chanted.

Steve pried her arms off. "Don't thank me yet. Let's get the hell out of here first."

"We can't leave yet! You're not going to believe who I found!"

"Tell me later. Did you see those things back there? They are waiting for me to slip up. I have to keep them in check at all times. We cannot let our guard down."

Steve grabbed her arm and pulled her toward the one tunnel that had wafts of fresh air coming from it. Lissa threw on the brakes and pulled him to a sudden stop.

"We can't leave. Not yet. I found Mina!"

"What? You found Luther's sister? Where is she?"

"I watched her haul away the carcass of a bolger a little while ago."

Steve shook his head. "There's no way she could do that. A bolger is way too big for a simple girl to handle."

"There wasn't much left of it," Lissa admitted with a shudder. "I tried talking to her. I asked her what her name was. She didn't answer me. Not at first. I think she had forgotten how to talk!"

"If you think you can find her, lead the way."

Progress was slow. Steve was forced to walk, backward, away from the main cavern's fire and the encroaching tribe of griskis. He let Lissa be his navigator. He noticed another group of the little monsters break off and rush toward them. One small group quickly became five rapidly moving targets. Steve fired a huge blast to keep the rest of the tribe at bay while he focused on the zigzagging griskis in front of him.

Steve grinned. Perhaps he was going about this the wrong way. He was trying too hard to hit the moving targets. Maybe if he tried to have a little fun at the same time, he'd have better results? Steve eyed the griskis running in no discernible pattern and waited. After three or four seconds of silence he fired five blasts in rapid succession.

The charred remains of five griskis met his eyes. The rest of the tribe fell silent as they stared at the burnt remains. Steve felt a light tap on his shoulder. Lissa was staring at him with huge eyes.

"That was incredible. Where did you learn to do that?"

"Duck Hunt. Years and years of playing that silly game."

Lissa blinked with confusion. "What? What's that?"

"It's not anything you'd know. It's an old game from back home. I got pretty good at it." Steve tapped the side of his head with two fingers. "It's nice to see all those useless skills I picked up from those video games I played are still lurking about up there."

Lissa shook her head, confused.

"Don't worry about it," Steve told her. He blasted a few more errant griskis. "Lead the way. Find Mina so we can get out of here."

Lissa carefully picked her way across the cavern, heading toward another tunnel. As if they sensed an attempted escape, a dozen griskis appeared in front of the tunnel, blocking their way.

"They're in front of us, too!" Lissa shouted, hoping she'd be heard over Steve's constant blasts of fire. When he didn't respond she tried again. "We've got trouble! They're blocking the direction we need to go!"

Steve glanced over. He motioned for Lissa to duck out of the way. The girl dropped to the floor and made herself as flat as possible. Steve fired a blast straight at the tunnel. He managed to hit three of the disgusting monsters while the other nine fled.

"Hurry!" Lissa urged. "They're going to come back!"

Steve backpedaled as quickly as he dared. Wave after wave of the nasty creatures rushed forward. The small monsters were literally throwing themselves at Steve, hoping that one of their number would be able to administer a crippling bite. However, no one liked being blasted by fire, not even the griskis. They ended up spending most of their time making sure they were out of firing range.

As soon as they were in the tunnel, Steve relaxed. Somewhat. A tunnel was much easier to defend than a wide-open cavern. He could see the griskis poke their heads into the tunnel and growl at them. However, as long as the tunnel remained straight, they wouldn't dare try a frontal attack.

Right on cue, the tunnel curved to the left. The mouth of the cavern disappeared from sight. Almost instantly, he could hear many hundreds of little feet rushing toward him. The first set of pointed ears poked around the bend. The griski squealed in fright as it leapt out of the way to avoid being fried to a crisp. It screeched angrily, causing its fellow griskis to join in.

The screeching became deafening in the enclosed tunnel. The griskis almost claimed another victory the instant Steve tried covering his ears. They had been watching, waiting. They swarmed the instant he had appeared disoriented.

Something brushed by his ear. He brought an arm up and was ready to blast whatever it was, point blank. He didn't care. He wanted sunlight. He wanted fresh air. He wanted to see his wife.

It was Lissa. She had torn off a tiny strip of her brown dress and ripped it into several pieces. She held up two of them and then tapped her own ears. Steve smiled and nodded. Ear plugs.

Lissa gently pushed the fabric into his ears, and the terrible screeching became way more manageable. Invigorated, Steve doubled his efforts at driving the bloodthirsty monsters away. He felt another tap on his shoulder. Steve glanced back at Lissa, who looked terrified and was now frantically pointing up the tunnel. Nearly a hundred griskis were packed inside, steadily advancing toward them from both ends of the tunnel.

There was nowhere to flee.

"What are we going to do?" Lissa wailed. "They tricked us into coming in here!"

The griskis, sensing fear and hopelessness emanating from the girl, surged forward, intent on ending this confrontation once and for all.

"Get on my back," Steve ordered.

"What?"

"Get on my back! Like I'm giving you a piggy back ride. Hurry!"

Steve held his arms out at ninety-degree angles and waited for the girl to jump on. As soon as she did, she wrapped her legs around his waist and held tight.

"How is this going to help us?"

"Whatever you see," Steve began, in an oddly calm voice, "whatever you hear, or whatever you feel, the thing I need you to remember is to *not let go*."

Growing more scared of Steve than the griskis, Lissa gulped nervously. "What are you going to do?"

"I can only protect you if you don't let go. This is important. Do you understand?"

"Aye."

Steve stood, motionless, in the middle of the tunnel and watched the two groups of griskis approach from either side. He lowered his hands and waited.

"Whatever you're going to do, do it now!" Lissa pleaded, as she twisted to look at the horde of monsters approaching them from behind.

Steve finally smiled. "I always wanted to do this."

Lissa returned her gaze to the front and leaned her head in close to Steve's. "Do what?"

The flames on Steve's hand began growing. They climbed up his arms and rapidly spread across his chest. Steve felt Lissa gasp in horror as she saw his body go up in flames. He felt her grip around his neck loosen.

"Don't you dare let go!" he snapped. "You'll be burned to a crisp!"

"But what am I —"

"Trust me."

Lissa stared, amazed, as the flames spreading across Steve's body finally hit her skin and, after a second's hesitation, began spreading across her body, too. She watched the flames creep down her arms and snake up her shoulders. Her entire body tingled as she became completely engulfed in flames, just like Steve.

"You are full of surprises," Lissa whispered to him, pressing her burning face next to his. "Did you know you could do this?"

"I did it once before," Steve calmly told her, as he turned on his heel and began striding straight down the tunnel toward the second griski horde. The monsters, in turn, had completely turned about and were fleeing as fast as they could.

"I had lost my temper," Steve continued, using the most casual tone imaginable. "I was trying to install a new dishwasher. That's, er, a device that literally washes dishes. The damn thing kept leaking water, the drain pipe wasn't fitting, and then it wouldn't fit properly under my counter. I didn't realize it at the time but my entire back was lit and burning. Then all of my chest was."

"What did you do?" Lissa asked.

"I ended up having to roll around outside, like they taught us in school. I couldn't let Sarah see me like that. I've since been working on my temper. Well, at least I'm trying to."

They finally came to an intersection. This new tunnel bisected their own, giving them two new possible avenues. However, the griskis were waiting for them. They swarmed in from both sides at the same time. Steve blasted jets of fire in opposite directions. He watched the little creatures shriek horribly at him as they tried to flee his flames.

Suddenly there was a commotion behind them. Steve twisted just enough to cast a look in the opposite direction. Those griskis were also rushing forward to attack. That would be three tunnels attacking at the same time. Steve was out of arms. He risked a glance down each of the two new tunnels. Sure enough he could see the griskis, just out of range, waiting for him to cease his attacks.

"I could use an explosion right about now," Steve angrily told his jhorun.

Evidently his jhorun thought he could handle this predicament on his own. No explosions were forthcoming.

He felt and heard a third blast of fire originate from behind him. He whirled around, expecting to see another person there but all he saw was the griskis rushing away. He resumed blasting the same two tunnels when he felt Lissa shift position on his back. The third blast appeared again. Steve craned his neck to look behind him.

Lissa was shooting out a jet of fire from her own hand!

"How in the world are you doing that?" Steve demanded. "I didn't even know someone else could do that."

"I didn't," Lissa told him between blasts. "You needed help. You're already helping me so I wished I could help you. My hand began to tingle and suddenly I knew I could shoot a blast of fire like you could. You're welcome, by the way."

"I'll give credit where credit is due," Steve told the girl. "That was quick thinking. Thank you."

"How are we going to get out of this?" Lissa asked. "They only retreat far enough to be out of harm's way. The moment we stop, they come rushing back!"

"Are you sure this is the tunnel that Mina went in?"

Lissa nodded between blasts. "Aye. Can't you smell it? That carcass she dragged in here must indicate a disposal site nearby. With all that's going on now, poor Mina must be frightened to death. I'll wager she's hiding."

Steve groaned. He was tiring. Now that a second person was using his jhorun it was depleting him much faster than he was accustomed to. They were going to have to wrap things up fairly quickly.

"How long can you keep this up?" the teenager asked him, as if sensing his thoughts.

"Not much longer. We need to find Mina and fast. Hold on, I have an idea how to buy us a little time."

Steve dropped his arms to his sides and then brought them up, cupping them together as though he was holding a basketball. He generated a huge chaser and flung it down the right-hand tunnel. He did the same for the left. He then eyed the tunnel Lissa had been attacking and did the same for it.

"That should keep them occupied for a few minutes.

Come on, we need to start searching."

"Are you going to douse these flames?"

Steve looked down at his engulfed body and then at Lissa's flaming arm.

"Best to leave it like this for a little bit. It's added incentive for those cretins to leave us alone."

"Where should we look for Mina?" Lissa wondered.

"You said there might be someplace where they dispose of the carcasses? Think you can find it?"

Lissa sniffed the air. The air was already foul but even more so in the left tunnel.

"Let's go that way," she suggested. "It smells really bad."

They headed down the tunnel, following their noses as they tried to find where the griskis dumped that which they didn't want to eat. Steve didn't want to know what fell into that category. They passed several offshoots and hesitated only long enough to verify no one was hiding inside.

They arrived at a subterranean cliff. The stench was so foul that Steve could swear he could see noxious gas rising up from below.

"This has to be it," Steve told the girl. "But I don't see anyone lurking about."

A pebble clattered noisily along the floor. The two of them whirled around. A thin, scrawny girl with matted black hair was standing behind them. She stared at them with wide, unblinking eyes. Her clothes were tattered and torn, and unbelievably filthy. She had sores all over her pale face and arms.

Not wanting to scare the girl, Steve reduced the amount of jhorun fueling the protective blanket of fire encompassing both him and Lissa, until his face and most of his torso appeared.

"Mina?" Steve inquired. "Is your name Mina?"

The girl was silent and motionless for at least ten seconds before she gave a barely perceptible nod.

"I'm a friend of your brother. Would you like to get out of here, Mina? If you'll let us, we'll help you escape. Would you like that?"

The girl nodded again, faster this time.

"Good. Can you lead us back to the surface?"

A look of sheer terror appeared on the girl's face.

"They won't touch you," Steve promised. "Do you know the way out or not?"

The trembling girl gave another slight nod.

"That's the best news I've heard all day. Lead the way. I'll be right behind you. If you see one of those griski things, then drop to the ground and lay flat, okay? Let me handle the rest."

Mina turned and with surprising assuredness, led them down the tunnel, back toward the main cavern.

"I hope you know what you're doing," Steve muttered uneasily. His jhorun was growing more tired by the second. He wouldn't be able to get more than a few blasts out before he'd keel over from sheer exhaustion.

They reached the main cavern as the griskis were regrouping again. They spotted the three humans and screeched their anger. Mina was absolutely terrified. She nervously inched closer to Steve, who waved his fiery arms a few times to get her attention.

"Mina! Which way do we go?"

Mina pointed at the tunnel they had previously headed to, the one with the fresh air coming from it.

"Good. Run. Run!"

Mina sprinted into the new tunnel. Steve struggled to keep up. Even though Lissa didn't weigh more than a ninety pounds soaking wet, she was dead weight on his back. He could feel every jarring footfall with each wheezing breath he took.

"Here they come!" Lissa warned, pointing back the way they had come. "What do you want me to do?"

"Blast 'em!" Steve promptly told her. "Keep them off our backs!"

Lissa fired off a blast, forcing the advancing monsters to reverse course and flee. On and on they ran, up one tunnel, then across a narrow stone bridge spanning a deep chasm, and then up another tunnel. The griskis followed, screeching and snarling their displeasure.

"I don't have many blasts left," Steve wheezed out as they

emerged from the sixth or seventh tunnel Mina had guided them through. He had lost count. "Use my jhorun sparingly."

Steve rounded a bend and almost cried with relief. He could see daylight coming from a narrow opening in the rock wall. He ran up to it and looked through. He could see the woods! Tall evergreen trees were everywhere. The sun was shining. He could hear birds chirping. Everything he had taken for granted outside now appealed to him more than he could ever remember.

Steve turned back to the dark tunnel; his face grim. Griskis were everywhere. They howled with rage at the sight of the sunlight and tried one last time to overtake them. He extinguished the flames that had been protecting the two of them.

"Okay, it's my turn. Lissa, I need you to get down."

"But…"

"No buts. Hurry!"

"But I'm not —"

"Now, Lissa! We're running out of time! You and Mina need to get out of here!"

The girl reluctantly climbed off his back. Steve called up his emergency reserves of jhorun and channeled every drop of power he had left into this final blast. He snorted. It was time to repay their gracious hosts for the wonderful hospitality during their delightful stay underground.

He waited as long as he could. The griskis were now close enough where he could see their blood-red eyes. He risked a glance behind him to see if the girls were still there. They weren't. They were safe! A smug smile appeared.

"A present. From me to you, you little pukes."

Steve's hands sprang open. A concussive blast rivaling that which killed the guur queen all those years ago ripped through the tunnel, incinerating everything in its path. It also knocked Steve through the opening in the wall and out into the woods.

A loud rumbling started and grew progressively louder. Steve painfully rolled to his feet and spat out a few pine needles. He blindly stumbled away from the jagged crack as several large stones broke off from the mountainside and fell dangerously close to where he had been lying. The rumblings grew louder. He risked a glance behind him and saw that the entire hillside was collapsing. Several thousand metric tons of rock came crashing down, as though a giant had mistakenly thought the small mountain was a button and had pushed it.

Steve detected movement in his peripheral vision and automatically moved toward it. He saw a flash of skin as a figure leapt out of the trees and latched onto his back. Two arms fastened around his neck and held on. "Oof! Lissa, what are you doing? Why are you on my back again?"

"I'm sorry, I have to!"

"What? Why?"

"My clothes are gone!"

"You took off your clothes? Why in the world would you do that?"

"I didn't! They must have burned off during the battle. That's not fair! Why didn't your clothes burn off, too?"

"My clothes are immune to the fire," Steve explained as he kept his eyes straight ahead. "My jhorun knows not to burn my clothes."

"So why did they burn mine?"

"I'm not sure," Steve admitted. "I asked my jhorun to protect you the same way it was protecting me."

"So, you are okay with my clothes burning off?"

"Uh … I don't suppose saying I'm sorry would cut it, huh?"

Mina appeared. She actually smiled at him. It was a start, Steve decided.

"Get off my back, Lissa. I'll give you my shirt, okay?"

A loud voice startled all three of them.

"Steve? Lissa? Are you there?"

"It's Cecil!" Lissa squeaked in terror. "I can't let him see me like this!"

"If you're not careful, then I'll see you like this," Steve cautioned. "Stay behind me. Here." He peeled off his shirt and held it out behind his back.

Cecil and Quinn appeared just as Steve's shirt slid into place past Lissa's hips. Cecil eyed the girl's bare legs and spun around to face the other direction. Still somewhat hunched over, Quinn mimicked him.

"Have we, er, interrupted something? Do we need to say something to your wife?"

"Nope," Steve answered. "Why? Because nothing happened. She lost her clothes and I'm just giving her my shirt until we can get her some more, okay?"

Cecil grinned. "She lost her clothes, you say?"

"They were burned off during our escape. Nothing more."

"So you say," Cecil chortled, clearly enjoying Steve's embarrassment.

Steve shook a finger at his companion. "You aren't gonna say a damn thing. Am I right?"

Cecil smiled and held a finger to his lips. "Your secret is safe with me."

"It'd better be, pal."

Chapter 3 — Runs in the Family

The door banged open in the small, three-bedroom cottage, kicking up a thick layer of dust. Four separate people sneezed. They all peered intently at the comfort of the small house and then looked at the sorry condition they were in. Steve was bare chested and doing his best to suck in his gut. Cecil's business attire looked as though it had tangled with a wildcat. Quinn's clothes were so torn and filthy that they barely resembled rags. The only thing Lissa was wearing was Steve's shirt. Thankfully Steve's 3XL tunic fell all the way down to a few inches above the young girl's knees.

"What a quaint house," Quinn observed. "Looks perfectly comfortable."

Steve harrumphed. "Based on what we've just been through it looks like a freakin' Hilton to me."

"What is a hilton?" Cecil wanted to know.

"A nice hotel," Steve translated.

Lissa noticed the home's rightful owner was doubled over in pain. She laid a hand on Mina's thin shoulder and gave her a friendly shake. "You're home. You're safe here."

Mina lifted her head and stared at Lissa with tear-stained eyes. She was rapidly blinking in a feeble attempt to clear her vision. Her gaze darted from one corner of the house to the other. She laid a trembling hand on the door frame and gave a heart wrenching sob. Lissa was instantly sympathetic.

"Here," she told the girl as she draped her arm across Mina's shoulders, "let's get you cleaned up. I think we could all use a bath after that ordeal."

"Is there a place to wash around here?" Quinn asked. He was almost back to walking fully upright. Clearly, the exercise was working wonders on his body. "Somewhere outside? I wouldn't dare soil anything in this lovely house until I'm clean."

Steve glanced down at his chest and noted the layers of dirt and grime.

"I definitely second that notion. Mina, is there a river nearby? Perhaps a tub or something where we could get clean?"

Mina turned to point back outside. "There's…" Her voice broke. She angrily cleared her throat and tried again. "There's a large basin in the back of the house, next to the well. There's a pump nearby. You may bathe there."

Steve shook his head. "This is your house. You've been through the most. I say you have first dibs. Lissa, perhaps you could give her a hand?"

Lissa nodded. "Of course. Mina, can you show me where it is? We'll get it ready for you."

The girls vanished around the back of the house. Quinn sniffed his shirt and recoiled with disgust. He noticed a large fire pit outside the cottage with several logs arranged in a circle for seating. Quinn peeled off his shirt and tossed it into the pit. He looked over at Steve. "Think you could burn that for me?"

"You don't want to try and wash it?"

Quinn shook his head. "I'd rather walk around as naked as the day I was born before I put that shirt back on. In fact…" He pulled the rest of his grubby attire off, leaving on a thin set of grimy underclothes. He tossed the decrepit pile into the pit. It landed in a sodden heap on top of what used to be his shirt. "Please. Do me another favor. Burn that. Burn it all."

Steve shrugged. "If we're all going to take baths then it'd be a good idea if we got a fire going. Cecil, see if there's a wood shed nearby. I'd like to —"

They all heard a loud shrill scream, definitely a woman's. Steve bolted around the house, heading for the girls. Had the griskis followed them here? Would they be bold enough to try and recapture them in broad daylight?

Steve rounded the corner of Mina's house and came to a sudden stop. Both eyes snapped closed. Mina was trying to lower herself into a large tub of water and evidently it was cold.

"What is it?" Cecil asked, trying to peer around Steve. "What has happened?"

Alerted to their presence, Mina screamed again, this time from embarrassment, and quickly submerged herself in the frigid water. The water sloshed over the edge as she thrashed about in the icy water.

"You shouldn't be back here," Lissa scolded. "Shoo! Go away!"

Following Steve's example, Cecil and Quinn closed their eyes the moment they saw the reason for the scream. Steve spun in place and had retreated two steps when Lissa pulled him back.

"Wait a moment. You can stay."

"Excuse me? I shouldn't be staying. I don't want to stay. You can't make me stay. I'm married!"

Lissa giggled as Steve tried to pull his arm free. "Don't be silly. We need your help. Do you think you could warm up the water? It's terribly cold."

"Oh. Uh, sure. I'm not opening my eyes so you'll have to lead the way."

"Sure. Take my hand."

"Nuh-uh. Guide my arm."

Lissa giggled again, enjoying Steve's discomfort. She guided him over to the large metal basin and pulled him to a stop.

"We're there. Stoop down. There you go. Can you feel the water?"

Steve nodded. "I'd say so. You just shoved my hand in it."

"Do your thing. Heat it up."

"Mina's in it now, right?"

"Aye."

"Okay. I'm going to go slow. Let me know if it gets too warm, alright?"

This time he heard Mina's reply. "I will. Thank you."

Several minutes later Steve returned to the front of the house and sank down onto one of the logs. He noticed that Cecil had loaded several split pieces of wood in the pit and had set them directly on Quinn's soiled clothes.

"Would you do the honors?"

Steve looked up as Quinn sat down next to him. He was still only wearing his underpants.

"Aren't you cold?"

"I won't be as soon as you light that fire."

"Ah." Steve's jhorun barely stirred. There'd be no more physical manifestations of his power until he had a chance to rest. However, he could still start a fire with minimal jhorun.

He eyed the fire pit and focused on one of the pieces of wood. Within moments it burst into flame and rapidly spread to the other tinder. Quinn nodded approvingly.

Ten minutes later, Mina came around the corner, wrapped in a thick, albeit dusty brown towel. She shyly smiled at Steve and then blushed when she saw Quinn's state of attire. She hurried into the house. Another ten minutes passed when Lissa hurried by, wrapped in a blanket.

"The bathtub is free," she informed the men with a giggle. "It has been drained and refilled."

It was nearly an hour before everyone had successfully scrubbed the grime from the griski cavern off their skin. Steve and Cecil had chosen to keep their clothes and scrubbed them clean as best as they could. Shirts and trousers were draped over one of the logs in front of the fire.

Steve tightened his hold on the thin blanket Mina had provided for him. Ordinarily he never had to worry about being cold; his jhorun saw to that. Now, however, he was fairly certain his jhorun was snoozing contentedly, somewhere in the recesses of his brain, so he was on his own with regard to keeping himself warm. He scooted a little closer to the fire.

"I can't even remember the last time I was cold," Steve remarked drowsily.

He yawned noisily and stretched his muscles. The sun had set moments before and with it came an instant drop in temperature. Lissa emerged from the house holding several small wooden bowls.

"What do you have there?" Cecil inquired. He stifled his own yawn and pulled up a corner of his blanket that had dropped low, exposing his shoulder. Running out of blankets, Mina had let the demure stranger use the bright pink quilt from her bed.

"I made a salve to treat the sores on Mina's arms. They're just simple lacerations and abrasions, but they had become infected." The teenager hefted a bowl. "This will clear them up."

Steve nodded his approval. "That's very thoughtful of you."

"It's the least I can do. What about you, Quinn? I made a bowl for you, too."

Quinn took the proffered bowl and inspected the contents. He brought the bowl up to his face and sniffed. "Hediondilla?"

Lissa brightened. "Aye! It's perfect for cuts, sores, and bruises on your skin. I found several plants outside."

"Impressive, young lady. You have become quite the healer. I don't know if you remember me, but I was once your teacher."

Lissa shook her head. "I'm sorry, I don't remember you. I was probably too busy studying to pay attention to anything else around me. There's still much I don't know. I hope to travel to R'Tal someday and ask for the king's permission to access the medicinal tomes in his library. They are equal to none. I could learn so much!" She set the final bowl down between Cecil and Steve.

"I will personally plead your case to Kri'Entu," Steve vowed.

Lissa curtsied. "Why thank you, kind sir." She giggled and ran back to the house.

Steve chuckled. At times she appeared as a well-adjusted young adult, confident in what she wanted to do with her life. Other times, as he just witnessed, proved she was still a little girl at heart.

Steve awoke the following morning stiff as a board, unsurprising, as he had slept on the floor

He softly groaned as he sat up, remembering where he was. He was definitely getting too old for this. His back was angrily protesting its recent treatment and was threatening to make his day miserable. Steve looked around the quiet room, noting it was still dark. However, it was growing brighter outside. Sunrise must be moments away.

"Oh, good, you're awake."

Steve glanced over and saw Lissa sitting in a nearby chair. "Where is everyone?"

"They're all outside. We've been chatting with Mina. Poor girl. She thought she was going to die in that horrible cavern."

Steve struggled to his feet, determined not to let Lissa know how sore he felt. "Everyone's outside? Why didn't you wake me?"

"We all felt you needed to rest. You are, after all, the oldest one in our group."

Steve's expression quickly soured. "Really? You're gonna hit me with the age jokes first thing in the morning?"

Lissa flashed him a dazzling smile. "Whatever do you mean?"

"Mm-hmm. How's Mina holding up?"

"Much better. The infections on her arms and legs have gone down tremendously. She should be completely healed in a few days."

"Good."

"We asked her about her jhorun."

"Oh? What'd she tell you?"

"She couldn't tell me what her jhorun is. She's never been able to make anything happen, so she doesn't know."

"Sounds like she's a gatekeeper to me. Their jhorun

doesn't really manifest itself."

Lissa nodded. "That's what we all told her. I guess her brother thought for certain she was a gatekeeper, too. He encouraged her to get some training from Zevern the Magnificent, but when he…"

"Don't call him that," Steve muttered crossly. "Drop the *Magnificent* part, alright?"

Lissa shrugged. "As you wish. Anyway, her brother insisted she get some training as a gatekeeper, just to see if that's what her jhorun truly was."

"And? Tell me you have some good news."

Lissa sadly shook her head. "She tried. She tried for a long time. Zevern the Mag — er, Zevern claimed she didn't have the skills needed to be a gatekeeper so he abandoned her training."

Steve scowled. "I seriously don't like that guy."

He rose to his feet and stretched his arms high over his head. Steve noticed how far his stomach was sticking out and quickly sucked it in. He also noticed that the thin blanket he had draped around his shoulders was pretty much the only thing he was wearing. Why had he taken off his clothes? Better yet, where were they?

Memories from last night's battle with the griskis slowly filtered into his brain. Ah. They were dirty. He had washed them when he was taking his turn in the tub.

"Are the clothes dry?"

"No. The fire died sometime during the night. Can you relight it?"

Steve ignited his right hand. His jhorun hadn't had adequate time to regenerate but it was better than nothing. "I can light it, sure. I'm just not at full power."

Lissa patted his hand. "We'll go easy on you today."

Steve grunted and headed toward the door. He walked to the fire pit and sat on one of the logs. Less than five seconds later a blazing fire erupted in the pit, casting its warmth in all directions. Steve picked up his sodden shirt and pants. He twisted out a few more drops of water before he applied his jhorun to his clothes. They were dry in no time.

Once everyone was dressed in their clean, wrinkly clothes,

they convened around the dinner table, located oddly enough in what Steve thought of as the living room. He turned his attention on Mina. He retrieved the dennai Kri'Calin had given him and passed it to the girl, who had hesitatingly accepted it.

"Do you know what that is?"

Mina looked at the miniature portal generator. "It's a strange mirror?"

"It can create a small portal between villages," Steve clarified. "It's called a dennai and it's used for delivering messages."

Mina nodded and held it out to him, frowning when Steve elected not to take it back.

"What am I supposed to do with it?" she asked. "I've never seen one of these before."

"It's our hope that you and your brother share jhorun."

Mina sighed. "We've already gone through this. I'm not a gatekeeper. I don't know what my jhorun is. I've never been able to tell. Luther tried to get me interested in gatekeeping, to see if I followed in our family's footsteps. Alas, I did not."

Not wanting to frighten the girl into silence, Steve switched topics. "I heard you started working for a scribe. How was that?"

"Monotonous," Mina instantly answered. She smiled moments later. "I loved it. My brother is the only family I have left. I fell into despair when Luther enlisted. He and I were very close. I threw myself into my work so I wouldn't dwell on Luther and what could be happening to him."

"Did he tell you why he became a soldier?" Steve asked.

"He did it for me. Becoming a king's soldier guaranteed we would be provided for, even in the roughest times. My jhorun hadn't manifested, and at that time I didn't know what I should do for work, so Luther joined the army as a way to secure our future. I owe him everything. Do you think we can give him a message? I want to let him know I'm alright."

Steve fidgeted uneasily. Mina noticed and went rigid. "Has something happened to Luther?"

"Well, it's like this. After you disappeared, he volunteered for a special mission."

Mina gasped with alarm. "Oh, no! He took *that* mission?"

Steve cocked his head as he stared at Luther's sister. "Before I say anything else I need to know we're on the same page. What mission are you referring to?"

"He told me that his captain wanted a volunteer to head a mission to another world. I think he said it was about some prophecy. I told him it was a foolhardy mission and he shouldn't go. He agreed with me. He agreed! Why would he change his mind?"

"He thought you were dead," Steve softly told her. "He didn't have any other ties to Lentari so he volunteered to complete a very important mission for the king."

"It's true," Cecil quietly told her. "Luther said to me on more than one occasion that he had no surviving family members left."

"My brother thinks I'm dead? And now I won't ever get to see him again. This is horrible!" Mina slouched over the table and let her head fall onto her arms. Her sobs were loud and heartbreaking. "I am truly alone now."

Steve cleared his throat. "Er, there's more."

Mina's head lifted. "What? Have you come to give me even worse news? I don't think my heart can take it. Not after what I've been through."

Steve worked up the courage to lay a hand over hers. "You and I are related."

Mina shook her head. "That's not possible. There are no other members of my family still living. You must be mistaken."

"I'm living proof you're wrong."

Mina gave him a skeptical look. Lissa and Cecil smiled. They knew the story. Quinn, however, did not and was waiting for Steve to explain.

"I saw Luther a few days ago."

"You did? How is he? Is he safe? Is he well?"

Steve smiled. "He's happily married."

"What? You're jesting."

"He married a wonderful lady by the name of Cora."

"He married a woman from another world?"

Steve nodded. "Yep."

"Why would he do that? Why would he go to another world for the sole purpose of linking it to ours unless…"

"He knew that more than likely he would never return," Quinn slowly answered.

"Was he put under some type of spell?" Mina demanded, growing angry. "Luther wouldn't choose to live on another world. He loves Lentari. And there are plenty of girls for him to choose from here. He has always been awkward around women. He'd never have the courage to actively court a woman, let alone one from another world."

"You need to trust me on this," Steve told her.

"Why?"

"Because I'm Luther's great-great-grandson."

Mina's mouth opened but didn't say anything.

"That's preposterous," Quinn finally said, breaking a full twenty seconds of silence. "What you suggest is impossible."

"Nothing's impossible, pal," Steve told him. He turned back to Mina. "My wife and I came here by way of something called an interdimensional portal, created by Zevern the Inept."

Lissa giggled. Steve pointed a finger at her.

"Lissa is also from that time. So is Quinn. They live in Lentari and Cecil lives in my world."

"You all went through this portal?" Mina asked, amazed.

"Yes. Um, except for Cecil. He's from my world just not from my time."

"What about your time?"

"The portal took us back over a hundred twenty years," Steve explained. "Long story short—"

"Too late," Cecil muttered.

"—we're here in Lentari trying to get another athe crystal."

"Why do you need an athe crystal?" Mina wanted to know.

"To power the portal that I will eventually use when my wife and I make our first trip to Lentari. If we can't get him another crystal, it's going to cause some serious problems for us in the future."

"How do I fit into this picture?"

"Mina, you are our only hope for getting back to our world. Luther can't link the portal until he gets a replacement power crystal. I've got the power crystal right here, but we can't get it to him."

"How did you get here if you didn't come by portal?"

"Sarah brought us."

"Your wife?"

Steve nodded. "Right. She's a teleporter."

Mina's eyebrows shot up. Quinn nodded smugly. He had heard of the caliber of Sarah's jhorun.

"That is very impressive. I would love to have her jhorun."

"You and everyone else. Now, back to the problem at hand." Steve pulled out the small leather satchel and held it up so Mina could see it. "We need to get this to your brother using nothing but the dennai."

"That's why you need me? I'm sorry, I am no gatekeeper."

"I think you are," Steve contradicted. "Could you please humor me and try?"

"Try what? I don't know how to make this work."

"Captain Sauer said you shouldn't have to worry about making the dennai work. You're just trying to change its destination."

"But I am no —"

"Yes, I know, you told me. You're no gatekeeper. Just try. Hold onto it and concentrate. See if anything happens."

Mina sighed. She leaned forward to rest both elbows on the table and gripped the mirror tightly in both hands. "Very well. I'll try."

Her eyes closed and she went still. Several minutes passed. Steve studied Mina's face closely. He could see her eyes moving under her eyelids. Her lips pursed and she frowned. A few seconds later she opened her eyes and apologetically shook her head. "Nothing happened. I'm sorry."

"I saw your eyes moving," Steve told her. "What were you thinking? Could you see anything?"

"I've been through a lot," Mina hastily reminded him. "I have a lot to think about."

"Whenever Sarah tells me about teleporting, she says she has to be able to clearly visualize where she's going."

"I'm no teleporter," Mina reminded him. "How does that help me?"

"From what I can tell, a gatekeeper also deals with teleporting. You have to concentrate. I'm willing to bet if you could quiet your mind, you'd be able to picture something. If that thing you're holding really does generate a small portal, maybe you would see where it has been preset to."

"How do you propose I do that?" Mina challenged. "I can't even begin to tell you how many thoughts I have running through my head right now. There is no way to quiet them all."

Lissa spoke up. "Perhaps I can help."

"What do you have in mind?" Steve wanted to know.

"I'll be right back. Let me see what I can find."

Lissa sprang to her feet and rushed outside. Four adults sat, motionless and silent, as they waited for the young teenager to return. She returned five minutes later, holding several long, brown, tuberous roots. She carefully washed the roots, chopped them into paste, and scraped a portion of the unappetizing goo into a large mug. She filled the mug with water and held it out to Steve. "Can you heat this, please?"

Steve took the mug and ignited his hand. Thirty seconds later he handed the steaming mug back to Lissa, who skimmed the remains of the root off the surface with a spoon. She handed the mug to Mina. "Here. Drink this."

"What is it?"

"It's a tea made from the roots of a type of gooseberry bush."

"What does it do?"

"It will help you relax."

Mina took a sip and made a face. "It doesn't taste very good."

"I'm sorry. I know it doesn't. But it'll help you clear your mind."

Mina took a few more tentative sips, making a face after each taste. "That really does taste quite horrid."

"How are you feeling?" Lissa asked.

"No different."

"Close your eyes and try to rest," Quinn suggested. "If

you start to think of something, allow it to come."

Mina settled back in her chair and closed her eyes. She took several deep, calming breaths.

"Feeling better?" Lissa asked again.

"Actually, I do," Mina admitted.

"Pick up the dennai," Steve softly told her. "Try again."

Without opening her eyes, Mina reached for the pewter object. She held it lightly in one hand. Steve watched her eyes. They weren't moving this time. Concerned, he looked over at Lissa and mouthed *is she sleeping?* Lissa leaned close and watched her breathe. She shook her head.

Mina's eyebrows shot up but her eyes remained closed. She switched the dennai from her right hand to her left.

"Do you see something?" Steve asked. Much to his delight, Mina nodded yes.

"I do see something, aye."

"What? What do you see?"

"Well, a thought just appeared. It's not going away."

"What kind of thought?" Quinn asked.

"It's like I'm remembering being in a room. It has such vivid detail it's as if I was there yesterday."

"And you were never there before?" Steve asked.

Mina shook her head. "I do recognize this room. And I was wrong. I have been here before."

"Where?" Quinn wanted to know.

"I'm not sure. I feel like I should know this, but I don't. I see an old scarred desk. I see a wall full of bookcases directly in front of the desk. Hmm, I also see a huge map on the adjacent wall."

"Can you tell us anything else about the map?" Quinn asked. "What does it depict? Is it topographical or political? Professional or amateurish?"

"It looks like a map you'd find in a constable's office," Mina decided. Her face lit up. "That's it! I'm looking at the inside of a constable's office."

"Do we know which one?" Steve asked.

"I'm looking at the map now," Mina informed them. "I should be able to … it's Capily! I can see the water and I can see islands."

Steve nodded, pleased. "That makes sense. If that dennai is designed to move communiqués from one village to the other then it should be pointed at a constable's office."

Mina opened her eyes and looked about the room. "You think I was tuning in to the dennai? Couldn't I have been remembering a simple visit from my own past?"

"How clear was the image?" Steve asked. "How well can you remember what you were looking at?"

Mina shut her eyes. "Quite well. I'm looking at it now."

"Sarah could do that," Steve told everyone. "Once she had something pictured in her head, it was there until she cleared it out."

Mina skeptically looked down at the dennai in her hands. "Does this mean I'm using my jhorun?"

Quinn and Steve both nodded. "It does, honey," Quinn agreed. "It means you're a gatekeeper, too. An untrained gatekeeper, but a gatekeeper nonetheless."

"You were right about me," Mina quietly announced. "I'm a gatekeeper. How does that help you? I don't know how to change this thing's final destination."

"Go back to the image," Steve instructed. He waited until Mina's eyes were closed. "You can see the office, is that right?"

Mina nodded. "Aye."

"Have you thought about forcing the picture to move?"

"How do I do that?" the girl wondered aloud.

Steve pondered for a moment. "Okay, try this. Imagine you're in that room. You really want to be in that room and have no desire to leave it. Suddenly someone comes up to you and wants you out, so they grab one of your hands and pull you toward the door."

"How does this help me?"

"Just try that. Tell me if anything changes."

Mina started to shake her head when her eyes snapped open. "I felt it!"

"You felt what?"

"I did what you suggested. I pretended I was there and that I wanted to leave. I felt something push back at me. It didn't want me to go."

"That'd be the dennai!" Quinn excitedly told her. "It's resisting your efforts to change it. Can you push any harder?"

Mina shrugged. "I don't know. I can try."

Mina closed her eyes and went still. Her brow furrowed. She grimaced and then gritted her teeth. Everyone sitting around the table leaned forward in anticipation.

Mina's eyes flew open and she bolted out of her chair. "It worked!"

Steve jerked back so violently he tipped himself over. Quinn leapt up, out of his chair, and smashed both knees against the table. Cecil squealed with fright and covered his face with his hands. Only Lissa remained unmoved.

Steve began laughing from the floor. He slowly regained his feet and righted his chair. He looked around the room. "No one saw that."

Mina gave a sheepish smile. "I'm sorry. I didn't mean to frighten anyone."

Quinn plopped back down on his chair and rubbed his sore knees. "No apologies necessary. We've all been on edge. Lissa, I'm proud of you. You didn't even flinch!"

Lissa sank a little farther down into her chair. "Don't be proud. I think I peed a little."

Mina slapped a hand over her mouth. She tried unsuccessfully to suppress her giggles. She looked, horrified, at the younger girl and gave her an apologetic smile. "I am so sorry, Lissa. I didn't mean to startle you."

Lissa shook her head and tried to wave off the apology. "It's okay. It's been a long couple of days."

"So, what happened?" Steve wanted to know. "You said it worked. What did you do?"

"I pushed harder at the force that was pushing against me. The picture moved from the constable's office to just outside the front door. The only thing I see now is a closed door."

"That means you successfully changed the dennai's destination!" Steve let out a victorious whoop. "Good work, Mina!"

Mina closed her eyes for another two minutes. Beads of sweat formed on her brow and trickled down the side of her cheek. "I did it again. Now I'm facing the water, with the constable's office directly behind me. I can see the beach! Oh, this is wonderful!"

"Remind me again to punch out Zevern the Inept the next time I see him," Steve said quietly to Cecil. "How that guy ever became a wizard is beyond me."

Quinn switched seats with Lissa and laid a hand on her shoulder. Mina looked up at him and smiled. "Okay, Mina," he began, "here's your next test. See if you can change villages."

Mina paled, but almost immediately regained her composure. It wasn't a difficult request. Would she be able to do it? She slowly closed her eyes, her right fist tightening around the dennai's pewter handle.

"I'm still looking at the shore," she told them. She was silent for a few more seconds. "I see one of the city's galleons moored at the pier. I know I'm still in Capily. I'm trying to bring up an image of R'Tal but nothing happens. What am I doing wrong?"

"Sarah can teleport only when she has a clear picture of where she's going," Steve told the girl. "Assuming you've been to R'Tal, try to visualize a location that you can remember in vivid detail. Can you do that?"

"I'll try." Mina was silent for a full ten minutes before she finally spoke. "I have an image! It worked!"

"What do you see?" Quinn asked.

"The drawbridge in front of the west gate. This is extraordinary! I can even see people walking across the bridge!"

"Can you substitute the picture of Capily's shore with R'Tal's western drawbridge? Is that possible?"

Mina was silent as she considered. She took a deep breath and held it. Her brow furrowed again. This time no fewer than five beads of perspiration formed and trickled down her face. Whatever she was doing, she was giving it her all.

"Don't hold your breath," Quinn warned. "Keep breathing, Mina. You don't want to pass out on us."

Mina slowly exhaled. However, she was slow to take another breath.

"Don't forget to inhale, either," Quinn reminded her.

Mina did so.

"Exhale," Quinn ordered.

Mina exhaled.

For the next ten minutes Quinn directed her breathing as she refocused the dennai on a different locale. Once she finished, she opened her eyes.

"Any luck?" Steve asked, certain the answer was negative.

Mina slowly smiled. "Aye. I did it!"

The table erupted with shouts, exclamations, and praise. Mina flushed with embarrassment as everyone congratulated her on her brilliant success. She set the dennai on the table and asked Lissa for a cup of water. The teenager was all too eager to comply.

"The dennai is now pointed at R'Tal?" Steve asked.

Mina nodded. "The image I see is the same that I saw before. It shows the western drawbridge."

"Outstanding. Was it difficult?"

Mina thought for a moment. "The most difficult part was being able to completely focus my attention. If an errant thought popped into my head, the image was gone and I had to start over. That's what took so long."

"You forgot to breathe," Steve informed her. "Quinn had to remind you to inhale and exhale."

"I have no recollection of that."

"It doesn't matter," Quinn excitedly said. "Do you think you can link this dennai to Steve's world?"

"How can I do that?" Mina asked, despair in her voice. "It was hard enough to visualize something I've seen before in R'Tal. I've never been to Steve's world. I have no idea what it looks like. How am I supposed to visualize something I've never seen?"

"Sarah did it once," Steve recalled.

"How?" Cecil asked.

Luther's friend had been so quiet that Steve had forgotten he was there.

"We showed her a map of another village. She was able to picture the village in her head without knowing what it actually looked like."

"Do you have a picture of your home world?" Lissa

asked. "If we can show Mina what your world looks like, she might be able to picture something."

Steve shook his head. "I don't even have my wallet on me, not that I carry around a picture of my home town."

"What do we do now?" Cecil asked. "We're so close. There must be something we can do."

Steve scratched his head and looked over at Cecil. "Do you think we could describe something on our world in enough detail that she might picture it?"

"Like what?"

"What about the manor?" Steve suggested. "I know it inside and out. I mean, I've lived there for a number of years now."

Cecil nodded. "That might work."

"But I'll need your help 'cause the manor I remember isn't exactly the same one we need to get to."

Cecil frowned. "That would be a problem. Very well. What can I do?"

"Let's do this. Let's just tell her everything we can remember about Idaho. The manor, the town, the people, the trees, woods, fields, etc. I'm hoping something will trigger an image."

For the next thirty minutes, Steve described the manor and the lands that surrounded it. He told everyone about the dusty, dirty streets and the worn-down, weather-beaten wood buildings that made up Coeur d'Alene. Cecil described his own home in as much detail as he could muster. He described barber shops, general stores, the telegraph office, even the county jail.

Mina hadn't given a single sign that she was listening. Her eyes were closed and she was sitting as still as a statue.

"Do we keep going?" Cecil asked as he looked over at Mina.

"Yes," Steve nodded, answering for her. "What else do you have?"

Cecil described banks, delis, hotels, and was halfway through describing the local butcher and the sights and smells associated with that shop when Steve popped him on his arm.

"No one wants to hear about that."

"Of course. I'm sorry."

Cecil started describing several of the saloons he frequented when he played poker. He expanded on sights, sounds, and smells frequently found in a bustling gaming hall. The clink of poker chips, the creaking of leather boots, the scent of stale cigarette smoke. Steve had to admit he was doing an excellent job.

Mina stirred. Cecil stopped talking and looked over at her. "Is everything alright?"

"I see something!"

Everyone was on their feet.

"What?" Steve demanded. "What do you see?"

Mina went silent as she inspected her vision.

"I'm not sure. It's too dark to make out many details. I see wooden chairs. One is broken. I see a sofa."

Another minute passed before Mina continued. "There's something on the sofa. A metal object. In fact, there are multiple metal objects."

"Describe them," Steve told the girl. "Tell me what you see."

"They are long, like walking sticks, but irregularly shaped. One end is wood and the other is metal. The wood end flares and is easily four times the size of the metal end, which stays the same shape."

"A stick with wood on one end and metal on the other," Steve mused aloud. "I have no freakin' idea what that is."

"There are more of these objects on the sofa," Mina announced. "I also see small versions of these objects."

Comprehension dawned. Steve smiled. "You're looking at a couch with rifles and pistols on it. Mina, you did it! I think you're looking at the snug in the Silver Spike. We disarmed a couple of the sheriff's men outside the manor. Sarah said she sent the weapons to the snug to keep them safe."

"I hate to be the bearer of bad news," Cecil hesitantly began, "but Luther doesn't frequent the saloons. He'll never get the crystal if we put it there."

"Can you try to see something else?" Quinn asked.

"Nothing else has formed," Mina replied. Her eyes were still closed.

"What does that tell us?" Quinn asked the others.

Cecil sheepishly shook his head. "It tells me that I spend way too much time at the saloon if I can describe it so well a foreigner can picture what it looks like."

Mina opened her eyes. She gave them a tired smile as she placed the dennai onto the table. "It's done. The dennai is linked to the last vision I had."

Cecil peered at his reflection in the dennai's surface.

"How do we turn it on? How does it work?"

Steve stood, disappeared outside for a few moments, and returned to the table. He showed them some small stones he had picked up. He dropped one on the surface of the dennai. It bounced off harmlessly and dropped to the wooden floor boards, clattering noisily.

Quinn slid the dennai over to Mina. "Put your hand on that and bring back your vision of the destination."

Mina laid her thin, delicate hand on the dennai's handle. She nodded at him. Quinn nodded at Steve. "Here goes."

He dropped another pebble onto the dennai's reflective surface. It vanished the moment it made contact. Steve was ecstatic. "Bingo! It's working! I need to leave a note for Rosamund."

"Who's Rosamund?" Quinn wanted to know.

"She's the lady who runs the Silver Spike saloon," Cecil immediately answered.

"Right. If she goes down into that secret little room and sees a strange leather pouch in there, she's going to open it up to see what it is. I guarantee it. So, I need to ask her to give it to Luther."

Mina disappeared for a few moments and then reappeared with a scrap of parchment and a quill full of ink. Steve thanked her and wrote out his simple message:

Rosamund —
Please give this to Luther Miller as soon as possible. Urgent!

"If that is an athe crystal, then you should tell her to keep the pouch closed," Quinn suggested.

Steve snapped his fingers and added another line to his message.

Very important. Keep this pouch sealed! - Steve

"Dude, that would have sucked. Thanks for reminding me." Steve folded the paper in half and then in half again. He tucked a corner of the paper into one of the pouch's leather folds and eyed Mina. "Are you ready?"

She nodded. She placed a hand back on the dennai's handle, closed her eyes, and nodded again at Steve. "It's ready."

"Perfect. Here we go!" Steve dropped the leather pouch onto the dennai's reflective surface and watched it vanish the instant contact was made.

"Now what do we do?" Cecil wanted to know.

"The only thing we can do," Steve answered. He clapped a friendly hand on Cecil's shoulder. "Let's hope Rosamund checks that snug sometime soon and she gets the crystal into Luther's hands."

"How will we know he has it?" Cecil wondered. "How will we know if he does what he has to do?"

Steve held up a finger to emphasize a point and hesitated, his eyes widening. "A very good point. We need to get our keesters back to the castle."

"What about the rest of us?" Lissa asked.

Steve, about ready to step outside, turned to look back at the small gathering of people still seated around the table. "I had assumed you're all going with me. Am I wrong?"

Lissa was on her feet in a flash. She rushed to his side.

"What about me?" Mina asked, growing tearful. "My only family lives in your world now."

Steve grinned. "Like I said, I figured everyone was coming."

Mina's face broke out into a smile. The next thing Steve knew Mina was on her feet and had thrown her arms around him. Steve shook his head.

"Yep. This is gonna take some explaining."

Chapter 4 — A Brand New Believer

Rosamund Jones was a woman who wouldn't back down from a confrontation, even if a buzzing rattlesnake was involved. On many occasions she had to confront non-paying patrons while her kind-hearted husband, Gerry, tended to look the other way. If she provided a service or a product, she fully expected to be paid for her services. End of story. There were no exceptions.

Therefore, the last Friday of the month saw the stern, but friendly, proprietor casually mingling with her regulars and handing them carefully calculated, thoroughly detailed bar tabs.

Rosamund had a mind for numbers and figures which she used to her advantage. She and Gerry had turned a profit every single month, other than their grand opening. Gerry was in charge of procuring the liquor, ordering whatever she said they needed for the month. He was also in charge of handling unruly patrons or anyone who tried to challenge her meticulous bar tabs.

She was responsible for everything else. Her husband loved playing poker, so while he typically could be found at one of the tables, beating the pants off anyone foolish enough to challenge him, she was responsible for the day-to-day operations of the saloon. Rosamund wouldn't have it any other way.

She had just collected on three of the bar tabs when she hesitated. She stepped up onto one of the boxes placed behind the counter and looked around. People were laughing and drinking; Willy was on the piano and her two girls, Kate and Peggy, expertly wove their way through the bustling crowds delivering drinks.

The noise level in her saloon was right where she liked it: too loud to think straight. Yet her ears hadn't deceived her. She had heard a loud clatter and then what sounded like a pebble being dropped. Had someone brought rocks into her saloon?

Rosamund frowned. She smoothed several wrinkles on the sleeves of her exquisite violet dress and tightened the strap holding her delicate Victorian hat in place. If she caught the jokester who had brought pebbles into her place then she would...

There! She had heard the clatter again. But it seemed not one other person had heard the noise. She thought for a moment. It almost sounded like a door opening and closing, or someone walking into a wall.

Her eyes landed on the thin gray rug concealing the snug's trapdoor. Her eyes narrowed. Yes, that could be it. However, there shouldn't be anyone down there.

She knew it wasn't Gerry, as his knees wouldn't allow him to descend the steep steps. Her eyes flicked up to one of the distant tables. She saw his familiar black ten-gallon hat bob up and down as he held conversation with another poker player. She worriedly glanced back down at the snug. The only people she had allowed down there were Sarah and her husband, Steve.

Rosamund finished ringing up her paid bar tabs and

closed her ledger, stashing it back in the hidden compartment under the counter. She patted her right thigh, verifying her loaded Remington dual barrel derringer was there. She called one of her two serving girls over and instructed her to man the counter.

"Is everything alright, Mrs. Jones?" Kate asked, anxious to return to the floor where she could be the center of attention.

"Everything is fine," she assured her. "I need to run down to the snug."

Kate briefly glanced down at the rug before returning her gaze to the handsome poker player who had attracted her attention that night. "Don't be gone long!"

Mrs. Jones harrumphed loud enough for the girl to hear. Serving girls didn't tell their employers how long they could step away from the counter. That was her job, thank you very much.

She slid the rug out of the way, unlocked the trap door, and opened it. Inside the dark opening she pulled the heavy wooden switch toward herself. She heard a loud click and then a single light bulb flickered to life. She held her breath as she quickly looked around the room. Her hand went to the concealed derringer.

Her breath caught in her throat. Someone *had* been there! There were rifles and pistols on her sofa! She carefully descended the steep stairs and peered around the small room. No one lurked in the shadows.

She wandered over to the sofa to stare at the weapons. Those hadn't been there when Sarah gave her demonstration, that's for sure. Sarah! She could move about using magic. But still, she *had* heard something.

Rosamund's eye was drawn to the floor. She stooped to pick up a pebble, then glanced at the ceiling. Had Sarah just been there? She hadn't seen or heard anything from the girl all day, assuming she was with Steve.

She had turned back to the stairs when she stopped. A leather pouch lay on the couch, a piece of paper sticking out from it.

She gingerly took the pouch and felt an object concealed within. She pulled the paper out, unfolded and read it. A message from Steve.

Rosamund clutched the leather pouch tightly to her chest and ascended the stairs. She groaned when she noticed that the number of patrons in her saloon had almost doubled. Steve had instructed her to deliver the pouch to Luther Miller as soon as possible. Rosamund frowned. She wanted to keep her pledge to help Sarah and Steve, but this was her busiest day of the week. A trip to the manor would consume at least an hour.

She drummed her fingers on the long counter and reread Steve's message. He said it was urgent. Rosamund sighed. She waved one of her two bouncers over and instructed him to have her buckboard ready.

"Would you like me to go with you, ma'am?"

Rosamund climbed up into the rickety wagon and took the reins. "That won't be necessary, Bart. I won't be gone long. Say, can you tell me if you've seen Sarah today?"

Bart's head shook back and forth on his thick neck. "No, ma'am. I don't reckon I have."

"Thank you. That'll be all."

"Yes, ma'am. You might ask Hank. I think he saw her yesterday."

Rosamund hesitated. "What time yesterday?"

"I don't know, ma'am."

"Please ask Hank to come here for a moment."

"Yes, ma'am."

Her mare chomped and pulled at the bit, anxious to get going. Rosamund leaned forward and laid a hand on the horse's flank. The mare calmed almost instantly. "There, there. We'll be off shortly."

"You sent for me, ma'am?"

Mrs. Jones turned. Hank was just as large as Bart, standing nearly six and a half feet tall. He was full of muscles and probably the most timid person she had ever met in her entire life. However, no one else knew that.

"Have you seen Sarah lately?"

Hank's face flushed red and his head fell.

Alarmed, Rosamund set the wagon's brake and hurried down out of the wagon to confront her employee. Hank was ashamed about something and that worried Rosamund more than anything.

"What happened? What did you see?"

"She was taken, Mrs. Jones."

Rosamund gasped. "By whom?"

"The sheriff's men, ma'am."

"Oh, dear. Where …? How …? Hank, when was this?"

"Last evening, ma'am. It was during the festival. Ms. Sarah and Mrs. Miller were trying to get away from Deke Babcock."

Rosamund scowled. "You saw that despicable Mr. Babcock forcibly abscond with Sarah and you did nothing?"

"He confronted her as they were leaving," Hank uneasily continued. "He slapped a rag over her nose and whatever it was knocked her out."

"Why didn't you do something, Hank? Sarah is one of ours! You should've told me the instant it happened!"

The huge man scuffed his feet, kicking up a cloud of dust.

"I should have, ma'am. I should have. I am so sorry. I tried to tell you that I lack the courage to —"

"Oh, don't give me that 'lack the courage' nonsense," Rosamund snapped. "Hank, you tower over everyone except maybe Bart. No one would ever wish to face you in a dark alley. I hope you'll forgive me for telling you this, son, but I need to pass along what I've heard Gerry tell many a person: you need to grow a pair."

If possible, Hank's cheeks reddened even further. "Yes, ma'am."

Rosamund jumped into the seat and urged the mare faster, a knot of worry in her stomach. Sarah kidnapped by the sheriff's men!

She looked at the leather pouch on the wooden bench beside her. Did Steve know something had happened to Sarah? Was that the point of the urgent request?

Her mind whirled. What had Sarah done to attract the attention of Sheriff Bixby? Had she not pointed out the sheriff on Sarah's first day and explained that people who crossed him simply vanished? Including his predecessor?

Twenty minutes later, she brought the wagon to a stop

before a set of sturdy iron gates in an enormous field of lupines. It was fastened with a chain and padlock. She stepped down from the wagon and inspected the name plaque: The Millers. This was it, alright, only the bars and gate were new additions.

"Hello!" Rosamund shouted. "Is anyone there?"

She caught sight of a rope hanging to the left of the plaque and gave it a quick tug. A bell, concealed on the flip side of the wall, gave off a single pure note. She waited a few moments then rang the bell again.

"Who's there?" a male voice called out. "What do you want?"

"It's Rosamund Jones, from the Silver Spike. I'm not in the mood for nonsense, young man. Open the gate. There are things you need to hear and see.

Luther Miller rounded the bend and peered suspiciously at her from safely inside.

"Mrs. Jones," Luther interrupted, "I'm sorry. This isn't the best time. We aren't really prepared to entertain at the moment. I hope you understand."

"Wait! Sarah's been taken and I have a message from Steve. He says it's urgent!"

Rosamund held the leather pouch up where he could see it.

"Where did you get that?" Luther asked, his eyes wide. "It's dwarven by design!"

Rosamund looked down at the pouch in disbelief. "A group of small people made this?"

"You didn't open it?"

"The message said I wasn't supposed to." Rosamund pulled out the folded piece of paper and held it up. "This one."

Luther unlocked the padlock and pulled the gates open. "Come inside. We need to talk."

Luther relocked the gates after the wagon passed through and then ran to catch up. He hopped up onto the seat and rode with Rosamund until they reached the house. Cora's tear-streaked face appeared in the manor's front door, followed closely thereafter by AnnaBelle's.

"You know about Sarah," Rosamund guessed.

Luther leapt off the wagon and helped Mrs. Jones down. He pointed up at the manor's front door. "Come. We should go inside."

"What's going on?" Cora wanted to know. She descended the short flight of steps and appeared at Luther's side. "Why is she here?"

"She delivered that," Luther answered, pointing at the small pouch.

AnnaBelle wiped her eyes and blinked, clearly confused as to what she was looking at. "She brought you a purse?"

"It's not a purse," Luther pointed out. "It's a dwarven travel bag."

Cora shrugged. "How does that help us get Sarah back?"

Luther held out a hand. "May I have the message, Mrs. Jones?"

Rosamund handed over the pouch and the note. Luther passed the pouch to AnnaBelle, who had joined the others at the bottom of the landing. She was about to open it when Rosamund gave a cry of alarm. She frantically pointed at AnnaBelle.

"Don't open that!"

AnnaBelle looked up. "What? Why not?"

Luther read the message and gave a cry of alarm. He whirled around, snatched the pouch back from AnnaBelle, and cradled it to his chest. He hurried up the steps and into the manor. The other three immediately followed.

AnnaBelle frowned. "I wasn't going to take it."

Luther hefted the pouch. He looked over at Cora. His wife returned his gaze.

"What is it, Luther? What do you have there?"

"It's from Steve! He's done it!"

"Done what? He's stranded. You said so, earlier."

"He's stranded *unless* we give him a way to get back," Luther explained, struggling to keep his voice calm. "This must be an athe crystal. It can power the portal! If I can get the portal activated, and linked, do you know what that would mean?"

Cora clapped her hands. "You can complete your mission!

Oh, honey! You must be excited!"

"Does that mean we can get Cecil back?" AnnaBelle asked.

Luther looked over at his friend's wife and smiled. "Aye, it does."

"Cecil is missing?"

Luther, Cora, and AnnaBelle turned back to Mrs. Jones. They had forgotten the tiny saloon proprietor was there. Mrs. Jones tsked loudly.

"I already know there's something special about Sarah and Steve. Your actions just confirm it."

"Do you know where they're from?" Luther hesitantly asked.

Rosamund nodded. "They told me they're from another time."

"And you know that Sarah has been taken? By the sheriff's men?"

Rosamund nodded again. "One of my bouncers saw the abduction take place. It shames me to think he could have prevented it, but didn't do anything."

"That sheriff is deplorable," AnnaBelle sniffed, dabbing her eyes with a handkerchief once more. "He must be stopped."

"And do you know who might be able to stop him?" Luther excitedly told the others. "A fire thrower."

Luther rushed up the stairs with the others in tow, all the way to the top floor. He dropped down to his stomach and inspected the bottom lower corner of the master suite's door frames. Carved dragons, griffins, swords, and mythological figurines decorated the ten-foot-high double door frames. Luther looked at the lowest carved figure, and gently twisted the tiny broadsword a quarter turn to the right. He heard a soft click.

A hidden panel popped loose and fell over, revealing a recessed indentation where something could be placed. Luther gingerly reached into the pouch and unwrapped a brown multi-faceted crystal so dark it almost looked black. He set the crystal in the holder and quickly slapped the panel back in place, twisting the sword back to its original orientation to lock the panel down.

The tiny broadsword began glowing, as if lit from the inside. The glow flickered up and across the frames, illuminating each carving it touched. When it reached the dual-bladed battle ax carved onto the opposite corner, the illumination faded away.

"Did everyone see that?" Cora asked, turning to them. "Can we assume the portal is now active?"

Luther nodded. "It is. Now all I have to do is link it to the portal key Kri'Calin gave me. Let me fetch it."

Luther disappeared into the huge master bedroom and came out moments later with a box made of pewter. He flipped the lid back and gingerly pulled out a green crystal key and a smoke-colored marble.

"How long will this take?" Cora softly asked her husband.

Luther closed the massive doors and ran his hands over the detailed carvings. It was a graphical representation of Lentari. There were the Bohanis, the northern mountains. There was Lake Raehón and the valley that bordered on the southeast. He could see the mighty Zylan River stretching across the entire kingdom. And there, nestled up against the forest in the northeast, was R'Tal, capital city of Lentari. In that city's eastern section sat the castle, complete with carved turrets, towers, and crenellated walls.

Luther zeroed in on the one window that wasn't a window, but a keyhole. He inserted the key but didn't twist it. The portal wasn't linked yet so there wasn't any point in trying.

"Not long. I need you three to be quiet. No noise. No interruptions."

Luther laid his right hand on the door and clutched the marble with his left. The marble, Luther knew, was a very powerful object, a jorii. Each sphere had the ability to magnify a person's jhorun to a level matched only by the wizards. This jorii, unfortunately, was almost spent. It had only enough power to allow his own jhorun to work one last time, for a few minutes. He had to link the portal quickly.

He closed his eyes and mentally probed the portal. No vision appeared in his head. It was waiting to be assigned a destination. He slid his right hand along the surface of the door until he made it to the carved castle. As soon as his hand closed around the crystal key, he sent his jhorun to investigate.

He took a few calming breaths and cleared any random thoughts from his mind. He waited for his jhorun to attune to the key. A vision formed, almost instantly. He was looking at a serene path through the woods. Which woods, he couldn't tell, but what he did notice almost immediately, it was undoubtedly Lentari. The trees, the flowers, even the kytes flying through the air indicated it was his homeland. What he wouldn't do to step foot on his native soil once more.

His thoughts shifted to Cora and were instantly quelled. His wife's home was here. He knew when he volunteered for this mission that he'd never see his home again. Returning there simply wasn't meant to be. He'd have to be content to look at pictures of it.

Holding the scene firmly in his mind, he switched his attention back to the portal. It was there, active, patient; it wanted a destination. He sent it the image of the woodland path and felt the inner workings of the portal powering up. The portal was chiming! Only active portals chimed. His heart sang with pride. Right on cue, the portal key began to glow.

AnnaBelle noticed first. "Look! Is it supposed to do that?"

Luther removed his hands from the two doors and pulled the key free from the keyhole. "I do believe we're ready."

"Try it out!" Cora urged, anxious to see her first glimpse of her husband's homeland.

Luther reinserted the key, twisted it clockwise for one revolution, and then pulled it free. He slid it into his pocket and stepped back a few paces, prompting the others to do the same. The two master bedroom doors fused together and began rippling, as if the surface had somehow become fluid. A few seconds later the doors fuzzed out and became a doorway leading into the woods.

Luther smiled. He had correctly tuned the portal back to Lentari. He approached the edge of the door and looked longingly at his home country. A single tear rolled down his cheek.

Cora took his hand in hers. "If it means that much to

you, why don't we visit for a few days? It looks like a nice place. Would that be possible?"

Luther sighed and shook his head. He started to poke his hand through the portal. It stopped less than an inch from the threshold, an invisible force resisting him. The harder he pushed, the stronger the portal pushed back.

Cora experimentally poked her own arm through the portal and encountered no resistance. She pulled it back. The path in the woods disappeared and was replaced by the carving of the kingdom.

"Why could I—? That makes no sense."

"It makes perfect sense," Luther contradicted. "It was programmed in to this portal as insurance."

He caught his wife's eyes and held them. "The king knew that the Nohrin must be non-Lentarians, and only they would be allowed to use the portal. The king explained to me that even if I became homesick, or wanted to abandon the mission, the portal would not allow me to pass. Besides, someone needs to stay here and see to it the portal remains unharmed. Since this was a one-way journey, the king saw to it that I had everything I needed. How? With gold. Lots of it. I've deposited a small portion in the bank, to maintain appearances. The rest is hidden here in the manor."

Startled, Cora's head jerked up. "There's gold hidden in the house? Really?"

"I'm sorry I didn't tell you. I wasn't sure how you'd react to learning an enormous stash of Lentarian grifs was hidden in our home."

"Grifs?"

"Gold coins minted in Lentari," Luther explained. "No one knew how long it would take before the Nohrin would find their way to our world. The king realized a Lentarian would have to stay behind and keep the portal active and out of the wrong person's hands."

"That's where you got your money," Rosamund observed. "I had wondered."

"Many people have wondered," AnnaBelle added.

"And that's something I'm trusting the two of you to keep to yourselves," Luther said, eyeing the two of them. "Cora has told me repeatedly that the two of you are trustworthy. Will you keep this to yourselves? I do not want to worry about whether or not Cora or I will be robbed at gunpoint at a later date."

"Of course," Rosamund said.

"I will, too," AnnaBelle agreed.

"Thank you. Both of you. Now, I see that you've got a confused look on your face, Mrs. Jones. I can't say that I blame you."

"You say you're looking for someone to go to your world, is that it?" Rosamund asked.

"The prophecy referenced the two Nohrin. They're the prince's bodyguards," Luther explained. "The prophecy was very specific, and the only way to get non-Lentarians to our kingdom was to create a link to another world. This particular world was chosen, and I was sent here with everything I needed to construct this manor and the portal."

"What did your king expect to happen?" Rosamund wanted to know. "Were people supposed to wander in here by mistake and accidentally activate your portal?"

Luther scoffed. "Of course not."

"Were you planning on kidnapping them and pushing them through?"

"Mrs. Jones! Really!"

"Tell me how your prophecy is supposed to be fulfilled," Rosamund insisted. "How can you expect two people from my world to find their way to yours? How would that even work?"

Luther smiled at the tiny woman. "I already know it worked, Mrs. Jones. Two people from Idaho journeyed through my portal and fulfilled the prophecy."

Rosamund's eyes widened with shock. "Sarah and her husband. They're these Nohrin people you're talking about?"

"Aye. Apparently, it won't happen for another hundred twenty years. That's where this crystal comes in. Until we powered up the portal and linked it to Lentari, their future was in jeopardy."

"Sarah is already in jeopardy," Rosamund coldly reminded him. "I look after my own, Luther Miller, and even though she wasn't born here, nor does she belong here, Sarah *is* one of my own. What are we going to do to help her?"

Before anyone could answer, they all heard the same thing: the portal was chiming! They spun about to see the two doors fuse back together and fuzz out, this time replaced by an entirely different scene.

Luther dropped to one knee. They were staring at the portal room inside the castle. Kri'Calin, Captain Sauer, and a whole room full of nobles stared quietly back at them.

"On your feet, soldier," Captain Sauer instructed.

Luther complied.

"Is it true? You've been there over three years?"

Luther nodded. "Aye, it's true."

"What happened to the first athe crystal? Why did we have to procure another?"

Luther's face colored with embarrassment. "I, er…"

Captain Sauer managed to bite back a smile. "I'm waiting, soldier."

"I, uh, did a mock proposal to my wife, Cora. I pretended the crystal was an engagement ring and proposed with it."

Kri'Calin snorted softly with amusement and looked away.

"I take it you did this outdoors?" Sauer dryly asked.

Both Luther and Cora's faces blushed bright crimson.

"Be that as it may, Luther Miller," Kri'Calin said, causing a lull in conversation, "you have completed your mission. Very well done, soldier."

Luther bowed. "I thank you, Your Majesty."

The portal faded back to the doors.

Cora turned to her husband and put both hands on her hips as a frown appeared on her face. "That was rude. Congratulations, you completed your mission, now go away? I have a mind to tell him that he should —"

The chiming began again and within moments they were once more staring at the king.

"As I was saying," Kri'Calin continued, ignoring the fact that his conversation had been interrupted, "you have completed your mission. You have earned my appreciation, and that of the kingdom."

"It was my pleasure, Your Majesty."

"Now, I believe there's someone here who would like to use your portal."

The king motioned to someone out of Luther's line of sight. A group of people appeared, and before anyone could say anything, they rushed the portal, anxious to get through before it could close again. Luther, Cora, and AnnaBelle were knocked off their feet and went down in a tangle of arms and legs. Rosamund wisely side-stepped out of the way.

Cecil made it to his feet first. "AnnaBelle!" he cried, crushing his wife in a hug. "I thought I'd never see you again!"

AnnaBelle was openly crying. "My darling! We were so worried about you!"

"Where's Sarah?" Steve demanded as soon as he regained his feet. "What's happened to her? Why didn't she meet us at the waterfall?"

Luther rose to his feet. "We have much to talk about. Come this way so we can…" He trailed off as he noticed three strangers had also come through the portal. The first was a teenage girl. She was staring around the house with huge eyes. The second was a thin man in his late twenties. He had promptly regained his feet and joined the teenage girl to look out the window, staring at the outside landscape with wide, wondrous eyes. The third…

All the color drained from Luther's face. The third person, a young thin girl, rose unsteadily to her feet. Her eyes locked on his and she began to cry. Luther began to cry, too.

"Mina!"

Chapter 5 — Misplaced Affections

"Well, what was I supposed to do?" Deke Babcock demanded with a scowl. He was pacing back and forth in the small room that served as the sheriff's office. "Tell him that you're holding a woman against her will, who is fighting back by magically throwing our men around like tennis balls? That she's the reason you saw him yesterday for your dislocated shoulder? Mick was the third injury the doc has seen in less than two days. I thought you said you could keep her in line, boss. So far, this woman has been nothing but a pain in the arse."

Sheriff Bixby sighed, leaned back in his chair, and lit the cigar he had been chewing on. He absentmindedly rubbed his right shoulder. "How much did you have to pay Doc Emerson to keep his trap shut?"

"Fifty dollars in gold coin," Deke spat out. "He wouldn't take any less. That woman now owes me fifty dollars! I'm gonna take it out on her hide!"

"If you touch her, I'll personally lop every one of your fingers off and then feed 'em to you," the sheriff coolly answered.

Deke fell silent, properly cowed.

"Miss Sarah is more of a handful than I originally gave her credit for, that's for sure," Bixby agreed. He stroked his handlebar moustache thoughtfully.

"Can't you give her more opium?" Deke asked, with enough of a sneer to insinuate the sheriff was a dullard for not coming to that same conclusion.

"She's already stopped eating. She barely drinks any water. If we increase the dose, she'll detect it and I assume she's stubborn enough to stop drinking the water, too. If she does that, she'll regain full control of her jhorun and teleport out of here. Do you have any idea what she'd do to us if that ever happens?"

"She'll starve herself to avoid cooperating, is that it?"

The sheriff leveled a stern gaze at his henchman. "You ain't ever been with a woman, have you?"

Deke's face reddened. "I have so. What's that got to do with anything?"

"If you had been with a woman, you'd know how stubborn they can be. I know this woman's type. She's strong-willed, and there ain't no place for that type of thing around here."

Both the sheriff and Deke cocked their heads at the same time. Several people were shouting. One voice had risen above the rest and sounded like a young child.

"Not again," the sheriff growled as he snatched his gun off the desk and slid it into its holster on his hip. "If she's hurt another of my men, there'll be hell to pay. Mark my words."

The sheriff yanked the door opened and stepped through at the exact same time Deke tried squeezing through. Both men became wedged in the doorway. The sheriff looked down his nose at his henchman and scowled. "Do you think I opened that door for you, princess?"

Deke mumbled an apology and stepped back as the

sheriff stepped forward. They hurried down the hall and rushed through the enormous lodge, pushing by several of the sheriff's men, who were strapping their gun belts around their waists.

"Get out of the way," the sheriff barked. "Step aside."

The crowd parted, right down the middle. The sheriff stepped outside and immediately headed to one of the other four buildings on his property. This one looked like a ramshackle shed, but the sheriff knew its only purpose was to conceal the bulk of his wealth, namely the entrance to a very lucrative, very deep silver mine. The mine's tunnels branched off in all directions and were the ideal place to stash a prisoner.

He barged into the shed, took a lantern from a row of them hanging on the wall, lit it, and descended into the darkness. A form materialized and rushed up the stairs at him. It was Elijah. His pants were around his knees, his face contorted in pain, and he was screaming like a little girl.

The sheriff cursed and pulled his gun from his holster, only to have Elijah rush by him and clamber up the stairs to disappear outside. The screams slowly faded away and utter silence fell again. The sheriff turned back to stare down at the inky blackness before him.

With one hand holding the gun and the other holding the lantern, Sheriff Bixby descended to the first level of the mine and surveyed the platform that stored equipment, mining carts, picks, shovels, and crates of TNT. Several tables and a row of lit lanterns met his eyes. The platform was nearly thirty feet long by about ten feet wide, with tunnels branching off to the west and east, while a third angled steeply down to the north, leading to the much deeper second level.

The sheriff glared at the two henchmen who were present. Both of them were scuffing their feet as they stared at the ground.

"What was that?" Bixby snapped. "What happened to Elijah?"

No one answered.

The sheriff pulled his gun and trained it on one of the men. "Dexter, you and Craig had better tell me what just happened. What's with all the damn shouting?"

Dexter's composure broke first. "I'm sorry, boss. We shoulda kept a better eye on Elijah."

"What happened?"

"He went to take the lady her lunch, but apparently he had other ideas."

"What? How dare he disobey me? I'll skin him alive!"

"You don't have to worry 'bout that, boss," Craig told him. He spat a stream of tobacco juice onto the ground. "She took care of that for you."

"What happened?" Bixby asked.

Craig scratched his head with a dirty hand. "Elijah made the mistake of lowering his pants."

"And?"

"Lunch today was chicken."

"So?"

"She made a chicken leg … uh, er, she took the chicken leg and…"

"And what?" the sheriff demanded.

"Let's just say Elijah won't be sittin' down any time soon," Dexter chortled.

The sheriff's bushy grey eyebrows rose with surprise. "Do you mean to tell me that she shoved a chicken leg up Elijah's —"

Both of his men started giggling like school girls. The sheriff slowly lowered his gun and returned it to his holster.

"I'm surprised to hear myself say this, but you may be right. I like the lady's punishment better than a bullet between the eyes. Where is she now? Did she make it out this time?"

Craig shook his head. "No, boss. She's just sitting on her cot, lookin' as pleased as she could be."

The impudence of the woman made him see red.

"I'll handle this," Sheriff Bixby growled.

He took the ring of huge, rusty skeleton keys off a peg on the wall and walked down the eastern tunnel. He unlocked the heavy iron door he had installed several years ago and walked into the room. Once he was seated, one of his henchmen reached inside to swing the door closed.

"This has got to stop, lady," the sheriff warned. "The

doc is gonna start askin' questions if he has to keep treatin' everyone you send his way."

"Then let me out of here," Sarah curtly responded.

"That ain't gonna happen, darlin'. I told you before why you're here. Once I secure enough capital to retire, then you're free to go."

"I'm supposed to believe you're going to just let me go when you've robbed enough banks? Is that it?"

The sheriff laid a hand over his heart. "You have my word."

Sarah gave him a scornful look. "You expect me to believe you'd keep your word? You really are as stupid as I think you look."

"You watch your mouth, girlie. I've tolerated your little outbursts but that ends now. I'm done negotiating. You will cooperate."

"Or what?" Sarah challenged. "You don't have anything to hold over me."

"The hell I don't," the sheriff disagreed. "You want to keep your husband alive? Play along or I'll bury both Luther and Cora Miller. You got that, darlin'?"

Sarah sighed. "You know, you keep threatening me with that very same thing. If you meant it you'd drag the two of them down here and show me what you're capable of doing. Since you haven't, I can only speculate you don't have the Millers and that you're bluffing."

"I ain't bluffin', darlin'. Push me on this and I will do 'em both. Right here, right now."

Detecting the cold malice dripping from every word the sheriff spoke, Sarah finally looked over at him. The lantern was yanked out of his grip and a small piece of gravel flew at it, colliding with one of the panels of glass, sending razor sharp shards of glass flying.

Every splinter was now hovering less than an inch from the sheriff's surprised eyes. One piece darted in and sliced a three-inch-long laceration on his right cheek. The sheriff howled with outrage. His hand went for his gun.

Sarah barely moved her hand. Now the shards were all making contact with his face. Drops of blood fell from fresh puncture marks on his nose and forehead as Sarah coolly stared at him.

"You'd never make it out the door," the sheriff calmly told her. He arrogantly pushed aside the shards of glass poking his face and wiped his bloody cheek with the back of a hand. "They're under orders to shoot to kill if I don't make it back outta here. You're good, darlin'. There ain't nobody that can say otherwise. However, you ain't *that* good. Now release me."

The glass fell to the ground and shattered into even smaller pieces.

"Let's be honest with each other," Sarah began, keeping her expression neutral. "It's obvious you're going to kill me. There's no way you'd let me live, especially if I do the things you want me to do. My husband isn't here, and there's no one to rescue me. Therefore, since I'm going to die anyway, I choose not to cooperate."

"You're right," the sheriff confessed. "Without leverage, I don't expect you to cooperate. If you want to be all noble, darlin', that's up to you. I suspect you'd willingly sacrifice yourself in order to protect the people you love. I can respect that. However, I don't see you actin' too brave when it comes to your own husband's life. I don't have Luther or his wife in my possession. Yet. But I will soon. Tonight, in fact. Then you'll see. Oh, yes, you'll see. I'll put a bullet between Luther's eyes myself if I have to. By heaven, you will help me retire."

Sarah adopted a bored attitude. "You expect me to believe you're going after the Millers? Tonight? There's no way you're going to convince your men to return to the manor. Haunted houses have a way of doing that to people."

"You scared them good, there ain't no doubt about it," the sheriff agreed. He chuckled. "All the more reason to prove to 'em that there ain't nuthin' there to be afraid of."

His prisoner stared at him for a few moments in silence. "You're Lentarian. Why are you doing this? Aren't you ashamed of yourself?"

"A man's gotta do what a man's gotta do to survive in this world, darlin'," he drawled.

"I can get us all back to Lentari. Don't you understand?

You could go home! Don't you want to see your family again?"

"My family thinks I am a useless waste of skin," the sheriff snarled. "My father thought I'd never amount to anything. Well, look how wrong he was. I am sheriff of this podunk little town. I run it. I can do what I want, when I want. How's that for having no career prospects?"

The sheriff's face softened. He then surprised her by sitting next to her on the cot.

"Look, perhaps we got off on the wrong foot. I think we can and should be friends."

"You just threatened my husband's very existence and you think the two of us can be friends?" Sarah asked.

"To prove my sincerity," the sheriff continued, ignoring Sarah's outburst, "what would you say to an evening out on the town?"

Sarah blinked her eyes and cocked her head at him. "Excuse me?"

"You heard me. I say we go to town tonight. That way you can see my intentions are noble."

"You don't have a noble cell in your body," Sarah heatedly countered.

"Let me rephrase that," Bixby smoothly added. "I'm going to town tonight. So are you. I very much would like it if you did so of your own free will. Or, you can be trussed up like a wild animal. It's your call."

"This is how you treat your friends?" Sarah asked sarcastically.

The sheriff smiled sardonically. "Only friends that don't see reason."

Sarah slowly smiled. Every hair on the sheriff's neck stood on end. He smiled his own lecherous smile, slapped a hand on his knee, as though he had just had a monumental breakthrough, and rose to his feet.

"You'll need your strength. Can I get you a plate of food? You'll forgive me if I don't offer you any more chicken."

"I'm not hungry."

"You haven't eaten in two days. You must be hungry. Do you still think I'd drug the food?"

"Of course, I do. You know that I do."

"What if I take a few bites for you?"

"I still wouldn't touch it," Sarah informed him.

The sheriff gritted his teeth. This woman really knew how to get on his nerves. "Suit yourself. Be ready to go in an hour."

"Only an hour? I have to get my hair ready, pick out my finest dress, do my nails, and … and is there anything else I'm forgetting?"

Bixby grunted with amusement. He had locked the door and was heading back down the mine tunnel when he heard Sarah's parting words.

"Go suck it."

An hour and a half later, the sheriff and fifteen of his men rode into town. Sarah, the sheriff, Deke, and four of his henchmen were riding in the double bench buckboard while everyone else rode on horseback. The townsfolk took one look at who was approaching and wisely vacated the area. Mothers ushered their children indoors, while the men anxiously stood guard in front of their shops and stores, hoping the sheriff would take his business elsewhere.

Sheriff Bixby dismounted at the start of one of the street's two boardwalks. He indicated several of the men should stay with the wagon, and the rest were allowed to do as they pleased. He, Deke, Sarah, and a contingent of a half dozen men leisurely strolled past the storefronts. Every person they encountered refused to look them in the eye. All but one, however.

"Sarah! You're here! You're safe!"

Bixby looked down his nose at the tiny middle-aged woman and scoffed loudly. "You may wait over there," the sheriff told her, pointing to the street.

Rosamund Jones ignored the sheriff and rushed toward Sarah. "We were so worried, my dear. Let me look at you. How are you feeling? Are you well?"

The sheriff stepped directly in front of the woman and waited for Rosamund to stop and acknowledge his presence. She didn't. She walked right around him and reached Sarah.

"Mrs. Jones. It's good to see you," Sarah said in a

somewhat slurred voice.

"What have they done to you?"

This time Deke stepped in Rosamund's path and pushed back the brim of his hat with his right index finger. "Afternoon, ma'am. Kindly step aside."

"I'll do no such thing. Sarah is coming with me."

Deke snapped his fingers. Two burly henchmen appeared at his side. "Escort the lady to … I'm sorry, where should we drop you off? Where have I seen you before, ma'am?"

Each goon hooked a hand under Rosamund's arms and effortlessly hoisted her into the air. Her legs continued to move, uselessly. One goon bent low to give her a closer inspection.

"I've seen her before. She runs the Silver Spike."

Deke turned to look at the sheriff, who gave him a thin smile in return. "Well, then, we should return her to her saloon. Take her back to the Silver Spoke."

"Spike," Rosamund crossly corrected.

"Whatever."

The two goons nodded. They walked off, carrying Rosamund right along as though she were nothing more than a sack of flour.

"Now, let's enjoy our evening, shall we?"

Sarah glared daggers at him. The sheriff took her arm and guided her toward a small fashion boutique.

"I'm told women enjoy looking at this sort of nonsense," he remarked nonchalantly. He held out an arm. "Shall we?"

The sheriff's arm slammed down against his side, as though it had been struck by a sledgehammer.

"Don't press your luck," Sarah told him. She stalked into the store as the sheriff massaged his sore arm and pulled Deke aside. "How much water did she drink?"

"Almost a full cup."

"Did you bring more?"

Deke pointed at a third man who was wearing a canteen strapped across his shoulders.

"Good. Keep an eye on her. If she tries to drink anything, make sure a cup of that water makes it into her hand. Got it?"

Deke nodded. "I got it, boss."

The sheriff stepped across the threshold of the store and saw rack after rack of women's dresses. Shabbily made dresses, he decided, as the patterns didn't match, sleeves were uneven, and the collars of several were asymmetrical. His eyes skimmed the racks to see where Sarah was. She stood there, talking to a frightened young girl who was doing her best to edge away from the counter.

"Just as I suspected, darlin'," the sheriff announced. "There's nothing here worth looking at. Let's go."

Sarah pushed the door open and stepped back onto the boardwalk. She let the door slam in his face. Bixby flinched and yanked his hand out of the way. He angrily eyed Sarah. When she didn't respond, he chalked the unfortunate incident up to an errant gust of wind.

The sheriff hadn't taken five steps when he felt a small tap on his left boot. His left foot hooked behind his right and he fell to the boardwalk with a loud crash. His henchmen rushed to his side, hands extended, to help him back up.

"Who did that?" the sheriff growled. He snatched his hat back and returned it to his head. "Who tripped me?"

His knees were throbbing and his hand stung where he had landed on it, but nothing like the fact that all his men had witnessed him tripping over his own two feet. He cast a quick look at Sarah, who was looking disinterestedly across the street at the entrance of a saloon. Was she responsible for this? Was her semi-stupor an act?

The sheriff scowled. She needed another dose of the tainted water; otherwise, she'd regain full control of her jhorun and all his plans would be for naught. Perhaps he could convince her she was thirsty?

"I need a drink," he announced, to no one in particular.

His entourage followed him to the closest saloon. The sheriff didn't even bother to see which one it was. He and his men drank for free everywhere. Those were the rules. His rules.

"What'll it be, sheriff?" the barkeep gloomily asked once they made it inside.

"Whiskey for me, beer for the boys, and water for the lady."

The young barkeep nodded and began filling the order. Sheriff Bixby nodded at Deke, who discreetly took the glass of water the barkeep had placed on the tray, dumped it on the floor, and filled it from the canteen. He quietly put the glass back on the tray and indicated the serving girl should deliver the drinks.

Sarah, who hadn't noticed the switch, eagerly gulped the water. The sheriff nodded appreciatively at Deke. Now, to wait for the opiate to kick in.

Ten minutes later, as the men laughed, drank, and traded insults, Sarah began to look drowsy. The sheriff smiled. It was showtime.

Bixby tapped Sarah on her shoulder. He pointed across the table at two men in a heated debate over who was the better poker player.

"Did you see that? Just then? That fellow on the left just admitted he was unfaithful to his wife. Can you believe that? What would you do to him if you were married to him and he said that to you?"

Sarah rubbed her eyes and focused on the two men. Her brow furrowed as she tried to think. "I'd slap him. Hard."

"Do it. Show me what you'd do to your husband if he ever admitted to cheating on you."

Sarah's eyes narrowed. Her hand made a slight twitch. Everyone heard a loud slap and watched, dumbfounded, as Dexter was knocked backwards off his chair and fell over on the ground, out cold. Sarah had barely moved! The men laughed. Bixby looked around the room. What else could he get her to do?

He spotted two men on the far side of the saloon. They saw him and both were now staring at their bottles, hoping to not attract attention. He nudged Sarah again. "Look over there. See those two?"

Sarah slowly nodded.

"They're known bank robbers. I've seen their mugs on wanted posters. They gotta be in town to rob our bank. You said you don't like the idea of stealing, so if we can't get their weapons away from them, they're gonna hurt a lot of people and do terrible things. What can we do?"

Sarah's glazed eyes studied the two figures. She gave a slight shrug and sighed, as though the effort to concentrate was tiring her. She gave the barest flick of her hand. Two pistols dropped to the floor. Their chambers sprang open, sending bullets tumbling everywhere.

The first man stared at the other. "What the…"

The men pushed back from their chairs and knelt on the floor, hastily gathering their guns and their bullets. The sheriff caught sight of one man's billfold, sticking up out of his back pocket.

"Didn't you just say one of those men owes your husband money? You did, right?"

Sarah's brow furrowed as she tried to think. "I don't…"

"Oh, trust me, darlin'. You just said they owed your husband money. Look, there's a wallet right there. Slide it over here. Hurry, before he realizes its missing!"

The billfold zipped across the room toward Sarah's hand, but he snatched it out of the air. He opened the wallet, extracted all the bills, and then folded it closed. He handed it to Sarah.

"Oh, my mistake. I guess not. You ought to send this back before anyone notices how suspicious it looks to have another man's wallet."

Sarah nodded. The billfold hurled back through the air and neatly slid back into place without him realizing what happened.

The sheriff was all smiles. It worked! In fact, it had worked so well that his mind was spinning with possibilities. She could steal him gold, silver, even diamonds! Oh yes, whether Sarah wanted to or not, she was going to help him retire!

He detected movement in his peripheral vision and turned to look at his table. Sarah had picked up her nearly empty glass and was swirling the contents around as she studied the clear liquid. Did she suspect something? Had the dose been too strong? Had Deke inadvertently tipped Sarah off? Had she been able to taste it?

"Come on, darlin'. I'd like to get some fresh air."

Sarah reluctantly set the glass down and rose to her feet.

She swayed a little, but managed to stay upright. The sheriff scowled. The water was definitely too strong. Now it was going to appear that she was intoxicated and might arouse suspicion.

The sheriff bristled. This was *his* town. He wouldn't tolerate anyone questioning him or his actions. If he had to remind the people, then so be it.

"We're done here," he told Deke. "Round up the boys. We're leavin'."

"You got it, boss."

"Be quick about it. Comin' to town with her was a mistake."

While men went to get the horses and wagon, Sheriff Bixby paced in front of the saloon, glaring. A smug smile formed on his face. No one looked his way, and no one was even bothering to look up. That was how you ran a town. That's how you kept people in line. With fear and determination.

"Sarah! Yoohoo! Sarah! There you are."

The sheriff turned at the voice. A brunette girl had come out of the fashion boutique and was eagerly hurrying across the street.

"I've been looking high and low for you. Where have you been?"

Sarah stared at the newcomer's face with a vacant expression. "Peggy, is that you?"

Peggy, one of Sarah's co-workers at the Silver Spike, finally noticed who was standing protectively nearby. "Sheriff Bixby, what are you doing here?"

The sheriff's cold grey eyes narrowed. "This is my town, darlin'. Get goin'. There ain't nuthin' for you here today."

The girl turned to look back at Sarah. Peggy's face was set. "No. I don't know what you've done to her, but you need to leave her alone. I don't abandon my friends and she clearly needs me."

Deke stepped directly into Peggy's path.

"Git on out of here, harlot. You heard the man. This doesn't concern you. Now git!"

Peggy jammed her hands into her hips and held her ground. "Not without my friend. You can't treat people this way. I think you are the one that needs to leave."

CRACK!

The sheriff backhanded the serving girl, easily knocking her to the ground. "Consider that a warning, darlin'. When I tell a woman to git then she had damn well better git. Oh, and just so you know, there is no second warning."

Peggy put a hand to the red welt on her face, her eyes tearing up. She tried to rise but her legs were too shaky. The young owner of the saloon rushed out and pulled Peggy to her feet and ushered her inside.

Satisfied, the sheriff turned to the sound of his wagon approaching. However, he frowned once he saw that he had an audience. A large audience.

Men and women were slowly pouring out of nearby buildings and were angrily glaring at the sheriff and his entourage. Everywhere he looked, the sheriff saw angry scowls and disapproving stares. For the first time ever, Bixby felt his control over the town loosen.

Deke scoffed loudly and strode confidently out to meet the crowd. "Who said you could come out here? Get out of here! Go home. This is the sheriff's private business."

No one moved.

"You heard me. Scram!"

"Need I remind you people who's in charge?" the sheriff challenged. He took a few steps toward the crowd of onlookers and drew his sidearm. "Do I need to make an example out of a few of you? Don't test me. I will not tolerate disobedience."

Several villagers hesitantly looked at each other. A few hushed conversations started. Unfortunately for the sheriff, no one moved an inch.

Growing angrier, the sheriff fired several rounds into the air. The crowd flinched but they still didn't back down. Quiet conversations turned into shouts and accusations. The sheriff stared incredulously at the impudent townsfolk. Fifty or more men were standing in the street, and over half of them had their hands resting on their firearms.

They dared to rebel? He was the sheriff! Everyone knew he ran this town. So why now? Was it the woman?

Bixby risked a sidelong glance at Sarah. Her eyes were blinking faster. She was shaking her head, fighting the effects of the opium. The last thing he needed was to have his prisoner tossing his men around like paper dolls. It was time to go, but not before he had the last word.

He brought up his gun and took aim at an incredibly large man who was giving him a hostile look. The huge man was surprisingly nimble, and leapt to the side, but not before taking a bullet in his shoulder. He hit the ground hard, causing the crowd to erupt into screams of terror. The people scattered in all directions.

Sarah remained motionless as she stared at the fallen man. "Hank?"

Hank twisted on the ground and turned to look up at her. "I'm so sorry, ma'am. I should've done something sooner. Don't worry about me. It's just a flesh wound."

"Oh, Hank!" Sarah gave her head a couple of violent shakes as she blinked and fought to regain her senses. At a signal from the sheriff she saw Deke pull out his gun and advance on her, gripping his pistol by the chamber, ready to slam the heavy wooden grip down over her head.

Sarah's foggy mind cast about for a way to overcome Deke.

For the first time, she noticed his immaculate appearance. Was Mr. Creepy some kind of germaphobe, afraid of getting dirty?

Her eyes dropped to the dirt road. She rallied all her mental strength and whipped a plume of dirt straight up at him.

He started howling as though he had been doused in fire.

Deke wiped his eyes with the back of a sleeve and glared at her. He gave a flick of his wrist, pointing the business end of the gun straight at her.

Sarah's eyes cast about, and fell upon a pile of steaming, fresh horse dung. Her expression changed to one of pure malice. The dung flew straight at Deke, who gasped with surprise. Too bad his mouth was open.

His screech could have shattered glass. He dove head first into the closest watering trough, swishing out his mouth.

Sarah turned back to see what the sheriff was doing but was surprised to find him missing. Where was he?

Suddenly, a sharp blow on the back of her head. She fought off the darkness but was no match for it. Sarah passed out.

The rest of the sheriff's men had drawn their guns. They were cocked, loaded, and ready to fire upon the townspeople, some of whom had returned and were helping Hank retreat into one of the shops. It was the new bakery. He saw the baker and his assistant usher the wounded man inside, then watched as the assistant ran off down the street, presumably to alert Doc Emerson. Bixby ordered his men to put Sarah in the wagon.

He came to a decision.

It was time to pull up stakes and abandon Coeur d'Alene. What did he need with his silver mine? He had a teleporter in his possession. He could clean out a bank without even stepping foot inside. Besides, he hadn't liked the looks people were giving him. They had just got their first taste of strengthened unity today. He could see it in their eyes.

He needed to get the Millers tonight, and by sunrise tomorrow he would be long gone. He could always find another little town to take over.

Sheriff Marcus Bixby smiled as they rode off into the sunset. Life was good.

Chapter 6 – The Approaching Storm

"Where is she?" Steve demanded. He followed the others downstairs into the living room and reluctantly sat down. His great-great-grandmother placed a gentle hand on his shoulder but whipped it away once she realized he was burning hot. "What's happened to Sarah?"

Luther sighed. "I'll tell you what we know. Just keep your jhorun in check. The portal is now active. We don't want to burn down the house it's sitting in, do we?"

Steve cast an irritated look down at his hands. They weren't lit. Yet. "Please, just tell me what happened. Did someone take her?"

Luther nodded.

Steve grimaced. "It's that damn sheriff, isn't it?"

Luther nodded again.

Steve rose to his feet. His hands balled into fists and instantly flamed up. Everyone else flinched. Luther held up both hands, signaling Steve to wait.

"Extinguish your flames. You're going to drive us out of the house if you keep that up."

Steve flicked his hands out. The ambient temperature dropped, but not by much.

"Listen to me, Steve. Please. Sit down. I know you want to rescue her. We all do. However, it'd be foolish not to think this through. You don't appear to be a foolish man, so will you listen?"

Steve reluctantly sat but the frown remained on his face.

"Thank you. Now, what we've learned is that Sarah was taken by the sheriff's men. They —"

"When?" Steve interrupted.

"Several nights ago. She and Cora were in town when they were attacked."

Steve looked over at Cora. "Are you okay?"

Cora nodded. She dabbed a handkerchief at the corner of her eyes. "I just hope she's safe. I've been worried sick."

"Where would he take her?" Steve wanted to know. "I'm going to get her back. That's a promise. I just need to know where she is."

Luther forced a smile. "I know you will, Steve. Hear me out. We know the sheriff has his own private compound on Jackknife Peak. I wish I could tell you more but unfortunately, I can't. I haven't personally seen it."

"No one has," Cecil muttered.

"Someone must have seen something," Rosamund snapped. Steve stared at her. "Mrs. Jones. What are you doing here?"

"She delivered the athe crystal," Luther said. "I don't know how you did it, or why you chose her saloon, but you did an admirable job of getting the crystal into friendly hands."

Steve's demeanor softened. He turned back to the small woman and smiled. "Thank you. I didn't want to involve you in anything else, but your snug was the only vision we could get from Lentari."

"I knew Mina was a gatekeeper," Luther said, beaming. "I knew she shared my jhorun. How she managed to home in on the snug at the Silver Spike is still beyond me."

"Right there with you, pal," Steve told him. He glanced

up at the ceiling. "How's she doing? You need to go easy on her. She's been through more than you could ever imagine."

"She's resting. Cora gave her something to eat and put her in one of the guest rooms. She was nearly asleep on her feet. I can't thank you enough for rescuing her."

"Hey, she's family. What was I supposed to do? Leave her there? Absolutely not. Now, back to the problem at hand, rescuing Sarah. I don't even want to imagine what that sheriff has planned for her."

"I want to know," Quinn began, as he leaned forward in his chair, "how did this sheriff fellow know Lady Sarah was the Nohrin?"

"Who said he did?" Steve countered.

"Why else would he want her?" Quinn looked around the room. "I may be an outsider here, but it certainly sounds like this unpleasant fellow knew Lady Sarah was a teleporter."

"How can Lady Sarah be abducted?" Lissa asked. She was sitting next to Quinn and had raised a hand. "Couldn't she just teleport herself back to safety?"

Steve nodded. "Yes, she could, and the fact that she hasn't concerns me more than anything else. That's why I think something has happened to her."

"I might be able to shed some light there," Rosamund announced. "One of my boys, the same one who witnessed the kidnapping and could have prevented it —"

"Could have prevented it?" Steve interrupted, frowning harder.

"Don't get me started," Rosamund warned. "Hank said he saw Sarah acting strangely. Peggy noticed it, too. She said Sarah and the sheriff were in town yesterday."

"When?" Steve wanted to know.

"Not long after sunset. The sheriff was parading her around town like she was a show pony. Peggy saw Sarah and tried to say hello. You know, make sure she was okay. Sheriff Bixby backhanded her and sent her to the ground."

Steve's eyebrows shot up. "He hit Sarah? You've got to be kidding! When I find that son of a..."

"Not Sarah," Rosamund corrected. "Peggy. He hit Peggy."

"Oh. Sorry. Is she okay?"

"She's bruised but she'll be fine in a few days."

"Wait a minute. Sarah was out in public? With him?"

Rosamund nodded. "Yes. Let me finish. Peggy told me that Sarah was not acting like herself."

Steve crossed his arms over his chest. "In what way?"

"As if she was drugged," the diminutive woman told him.

"That's how he's keeping Lady Sarah from teleporting," Quinn announced.

Steve looked over at Quinn and waited for an explanation.

"Teleporters must be able to visualize where they're going. Without that reference point clearly ingrained in their mind, a teleporter would be rendered powerless."

"He's drugging her," Steve repeated.

"You must be prepared," Luther insisted. "You cannot blindly rush in."

"Easy for you to say," Steve angrily shot back. "Your wife is sitting safe and sound right next to you. Mine is going through who knows what."

"You're not in Lentari anymore," Luther reminded him.

"That's something Sarah would say," Steve accused.

"Then she'd be right. Think about where you are. Your flames will not stop bullets. Arrows, aye, but not bullets."

Steve dropped his arms to his sides. He groaned. "What do you suggest?"

"We need to know exactly where she is, who Sheriff Bixby has up there with him, what type of weapons he has, and so on. We need inside information."

"Good luck," Rosamund scoffed. "You're an outsider, Steve. Sheriff Bixby has got everyone in town completely petrified of him. You're going to be hard pressed to find someone willing to talk."

Steve slowly stood. Cecil, Quinn, and Lissa immediately followed suit. "Then we find someone."

"And if they don't want to talk?" Rosamund asked.

Steve ignited both hands and smiled. "Then we persuade him."

"Do you have someone in mind?" Luther asked.

Steve shook his head. "Not really. Any one of the sheriff's

men will do."

"How are you going to find one of them?" Cecil wanted to know. "Better yet, how will you get one of them alone?"

Steve headed for the door. "Haven't a clue. All I know is I'm going to town. The last time I was there they seemed to be everywhere. You all are more than welcome to come along."

Rosamund rose to her feet with a determined expression on her face. "I'll take you. My wagon is right outside."

Luther and Cecil rose to their feet. "We're coming, too."

Quinn started to say something but Luther hushed him.

"You are too weak, Quinn. Stay here and rest. Get your strength back. And no, Lissa, don't even think about it."

The teenager sulked as she sat back down.

"Follow us in your wagon," Steve instructed, as he climbed up into Rosamund's buckboard. "We're going to need a way to get back here."

Luther and Cecil immediately changed course and veered toward the barn.

"We'll meet you at the Silver Spike," Cecil called out.

* * *

Steve followed Mrs. Jones into the saloon, reaching out to hold one of the swinging saloon doors open for her. The tiny proprietor's head didn't even show over the top of the swinging doors. Several feathers sticking out of the top of her hat did make it over, and Steve briefly wondered what her approach must look like from someone already inside the saloon.

Hank and Bart appeared and nodded their heads.

"Hank, find Peggy and join us down in the snug. Be quick about it. I know you were shot in the shoulder, so I meant what I said. If you're not feeling up to this, then you should go home. No one will think any less of you."

Hank shook his head vehemently. "No, ma'am. I will see this through. I—I caused this problem. I need to see this through."

"Good for you, Hank." Rosamund eyed Hank's broad

physique and reconsidered. She looked around her saloon. It was past noon, squarely in the middle of her slow time of the day. As a result, there were only a few of her regular patrons on the floor. "I've changed my mind. We'll be more comfortable up here. I want everyone up at the bar."

Fifteen minutes later, Rosamund, her two bouncers, plus Peggy, Steve, Luther, and Cecil, were all seated side-by-side at the bar. Rosamund was pacing back and forth behind the counter, which meant the only thing most of them could see was the top of her hat bobbing back and forth. A moment later, she stepped up onto one of the boxes and eyed the people eyeing her back. She caught Hank glaring at Steve. Her bouncer saw her looking at him and hooked a thumb in Steve's direction.

"What's *he* doing here, Mrs. Jones? This was the man bothering Miss Sarah several days ago."

Steve shot the huge man a look of disbelief.

"He's Sarah's husband," Rosamund quickly answered. "This is Steve. We are going to help him rescue Sarah."

Hank's darkening attitude skyrocketed straight up. "You are Miss Sarah's husband? I apologize for my actions."

"Don't worry about it," Steve told the enormous man.

"It was my fault she was taken," Hank miserably admitted.

"Did you take her?" Steve asked.

Hank shook his head no.

"Then you're not at fault. You want to make it up to me? Help me get her back."

A look of grim resolve appeared on Hank's broad face. "Consider it done."

Rosamund nodded. "Now, here's the situation. The sheriff is more than likely holding Sarah at his compound up on the mountain. We need to know more about it. We need to know exactly where she's being held and what the sheriff is planning on doing with her."

Peggy absentmindedly touched her swollen face. "What can we do to help, Mrs. Jones?"

"Find me someone who can answer those questions," Steve answered flatly.

"None of the sheriff's men will talk," Peggy tried to

explain. "They're too afraid of him. I doubt very much they'd even talk at gunpoint."

"Then it's a good thing I won't be using guns," Steve informed her.

"How are you planning on persuading someone to talk?" Hank wanted to know. "What do you know that the rest of us don't?"

"I know that practically everyone is afraid of fire."

Hank spread his hands. "How does that help us?"

Steve looked over at the large fireplace in the middle of the room. It was loaded with wood and was burning fast and furious. He held up a hand. The fire in the fireplace jumped straight up and slowly approached Steve's outstretched hand. Steve turned to see what the bouncer's reaction would be and was startled to see that two stools had been knocked over as his two newest companions had beaten a hasty retreat.

He rotated the large ball of flames this way and that before instructing his jhorun to push the fire back into the fireplace and allow it to resume burning the wood. As soon as the fireplace had been set back in order, Steve looked around the room to see what had happened to Hank. He found the giant man, along with Peggy and Rosamund, cowering behind the bar. As one, their heads peeked up and over the counter to stare at him with wide eyes.

The four patrons who were enjoying their drinks had tipped over their table and were hiding behind it. Four grizzled faces peered anxiously at them.

"Perhaps a warning would have been in order," Rosamund suggested, as she regained her feet. She waved apologetically at her regulars. "I'm sorry about that. The fireplace appears to be faulty. I'll have that looked at."

"The damn fire done jumped out of the fireplace!" one of her regulars exclaimed. He pointed at Steve. "You did that!"

Steve nodded. "Yes, I did."

"How did you do that?" the man wanted to know.

"I can't explain and even if I could, I don't have the time. I have to get Sarah back."

"The lovely young gal that worked here?" another of the

regulars asked. Together the four men carefully stood and righted the table. They pulled their chairs back over and sank heavily down on them. "What happened to Sarah? You kin to her?"

"She's my wife."

"She's married? Damned if I knew that."

"You guys were here the whole time we were talking about it," Steve pointed out.

"Weren't payin' attention to you, friend. What goes on at tables other than ours, well, it be none of our business."

"She kept it quiet," Rosamund told them. "It's not important. She's been taken by the sheriff, Ronald. We're going to get her back."

Ronald, the first patron to have spoken, rose to his feet. "I'll help. I liked her."

The other three men pushed away from their table and rose to their feet, too. "We'll help. What do you need us to do?"

"Thanks for the offer, guys, but … wait. You know what? I do think I have something for you to do."

"You do?" Ronald eagerly asked.

"You do?" Rosamund, Luther, and Cecil echoed.

Steve nodded. "I do. Listen, do you think you can find one of the sheriff's men for us? I don't care who. Any of them will do. Go out together as a group and look around town. As soon as you spot one of them send someone back here, okay?"

Ronald nodded enthusiastically. "Yes, sir! We can do that! Come on, fellers. We got a job to do."

"Thank you, Ronald," Rosamund called out as they exited the saloon. "Drinks are on me today! Now then, since there's no one left in here and Gerry is out fishing today, we're going to close. Bart, Hank, you know what to do."

The two burly men began the tedious job of securing the saloon. Windows were closed and shutters were bolted in place. As he locked one of the shutters, Hank looked over at Steve. He shook his head.

Steve noticed. "What? What is it?"

"A little feller like yourself ain't gonna be able to take

on the likes of the sheriff. I hope you're good with a gun, buddy."

"I don't think I've ever been called little before in my entire life. Hmmph. Doesn't matter. No guns. I hate guns."

Hank's eyebrows shot up. "No guns? What are you plannin' on doin'? Politely ask him to let your woman go? He's gonna put up a fight. I hope you know that."

Steve ignited both hands. "I certainly hope so."

Finished with locking up, Hank and Bart went out to help Ronald and the regulars in locating someone, anyone, from the sheriff's gang. The reports coming in were less than promising. The sheriff's gang of deputies had vanished.

"Where are they?" Steve demanded, nearly an hour later. He was pacing in front of the fireplace; the flames doubled in size every time he passed. "Where is everybody? It's like he's abandoned the town. Why would he … Oh, no. He's jumped ship, hasn't he?"

"He wouldn't do that, Steve. He has the richest silver mine in town. He wouldn't leave that behind."

"He would if he had a teleporter under his control," Luther countered. "If he thinks he can control Miss Sarah, all the silver in the world would mean nothing to him."

Cecil stared at Luther in shock.

Luther explained. "A teleporter could get him more silver at a moment's notice. She could teleport into the most secure bank vault and back out before anyone would know about it."

Steve cursed softly to himself and looked Luther in the eye. "If the sheriff leaves town, and abandons his compound, then we'll never find her again. We need to find out what's going on and we need to do it *now*."

"We're trying, Steve," Luther snapped, displaying a rare bout of exasperation.

Steve studied his ancestor closely. The man was frustrated, distraught, and clueless as to what to do next. His gaze swept around the room. No one had any idea.

Steve came to a rapid decision. He stopped his pacing and headed toward the door.

"Where are you going?" Luther asked, hurrying to catch up.

Steve held up a hand, signaling him to stop.

"You and Cecil stay here. I'm going to find us a snitch."

"Not by yourself you're not," Luther told him in a stern voice.

"I second that," Cecil told him.

"Luther, you're too important for me to risk. You're staying put. Cecil, I appreciate what you've done for me, but I can work faster if I don't have to worry about you."

Rosamund pushed her way through the tall men and regarded Steve. "Then take someone you don't have to worry about."

Steve met the tiny woman's gaze. "Like?"

"Me," a deep voice rumbled.

Steve turned to look at Hank, who had just crossed his big beefy arms across his chest.

"Didn't I hear you were shot? I know you're tough, and you probably can't tell you have a hole in your shoulder, but I don't want you getting hurt any more than you already are."

Hank shook his head. "Every time I close my eyes, I see Deke carrying Miss Sarah away while I couldn't lift an arm in protest. I want retribution. For myself. For Sarah. For you. This wound? I'll proudly wear it as a battle scar."

He held out a hand that was bigger than most dinner plates. Steve took it and winced as Hank crushed it in an eager handshake.

"Where are we going?" Hank wanted to know.

"The jail. I'll bet we can find someone there."

"There's bound to be more than one," Hank advised. He cracked his knuckles. "I certainly hope so."

Steve followed Hank to the door. Just before he stepped outside, he looked back at his circle of friends.

"Be ready to move. Chances are we're going to be moving pretty fast when we come back here."

"Then don't bother coming back here," Rosamund instructed. "We'll meet you at the jail."

Steve nodded. "That'll work. Give us half an hour and then come get us."

"We will."

Twenty minutes later, the two of them were safely

concealed within the nearby trees, staring at a familiar two story building. Hank tapped him on the shoulder and pointed to a single man who had just come down the steps of the county jail. Steve recognized the deputy. It was Gabriel, the same one who had arrested him before.

"He's perfect," Steve whispered to his hulking bodyguard. "He's our guy. Let's go get him."

Hank growled. "With pleasure."

Steve and Hank stepped out into the open and began striding confidently toward the jail. Sensing movement, the deputy looked over in their direction and paled. His eyes widened as he recognized Steve and instantly turned tail and fled. He was screaming profanities as he disappeared into the nearby woods.

Steve frowned. "Hmm. Flaw detected. I didn't think he'd do that."

"I'm sorry," Hank began. "Many people are intimidated by my size."

"Believe it or not, I don't think he was running from you." He gave a quick recap of his earlier jailbreak.

Hank chuckled. "Serves him right."

Alerted by the commotion, two more men appeared at the jailhouse door. They spotted Steve and Hank and ran down the steps, drawing their guns.

Hank stiffened with surprise. Steve even heard the big man growl.

"It's him," Hank whispered.

"Who?" Steve whispered back.

"It's Deke Babcock. He's the one who kidnapped Miss Sarah."

"Is he now? Change of plan. There's our snitch. He's going to tell us everything he knows."

Deke and the second man now had a pistol in each hand, trained directly at them.

"If he resists," Hank murmured, "then I get to be the one to persuade him."

"He took my wife," Steve answered, not bothering to lower his voice. "I have first dibs."

Deke cocked both pistols and leered. Hank slowly raised

his hands.

"Lookee what we got here, Sirus. I remember this feller. This is the yellow-skinned pea-brain from the Silver Spike. He's all bark but no bite."

Steve deliberately crossed his arms over his chest and scowled.

"Get your hands up, fool. I … yeow!"

Both men dropped their guns to the ground. Together they stared in amazement; all four guns glowed red.

Steve dropped his hands back to his sides and ignited them. He pointed a flaming finger at Deke. "You and I need to have a little chat."

"Who … who are you?" Deke stammered.

"My name is Steve. Sarah, the woman you kidnapped, is my wife."

Deke's eyes shot open. He turned on his heel, shoved Sirus to the ground, and bolted. Doors slammed as he barricaded himself inside the jail.

Sirus scrambled to his feet and hesitantly backed away from them. Steve looked up at Hank. "Would you take care of him, please? I'll take Deke."

"It would be my sincerest pleasure," the huge man rumbled.

Sirus bolted, with Hank hot on his heels. Steve turned to look up at the closed front door. He walked up the steps and tried the handle. It was locked.

Steve pumped his jhorun into his hand and pulled the handle. After a few moments the metal handle and the lock's inner workings were forcefully yanked out of the door. It creaked open.

"Stay away from me!" Deke's high-pitched voice screamed. "Someone get the sheriff! I need backup! Hurry!"

Steve checked the small jailer's office and found it empty. He moved toward the large holding cell in the middle of the building. Three scruffy men immediately pointed up at the second floor. Steve nodded and started to head toward the stairs when he paused. He looked back at the three men who were desperately staring back at him.

He grabbed the locking mechanism on their cell with both

hands and waited for the metal to heat. Ten seconds later he gave a violent twist. The entire lock came away from the door. He dropped the misshapen ball of metal and opened the cell door.

"Get out of here, guys."

The men didn't need to be told a second time. They practically tripped over each other in their haste. Once they had disappeared outside, Steve grabbed a pair of handcuffs from the desk and climbed the stairs to the second floor.

Having recently been repaired, after he had successfully freed Luther and several others from this very jail, the cells on the second floor were empty.

All but one.

Deke had locked himself into the farthest cell, the one where Luther had been held, and had dragged the cot over to wedge it up against the cell door. Steve peered angrily at the smarmy looking individual who was crouching fearfully behind the thin cot.

"You and I have a lot to talk about," Steve told the trembling man. He caught sight of a dagger sticking out of Deke's right boot and stepped a few paces back. "You're going to remove your weapons and drop them through the bars here."

When Deke didn't move, Steve smacked a fist against the bars, making a loud clang. Deke jumped.

"I said, drop your weapons. Now. Any metal on your body is going to heat up in about five seconds. Your choice."

Deke still refused to cooperate. Steve shrugged. "Suit yourself."

The dagger in Deke's boot was the first to be yanked off and thrust through the bars. Then a second dagger, hidden in his other boot, joined the first. An ammo belt, his regular belt, and a pocket watch followed moments later.

Steve kicked the items across the floor and watched them fall over the edge of the balcony onto the ground floor below. He turned his gaze back to Deke, who had fallen to his knees.

"Please don't kill me."

"Why would I do that? You're much more valuable to me alive."

"What do you want?"

"Information. You are going to tell me everything I want to know about the sheriff."

"I can't do that."

"I'm sorry, but did I phrase that in such a way where I insinuated I was giving you a choice? You will tell me what I want to know."

Deke swallowed nervously. "Why would I do that?"

Steve grasped two of the metal bars in his hands and leaned forward to glare at his wife's abductor. "Because I'm going to say *please*."

At the exact instant he said 'please' he yanked the bars right out of the wall. He looked at the blisteringly hot bars in his hands and then pointedly looked back at Deke. He tossed them inside Deke's cell and watched with grim satisfaction as Deke dodged the smoldering bars.

Five minutes later, with his arms shackled securely in place behind his back, Deke was led out of the jail and down the street, toward the heart of the town. Hank appeared, with an unconscious man draped over his shoulder.

"Is that our friend Sirus?"

Hank nodded. He poked a threatening finger at Deke, who shied away from him. "Was he much trouble?" the big man asked.

Steve shook his head. "Not really. For some strange reason he didn't want to come with us. Thankfully it didn't take much persuasion. Personally, I was hoping he'd put up more of a fight."

Deke's head hung a little lower. Steve knew he had seen the people gawking at him as they slowly walked by. They stared at the sheriff's deputy and started whispering amongst themselves.

"You're never going to get her back," Deke mumbled.

Steve motioned to Hank, who reached out a huge hand to smack Deke's head.

"Let's agree to disagree, pal."

"I've never seen him so obsessed with one person before."

"It's because he knows what she can do," Steve told him.

Rosamund and her wagon appeared. She pulled her

buckboard to a stop next to them and smiled appreciatively at Hank and his captive. "You're looking good, Hank. How are you feeling?"

Hank grinned at his employer and tipped his hat. "Mighty fine, ma'am. Thank you."

"Deke Babcock, is it?" Rosamund turned in her seat and watched Hank dump Sirus in the back, then single-handedly tossed Deke in, too. "I don't think we've been properly introduced."

"I know who you are, woman," Deke sneered. "You're the b—"

An insanely huge hand appeared on his shoulder and squeezed so tightly that Steve was afraid he'd hear snapping bones any moment. Deke fell silent and gritted his teeth through the pain.

They made it back to the Silver Spike without any further incidents. Hank dropped Sirus by the fireplace and trussed him up tighter than a fly caught in a spider's web. Hank looked over at Deke and pointed at a chair. Deke didn't offer a word of protest as he reluctantly sat. Within moments he had so many strands of rope encircling his body that he could barely breathe.

Steve slid a chair over, flipped it around, and straddled it as he sat down. Luther and Cecil also pulled up chairs. Rosamund continued to pace. Steve looked up at her.

"Do you think you could find a map of Coeur d'Alene?"

"Sure. Gerry has one. I'll go fetch it."

"What do you need a map for?" Cecil wanted to know.

"Our new friend here is going to point out where the sheriff's compound is, where the best place to mount a rescue should come from, where they're holding Sarah, and so on. Isn't that right, Deke?"

Deke glowered at Steve but didn't say anything.

Steve blasted out a jet of fire and twirled it around Deke a few times before pulling the flames back to his hand. Deke actually screamed like a small child. For that matter Luther and Cecil had both let out cries of shock.

Luther backhanded Steve's arm. "Don't *do* that!"

"Fine! Fine! I'll tell you what you want to know!" Deke

cried out.

Rosamund produced her map and they spread it out on the table before them. Hank gave a gentle push on Deke's chair and slid him the ten feet so that he could see too. Steve pointed at a spot on the map.

"Here's Jackknife Peak. This here is the summit. Where does the sheriff live?"

When Deke wasn't forthcoming with the answer, Hank slid a chair over and sat down next to him.

"It's there, on the western mesa," Deke hastily offered.

Steve, Luther, Cecil, and Rosamund leaned forward to look at the map. Rosamund tapped an area on the mountain. "Here?"

Deke nodded. "Yes. His lodge faces the western sun. He told me once it was so he could keep an eye on his town."

"Is that where he's holding Sarah?" Steve asked.

"No. In the mine."

"What? He's got her down a mine?"

Deke shook his head. "The sheriff's mine is enormous. Most of the first level has been adapted for his own personal use. The second level extends much deeper. That's where the silver starts. He has your wife in one of the tunnels."

"Has he been drugging her?"

Deke sighed. "He has, yes."

"Did he tell you why?" Luther asked.

Deke shrugged as best he was able to. "The only thing he kept saying was that if she came to her senses then there would be hell to pay."

Steve looked at Luther, amazed. "That confirms it. Quinn was right. The sheriff knows about her. How is that even possible? Sarah wouldn't tell anyone about her jhorun."

Luther sadly shook his head. "I don't have an answer for you."

"What's he drugging her with?" Steve snapped.

"Opiate."

Steve groaned. "Oh, that's just great."

Rosamund laid a hand on Steve's arm. "She'll be alright. The effects of opium will wear off eventually."

"Any residual damage or side effects?" Luther asked,

unfamiliar with the drug.

"Aside from it being an addictive substance and illegal?" Steve asked, looking incredulously at his ancestor.

Cecil hesitantly spoke up. "What are you talking about? Opium isn't illegal."

"It most certainly is," Steve argued.

"Perhaps in your time," Luther quietly told him, "but not here."

"Oh. Okay, I'll let that one go. Be that as it may, I can't imagine Sarah would willingly take that stuff."

"He's spiking her food?" Rosamund suggested.

"She suspected that and wouldn't eat," Deke told them. "So we spiked the water in very low doses. She resisted. I tried to tell the sheriff she was bad news but he wouldn't listen. He kept saying he was going to use her so he could retire."

"And then what?" Cecil asked in a quiet voice. "Was he going to let her go?"

"Now what do you think, idiot?" Deke snapped. "She sent so many men to Doc Emerson that we had to start paying him off."

"Miss Sarah was hurting people?" Rosamund asked, certain she had misheard or else Deke had misremembered.

"She was moving things around without touchin' 'em," Deke recalled. "I don't know how she was doin' it."

"Why aren't the sheriff's men in town?" Rosamund asked. "Do you know what he's doing?"

"Sheriff Bixby has decided to ditch this flea-bitten town," Deke smugly told her. "He's gonna be gone by sunrise."

Steve lurched to his feet. He slid the map over to Deke and pointed down at the mountain.

"Where's the mine?"

Chapter 7 – Siege on Jackknife Peak

Nearly an hour before sunrise, the sky was dark and riddled with thousands of stars. The moon had long since gone to bed for the night, affording the perfect conditions to sneak undetected up the side of a quiet mountain.

There were no warbling birds, or rustling crickets. Hank stepped on a twig and smiled sheepishly at his two companions.

"Dude, that sounded like a gunshot," Steve whispered, crossly. "Seriously, watch where you're stepping."

The big man to his left grunted once in apology.

"I still say we should have left much earlier."

This time the voice came from his right. Steve glanced over his shoulder at Bart, Rosamund's other bouncer. The behemoth of a man stood easily seven feet tall and tipped the scales at well over three hundred fifty pounds, yet there he was, tiptoeing through the grass as though he was afraid to step on a flower. Steve chuckled to himself. At least he was trying.

"I told you before, we needed more time to plan. It's better to be safe than sorry."

Following Hank's lead, Bart grunted once. Hank held up a hand. Steve and Bart froze in their tracks.

"What is it?" Steve whispered. "What do you see?"

"A lookout."

"Where?"

"Three hundred paces up the road, sitting against a tree."

Steve peered at the dark countryside. He could make out shapes, but his eyesight was nowhere near good enough to spot someone sitting against a tree trunk. A spark of light appeared and disappeared almost as quickly. Someone had lit a cigarette.

He gave the signal to Hank, who edged his way as close as he dared to the smoking man.

They heard a strangled cry and then Hank's 'all clear' whistle. They started on their way again, keeping to the damp underbrush, rather than risk venturing into the open. As Steve had repeatedly warned, he couldn't melt bullets fast enough to be of any use, so it was best to stay out of the way.

They incapacitated two more guards before they finally saw the sheriff's private home. Steve stared at the enormous A-frame lodge in shock. It was easily twice as big as the manor, which was truly saying something. The large main window was pointed straight at them, giving a view of the lake and town.

Three smaller buildings sat nearby. The northernmost one, Steve knew, hid the entrance to the mine—and Sarah. The lodge faced town, which was directly behind him, so that meant the northern shack should be … Steve peered at the three tiny shacks and grumbled. Any of them could be considered northern.

"Do not light anything on fire," Hank reminded him. "Not yet. We'd be seen."

"You think?"

Hank turned to him strangely. "Yes. Yes, I do think."

"Wow. We need to work on your sarcasm skills. Okay,

we're going to have to mmmf!"

Hank slapped a hand over Steve's mouth, instantly cutting him off. He pointed at the main lodge. Three men had just come out the front door and split up. Two went to the shack on the far right and one went to the shack in the middle. Steve eyed the small building on the right.

"It's that one."

Bart shook his head. "You don't know that for sure."

"Sure, I do. Two people just went in. That's gotta be the mine."

One person emerged from the shack on the left, carrying an armful of gear. He disappeared into the lodge. A few minutes later four men emerged from the lodge. Three went into the far-left shack while one went to the one in the middle.

"Is this some type of joke?" Steve grumbled to himself. "Why do I feel like we should be keeping track of how many people went into each building?"

They watched as teams of horses were hitched to three wagons which, Steve noted with dismay, were fully loaded. A fourth wagon and team pulled up. The men began loading this wagon, too.

"He's certainly planning on leaving." Steve scowled. This wasn't what he wanted to see. He was hoping they'd be early enough to slip in and out completely undetected.

"Hank, we have to act quickly. You and Bart are up. I need a diversion. You said you could create one mother of a distraction. Let's see what you can do. Remember, be subtle."

Hank and Bart reached behind their backs and from under their coats produced two sticks of dynamite.

Bart grinned at him. "I've always wanted to do this."

"No blowing up any buildings until we get Sarah," Steve warned. He turned to look up at each of his companions. "I mean it, guys. We're here to save Sarah. She's our priority."

"You got it, boss," Hank jovially told him. He and Bart stepped back into the woods and disappeared.

Steve eyed the three small shacks. Which one should he try first? He hadn't realized how long he had been squatting on the ground amidst the damp plants until the shack in the middle suddenly vanished in a brilliant flash of light. In the quiet stillness of the pre-dawn morning, the ear-shattering explosion ripped through the countryside, rattling windows and shaking trees.

Steve rolled his eyes. "Subtle. Really freakin' subtle. Did I, or did I not tell those guys to wait until we knew which one was the mine?"

The lodge door banged open and a whole slew of men came pouring out. One, an older fellow in his fifties, began shouting orders.

"Put that out! As quickly as possible! They'll be seein' that all the way from town. Hurry, you ignorant louts!"

Steve's eyes narrowed. It was the sheriff. Who else would snap out orders and insults like that and not expect to get a bullet in return? He's the one who was responsible for Sarah's capture. Steve clenched his fists, which had immediately turned dark red.

A bucket line was quickly formed. While one man furiously cranked a water pump, another man filled buckets and passed them down the line. It wasn't the most effective way to put out a fire, but if the building was small enough, then it would suffice. In this case, there wasn't really anything left of the small tool shed. All they had to do was douse a few lingering fires.

The sheriff returned to the lodge, shouting orders the entire way back. "Make sure you get it all the way out. If there are flare ups it'll be seen from town. Find out who was on duty and bring them to me. And for the love of God, find out what the hell happened to Deke! Tell him to get his sorry butt up here as soon as possible. I won't be waitin' for him. If he gets left behind, then he's outta luck. You got that?"

The small group of men flanking the sheriff all nodded and eagerly rushed off. Four men disappeared into the shack on the left and the remaining two went into the shack on the right. Steve eyed the two buildings. He looked at the one on the right. More people were going into that one than the other. That had to mean they were checking out the mine and presumably on Sarah. That had to be the right one.

Steve snuck in as close as he dared in the woods and before he lost his nerve, he sprinted for the shack and slipped inside.

"The sheriff was right," he heard a smug voice say. "He's very predictable."

There was a single lantern in the small utility shed. It was enough to illuminate all four corners of the tiny building and show Steve that there were not four but at least a dozen men all hiding inside, presumably waiting for him to 'sneak' in.

Unfortunately for the men, Steve's patience had just worn out. He smiled at each of the burly men and dropped his arms to his sides.

"Before we get started, would anyone like to leave?"

Had someone been there to drop a pin it would have been heard by all. Steve shrugged. "Alrighty, then. Suit yourself. Let's have some fun, shall we?"

A pair of arms grabbed him from behind. The others pulled their guns to shove them in his face.

"Last chance, guys."

No one moved. A few of them even snickered derisively.

The howls and screams began. The man holding him suddenly couldn't let go fast enough. Those holding guns instantly dropped them and screamed in pain as the white-hot metal burned their hands. Steve's fists ignited and traveled up his arms to encompass his chest. Deciding a good show was in order he allowed the flames to completely cover his body.

No burning my clothes like you did with Lissa, Steve instructed his jhorun. *I'm not doing this in the buff.*

The men scrambled for the door, yanking it off its hinges and tossing it aside as half a dozen men ran, screaming, from the shed. The other six decided that departure via the main door wasn't fast enough and instead punched their way through the thin wooden walls. Steve debated destroying it with a chaser, but the flimsy structure collapsed before he could.

Steve eyed the third shack. Figures. Of course, it'd be the last place he'd check. He rushed to the small dilapidated building and reached for the handle. A bullet plunked into the wood inches from his hand. Steve turned and saw someone crouching by the corner of the lodge. That person was raising a rifle for another shot.

Steve generated a chaser and flung it straight at the shooter. The man dove to the ground, thinking that it'd simply pass over him. The chaser flew over and instantly swung around to home in on its target. Steve halted it less than a foot from the man's face.

"You fire another shot at me and next time I won't stop it. You got that?"

Terrified, the man nodded.

"Start running, in case I change my mind."

The man complied. He was at least a hundred feet down the road by the time Steve called the chaser back to his hand. He opened the door and went inside.

Rows of lanterns hung on pegs inside the dark shack. He noticed the fat wicks inside each of the lanterns, and lit them all simultaneously. Once the tiny room was properly illuminated, he saw the dark staircase leading down. Anyone could be lurking just out of sight.

Steve formed a large chaser and instructed it to lead the way. He emerged onto a landing without a single shot being fired. Then, he ordered the large fireball to split into smaller, regular sized ones and spread out.

Steve groaned. Where was he supposed to look? Mines could extend for hundreds, if not thousands, of feet below the ground. He could spend days searching.

Steve chose the closest tunnel and stepped foot inside. He took a few steps before drawing a fire arrow on the wall, indicating which way he had come.

He spent the next twenty minutes hastily exploring several tunnels, but to no avail. He chose the next tunnel at random and fired a chaser in that direction.

CLANG!

His chaser, at least twenty feet out in front of him, had slammed into something hard. Whatever it impacted, it sounded metallic in nature and worth checking out.

The source of the obstacle appeared. The tunnel had been sealed by a thick circular door. He inspected the surface of the heavy iron door before giving it an experimental tug. That's when he noticed the keyhole.

The door was locked.

He heard another shout, followed closely thereafter by a shrill scream. The scream hadn't sounded like a woman's. The shouting, though, definitely sounded like a woman's voice. A supremely pissed off woman. Could it be Sarah?

"Sarah?" Steve called out. He pounded the surface of the door with his fist. "Are you in there?" He heard more shouts, but nothing he could decipher.

"Sarah! If you're in there, answer me!"

Just then he heard tapping.

Tap taptap tap tap…

The noise disappeared. Steve breathed a sigh of relief and grunted. He couldn't remember the last time he hadn't been worried about his wife. Had it only been a few days ago?

Tap taptap tap tap…

"Two bits," Steve mouthed, rapping twice on the door.

The simple 'Shave and a Haircut' tune was their sign to each other.

"Step back!" Steve shouted, cupping his hands on the door and shouting into his makeshift megaphone. "I'm going to try and burn my way through."

"Brackets!" came Sarah's muffled reply.

Brackets? Steve looked up at the thick iron brackets holding the door securely in place.

"Melt brackets!" Sarah's muffled voice urged. "THEN STEP BACK!"

"Get ready!" Steve shouted, igniting a hand.

He targeted the first bracket and blasted a strong jet of fire at it. Fifteen seconds later the bracket literally melted off the tunnel wall. He attacked the other six brackets and then raced back down his side of the tunnel.

"Ready!" Steve shouted as loud as he could. "Give it your best shot!"

Metal groaned. The top of the circular door inched forward, scraping noisily along the stony wall.

"Get out of the way!" Sarah shouted, her voice clearer now.

Steve retreated another hundred feet down the tunnel. "I'm clear!"

The circular metal door was punched free of the tunnel and fell to the ground with a loud crash, sending up bits of pulverized stone and gravel. Sounds of the epic crash echoed throughout the tunnel.

Sarah rushed across the fallen door and threw herself into his arms. "I thought I wouldn't see you again!"

Steve wrapped his arms around his wife and held her tight. "I've told you before and I'll tell you again: you're stuck with me, lady. You've got to do better than that if you think you're going to drive me away."

He looked into his wife's glazed eyes and frowned. "I need to have a little chat with him."

Sarah put a restraining arm on his. "Don't. He's smarter than he looks. And he's Lentarian! Or he used to be."

That got Steve's attention. "What? Are you kidding? Did he tell you that?"

Sarah nodded.

Steve scowled. "That explains how he knew who you were."

"That's right. Honey, he's one of the people who fell through the portal. He's been here for over twenty years. I volunteered to take him back to Lentari."

"Oh, *hell* no," Steve vowed, frowning.

"Don't worry. He wasn't interested. He's grown fond of the power he wields in this town. He thrives on fear."

"If he loves it here so much then why is he leaving?"

"Bixby's a bully," Sarah answered. "He knows the people are starting to turn on him. My memory is a little hazy on this next part, but I think he struck a woman. He was cursing about it all the way back here."

"There's nothing wrong with your memory," Steve told her. "He hit Peggy."

"Peggy from the Silver Spike? Oh, no! Is she okay?"

"She's got a bruise but she'll be okay. Come on, let's get out of here."

Steve took his wife's hand and led her toward the surface, following the fire arrows to the small shack.

Sarah smiled at him as they passed one of the arrows. "That's a smart idea."

"The last thing I wanted to do was get lost down here," Steve told her. "What good would I be if … whoa! Back up, back up!"

Outside the shack several dozen men were running toward them, guns drawn. He slammed the door closed.

"Get back and get down!" Steve snapped. He ignited both hands and glared at the men through the chinks in the shabbily constructed wood walls.

"Do you have a plan for getting us out of here?" Sarah placed a hand on the side of her head and gave it a few shakes.

"Are you okay?" Steve asked her. The first bullet slammed into the side of the shed. They both dove to the ground.

"I'm just dizzy. I'm so tired of not being able to think straight. Honey, what are we going to do?"

Steve slowly shook his head. "I don't know. If we … wait. Wait a minute! You can still use your jhorun to move things around, right?"

Sarah leveled a gaze at him. "Obviously."

"Wait here."

Steve crawled back to the stairs and scrambled down. He made it back to the landing and inspected the crates he had seen before. Yes! There it was!

Steve snatched one of the crates and raced back up the stairs. He crawled into position next to his wife. He proudly showed her the crate.

"Let's take this up a notch, shall we?"

Sarah eyed the crate full of dynamite. She looked up at him and smiled. She nodded.

"I'll open the door and you fling this up into the air. I'll handle the rest. Can you do that?"

He started for the door but Sarah held him back. She focused her attention on the door. Moments later it ripped off its hinges and flung out toward the men, who cursed and scrambled for cover.

Steve ducked as a stick of dynamite whizzed by his ear. It sailed straight up, thirty feet in the air. Steve hit it with a chaser. The explosion illuminated the entire compound.

Steve saw men hiding behind trees, crouching behind large boulders, and satisfactorily enough, he could see a number of men running down the road back toward town.

Two more sticks flew by him. He fired off two blasts but missed the second stick. One man, picking himself up from the ground, saw that the fuse wasn't lit and held it up.

"It ain't lit! Who's got a match? We'll use this on them bastards just like they was tryin' to use 'em on us!"

Before anyone could find a match, the fuse flared to life and began burning down. The man turned to his friends and questioningly held up the burning stick.

"Throw it, ya damn fool!" one man hissed. "Get rid of it! Throw it away!"

That seemed to snap the man out of his trance. He pivoted until he was facing the mine entrance and tossed the stick straight at Steve. Sarah caught the stick with her jhorun and it punched through a window in the lodge. Two seconds later, the entire southeastern corner of the lodge exploded apart. Tiny bits of charred wood rained down.

Hank and Bart appeared. They looked at each other, shrugged, and lit sticks of dynamite, hurling them at the lodge. One bounced off the lodge's perimeter wall, but the other broke through a loft window on the second floor.

The explosive that landed outside shattered every window within two hundred feet. The second explosion ripped part of the roof off and blasted a huge hole in the lodge's attic. Steve and Sarah carefully emerged from the shack. Steve held onto the crate, unwilling to let the TNT fall into the wrong hands. They ran toward the lodge.

Another two dozen men fled down the mountain.

A few gunshots rang out. Steve pointed at two men who were crouched behind a large oak tree.

"You've got ten seconds to clear out!" Steve shouted at the two deputies. "Otherwise, want to see how well a tree burns?"

The two deputies unbuckled their gun belts, snatched their badges off their chests, and flung them to the ground. Without another word they walked, unhurried, down the road.

Bart appeared. He saw the half full crate of TNT and eagerly grabbed a few more sticks.

"Where's Hank?" Steve asked, looking around. The bouncer couldn't have gone far.

They heard the commotion before they spotted it. Hank was backing away from the damaged corner of the lodge. Three men were advancing on him. They had their fists up and were taunting him with insults, trying to provoke the huge man into fighting.

Steve frowned. He looked up at Bart and then at Sarah. "Keep her safe. I'll deal with this."

Sarah started to rise until Bart placed a huge hand on her shoulder.

Steve ignited his flames. He eyed the three assailants. One of them glanced his way. His eyes widened with disbelief. Steve glanced at his hands and then noticed he had let himself be completely engulfed in flames once more.

Steve targeted an undamaged section of the lodge and blasted a hole in it. He released his jhorun into both hands and his fire whips sprang into existence. He cracked the whip over his head and advanced on the three men, who were now cowering on the ground.

Hank backed off a few paces.

Several shots were fired. Steve felt a slight tap on his left shoulder. He reached back to touch the affected area and briefly wondered if he had been shot. He felt something on his fingertips but couldn't identify what it was as his fingers were glowing red and readily burning.

Steve looked over at Hank, who was pointing back at the last remaining shack. Half a dozen men were firing off shots.

"Hank, find cover," Steve promptly told his companion. "I don't want you getting hurt."

"What about you? You said before, you can't stop a bullet."

"I don't think I can. I think I might've been grazed by a bullet; I don't know. I can't tell."

Hank scoffed. "You'd know it if you had been shot."

"Whatever. I'll worry about that later. Take cover. Now!"

"What about those men in the mine?"

Steve held both hands out in front of him and generated the largest chaser he could, a fireball about two feet in diameter. It rose into the air and hovered, waiting for a command. Steve looked over at the mine and smiled. The men bolted from the shack, running as if their very lives depended on it.

Steve looked at the mine entrance and then back at the enormous chaser. He pointed at the shack. "Destroy it."

The huge chaser sped off. It collided with the tiny shack and detonated, blowing the four walls in separate directions. The mine entrance collapsed as tons of rock slammed down. Once the smoke cleared, there was only scorched bare rock.

"Now *that* is closure," he heard Sarah say. He pulled his jhorun back and extinguished his flames. She appeared by his side and took his hand in hers.

Hank and Bart stepped closer. Hank had a split lip while Bart had a smear of blood on his neck, but otherwise the two of them looked to be okay.

"We need to find the sheriff," Steve told his two accomplices. "Bart, would you wait here with Sarah while—"

"You're leaving me?" Sarah interrupted, frowning. "Again?"

"What I meant to say," Steve hastily corrected, "was that I won't rest easy until I know Sheriff Bixby has been found and dealt with."

"What should we do with him when we find him?" Hank wanted to know.

"Hold him accountable for what he's done," Bart instantly answered, sounding surprisingly eloquent despite his formidable appearance.

Steve pointed at the lodge. "We have to find him first. Look at the size of that place. He could be hiding anywhere."

"Then we should split up," Hank suggested. "We can cover more ground."

They stepped through the lodge's main front doors and looked around. They were in a great room with a thirty-foot ceiling. A huge fireplace of locally quarried granite sat against the far wall. The room also held more than twenty taxidermy animals, from a buffalo head to a bobcat. A great horned owl sat on a tree limb and regarded them with large unseeing eyes.

"It's creepy as hell in here," Steve muttered, rubbing his nose. "Wouldn't want to be caught in here in the dark."

"I'll check the loft," Bart announced. He headed for a large curved staircase. "If I find anything I'll give you a shout."

Steve nodded. "Be on your toes. You never know what could be lurking in the shadows."

"I'll take the south side," Hank decided. He passed a display case of ancient weapons. He smashed it open and reached in to grab a huge studded club, which he rested on his shoulder, looking just like a caveman.

"Not many people could pull off that look," Steve whispered to his wife, who stifled a giggle, "but he certainly nailed it."

A soft clunk got their attention, coming from somewhere down the long corridor. One room housed a collection of guns and rifles while another seemed to be devoted to nothing but maps. Steve eyed his wife. His jhorun, while starting to tire, was still active and standing by, ready to be called into action again.

His hands turned red.

The room at the end of the hall was the sheriff's private office and he was sitting behind his desk, smoking a cigar as if he didn't have a care in the world.

"You must be Steve, the fire thrower, am I right?"

Steve reached out with his jhorun and extinguished the pompous man's cigar. "Yep. You must be the sheriff. Am I right?"

"Marcus Bixby, Sheriff of Coeur d'Alene."

Steve shook his head. "Not any more you're not, pal."

The sheriff flashed him a smug smile. "Seems that my men have all deserted me. I guess I have you to thank for that, partner."

Steve bowed. "It's been my pleasure. It's the least I can do for the person who kidnapped my wife. So, tell me something, ex-sheriff of Coeur d'Alene, who are you? I don't want the name you made up for yourself. I want to know what you were called in Lentari."

The sheriff fixed him with a steely glare. He scowled.

"Melvyn."

Steve nodded. "Well, Melvyn, I have something for you."

"Oh? And what would that be?"

Steve caught the sheriff's jaw with a right hook that knocked him clean out of his chair and slammed him up against the wall. The sheriff crumbled to the floor in a heap.

Steve massaged his stinging right hand.

"Oh, consider it my way of saying thanks."

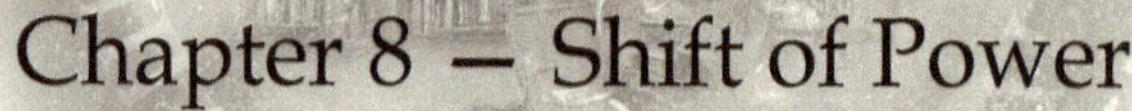

Chapter 8 — Shift of Power

"What are we supposed to do with him now?" Cecil asked, as he followed Steve up the front steps and disappeared into the large manor. Draped across Steve's shoulder was the unconscious form of Sheriff Bixby. "We can't really leave him like that, can we?"

"Why not?" Steve called out, navigating his way past Quinn and Lissa, who rose to their feet staring uncomprehendingly at the strange procession coming in the door. "He had worse things planned for Sarah, so I think a brief stay as our *guest* wouldn't be out of order."

"Where are you going to put him?" Luther asked.

"I'll stash him in one of the rooms on the second floor. Before I do that, I'll need some rope. Got any lying around?"

Luther nodded and hurried outside.

"I'm not really comfortable having that man inside my home," Cora announced.

"I'll second that notion," AnnaBelle added.

Rosamund appeared at the door, holding Sarah's arm to

keep her steady. The tiny woman guided Sarah to the closest chair and sat her down on it. Cora and AnnaBelle let out cries of relief and rushed to embrace Sarah in a hug.

"We were so worried about you," Cora admitted. "When I saw that man walk off with you, I feared the worst."

Sarah hugged each of them in turn.

"Thanks. I'm glad to be back. I have had the worst headache for several days now."

"I might be able to help with that," a soft, quiet voice piped up.

Sarah turned to see a young teenage girl silently observing them from the kitchen door.

"Who are you?" Sarah asked her. "Have we met?"

The young girl shook her head, sending her brown tresses tumbling about. "We haven't met. I'm Lissa. I already know who you are."

Sarah stared at the girl with amazement. "The constable's daughter! You're that Lissa?"

Lissa's eyes widened. "You've heard of me?"

"You were the last one to fall through the portal, save myself, of course. Your disappearance led to the king's decision to seek my help in figuring out what had happened to you and what we were dealing with in regard to that portal."

"You're here because of me?"

"Both of us are," Sarah confirmed. "I felt horrible, knowing the king decided to seal the portal so no one else could suffer the same fate."

Lissa's young face appeared troubled. "The king sealed the portal?"

Luther emerged, holding several coils of rope. He hurried up the stairs and disappeared into one of the rooms. Quinn appeared and quietly leaned against the doorway.

Sarah nodded. "When it became apparent that there was no way to safely mount a rescue mission, the king decided to have a building constructed over the portal, effectively sealing it off from the rest of the world. So, umm, did you mention something about knowing what would get rid of a headache?"

Lissa nodded enthusiastically. "Cora has quite a collection

of tea. I could brew you some that would help clear your head."

She smiled tenderly at the young girl. "I would be forever in your debt."

Sarah then noticed the newcomer. "Would you introduce us?" Sarah asked the girl.

"Sarah, this is Quinn. He's a schoolmaster from Capily. He's another victim of the portal. Quinn was captured by the griskis. Quinn, this is…"

Quinn rushed forward, took Sarah's hand, and brought it to within an inch of his mouth.

"I know who you are, Lady Sarah. You're the female Nohrin. You're the teleporter, am I right?"

Sarah nodded. "It's nice to meet you, Quinn. You, too, Lissa. You both fell through the portal? You went through the portal and appeared in Lentari? Steve and I went through and appeared on our world. I wonder why?"

Lissa darted off to the kitchen.

Quinn shrugged. "I don't know. I can only suspect the portal isn't stable. It seems the portal has deposited people in multiple worlds and in multiple times. I personally don't see how that's possible."

Steve and Luther emerged from the room they had thrown the sheriff in and walked down the stairs together.

"It's possible," Steve began, "because Zevern, the wizard who created it, didn't really know what the hell he was doing in the first place and pretty much threw things together in the hopes that something he tried would work."

"You don't know that for certain," Quinn accused, trying to suppress a smile.

"It's true," Cecil told him. "We heard it straight from his mouth. The king wasn't very pleased."

"The wizard admitted to his king that he didn't know what he was doing?" Quinn asked, skeptical. "I'll bet he loved hearing that."

Both Steve and Cecil nodded. Steve turned to Cecil and slapped him on the back.

"Wasn't that fun? Making Zevern sweat?" Steve turned to Sarah. "You should have seen the look on his face, hon.

His eyes became as big as saucers when I asked him to create another portal so we could get back. His face turned bright red and he began stammering. The king said that the two of them were going to have a conversation that he wouldn't enjoy. I wish I could have seen it."

Steve took his wife's hand and pulled her to her feet. He led her to the large living room, prompting the rest of the group to follow. Lissa appeared a few moments later to present a steaming cup of tea to Sarah.

"Drink it all," the teenager instructed. "It'll make your headache go away."

Sarah gratefully took the tea and took a small sip. She recognized the tart flavor of lemon, followed by a healthy dose of the one ingredient she detested most in tea: ginger. She managed to keep her expression neutral. She nodded her thanks to the girl and then patted the seat next to her on the couch. Lissa accepted. Once they were all seated, Steve cleared his throat and asked the question that had been on everyone's mind.

"What should we do with the sheriff?" Steve frowned, as a mental picture of the sheriff's smug smile appeared in his mind. "I imagine we can't keep him locked up in this house forever."

Luther looked at Steve. "He's from your time. Are you planning on taking him back with you?"

Steve shrugged. "I hadn't really thought about it."

Luther smiled. He glanced up at the ceiling above their heads. "Now might be the time to do just that."

"If we leave him here," Steve began, fidgeting uncomfortably on the sofa, "we risk him doing something that would have repercussions on future generations. He's already changed the future. I guarantee you there's no mention of a person from another world being elected sheriff of a small town in Idaho, let alone one as crooked as he is. We can't go back and prevent him from ever arriving, so we would have to—"

"Yes, we could," Sarah interrupted.

Steve blinked at her. "What was that?"

"We could prevent him from ever using that portal in the

first place."

"How?"

"By getting the present king to do what Kri'Entu wanted to do in the future."

"Sealing the portal?"

Sarah nodded. "Right. That way no one would ever mistakenly fall into it in the first place."

Luther frowned. "If the portal were sealed now, it would mean no one would ever stumble across it. If no one falls through then there'd be no need to ever go through it yourself, Steve. I believe you'd cease to exist."

Steve's eyebrows shot up. "What?"

Cora came into the room with a glass of water, which she offered to Sarah, who gladly accepted.

"Think about it," Luther continued. "If the portal is sealed in my time, then Sarah would never fall through it in the first place and therefore you'd never go in after her. Am I right?"

Steve shrugged. "Yeah, I can follow along with that."

"Very well. Using that same logic if you never make it to the past, as you've done now, what do you think would happen to you? That is, the *you* of right now?"

Steve looked over at his wife. "What would happen to us?"

Sarah downed half of her water and considered. "From their perspective, I imagine we'd vanish."

A loud commotion reached their ears through the open windows, the sound of the front gates being forcefully pushed open.

Steve groaned. "Don't tell me that after all we've been through, we forgot to lock the damn gate after we came in. Man your battle stations, guys. I think we're about to have company."

They heard horses neigh loudly, followed by the muffled curses of their riders. Steve hurried to the window and peered outside. Luther, Cecil, and Quinn joined him moments later.

"Who is it?" Quinn nervously asked.

Steve pointed up at the second floor. "I'm willing to bet it's some of the sheriff's men."

Sarah appeared at his side. She scowled. "I thought for certain we scared them away from ever coming here again."

Steve eyed his wife speculatively. "Really? You'll have to tell me what you did."

A dozen horsemen appeared and each was peering anxiously about, as though expecting the boogeyman. Sarah suddenly smiled. She pulled her husband close.

"I have an idea. Listen closely."

While Sarah relayed her idea to her husband, the nervous band of men inched closer to the manor, checking the surroundings, fully expecting spooks to emerge and make a run for them. Scared eyes darted from one tree to another. Shaking hands held trembling guns as twelve different guns were pointed in twelve different directions.

The front door of the manor banged open and a single man emerged, blinking in the bright sunlight. A dozen guns suddenly found a new target to take aim at. Steve smiled at the men and waved a friendly arm in their direction.

"Afternoon, gents. Are you guys lost? Is there something I can help you with?"

"We know you got the sheriff in there," one man brazenly told him. "Let him go. You ain't got no right to hold him against his will."

Steve kept his smile plastered to his face. "Let's agree to disagree."

Steve counted half a dozen metallic clicks as a number of guns were cocked. Ignoring the seriousness of the situation, Steve turned to look back at the manor and then returned his gaze to the riders.

"What are you doing all the way over there? Why don't you come on over here so we can talk this thing out."

"There ain't no way in hell I'm goin' over there, fella. Send the sheriff out here now and you might jus' live through this. You understand me, bub?"

"Bub?" Steve repeated, feigning anger. "You dare to call me 'Bub'? What did I do to deserve that?"

"Listen, pal," the lead rider angrily exclaimed, "if you don't..."

The leader trailed off, his face becoming as pale as chalk.

The rest of the men stiffened in their saddles and gasped with shock.

Knowing full well that Sarah had found a few of her 'ghosts' and had sent them out the window, Steve ignored what was happening behind him. The group of riders fell completely silent.

"What's the matter? There's nothing to be afraid of. I'm sure we can work this out. Come on in. I'm sure I can dig up a few beers. What do you say, pal?"

Behind Steve, a couple of the ghosts played peek-a-boo behind trees and bushes while candlestick holders, small picture frames, and a few pots and pans circled above the riders' heads. The lead rider began stammering incomprehensibly and was frantically gesturing at the floating items. The rest of the gang was slowly edging away, eyes open wide with fear.

Sarah, concealed behind a curtain inside the manor, made two of the ghosts twitch uncontrollably, while the pair of candlestick holders were directed to swoop dangerously close to the riders' heads. Three of the men turned about and galloped back toward the gates. Going along with the gag, Steve stiffened with surprise and turned around. He gave a scripted shout of terror.

"No! Not again! Leave us alone, you demons! You have no business here! Go back to whatever hell you came from!"

He waited for Sarah to raise one of the ghosts higher into the air. As soon as he saw it, he generated a chaser next to the ghost and instructed his jhorun to hold it there in place.

"Oh, no! What are you doing? I won't let you hurt these men! You can't do this. Not again! Go away!"

By this time, the horses were picking up on their riders' jitters. The horses were chomping at the bit, shaking their manes, and letting out nervous nickers.

Steve bit his lip to keep from smiling. He told his jhorun what he wanted it to do. The chaser soared straight toward him. It impacted his chest, which to him felt like a friendly slap on the back. He ignited his hands and quickly allowed the fire to envelope him.

"No!!!" Steve wailed. He dropped to the ground and tried rolling. "This can't be happening! No! Please make it stop!

Help me! Oh, the agony!"

He increased his flames, giving everyone the impression that he was succumbing to the fires. He let out a final wail and then lay still on the ground, his body burning hot and fast.

The men screamed in terror, pulled their horses around, and spurred their mounts away from the burning body.

Once the men were gone, the ghosts dropped to the ground, like one vast multi-stringed marionette with its strings cut. Slowly, and carefully, the rest of the items were placed on the ground. Sarah rushed out the door and stopped at the blazing form of her husband. "Okay, show-off, you can cut that out now."

The flames rapidly became absorbed back into Steve's body. He was rolling on the ground and laughing so hard he had tears streaming down his face.

"Woohoo! Did you see their faces? I think they probably peed themselves!" He chortled some more as he regained his feet. "Man, that was fun."

"You should have seen what Luther, Cora, and I did to them."

Steve dusted himself off. "I'm still waiting to hear that story."

"I'll tell you tonight."

Steve smiled and hooked his arm through his wife's. Together they walked back inside the manor. "I'm looking forward to it."

Inside, Cora tapped Sarah on her shoulder and pointed back outside. "Do you think you could bring them all back in? Those are my towels and linens out there on the ground."

Sarah cringed. "Oh. That's right. I'm sorry."

Once her linens were safely back inside the house, everyone sank back into their chairs in the living room. Practically everyone was still laughing after what they had just witnessed outside. Rosamund wiped the corner of her eyes with her handkerchief.

"Simply incredible," she was saying. She folded her handkerchief and tucked it back into a pocket on the front of her dress. "What I would give to have a gift like that."

"I'll second that notion," Cecil softly murmured.

"So where were we?" Steve asked. "Anyone remember where we left off?"

Quinn cleared his throat. "I believe you and Luther were discussing what would happen if the portal were to be sealed, in this time, thus preventing anyone from falling in at a later time."

Steve nodded. "That's right. I was curious what would happen to us if we'd never gone into it."

Sarah shrugged. "Logically I would imagine we'd reappear in our own time."

Steve smiled and nodded. "So that's how we can get home! Awesome! We just need to get Kri'Calin to seal the portal. That shouldn't be too difficult."

"But then you'd be changing your own future," Quinn pointed out.

Steve's surprised eyes looked up at the Lentarian teacher. "Care to run that by me again?"

"The normal course of time can be represented by a straight line," Quinn began, sounding very much like he was addressing a group of school children. He drew an imaginary line in the air for added emphasis. "That line has already been drawn, since the existence of the portal has survived for over a hundred years. If the portal is sealed at this point in time," Quinn drew another imaginary line but this time added a few dips and turns, "then a different set of events will transpire and could conceivably have more negative repercussions than positive ones."

"What do you suggest?" Steve asked the teacher. "What would you do if you were me?"

"Leave this time line alone and figure out what to do without altering it any further than it already has."

"What about the people who fell through and were never heard from again?" Sarah sadly asked. "Isn't there a way we could help them?"

Rosamund, who had been quietly sitting on an overstuffed arm chair, cleared her throat. "I might be able to help with that."

Everyone turned to the diminutive saloon owner.

"I was asked to see if I could locate anyone in town that

might have appeared under strange circumstances."

"And?" Luther prompted.

"I'll relay what I have learned," Rosamund informed the group. "A man had appeared in the middle of town. People swear one minute no one was there and the next, a man was seen sprawled out on the street. He was dressed strangely, they said. He had a foreign bow, a quiver full of arrows, and several knives with strange markings on them. Once the man awoke, he appeared to have no recollection of how he got there."

"How long ago was this?" Steve asked.

"Nearly thirty years ago."

"I wonder who it was." Sarah softly asked, not really expecting an answer.

"I can even answer that, too," Rosamund proudly announced. "I asked him that yesterday when I saw him. I've known him for years and never knew his history."

"Who is it?" Steve pressed, curious.

"You've met his son."

"We have? Who's his son?" Steve wanted to know.

"Hank."

"Hank's father is Lentarian?" Sarah asked, amazed.

"Hank's father is a man by the name of Ruan. I told him others from his world were here, looking for a way back."

Quinn leaned forward. "Ruan? You said his name was Ruan? Oh, that makes perfect sense."

"Do you know him?" Sarah asked.

"By reputation only. I heard the story of Capily's most skilled hunter, and of his disappearance, the moment I accepted the position of schoolmaster. I didn't know him personally."

Steve waited with bated breath. When nothing else was forthcoming he let it out.

"Well? What did Ruan say to the notion of returning home to Lentari?"

Rosamund smiled. "He gave me a message to pass along to you. He knew who you and Sarah are. He said that he wishes you the best of luck and to not worry about him. He would much rather remain here, with his family, rather than return to Lentari where he lived by himself."

Quinn drummed his fingers on the arm of his chair. "Even more of the future has been changed. A man who wasn't supposed to be in this time has appeared and had children. What if one of them becomes a bank robber? What if one of them becomes a murderer?"

Rosamund's face became stern, her thin lips pursed together. "Hank is neither a robber nor a murderer, Mister Quinn, and I'll thank you to not judge a person's character without having met them before."

Quinn's face reddened. "My most profuse apologies. What I meant was, what if a descendant of Ruan's does something that affects Steve and Sarah back in their own time?"

Rosamund's expression softened. "Oh. I misunderstood. I think I understand your concern. I am unsure what can be done about it."

"We can go crazy if we stop to think about all the possible ramifications," Steve told them. "The only way to prevent that from happening is to seal the portal and thereby create even more problems. It'll have to be one way or the other. I say we take our chances and hope everything turns out alright."

"You're taking a big chance," Sarah whispered to him. "Quinn has a point. We could seriously jeopardize our future."

"It's a chance we have to take. If that portal is sealed on Lentari then we'll cease to exist. I personally don't want that to happen, thank you very much."

"We wouldn't cease to exist," Sarah chided. "Stop overreacting. We'd just appear back home with no memories of this ever happening."

"That's right," Steve said, nodding. "But us right now, us with all of our memories of what's happened, that'd be gone forever. We'd essentially be dying."

"I think that's a bit on the dramatic side," Sarah confided, "but I do see your point."

"Good. Then it's settled, right? The portal stays as it is and the sheriff should come back with us."

Luther cleared his throat to signal he wanted to say something. "Speaking of the sheriff, who will take over his duties in town? The mayor is going to want to know what happened to him."

"We tell him the truth," Sarah decided. "He was corrupt and decided to skip town before he could be brought to justice."

"Would the mayor be the one who would appoint a new sheriff?" Steve asked.

Cecil shook his head. "It doesn't work that way. The position of sheriff is determined by election."

"In that case, how in the world did he ever get himself elected?" Sarah wondered aloud. "How did he remain in office?"

"By fear," Rosamund answered. "Fear, threats, and his influence. I will say that you're almost right, Steve. A mayor can appoint an acting sheriff until such time as one is elected by the people."

"Do you think the people are ready for a new sheriff?" Sarah asked.

Luther, Cora, Cecil, AnnaBelle, and Rosamund all scoffed.

"Of course, they are," Rosamund confirmed. "They'd be ready and willing to elect a new sheriff, and they would throw a parade in your honor if they learned you were responsible for his ousting."

"I wonder who they'll pick for an acting sheriff," Cecil mused.

"I already have a person in mind," Rosamund announced.

The entire room full of people stared at her in silence.

"I'm friends with the mayor," Rosamund explained. She smiled at each of them. "I can't make any guarantees, but I feel confident the mayor will listen to my suggestion."

"And who will you be suggesting?" Steve asked.

"Hank."

"Hank is too timid to be sheriff," Sarah told Rosamund. "I don't think he has the temperament for the job."

Rosamund shrugged. "Not yet, but he will. You don't know the boy like I do. He'd be perfect."

Steve took his wife's hand and turned to Luther. "Well, the future is as secure as we can make it. I'd say we need to figure out how to make it home. Don't get me wrong, Luther; you and Cora are living in a much simpler time and I think you're very lucky to be living here. However, this isn't for us. Speaking for the two of us, we would like to go home."

"Me, too," Lissa quietly added. "I miss my father. I'm all he has left. He must be devastated."

"I am unmarried, so I don't have anyone waiting for me back home," Quinn admitted, "but I would like to see my parents again. I don't want to stay here, either."

All eyes turned to Luther, who turned to regard Steve.

"Were you able to get a jorii?"

Steve slowly shook his head. "I asked. The king said he was out of them. I asked how he could get more but was told that it wasn't an easy feat."

Luther's face became stern. "Be that as it may, Steve, if there is to be any chance of my being able to change our portal's destination and have it deliver you to your world, then I am going to need a jorii. I will need my jhorun's full strength and even then, I'm not sure I can do it. But I will try."

"You said the king is out of jorii?" Sarah asked Steve. Her husband nodded. "How does he get more?"

"You know what? Kri'Calin asked me that same question. He claims that a jorii is made or created by some special process. He elected to keep the procedure to himself."

Sarah's surprised expression made him smile. "Why would he do that?"

"That's a question I've been asking myself over and over. He's piqued my curiosity, no doubt about it. The jerk."

Sarah giggled. "I doubt very much the king would allow their supply of jorii to simply become exhausted."

Steve shrugged. "Hey, he told me they were out and didn't have any to spare. Why? Do you think he was holding out on me?"

"He has to have at least one of them lying around," Sarah insisted. "Something. Anything! Even if he has a partially used one. Something is better than nothing."

"I agree," Luther agreed.

"Well, I have to go back to Lentari anyway," Steve admitted.

"You do? Why?" Sarah wanted to know.

"I, uh, created a little bit of a mess for Pryllan. I can't

leave things the way they are. I have to find a way to fix it."

Sarah fixed him with a gaze. "What did you do?"

"Hey, it wasn't my fault. The only way for us to get an athe crystal in a timely manner was to arrange for a little dwarf girl to ride on a dragon. I had to convince Pryllan-that's the Pryllan of the past--that she and I would become friends and that she, in the future, trusted me implicitly. Thankfully she agreed and she allowed the little girl on her back."

"So, you owe Pryllan a favor? That's not too bad."

Steve shook his head. "No. You didn't let me finish. The little girl was dying, and by putting a dying child on a dragon's back created something called a shachar."

"What's that?" Sarah asked.

"It's some type of life-debt," Steve answered. "Until the girl can repay the favor, she's indebted to Pryllan and her life is going to be miserable until the shachar is either lifted or absolved."

Sarah stared at him in shock. "You've been busy."

Steve grinned. "Lady, you have no idea."

"How are you going to break this debt?" Sarah asked. "How are you going to free this little girl? Speaking of which, was the girl cured?"

Steve nodded. "Little Aislinn is alive and healthier than she's been in her entire life."

A loud thump echoed throughout the room, rattling pictures on the walls. Everyone's attention went to the ceiling. Softer thumps were heard as someone began walking across the floor. Luther and Steve eyed one another.

A distinctive chime sounded from upstairs.

Steve tore past Luther and took the steps two at a time. Continuing to the top floor he skidded to a halt. Luther, Cecil, and Quinn were directly behind him, just as the women neared the top floor.

Steve blinked, trying to process what he saw.

The sheriff stood before the activated portal. He turned to his audience and gave them a lofty sneer. He raised his hand and touched two of his fingers to his forehead in a mock salute and stepped through the portal. Steve and the others rushed forward, intent on making it through the portal before it deactivated.

They didn't make it.

Just as Steve bunched his legs and prepared to launch himself through the portal, the visible path in the woods, was replaced by two impenetrable wooden doors. Steve slammed on the brakes and angrily turned to his companions.

"The sheriff knew about the portal? How the hell did he know that? And how could he have possibly found the portal key? This isn't making any sense whatsoever!"

Luther nervously cleared his throat. "The portal key is my fault. I hadn't put it away since I talked to the king. I was caught up in the excitement of seeing everyone again and must have set the key down. I don't know how the sheriff knew it was up here. Perhaps he saw it when we brought him upstairs?"

"Weren't you carrying him?" Sarah asked, confused. "There was no way he could have seen the key if he was unconscious."

"He must have been faking," Steve surmised. "Damn that guy. How'd he get loose? Did he have a knife hidden up his ass?"

Luther hurried off. When he returned, he was holding a set of cut ropes. "He had a knife, that's for sure. I'm sorry, I don't know where he was hiding it."

"We have to go after him!" Steve insisted. "Where's the key now?"

A quick check of the surrounding area gave them more unwelcome news. The green crystal key was nowhere to be seen.

Steve groaned. "He took the damn key, didn't he?"

Luther was crestfallen. "I am so sorry. This is all my fault."

Steve shook his head. "Don't worry about it. Sarah is here. She can get us to Lentari."

Sarah frowned. "Not right now I can't. I'm sorry, I still can't focus enough to bring up a vision."

Steve cursed. "I am really hating that guy right about now."

"That'll give him a long head start," Quinn observed. "Do you think he knew that would happen?"

Sarah nodded. "He knew I was still drugged. Until that opium is out of my system I can't focus enough to teleport. He knows that. He must also know that I'll eventually get full control of my jhorun again. It's why he chose now to escape. I'm afraid, based on how slowly I'm getting my senses back, I won't have full control for at least another few hours."

"So we can't do anything until morning," Steve deduced. He cursed softly. "That gives the sheriff way too long of a head start, if you ask me."

"What else can we do?" Cecil asked, exasperated.

Steve shrugged. "There's nothing we can do about that now. Sarah needs to get her full strength back. I can't get to Lentari without her. This is literally a waiting game now."

Luther gasped aloud. Without another word he bolted downstairs. After a few seconds of stunned silence, Steve motioned for the girls to stay put and he followed Luther down to the second floor. Steve slid to a halt. He looked down at his hands and noticed both had ignited. He flicked them out.

Luther had gently opened one of the bedroom doors and was silently observing the person within. Steve came up from behind and peered over Luther's shoulder. Both men breathed a sigh of relief.

Mina was fast asleep on the bed. Her mouth was partially open and a thin line of drool was visible dripping from the corner of her mouth to the pillow her head was resting on. Luther gently pulled the door closed and turned to face his descendant.

"She's safe. I'm sorry I startled everyone. I feared the worst. However, once more your own future is in jeopardy and I have no one to blame but myself. What should we do?"

"Is everyone alright?" Cora called down from the floor above them. "Is Mina safe?"

"She's safe," Luther assured her. "I don't think the sheriff knew she was here."

"Even if he did, he wouldn't know who she was," Steve told him.

Luther gave him a sardonic look. "Do you think that would stop him?"

"Probably not. Hey Lissa, are you up there?"

"Aye, I am here," the youngster's startled voice came down to them.

"Could you come here a moment?"

As soon as the girl appeared, Steve issued his next set of instructions. "I need you to do me a favor."

Lissa nodded enthusiastically. "Of course. What can I do?"

"Make Sarah another cup of tea, but this time knock her out. She needs to sleep and regain her strength. I don't want her tossing and turning and worrying about what will happen. She needs some good, solid rest and to be at full strength tomorrow. Will you do that for me?"

"Aye." Lissa smiled. "Leave it to me."

Chapter 9 — Mischief Maker

"What was in that tea last night?" Sarah wondered again. "I haven't slept that well in quite some time. Wait. Did you have something to do with this? Did that little girl put something in my tea?"

Steve smiled. "Guilty as charged. I needed you to get a decent night of sleep, so I asked Lissa to make you an herbal tea full of who knows what."

Sarah frowned. "I've had it with being drugged. I don't want you drugging me anymore. I don't care if you think it's in my best interest or not. Promise me, okay?"

"When it comes to your safety and well-being," Steve said slowly, choosing his answer with care, "I make no guarantees."

Sarah shot him a side long look. "You're probably the only person who could get away with a comment like that."

"As well as I should be," Steve politely informed her. He glanced around the area. The portal had just disappeared, bringing back a brief bout of uneasiness, just like the first time years ago when they had accidentally activated it.

"Where do you think he went?" Sarah asked as she looked around the silent woods where she and her husband were standing. The path looked just like it did over a hundred years from now when they would first step foot on it. "Obviously he knows Lentari very well. He's from Capily. Do you think he might have gone back there?"

Steve shook his head. He squatted so he could inspect the leaf-strewn ground. "I doubt it. He told me that his family doesn't think too highly of him. Besides, none of his family would be alive then. I don't think he'd go back there."

"What if he tries to look up an ancestor of his and, armed with what he knows, tries to change his own future?" Sarah argued.

"How?"

"Maybe he knows where certain valuable artifacts could be found? What if he blackmailed someone from this time using some tidbit of information he had learned back in the present?"

"Couldn't he run the risk of screwing up his own present just as much as someone else's?"

"Don't you mean future?" Sarah teased.

"Whatever," Steve grumbled. "All I'm saying is that guy is a real pain in the butt. We have to find him and put an end to this once and for all."

"So where should we start?" Sarah asked. "Avin's about an hour from here. What about trying there?"

"Possibly. Let's check out the waterfall first, okay?"

Sarah took his hand. "One waterfall coming right up."

It happened quicker than the blink of an eye. One second, they were standing on the path in the middle of the woods, and the next they were standing at the base of a waterfall, staring around at an area of the woods that had remained, and would continue to remain, relatively untouched by the passage of time. Steve squatted down again and looked for footprints, broken twigs, anything that would indicate someone had recently been there.

"Do you see anything?" Sarah asked hopefully. She knew Steve was nowhere close to being an expert tracker, but he had managed to help point them in the right direction in the past when they had been tracking a band of fugitives.

Steve shook his head and scowled, as he straightened back up. "Not a damn thing, I'm afraid. No prints, no disturbed dirt, no nothing. It doesn't mean he didn't come through here but if he did, I can't tell."

"What do we do now?" Sarah asked. "Why do I get the feeling that we can search for hours and not find a thing?"

"Because you'd be right," Steve agreed. "We need someone who's a lot better tracker than I am, which is probably just about anyone."

"Where do you think we could find one?"

"R'Tal. We can kill a couple of birds with the same stone. We need to let the king know what's going on, as well as ask his opinion which tracker we can use."

Sarah nodded. "One castle coming right up."

Steve shook his head. "I'm not coming here without you again. I sure could have used you a couple of days ago."

Sarah blew him a kiss. "Agreed. I hereby veto any more attempts at splitting up."

The waterfall and the sounds of splashing water were instantly replaced by a much more serene setting. It was dark, it was dead quiet, and there were people everywhere. In fact, everyone was frozen in place as though the entire crowd was unsure what had just happened or what to do next. Sarah had teleported them straight to an occupied Great Hall.

Kri'Calin sat back on his throne, surprised. A matronly-looking woman was sitting next to him. She, too, wore a bemused expression on her face as she studied the two newcomers.

Steve cleared his throat and grinned sheepishly. "Beg your pardon, Your Majesties."

Kri'Calin smiled, which brought a wave of relief to both husband and wife.

"Greetings, fire thrower. May I assume this is your wife?"

Sarah faced the two thrones and gave them her best curtsy. Steve put an arm around her and gave her a side hug. "She is. May I introduce my wife, Sarah. Sarah, this is Kri'Calin, the king. I'm sorry, you never told me the queen's name."

Surprised, the queen lifted an eyebrow and glanced over

at her husband. It was the king's turn to look sheepish.

"That's right, I haven't. Very well. Steve, Sarah, this is my wife Ny'Alena. My darling, this is Steve, the fire thrower I was telling you about, and his wife, Sarah."

"I am pleased to meet you both," the queen regally informed them.

"What brings you here?" the king asked, curious. He suppressed a smile. "Again."

Steve fidgeted uncomfortably. He nodded in the direction of the Antechamber. "Perhaps we could discuss this in a more private location?"

"What you need to say can be said here," Kri'Calin politely informed him. "Just don't tell me you need another athe crystal. That's all I want to hear."

Steve took a deep breath and let it out slowly. "We don't need an athe crystal. We, uh … hmm. Someone from, uh, my home has come here to, er, your home and needs to be found. Immediately."

"Someone from your home," the king slowly repeated, "has found their way here and you need to find them so you can take them back? You fear for his or her safety?"

"His," Steve clarified, "and no, I do not. Quite the contrary, I'd love it if he tangled with a dragon."

"You surprise me, fire thrower. I didn't think you'd be the type of person who would willingly seek out harm for a friend."

Steve shook his head. "I never said he was a friend."

The king looked thoughtful for a few moments before rising to his feet. "I believe I will speak with you in private. My darling, would you care to accompany us?"

The queen smiled and shook her head. "This concerns me not, Calin. I trust you will handle the matter."

Steve and Sarah followed the king into the Antechamber. Once they were sealed inside, the king sank down behind his desk and eyed his two guests.

"Very well. We're alone. Now out with it. What has happened?"

Sarah took a step back and pulled Steve with her. "How much does he know?"

"Everything."

"Oh." She flashed a smile at the king, who patiently smiled back.

"A Lentarian from our time has stolen our portal key and has come here, to the Lentari of the past."

Kri'Calin frowned. "That's not something I was expecting to hear."

"Trust me, it wasn't something I wanted to share. However, this man is smart and ruthless, and has already proven he'll do whatever it takes to get what he wants."

"What do you think this person is capable of doing?" the king asked. "What do you *suspect* he'll do?"

"I think he'll try to change something now, in order to benefit his future self back in our time," Steve answered.

"How could he possibly do something to benefit himself in the future when he's already here?" Kri'Calin asked, puzzled.

Steve shrugged. "Let's say he finds a place to hide here. He gets married and starts a family. Let's also assume he knows his Lentarian history and therefore knows who the future monarchs will be. What if he tracks down the parents of a future queen and kills them? What if he tries to manipulate the throne so that his own offspring becomes a future queen? What then?"

"That's a mighty big what-if," Sarah gently told her husband.

"But would you put it past him to try something like that?" Steve argued.

Sarah gave a slight shake of her head. "No, I wouldn't."

"I am liking this person less and less," Kri'Calin told the two of them. He was frowning and reaching for a quill and paper. "What do you need of me?"

"We know where he arrived," Sarah told the king. "We just need to find someone who can track him."

"Who's your best tracker?" Steve wanted to know.

"Captain Sauer," the king immediately answered.

Steve groaned. Of course, it was. Captain Sauer had appeared to take an instant dislike to Steve the moment they had met. Then again, it might have something to do with the fact Steve had encouraged the captain's men to either jump into the moat or do a striptease in front of the king by heating up their armor. Perhaps that might not have been the best thing to do but, then again, he had been in a rush to find out what had happened to Sarah.

"Do you have some type of aversion to the captain?" Kri'Calin asked. He had seen Steve's expression.

"Not really. I just get the impression he doesn't like me too much."

The king leveled a stare at him. "Does that matter?"

"If he can track this guy down, then he'll have no quarrel with me," Steve promised.

Kri'Calin nodded. "Good. You'll find no better tracker in all of Lentari."

The king sent a messenger off with instructions for the captain of the royal guard to report to the Antechamber. A few minutes later the door opened and Captain Sauer entered. He gave Steve a quick once over before his eyes fell upon Sarah.

Introductions were made and the situation was explained to the captain. Sauer frowned as he listened to Steve describe the quarry.

"He's killed, he's manipulated," Steve was saying, "he's kidnapped, and he's stolen all manner of things."

"This is a Lentarian we're talking about?" Captain Sauer reiterated. "This isn't a vigilante from your world?"

"He *is* a vigilante from my world," Steve confirmed. "But he started on your world."

"You just said he came from your world to ours," Kri'Calin reminded them, confused.

"He's Lentarian by birth," Sarah clarified. "He's one of the villagers who fell through the portal from our time but ended up on our world in the past. He's been there more than twenty years now."

"And now he's found his way here?" the king asked.

Steve nodded once. "That's right. He stole our portal key, used the portal, and came here. We tried, but were unable to follow him."

Sauer motioned one of the guards over. "Saddle my

horse. I will be leaving shortly."

The guard nodded. "Aye, sir."

Sarah held up a hand. "Wait. You don't want to do that."

The guard had reached the Antechamber's door and had a hand on the door knob. He turned questioningly to the captain, who had turned to Sarah.

"I mean to pursue," Sauer informed her, his face set and determined.

"I'm glad to hear it," Steve told him. "But you're going to be coming with us. Sarah doesn't ride horses. She teleports."

Sauer nodded, as if Steve had just made his own point for him.

"Exactly, but we don't. Therefore, we'll be making the journey on horseback. I assume you can ride?"

"Actually, I can, but that's not important. What I mean to say is, when Sarah teleports, she can take other people with her."

Sauer's eyebrows shot up. "At the same time? How is this possible? I was under the impression that teleporters barely have the strength to teleport themselves across the kingdom, let alone anyone else."

"Ordinarily you'd be right," Sarah told the captain with a smile. "Long story short, my jhorun was given a boost by a sorceress. Just trust me when I say I can easily take the two of you with me when I teleport."

"Incredible," Sauer breathed. "Is this a skill other teleporters could learn? There are a few here who could benefit greatly from their jhoruns becoming amplified."

Steve shook his head. "Nope, sorry. It doesn't work that way. Come on, we'll tell you all about it on the way."

Ten minutes later, Sarah returned them to the path in the woods where they had first arrived in Lentari. Sauer, much to Steve's surprise, had weathered the jump from R'Tal with ease. Most newbies became nauseated. Captain Sauer, on the other hand, looked none the worse for wear. He immediately dropped to one knee and began inspecting the ground.

"I see footprints," Sauer reported, more to himself.

"Can you tell how many there are?" Steve asked.

Sauer briefly glanced over at the two of them and then

down at the ground, noting the size and shape of their footprints.

"Three."

Steve nodded. "I knew it. Which way did he go?"

Sauer pointed south. "The tracks lead that way."

"Toward the waterfall? Makes sense. Hon, will you do the honors?"

Sarah nodded. She took her husband's hand and waited for Sauer to lay his over theirs. The quiet forest was replaced by a small lake and the waterfall that had created it. Sauer reclaimed his hand and began inspecting the environment.

Husband and wife remained in place. There was no sense wandering around the area, possibly disturbing signs that the sheriff had been there. So they waited and watched as Sauer bent down to inspect the rocks, rub handfuls of dirt, and finally individual blades of grass in front of the lake. After twenty minutes of meticulous examination of the small glade, Sauer rejoined them. He gave Steve a scrutinizing look.

"What?" Steve automatically said. "Why are you looking at me like that?"

"You never told me the person we're looking for is a master tracker."

"I didn't know. What makes you say that?"

"Am I correct in thinking the two of you did not walk away from here?"

Sarah nodded. "That's right. Our portal deposited us on the path where we showed you, then I teleported my husband and myself here, then we…"

"Checked along the water's edge," Sauer promptly finished for her, "but not before Steve stopped right here, squatted down for a few moments, and then straightened back up. The two of you wandered over to here," Sauer pointed to a spot on the ground that looked no different than any other, "turned to face the water, and then you disappeared."

Surprised, Steve went over to the spot. He could barely make out the faint image of a single footprint. He looked up at Sauer and nodded appreciatively.

"I can see why the king recommended you. Damn, dude, you're good."

"Was the sheriff here?" Sarah wanted to know.

The captain nodded. "Aye. His tracks were older, by about eight hours, I'd say. The only thing he did here was to walk straight to the water's edge, kneel down, presumably to take a drink, then he headed east."

"You can see all that by looking at the same ground that I'm looking at now?" Steve asked, bewildered. "Just when I think I'm getting better at tracking, someone like you comes along and definitely proves that I don't know what I'm doing."

Sauer finally cracked a smile. "I have been hunting my whole life. I have more experience than you do."

"No arguments there."

"Your sheriff also has more experience," Sauer continued, "as he did an expert job in covering his tracks. There are virtually no signs he has been here at all."

"Then how could you tell?" Steve demanded.

Sauer knelt and pointed at a small, oval river rock just below the water's surface less than six inches from the shore.

"Your man took great care not to disturb anything on the ground while he drank," Sauer pointed out. "He leaned out over the edge and propped himself up by sticking an arm into the water. It rested up against that stone, and if you look carefully, you'll see that it has been moved from its original resting place."

Sarah blinked, staring at the smooth rounded stone, that must have moved no more than an eighth of an inch.

"Impressive. I should have known the sheriff would be a good tracker."

Steve stared at his wife. "Why? You knew him just as well as I did."

"Well, I have been in this timeline six months longer than you, you know."

"So?"

"Think about it. There are no grocery stores in the nineteenth century, not like we're familiar with. It means Sheriff Bixby would have had to ... I mean Melvyn. I need to start calling him Melvyn. It means Melvyn would have had to hunt and take care of himself. His jhorun wouldn't have worked there, so he'd be entirely on his own. And, since he's had over twenty years of practice, it's understandable that he would become good at it."

"You speak of tracking as though it's something your world no longer does," Sauer observed. He had wandered toward the east and stopped by a section of tall grass. He reached inside the clump of tall green blades to pull out a small broken tree limb. He inspected it closely for a few moments before discarding it.

"There are still people who hunt in my world," Steve pointed out, "but not many. Hunting just isn't necessary, not when you can get everything you need without killing anything."

"You live in a strange world," Sauer decided.

"Says you," Steve countered. He finally offered the captain a smile. Sauer nodded in response. "So, what lies in that direction?"

"Donlari, and the main road to R'Tal," Sauer answered.

"Should we check Donlari first?" Sarah asked.

The captain turned to look in the opposite direction. He hesitated a few moments before looking back down at the ground.

"What is it?" Steve asked.

"I can see traces of where he left the glade," Sauer began, frowning, "but I don't see anything else. Did he continue or did he circle back?"

"You think he might have double backed to Avin?"

"Aye. From what you have told me about our fugitive, it's a distinct possibility."

"Then let's be certain we're heading in the right direction," Sarah decided. She held out her hand and waited for the two men to grasp hers. "Everyone ready?"

The waterfall winked out and was replaced by a quiet town nestled in the heart of the forest. Thatched cottages dotted the landscape, connected by quaint cobbled streets. The streets converged into one main thoroughfare that, for several hundred feet, was lined with picturesque shops and single-story buildings. The constable's office was in a large abode with three chimneys on the roof and large open windows facing in all directions. It was located near the center of what Steve thought of as downtown Avin.

A quick check with the constable confirmed no such outsider had appeared within the village. As a precaution, as soon as Sarah had given the constable a full description of Melvyn, a village-wide alert was issued and the number of soldiers protecting the small village was doubled.

"Are we heading to Donlari next?" Sarah asked.

Sauer nodded. "Aye. The sooner we can spread the word about his existence, the sooner we can have every single person in Lentari looking for him." The captain laid a hand on Steve's arm, drawing him up short. "Level with me. What kind of mischief can one person make? Is all of this worth the effort?"

Steve sighed. "It is, and I'll tell you why. The worst-case scenario is that Melvyn could change the future by altering the past. He's already proven to us what he's capable of. He won't think twice about killing someone if they get in his way. You see, that's what concerns me the most. Let's say he encounters someone, maybe a guard or a soldier, in Donlari and that soldier tries to stop him. Now let's assume Melvyn gets angry and fights for his freedom, and ends up killing the soldier. Accidentally or intentionally, it doesn't matter. This soldier could be the future parent of someone important in our time. We're good friends with a man by the name of Rhenyon. He happens to be commander of the king's armies. What if that soldier who ends up getting killed is Rhenyon's great-great-grandfather?"

Sauer stared at him in silence for a few moments before gently clearing his throat. "I can understand why you want to find this man."

"Find him and stop him," Steve corrected, "at all costs."

Their next stop was the river town of Donlari. The village Steve and Sarah were used to in their time was only slightly different than the one they were staring at now. There were fewer buildings and homes on each side of the river, but aside from that, everything looked the same. Steve had even spotted the building that would eventually become Thacken Inn, where he and Sarah stayed during their first trip to Lentari. Steve squinted at the sign as they approached.

Apparently, it was called Sebastian's during this time.

"Do you want to check there?" Steve asked Sauer.

The captain shook his head. "We need to check in with the constable first."

The constable, an older gentleman in his mid-to-late sixties, listened to Sarah's description of Melvyn and was scowling before she had finished.

"What?" Sauer pressed. "Does the description sound familiar to you?"

The constable nodded. "Aye. There was a disturbance this morning."

"Tell me about it," Captain Sauer impatiently demanded.

"A traveler, such as you described, was at the tavern and ordered refreshments. When presented with the cost of his drinks, he became belligerent and refused to pay."

"Sounds like that arrogant putz," Steve grumbled.

"Why would he draw attention to himself?" Sarah asked. "If he's trying to hide, I would think the last thing he'd want to do is make a scene."

"Did he end up paying for his drinks?" Steve asked the constable. "Or did he make a run for it?"

The constable blinked with surprise. When no answer was forthcoming, Sauer cleared his throat and repeated Steve's question. The village constable was at a loss for words, and everyone could see it. What had happened?

"I don't … I don't honestly remember," the constable admitted, his face reddening with shame. "Why is it I don't remember?"

Sauer was instantly heading toward the door. "This warrants investigation. We must check with the tavern owner."

Unfortunately, the answer they received from Sebastian himself was no less reassuring.

"I, uh…"

"You don't remember, either," Sauer guessed.

Surprised, the barkeep shook his head. The captain turned back to his companions. "Jhorun is at play here. Do we know what Melvyn's jhorun is?"

"I don't," Steve admitted. He glanced at Sarah. "Did he ever mention it to you?"

Sarah slowly shook her head. "I don't recall if he ever did. I think it's safe to say that his jhorun has something to do with making people forget."

"That's an odd jhorun to have," Steve commented.

"Odd, but effective," Sauer observed.

"His jhorun can't be that strong," Sarah deduced, "otherwise the constable and the barkeep wouldn't have remembered him at all."

"What does that tell us?" Steve asked.

"It means his jhorun can only make people forget small, trivial things."

"Like getting out of paying for your bar tab?" Steve guessed.

Sarah nodded. "Exactly. Since he used his jhorun once here already, I doubt very much that he'd still be in the area."

"Where do you think he's gone?" Sauer pointedly asked. "Where do we search now? R'Tal? The city is huge. He could easily hide in plain sight and no one would be the wiser."

"It'd be the best place to hide," Steve admitted. "We need to find him before he gets settled someplace. You need to alert the king."

Captain Sauer nodded. "I will. We can alert the ... are you not coming to the castle with me?"

"As far as I know we are," Sarah told him, confused. She looked at her husband and noticed a determined look on Steve's face. "Can you give us just a moment?"

Sauer nodded and wandered a few paces away.

"What are you doing?" Sarah whispered. "What's with that look on your face?"

"We need to ditch him."

"Excuse me?"

"I think we need to call in an even better tracker than he is."

"The king said Sauer was the best tracker."

"The best *human* tracker," Steve corrected.

"Who do you have in mind?" Sarah asked. She shielded her eyes with her hand and glanced around the riverside village, as if expecting to see someone else waiting their turn at tracking the truant sheriff. Sarah's eyes widened. She quickly looked at the captain, who was looking northeast, as if he could see the castle. "You want to contact Pryllan, don't you?"

"A dragon's sense of smell is much greater than that of the best bloodhound," Steve whispered to her. "Their sight and hearing are also much better. No one can beat a dragon when it comes to tracking someone."

"Will Pryllan help us?"

"What's the worst that could happen? Telling us no? I think it's worth asking her."

"Ask her then," Sarah told him. "If she agrees to help, I'll drop Captain Sauer back at the castle so he can warn the king."

Pryllan? Are you there?

Sarah tapped his shoulder. "Are you going to ask her or not?"

"I am asking her. She hasn't responded yet."

Pryllan? Can you hear me?

I am still acclimatizing to the shock of being contacted by a human.

I know. I'm sorry, my friend.

You want to ask another favor, is that so?

Are you reading my mind right now?

No. There is no need to.

Yes, you're right. I need to ask another favor.

I'm still trying to figure out how to undo the last favor I granted you.

I know you are, Pryllan. I told you before that I won't abandon you. We're in this together.

What is it you require?

We need your help searching for a fugitive.

A fugitive? Suggesting you wish to apprehend this person once their location has been determined?

That's right. This is a bad man, Pryllan. We need to find him just as soon as possible.

What has he done?

He's from the same time I am. I'm afraid if we don't capture him he will try to alter the present to change the future.

You're certain of this?

I wouldn't put it past him.

But you don't know for certain?

Steve sighed, drawing a speculative look from Sarah. *You're right. I don't know if he'd do that. However, he has shown that he is an opportunist and lacks a conscience.*

Pryllan was silent as she considered. **What do you suggest?**

He was last seen in Donlari. Chances are he's headed to R'Tal. It's a large city. He could hide anywhere in the crowds.

Pryllan was silent as she continued to consider the consequences of getting involved.

He knows the humans and wyverians have become allies in my time, Steve reminded her. *If left unchecked, Melvyn could interfere with our future alliance. Do you want to risk that?*

Help him, Kahvel's voice commanded.

Kahvel? Is that you?

Aye. I have been monitoring.

Why? Pryllan inquired. Steve could feel a sense of irritation creeping into the green dragon's mind. **Do you not trust me to make the proper decision?**

Of course. In this case, a human could have dangerous repercussions to wyverians. This human must not be allowed to do as he pleases.

Thanks, Kahvel. I owe you one.

Fear not, human, the gold dragon smugly thought to Steve. ***I will collect.***

Steve smiled. Sarah, who had been watching him closely, also smiled. Captain Sauer had rejoined them and was giving Sarah a questioning look. Sarah held a finger to her lips and indicated he still needed to be quiet.

Very well. I will assist. What do you need me to do?

We're in Donlari right now. We'll head west, following the river, until we're out of sight of the village. Pick us up there.

Do you know for certain this fugitive will go to R'Tal?

That would be our best guess, Kahvel.

I will search west of the river village. Sarnau will search north.

Sarnau?

He is a friend.

How do you know who to look for? I'm not sure I could describe him with any amount of certainty.

Pryllan, please pull an image of who we're looking for.

Aye. Steve, please think about this fugitive. Show me what he looks like.

Steve shook his head with amazement. *I didn't even know you guys could do that.*

Think about his face, Pryllan urged. **What does he look like? Think about the last time you saw him.**

Steve took several breaths and thought about the last encounter he had with that self-serving smug son of a b... An image formed. He was looking at the sheriff casually smoking a cigar in his office after he had rescued Sarah. He smiled as he remembered smashing his fist into the sheriff's face, knocking him out cold.

I believe I have it. We're looking for this human.

The image of the sheriff's face returned, but this time frozen in place, as if someone had hit the pause button on a movie.

I have it as well. I will relay this image to Sarnau. Do we have his scent?

Steve automatically shook his head. *I'm no bloodhound, sorry. I have no idea what he smells like.*

A series of images flashed through his head. Memories of Sarah, their time in Idaho, their visits to Lentari, and this most recent excursion all zipped through his mind, as though the person who hit the pause button had now pressed the fast forward button.

"What's the matter?" Sarah gently whispered. "I can see your eyes jumping around like crazy under your eyelids."

"I'll explain later," Steve quietly answered. "Wow, this is weird."

After a dizzying amount of forgotten memories had flashed through his brain, the images all stopped, as though someone had flicked a switch. Steve shook his head to clear his thoughts.

Well, that *was unpleasant.*

It was Pryllan's turn to apologize.

I am sorry. I should have warned you that when we're

mentally connected, I can easily access your thoughts, too. I made the mistake of wondering if you had ever smelled this person we're looking for.

I could've saved you the time, Pryllan. I haven't.

Except you have, Pryllan corrected. **I found his scent and have already relayed it to Kahvel.**

You did? You know what he smells like?

Aye. It was more than enough to begin our search.

I love your Collective.

It has its moments.

Steve opened his eyes and smiled at his wife. He noticed the captain standing nearby and smiled sheepishly. "We're going to take you back to R'Tal so you can warn the king."

"What will you do?" Sauer inquired. "What were you just doing with your eyes closed like that?"

"It's nothing you need to worry about," Steve assured him.

"You were communicating with someone," Sauer accused. "Who was it?"

"I can't tell you, man," Steve apologized. "I'm sorry. I don't want to risk screwing up something in the future. Can you let that one go?"

Captain Sauer stared at him for another minute or two before finally shrugging. "Very well. If you take me back to R'Tal, I'll inform the king."

Sarah nodded. She took the captain's arm and cast a look over her shoulder at Steve. "I'll be right back. Don't go anywhere."

Steve smiled. "You're ditching me already, is that it?"

"Don't wander off and you won't get lost. It's that simple."

"Must you inform everyone we come into contact with that I get lost easily?"

Sauer suppressed a smile. "You do?"

Steve scowled. "Now look what you've done."

Sarah and the captain vanished. Steve wandered over to the river's edge and looked down into the slow-moving water. He could see silvery shapes gently undulating back and forth as the currents tried to push the fish farther downstream.

Steve squinted at the closest fish. It looked like it had short stubby legs beneath its body. Was it a rypo? The multi-legged fish was known to frequent the river and had proven itself as a suitable source of food for the people living nearby.

Steve briefly thought back to Kornal and his wife, Nilhanu, and their first visit to Lentari all those years ago. Kornal, Steve remembered, could accurately predict where the elusive rypos were going to be, thus making them easier to catch. It was the first example of jhorun he had ever seen.

Sarah reappeared.

"Is everything alright?" Steve saw her look of concern.

"Everything is okay," Sarah assured him. "The king has the entire city on high alert. He's called for the guards to be tripled, as he wants to take no chances with Melvyn, either. He wants him found."

"Good."

Sarah held out her hand. "Ready to find Pryllan?"

"Yes."

Sarah squinted as she stared at the western horizon. She could see rolling hills and a single large tree. Moments later they were standing next to the tall silver-grey trunk of a lone beech tree. They turned to look back at the distant village.

"Do you think this is far enough?" Sarah asked.

Steve pointed at a group of three to four similar trees visible in the distance, away from the village. "Let's go there. That should be far enough."

Pryllan arrived less than ten minutes later. She scooped up the husband and wife team in her talons and retreated to the safety of the sky.

"Sarah knows you, but you've never met her before now," Steve said. "Pryllan, this is my wife, Sarah."

"Hello, Pryllan. It's good to see you."

"Incredible. I now know *two* humans. What is this world coming to?"

"One where everyone—usually—gets along with one another."

"Where would you like to search first?" Pryllan inquired.

Steve pointed east. Pryllan banked left and flew out over Donlari. "You do realize that the humans in the village certainly will see me?"

Steve shrugged. "It can't be helped. They live in Lentari. They've gotta know that dragons live here, too."

Sarah laid a hand on his. "But we don't want to frighten anyone, do we?"

"Not on purpose, no," Steve admitted. "If we can, Pryllan, let's keep human contact to a minimum, okay?"

Pryllan grunted in response. For close to two hours, they canvassed the wide-open prairies and fields east of Donlari, looking for some sign that Melvyn had passed through. Thus far, they had been unable to find anything.

"What is the status of absolving the shachar, may I ask?"

Steve looked up at Pryllan and grimaced. He had been afraid Pryllan was going to ask about that.

"Can I assume you are no closer to the answer than you were?" the dragon dryly asked.

Steve sighed. "That's right. I told you I wasn't going to abandon you. I meant it. I'll figure something out. I promise."

"Do you mind if I ask you about this shachar?" Sarah asked.

"Go ahead," Pryllan answered.

"Has a shachar ever been broken before?"

"I asked that already," Steve quietly told her.

"I wasn't there, was I? Now hush. Pryllan, what would it take?"

"An equivalent act of valor."

"From the little girl?" Sarah asked.

"Aye."

"But she's just a little girl!" Sarah protested. "She's not going to be able to do that."

"You asked what would absolve a shachar. I answered. I am well aware of the remote possibilities of a young dwarf underling accomplishing such a feat."

"Steve has mentioned that until the shachar has been absolved, then the girl will feel unsettled and restless."

"Aye, that is correct," the dragon agreed. She dipped her wings and circled for another pass over the endless prairie.

"Have you been inconvenienced at all?" Steve asked. "What's it like for you to be the recipient of the child's affections?"

"My emotions are nothing compared to what the child must be experiencing at this time."

"So, you can feel it?" Sarah insisted.

"Aye."

"How—"

Pryllan started growling. Thinking she was angry with her for asking too many questions, Sarah fell silent. She looked at Steve, who returned her concerned look. Had Pryllan found something?

"What is it?" Steve finally asked.

Pryllan tensed and became almost as still as a statue. Thankfully, there were enough air currents to keep her aloft, but it still didn't do anything to allay their concerns. Something had riled up their wyverian friend.

"What is it?" Steve repeated, growing concerned. "What's wrong?"

"Kahvel has informed me that there is a noticeable increase in dwarven activity up in our valley."

"Okay. Is that a bad thing?"

"Do you recall the stump door that the Kla Guur use?"

"What of it?" Sarah asked.

"For the past hour, dwarves have been seen pouring steadily out of it."

"How is that a bad thing?" Steve wanted to know.

"Dwarves are emerging Topside," Pryllan explained, "and they are fanning out, as though they are searching for something."

"Why does that concern you?" Sarah asked. She shared a look with her husband. There was something that the dragon wasn't telling them.

"Sarnau has overheard several conversations, which he has relayed to Kahvel, and he, in turn, has relayed them to the rest of the Collective."

Still confused, Steve waited for a further explanation.

"The dwarves are grouping together and forming search parties."

"What are they looking for?" Steve asked. He had a sinking feeling in his stomach that he wasn't going to like the answer.

"They are looking for a missing person. A child. It would seem young Aislinn has run away from her family."

Steve closed his eyes and groaned. They didn't have time for this. Not here, and not now. They needed to find the sheriff first. However, judging from Pryllan's reaction, their own search had just been preempted by the dwarven one. He sighed.

"We'll go search for Aislinn," Steve promised their wyverian friend. "We'll find Melvyn as soon as we know Aislinn is safe, okay?"

Pryllan continued to growl. "Sarnau has confirmed it. The underling is searching for me."

Chapter 10 — An Aislinn Alert

What the hell was she thinking?" Steve swore. "A tiny young dwarf girl is not going to have a snowball's chance in Nevir trying to survive out there on her own. She has to know that, doesn't she?"

"Remember what Pryllan said," Sarah softly added. "She won't be at peace until the shachar has been absolved. The poor little girl must be going out of her mind trying to figure out why she has this inexplicable attraction to Pryllan."

"The underling must be found," Pryllan agreed. "Steve is right. There are many unthinkable dangers that await."

"Do all the dragons know that the dwarves are looking for a missing child?" Steve asked, curious.

Pryllan's enormous head nodded. "Aye."

"Does Rinbok?"

Pryllan nodded again. "Aye. The Dragon Lord knows."

Steve cursed silently to himself.

"She said Rinbok knows the dwarves are looking for a missing underling," Sarah clarified. "He doesn't know about the child's connection to Pryllan."

"That is correct," the dragon confirmed. "And we must keep it that way."

"How fast can you get back to the valley?" Sarah asked.

"Flying at normal speeds the journey would take about two hours."

"I know you're capable of flying faster than that," Steve confided to her. "We've flown that way a number of times before."

"Perhaps a half hour," Pryllan amended. "Brace yourselves."

Sarah scooted closer to Steve and wrapped her arms around him. Steve hugged his wife close and waited. Within moments, the passing landscape was flashing by so fast everything had been reduced to a dizzying blur. The howl of the wind was so bad that Sarah buried her face in Steve's chest and gripped him in a death grip, afraid she'd be torn from his grasp.

"Hang in there!" Steve tried shouting to her, but his words were lost to the wind.

Thirty-five minutes later Pryllan decelerated. Steve risked a glance through the dragon's massive claws. They were back in the valley and were flying at a much more comfortable speed. He risked a glance at Sarah.

Sarah was glaring at him. Her ponytail scrunchy was long gone, and the long brown strands were in an impossible tangle, Bride of Frankenstein style.

"Not one word," Sarah warned him. "I must look terrible. Let's not do that again."

Not trusting himself to speak, Steve gave her a noncommittal grunt and tried to ignore the mess. "I don't know what you're talking about," he mumbled, fighting valiantly to keep his voice from quavering. "You look great, hon."

Sarah tried to smooth down her windswept hair. It was a losing battle.

"Where would you like to start searching?" Pryllan asked, angling her head to inspect the passing countryside.

"Head toward that stump door of theirs," Steve

instructed. "See if you can pick anything up there."

The emerald green dragon adjusted her course and banked right. Once Lake Raehón was behind her, she flew over the border of the forest and began circling. The stump, one of many subterranean entrances the Kla Guur regularly used, was inside the forest, less than twenty feet from the edge of the valley. They found the stump but it appeared deserted.

"Where's the closest dwarf?" Steve asked.

"Can you smell the girl?" Sarah asked, at the same time.

"There are three dwarves less than a league away, slowly heading east. As for being able to tell if the scent of the underling is there, I cannot say. Too many other scents are more prevalent."

"What if you were closer?" Steve suggested. "Like on the ground. Would you be able to tell then?"

"You want her to land?" Sarah asked. "Won't that look suspicious if someone were to see her?"

"Like who? Another dragon? She can just say that she had smelled something unusual and was investigating."

"She'd be grounded," Sarah was saying. "The trees are growing too thick in there. She'd be trapped."

"No, I wouldn't," Pryllan disagreed. "While it wouldn't be the most graceful of takeoffs, I could push my way through that canopy if I needed to."

Satisfied, Steve turned to Sarah. "There. Happy? She'd be fine."

"Ask her, don't tell her," Sarah scolded. She patted her seat, which was Pryllan's right claw. "Pryllan, would you consider walking along the ground for a little while?"

"That was essentially what I was asking her," Steve grumbled.

"But you didn't," Sarah pointed out. "What do you say? Would you do that, Pryllan?"

They felt Pryllan's body give a slight shudder as the dragon gave the approximation of a shrug.

"Of course."

She circled back to land at the edge of the valley and deposited husband and wife onto the soft grass-covered ground. Steve stretched while Sarah looked around.

"I've always thought this valley was pretty."

Steve took her hand and pulled Sarah into the forest. "Well, right now none of the dragons save Pryllan knows us. I'd just as soon not have to tangle with another dragon, let alone get Pryllan into more trouble by explaining what she's doing hanging around two humans."

"Good point. Which way to this door of theirs?"

Steve pointed straight ahead. "It's just over there. Not far."

Progress was a little slow, but Pryllan was able to squeeze her bulk through the trees to follow the two humans. They stopped at the huge stump and slowly inspected the disguised doorway.

"Can you smell anything now?" Steve wanted to know as he looked up at Pryllan.

Pryllan leaned her head down low and gently sniffed the stump. Her eyes closed as she sniffed a second time. "I can distinguish eleven different dwarves who have used this door in the last twelve hours," the dragon informed them. "The number increases to over two dozen if I go back another twelve hours. However, Aislinn is not one of the scents. She has not used this entrance in the last twenty-four hours."

"You said three dwarves were still nearby, moving slowly?"

Pryllan's head lifted and she sniffed again. "Aye. They are no longer traveling together. They are close to one another, but they do not travel together."

"They're looking for Aislinn," Steve told the dragon. "They've split up so they can cover more ground."

"Ah."

"Can you tell if one of them is Selwyn?" Steve asked.

"Who's Selwyn"? Sarah wanted to know.

"Aislinn's father," Steve told her.

"The child's father is one of the three," Pryllan confirmed. "His scent moves north."

Steve took Sarah's hand and headed off. "We should see if we can find him. We need to let him know that we're searching for her, too."

Sarah pulled him to a stop. "Pryllan said north. You're headed east."

"Whatever," Steve said, crossly.

Sarah shared a bemused look with Pryllan. She held a finger to her mouth and smiled at the dragon, shaking her head. Pryllan nodded, understanding. It was not the time for humorous comments about Steve's lousy sense of direction.

"Smell him out," Steve called back to Pryllan, as he pushed his way farther into the forest. "If we're getting close then let us know."

"Understood," Pryllan's strong voice answered.

Less than an hour later Pryllan froze in mid-step, forcing the two humans to halt and look back at her with curious stares.

"The girl's father is nearby," she softly told them. "He is frightened and distraught. Many sentient beings will behave irrationally when confronted with such circumstances."

"She means don't spook him," Sarah translated.

"Selwyn?" Steve softly called out, unwilling to shout. "Selwyn, are you there?"

"Who's there?" a gruff voice demanded.

"It's a friend. A couple of friends, actually."

"I know that voice. Steve, is that you?"

"Yes. Come out here where we can see you, okay?"

Selwyn appeared. He had been crouching behind a large tree trunk, gripping his axe tightly in both hands. He gasped with shock as he saw two humans and an enormous green dragon staring intently at him.

"You are responsible for this!" Selwyn shouted accusingly at Pryllan. "You are the reason my little Aislinn has run away!"

"Cool your jets there, Sparky," Steve snapped. "We warned you this was going to happen. Pryllan saved her life. You know it and I know it. We're going to break this thing but we're going to have to do that together, okay?"

Selwyn's angry glare fell on Sarah and he instantly softened. A little. "Who are you? I do not believe we have met."

Steve stepped forward. "Selwyn, this is my wife, Sarah. Sarah, this is Selwyn, Chief of Security for the Kla Guur, and father of Aislinn."

Sarah smiled at the dwarf, who was looking at her with an almost accusatory look. The dwarf swung his axe around his back in a practiced move and hooked it onto its holder. He finally returned Sarah's smile, although it did look a bit forced.

"Greetings. Please forgive my rudeness. You haven't caught me at my best."

There was a sharp gasp followed closely by two curses so vile they would have made a sailor blush. The other two dwarves, alerted by Selwyn's conversation, had found the group and were struggling to pull their axes.

Selwyn rushed to throw himself between his two fellow dwarves and the three of them. "Put those axes away," Selwyn snapped. Both dwarves looked as though they wanted to rebel but Selwyn's authoritative tone convinced them otherwise. Weapons were reluctantly returned to their holders. "Harrig, Galman, these are friends."

One of the dwarves, attired in solid black, wordlessly pointed up at Pryllan.

"Yes, Galman, it's a dragon. She's a friend. I do believe they're here to help us look for Aislinn, am I right?"

Steve and Sarah nodded.

"We are," Pryllan agreed. She lowered her head until she was practically nose to nose with the dwarves. She inhaled their scent.

"Why must you get so close?" Harrig demanded. His hand, slowly reaching for his axe, was swatted away by Selwyn.

Selwyn shot his fellow dwarves a disbelieving look. "Would you prefer she doesn't learn our scent and mistakes you for an enemy?"

Both newcomers dropped their objections and let Pryllan learn their scent. Then they turned to the two humans and gave them questioning looks.

"We're all friends," Steve told the two dwarves. "We can trust each other. We're here to find Aislinn, just as you are."

Galman was finally convinced. "Very well. We appreciate the help."

"How can you help?" Harrig wanted to know. "No

offense, human, but we know these woods much better than you do. We can cover more ground much more effectively than you. How do you think you can help find my niece?"

"In searches, the more eyes the better," Steve began. He hooked a thumb in Pryllan's direction. "But that doesn't matter. Pryllan has a much more advanced sense of smell and hearing. Trust me, you want her on your side." When neither dwarf objected Steve continued. "We know Aislinn didn't use your stump door. Do you know where she came out?"

Selwyn nodded. "Aye. There's a door less than a league from here, due south. It will look like a large flat rock. Trapezoidal, not rectangular. There are three other similar rocks nearby, but much smaller. You can't miss it." Selwyn sighed loudly. "I didn't even know she knew about it, but obviously she did. We followed her footprints into the woods before we lost her."

"We *will* get her back," Galman insisted, staring hard at the small group of rescuers as if daring them to say otherwise.

"Keep searching," Steve told Selwyn, as he and Sarah walked over to Pryllan. "We'll backtrack to the door and see if we can pick up her trail."

Selwyn nodded fitfully. "Thanks again for helping us search. And you, Pryllan. The generosity of the wyverians is something I will not be forgetting any time soon."

The band split up. The three dwarves trudged off, each angling in a slightly different direction. Pryllan stared down at the two humans and cocked her head.

"What?" Steve asked. "What's the matter?"

"How are we going to do this? I cannot move about on the forest floor with the two of you in my talons. You would be squished flat."

"Couldn't we just walk next to you?" Sarah asked. "I mean, we don't walk that slowly. I'd be more concerned about you."

"Why?" Pryllan asked, confused.

"It can get tight in here," Sarah told the dragon. "You're huge. What happens if you don't fit?"

"Then I'll either go around or push my way through," the dragon vowed. "As such, I don't want to worry about whether or not I'll step on you."

"What do you suggest?" Steve asked.

"I suggest you ride on my back. It'll get you out of harm's way."

"And if we're seen?"

"Then I'll leave it to Sarah to teleport the two of you to the ground."

Steve shrugged. "That'll work."

The three of them found the concealed dwarf door without any incidents. Pryllan sniffed the surface of the door and instantly reported smelling Aislinn's scent. With her nose to the ground, like a huge bloodhound, the dragon slowly headed northeast, as the child had wandered aimlessly about.

Pryllan squeezed through two long rows of pine trees, snapping off lower limbs in the process. The commotion was probably heard for miles in all directions. Steve chuckled.

"What's so funny?" Sarah wanted to know.

"I thought dragons always moved about in utter silence. Pryllan is definitely proving me wrong right about now."

"Let's see you try and navigate through such tight confines," the dragon promptly told them. "I challenge you to do better."

One dead tree, long since dried up, and as brittle as parchment, collapsed noisily to the ground as the giant dragon passed by. Pryllan hesitated only long enough to give the fallen tree a passing glance. She was about to take another step when she froze in place. Pryllan's massive head jerked up and stared at the forest's canopy high above their heads.

"Get down," Pryllan whispered to her riders. "Hurry!"

Sarah, ready for such a command, instantly teleported the two of them off of Pryllan's back and onto the forest floor. She and Steve began walking by her side as though they'd been doing that all along.

"Is everything alright?" Steve asked as he looked up at the towering dragon.

Pryllan gave a slight, almost imperceptible shake of her head. Something was happening, only she wasn't at liberty to say what. At least, not yet. A minute or two later Pryllan breathed a sigh of relief and resumed walking.

"What was that all about?" Steve asked.

"I had to convince my fellow dragons that I was not in peril. It's not often winged dragons are found inside a forest. It was believed I was in danger, or had been injured and therefore grounded. I told them I wasn't."

Steve let out a shaky sigh. "That was a close call."

"Did they ask what you were doing?" Sarah inquired.

Pryllan nodded. "Naturally. I told them I thought I had heard a sound of distress and I was investigating."

"That's some quick thinking," Sarah softly murmured. "Is Rinbok Intherer still in the dark about this rescue attempt?"

"We have done nothing to arouse his suspicions," Pryllan answered. "He remains unaware."

"You sure about that?" Steve asked, raising an eyebrow.

Pryllan snorted, sending out a thick jet of smoke from each nostril. "Are you not familiar with the Dragon Lord's temper? Trust me when I say he suspects nothing."

Steve gestured at the surrounding trees. "It's getting rather thick in here. Think you can still move freely enough to follow Aislinn's scent?"

Pryllan looked at the closest tree, only a few feet from her right flank. She reached out to grasp the trunk with one of her mighty claws. She gave it a quick jerk. The entire tree snapped off at the trunk. Pryllan let it drop to the ground and gave Steve a look.

Steve cleared his throat. "Alrighty then. No worries."

Sarah teleported the two of them to her back just as Pryllan headed off, following her nose southeast. The child's path was incredibly erratic. Aislinn had wandered straight south and then doubled back to head north. Half a league later, she'd turned and headed west, only to change direction yet again and head north once more.

Watching Pryllan hesitate as Aislinn's trail had changed direction again, Steve chuckled. "She really didn't know where she was going, did she?"

"She's a little girl," Sarah admonished. "She's probably scared out of her wits by now."

"Something else is tracking her," Pryllan announced, coming to a halt. She dropped her head a bit lower and inhaled, filling her lungs to full capacity. She waited a few moments before exhaling.

"What is it?" Steve asked. "What do you smell?"

Pryllan growled. Both Steve and Sarah could feel the deep rumblings as the dragon's low guttural growl rumbled across her body.

"Shabewts."

Steve blinked with surprise. He glanced at Sarah. She was just as surprised as he.

"Umm, shab-whats?" Steve asked.

"Shabewts. They are shaggy, squat, land bound predators that hunt in packs."

"So, they're like wolves," Steve decided, bringing up a mental picture of one for Pryllan to look at.

"No," Pryllan disagreed. "They look nothing like that creature. They have thick limbs, muscular haunches, short rounded ears, and…" The dragon trailed off as she detected Steve mentally reviewing different creatures. She selected one image and presented it back to him. "It is a closer match to this one, only the tail is wrong. The tail curves upward and is just as shaggy as the rest of its coat."

Steve reviewed the picture Pryllan gave him and paled.

"That's a bear. Bears don't travel in packs."

"They clearly do here," Sarah added.

"If a pack of bears are now trailing Aislinn, then we need to double-time it. She's in danger."

Pryllan hurried through the thick forest, snapping obtrusive branches and completely uprooting several trees. The racket could undoubtedly be heard for miles. She had just pushed her way through two large oak trees when something flew up off the branch and began squawking angrily at them.

Pryllan hesitated. It was a griffin. Judging by the dark red coloring on most of its pinfeathers, this one was an adolescent. The juvenile griffin angrily flapped its wings as it rose up to confront Pryllan eye-to-eye. It let loose a string of squawks and trills that didn't need to be translated. It was angry. Apparently Pryllan's passing had disrupted the griffin's nap and frightened away the rest of his flock. Only he was brave enough to stand his ground.

The griffin spied Steve and Sarah and fired off a litany of insults in their direction, too. A few moments later a second griffin appeared, followed closely by a third. Soon the sky was filled with loud angry squawks as the griffins all voiced their displeasure at Pryllan.

Pryllan, on the other hand, gave the upset griffins a quick cursory glance and decided to ignore them. She had no quarrel with them and elected to leave it that way.

Steve, ready to come to his wyverian friend's aid should the need arise, was carefully watching the griffins as they did their best to provoke Pryllan. Why would a mere griffin challenge a dragon? It'd be no contest. The dragon could easily best half a dozen griffins without even trying.

There was a flurry of flapping wings as more griffins emerged from their roosts on nearby trees. In less than ten seconds, there were no fewer than two dozen griffins, all squawking irritably and all trying to provoke Pryllan into starting a skirmish. The dragon turned to look at the two humans on her back.

"I might have to call for help," she softly told them. "I do not think I could handle that many by myself."

"You're not by yourself," Steve answered. He ignited both hands. "You have a fire thrower and a teleporter that will quite literally cover your back."

"I don't want to hurt a griffin," Sarah complained, eyeing the angry griffins. She quickly put her hands over her husband's, forcing him to extinguish them. "They didn't do anything to us."

"We didn't do anything to them," Steve pointed out, "yet there they are, trying to pick a fight."

"Can't we just make them leave us alone? We're friends with the griffins. We shouldn't hurt them."

One griffin broke away from the flock and deliberately flew past Pryllan's face, brushing the tips of its feathers along her nostrils, which both flared open in surprise. The dragon looked down at the two of them.

"They are trying to provoke an attack. I will ask for assistance."

Steve rose to his feet. "Hang on a sec, Pryllan. Let's see if we can get them to leave us alone." Steve smiled nervously at his wife. "We'll try to ask nicely."

Pryllan inclined her head, as if to say *you first.*

"Hey up there!" Steve called out, projecting his voice as loudly as he could. "We're not looking for trouble. We're just passing through. Leave us in peace and we'll do the same for you, okay?"

Three griffins let out derisive trills. Two of them tucked their wings close to their bodies and dove straight at him. Steve looked over at his wife.

"Thoughts?"

"Just try to not hurt any of them, okay?"

Steve ignited his hands and blasted a huge wall of flames directly above Pryllan's head. The diving griffins screeched with alarm and hastily changed course. Both of them crashed into nearby trees and disappeared. Steve pulled back his jhorun and let the wall of flames poof out.

"Do you guys really want to do this? You're facing a dragon and a fire thrower. Oh, and a teleporter, too. Think about that before you attack us again. Let us leave, and we'll go. Alright? There's no need for this to go any further."

Most of the circling griffins fell silent as they decided amongst themselves whether or not to pursue the matter. Just then two fallen trees and one huge boulder lifted off the ground and rose steadily higher into the air. One griffin squawked with terror as a boulder easily three times its size soared precariously near him. The rest of the griffins stopped circling and hovered, furiously flapping their wings, as they all spied the immense objects steadily rising toward them.

Evidently the griffins decided they had business elsewhere. One by one they disappeared into the nearby trees. Even then, Steve felt as though dozens of beady griffin eyes were watching him. He smiled appreciatively at his wife.

"Next time let's open with a demonstration of your jhorun instead of mine, okay?"

Sarah shrugged, as though fending off a band of unruly creatures was something she did on a daily basis. "It would probably save some time."

"We should keep moving," Pryllan informed them. "The

dwarf underling's trail is growing stronger."

Steve nodded. "That's a good thing, right?"

"More shabewts have converged on this spot," Pryllan growled. "The child's life is in imminent danger. We must hurry."

Pryllan crouched lower to the ground and hurried off. This time, Steve noted with surprise, she made no sound whatsoever. Steve leaned over Pryllan's side to see for himself that she was still walking and not somehow floating along the ground. He didn't know how Pryllan was doing it, but her movements now had an almost serpentine feel to them, gently undulating as she effortlessly snaked her way through the thick trees. No trees were knocked over. No branches were snapped in half. The forest was utterly quiet, except for an occasional chirp from a nearby kyte.

"That has got to be the coolest thing ever!" Steve excitedly whispered to Pryllan. "How are you doing that?"

Pryllan shushed him. "Now is not the time to discuss wyverian locomotion. We must approach in stealth. If the shabewts sense impending danger, they might be tempted to do something drastic. Usually when they hunt, they will wait for an adequate number of their kind before attempting a frontal attack."

"Aislinn is tiny!" Steve protested. "Why would they need more of those bear things?"

Pryllan shushed him again. **We are gaining on one of the shabewts.**

Where?

Pryllan shared her senses and looked straight ahead. There, partially concealed behind a tree, was one of the furry predators. It had its back to them, so all they really saw was a fluffy brown backside with an even fluffier tail curving up and over onto its back.

From this angle it doesn't look too dangerous, Steve decided.

It looks like a cuddly teddy bear, Sarah added.

Is Pryllan sharing her eyesight with you? Steve asked with a touch of bewilderment in his thoughts. *I thought she only did that with me.*

I'm not sharing my senses with her.

Steve heard his wife's laughter in his head.

Geez, take it easy. Jealous much? I don't need to borrow her eyesight. I see it just fine.

Showoff.

Steve watched the shabewt through Pryllan's eyes. The creature was sniffing the air and was shuffling about, as if it couldn't decide which direction to turn. Sarah was right. It did look like a harmless, fluffy teddy bear that should…

The shabewt finally turned around and stared directly at them. Its mouth opened, revealing rows of razor-sharp teeth. It gave out a tremendous roar, sounding very much like a bear. It left the safety of the trees and sprinted straight for them.

Steve readied his jhorun. Even though he knew there'd be no way Pryllan would be concerned about a single shabewt attacking her, she had mentioned the fuzzballs traveled in packs. Where there was one, there were bound to be others, perhaps hiding in the trees.

He fired off a warning blast, which slammed into the ground less than a foot from the shabewt. It kept running toward them, now faster, its black eyes trained on the dragon. Flecks of drool dripped off its fangs and were whisked away by the blowing wind.

The creature was now less than twenty feet from Pryllan. Steve watched. What would she do? Those teeth looked vicious. He generated a chaser, just in case.

The shabewt leapt for Pryllan's closest foreleg. She snatched the snarling, gnashing monster from the air. Holding the shabewt firmly in her left claw she brought the creature up to her face and studied it. It struggled to free itself and sink its fangs into Pryllan's flesh.

Pryllan's slitted eyes narrowed. Steve wondered if she would simply bite the monster's head off. She gave a low growl. The shabewt ceased struggling and moaned pitifully

Sarah quietly observed. "You're not going to hurt it, are you?"

"I have every right to," Pryllan growled. She eyed the creature, then opened her claw and dropped the shabewt as though she was discarding an insignificant rock she had picked up from the ground.

The shabewt scampered off and disappeared into the woods without another trace. Steve looked appraisingly up at the huge dragon.

"I thought for sure you were going to bite its head off. Let me guess. It doesn't taste very good."

"Not hungry," Pryllan nonchalantly told him.

"Ah."

Satisfied that the threat had been removed, the trio continued to head east. During the next fifteen minutes they encountered—and scared away—two more of the shaggy shabewts before Pryllan came to a stop.

The child is nearby.

How close is she? Steve wanted to know.

Less than a hundred feet.

Good job, Pryllan, Sarah happily told her.

The child isn't out of danger yet. At least a dozen shabewts are converging on this very spot.

Steve quietly looked around from his vantage point on Pryllan's back. He couldn't see a single one. *Do they know you're here yet?*

The shabewts suspect nothing.

They all heard the shrill scream of a young girl. Sarah teleported the two of them to the ground as Pryllan surged forward. Husband and wife watched the dragon push her way through a thin line of trees and roar her challenge to the bear-like creatures. A large dark gray stone hill, devoid of plant life, was directly before them. The narrow mouth of an ominous cave was also visible. Unfortunately, they still couldn't see Aislinn anywhere. Had she chosen to hide in the cave?

Steve ignited both hands just as five shabewts rushed to attack Pryllan. The mighty dragon squished one flat and snapped her jaws at two more who tried to dart in close to her abdomen. The uncanny creatures darted away at the last second. One of the two, who narrowly avoided being bitten in half, tried to attack Pryllan's long, serpentine tail, but was blasted by a well-timed jet of fire from Steve.

A pair of shabewts focused on the single human standing off by herself. Both sprung forward at the same time. At that moment, a nearby tree bent sharply and was broken off at the trunk by an invisible force. The large trunk whooshed through the air and made contact with one of the shabewts. The howling creature flew up and over the gray hill.

The floating broken tree suddenly reversed direction and swung again. The second shabewt took the blow lower and the monster was sent rocketing off through the trees. Branches and small trees snapped in its wake.

In a blink of an eye, the number of shabewts doubled. Half a dozen of the snarling creatures began circling Pryllan, waiting for the exact moment when the dragon would drop her guard.

Pryllan blasted out a huge wall of flames. The shabewts scattered but quickly reformed their ranks. One darted in to take a bite out of her tail. Sarah shouted a warning just in time for Pryllan to flick her tail out of the way. Steve managed to blast two more of the shabewts, but the shaggy bears kept getting bolder by the second.

"Get on my back," Pryllan ordered, as she noticed the monsters focusing on the two humans.

Steve threw a chaser at one shabewt as it ventured too close to his wife. Thankfully, the monster was too busy salivating over what it thought was an easy meal to take notice of the burning fireball speeding toward it. The chaser struck a split second later.

Steve turned in time to see three of the shaggy creatures leap toward him. All three hung suspended in mid-air a few moments, before they were all slammed together and dropped to the ground. He turned back to his wife in time to see her give him a thumbs-up.

The shabewts returned, this time slowly circling around Pryllan. Steve readied several chasers while Sarah scanned the area looking for other objects she could use as weapons. Pryllan, slowly circling in place as she watched the brown shaggy animals pace by, hesitated.

"What is it?" Steve asked, alarmed. The last thing they needed to see was another adversary.

"Do you feel that?" Pryllan asked him. She quickly flicked her tail across the ground, managing to sweep away three of the shabewts in the process.

"I don't feel anything," Steve told her. He looked at Sarah. "You?"

Sarah nodded. "Actually, yes, I do. What is that?"

They felt it again. The tremors were becoming more pronounced. Whatever was making them was coming closer! Steve eyed the dark opening and groaned.

"I don't know what's coming out," she softly whispered, "but if it's bad, then I'm getting us out of here. All of us."

"Pryllan, too?" Steve whispered back.

Sarah brought up a mental image of the serene valley she knew was nearby. "Right. All of us."

A thick jet of dark smoke shot out of the mouth of the cave and obscured everything, even the light of day. Steve coughed and pulled his shirt up over his nose. Sarah did the same.

"It's a dragon!" Steve smiled with relief. "At least I think it is."

Do not speak. Whoever this dragon is might not have seen the two of you on my back.

You can't tell who it is? I thought everyone knew everyone else.

The smoke has reduced visibility, not to mention the other dragon isn't presently using the Collective. I have no idea who it is.

Steve groaned. *That's just swell.*

They heard several shabewts roar as they attacked the new dragon. Then they heard several surprised squeals of pain, followed almost immediately by several seconds of utter silence. They felt Pryllan go into action as well.

Pryllan! I need you to fan your wings or something. It's getting hard to breathe in here.

They felt Pryllan spread her wings, dig her talons into the ground, and pump her wings several times. Most, if not all, of the smoke was blown away.

Steve blasted a shabewt with each hand before the shaggy bears could recover. In unison, they roared angrily and split their forces. Two tried to sneak into the cave. Three foolishly attacked Pryllan, who squished one flat as she turned her bulk around to face the threat head on. Pryllan opened her jaws, ready to bite the remaining two creatures in half, when a wall of flames appeared between her and her two attackers.

They turned to the cave's occupant. This dragon was as white as snow. However, the scales of its front forelegs were green.

I didn't know dragons could do that.

That is a trait available on only a select few of us. Most of us, when shedding scales, will still be the same color as we are now.

Oh.

The two shabewts that had chosen to attack the white and green dragon darted in to take a bite of the dragon's underbelly, not knowing that a dragon's stomach was just as armored as the rest of it. Just as the two shabewts readied themselves for a bite the wyverian standing over them suddenly came crashing down. A few seconds later they could hear the reason why: it was snoring.

That appears to be all of them. I do not smell any more in the area, aside from those that we have already dealt with.

They're all gone? Really?

Aye.

A western breeze appeared. Steve noted, with dismay, that the large cloud of smoke Pryllan had driven away was threatening to head in their direction again. They felt Pryllan arch her back, then jumped with surprise as the dragon snapped her wings open and then closed, all in less time than it takes to snap your fingers. The smoke cloud all but exploded apart.

The cave's inhabitant was lying, motionless, directly in front of its cave. Of the two attacking shabewts there was no sign they had ever been there. In the bright sunshine, Steve could see that the new dragon had another surprise in store for them: it had not two but four horns sticking out of its skull. The two large 'primary' horns on the outside of the skull extruded at least three feet while the smaller 'secondary' horns were less than a foot long and were sticking straight out.

Steve studied the motionless dragon. What was it doing

now? Was it lying in ambush for them? The dragon's white head was slowly lowered back to the ground. Its wings were folded flat against its back and it was making an intermittent buzzing sound. The odd thing was, it only lasted three to four seconds before it vanished. Perhaps the dragon had allergies?

Pryllan was standing just off to the side of the white dragon and hadn't moved a muscle. Now that the smoke cloud had cleared, she was waiting for a sign of acknowledgment from the new dragon, but hadn't received it yet.

Is he friend or foe? Steve asked.

Does it matter? Sarah's thought cut in. *We need to get off of Pryllan's back before that other dragon sees us. We don't want to get Pryllan in trouble.*

Be at ease. This is Vanze. He is a friend.

We need to get down, Steve reiterated. *Friend or not, we can't let him see us on your back.*

There is nothing to be concerned about. He sleeps a lot.

Steve stared at the large white dragon. Sure enough, the eyes were closed. Was that the source of the buzzing? Was Vanze snoring?

Do you think he was helping us with our fight, or do you think it was blind luck he ended up taking out several of those shabewts?

Unknown. If I were to venture a guess, then I'd say it was luck.

You mean we finally caught a break? There's a first.

Sarah, be ready to teleport down in the event Vanze starts to awaken. I do not believe he will, if his previous behavior holds true.

Sarah agreed. *You got it.*

Movement in his peripheral vision caused Steve to look down near the mouth of the cavern. Little Aislinn, looking even more improved than the last time he had seen her, was seen staring up at Vanze with wide, frightened eyes. Her terrified glance shifted to Pryllan and the little underling's eyes teared up. She began crying as she ran over to Pryllan and threw her arms around her right foreleg.

"What's wrong with me?" the girl sobbed. "Why do I feel so restless?"

Steve and Sarah shared a look before they both turned to look up at Pryllan. Steve gave the girl a few awkward pats on her back. Aislinn wiped her eyes with the back of her sleeve. She pulled away and looked adoringly up at Pryllan, who was giving the child a disconcerting stare.

"We'll get this figured out, Aislinn," Steve promised. "You just have to give us a little time."

"I'm never leaving Pryllan's side again," the underling tearfully vowed.

We need to resolve this, Pryllan's gentle, but firm thought spoke.

I know, Pryllan. I know.

Chapter 11 — You Can Run

You found her? Is she safe? Is she well? We found signs of shabewts, so we feared the worst. By the wizards! I am so relieved that I cannot think straight. Where is my little princess?"

Selwyn emerged from within the woods and practically collapsed to the ground when he heard the good news. Steve appeared in front of the dwarf, holding Aislinn in his arms. He dropped down to one knee and held the girl out to her father. Selwyn crushed her to his chest and gently rocked her back and forth. A single tear slid down Selwyn's face as he gently crooned a lullaby to his one and only daughter.

"You scared me, little princess."

Aislinn sniffled back. "I'm so sorry, Father."

"Why did you do it? Why did you run away?"

"I had to see her again. I just had to!"

"Who? The dragon?"

Aislinn eagerly nodded her head. "Aye. I had to see that she was safe. I remembered thinking that I would feel better if I could just see her again."

Selwyn's older brother, Harrig, came crashing through the brush, his axe gripped tightly in both hands. "Did I hear that right? Has Aislinn been found?"

Selwyn nodded. "Aye."

"Where?"

Selwyn shakily regained his feet. "I am not sure. Aislinn found a cave to hide in, so she…"

"Dolt," Harrig interrupted. "Where is your daughter right now? I want to see for myself that she is well."

Aislinn stepped out from behind her father and timidly approached her uncle. Relief washed through the older dwarf's face as his axe slipped through his fingers and fell to the ground. He pulled his niece into a fierce hug.

"Don't you ever do that to us again, do you hear me?"

Aislinn began crying again. "I'm sorry, uncle."

Selwyn cuffed his brother on the back of his head. "I just got her calmed down. She's already upset. Let's not make things worse, agreed?"

Harrig grabbed his axe as he rose to his feet. With a practiced swing he returned his weapon, stowed in its holder on his back. At that moment Galman, Selwyn's other brother, the eldest of the three, emerged from deep within the forest. He was gripping his battle axe tightly in one hand and had one of his daggers in the other. There were several fresh gouges and scratches in the eldest dwarf's leather armor.

"Were you attacked?" Selwyn asked, worried. "Are you well, brother?"

"Forget about me," Galman exclaimed, brushing aside Selwyn's concern. "Has Aislinn been found?"

"She has, aye. She's over there, next to the dragon."

"What the ruddy hell is a dragon doing here?" Galman demanded, slowly turning to face Pryllan. "Is it not bad enough that we were trying to come to the aid of a family member? The last thing we need right now is —"

"Quiet," Harrig snapped. "The dragon aided in the search. Judging from the scorch marks I'd say it was entirely responsible for driving away the accursed shabewts."

"It was a collected effort between us all," Pryllan curtly

informed them, as her long supple neck twisted to face the newcomers. "No one person was responsible."

Galman eyed the two humans for a few seconds, before he nodded his head and then bowed. "I don't know why you are here, but I am glad that you are. Thank you for coming to the aid of my niece."

"That goes for me, too," Harrig added.

A twig snapped loudly behind them. All three adult dwarves whirled around, weapons drawn, to face what they assumed to be a new group of the terrifying bear creatures. Pryllan bared her fangs and gulped air, fueling her flames in preparation for an imminent attack. Steve ignited both hands while Sarah used her jhorun to pick up the same broken tree she had used before. Everyone was silent as they waited for the newest aggressor to appear.

More twigs snapped. They heard something grunt loudly, followed by a few low growls. Straight ahead of the mixed group of companions, they caught signs of movement. Something was there, just beyond the trees.

Pryllan's nostrils pinged closed.

Half a dozen dwarves appeared. None were armed. In fact, all were wearing the decorative ceremonial robes that denoted their position on the Council. Each elder had the exact same reaction as they emerged into the clearing and saw what was waiting for them. Eyes shot open and arms were lifted.

"Selwyn!" one of the elders called as he, too, lifted his arms into the air. "We come in peace! Call off your dragon!"

Selwyn glanced back at Pryllan, whose jaws were open and ready to fire. Literally. Flames had appeared in the back of her throat and were rapidly expanding.

I cannot call the flames back! Pryllan worriedly thought to her two human friends.

Steve pointed straight up. *Aim high! Blast it into the sky. No one is up there.*

Pryllan angled her head and belched a huge blast of fire skyward. The impressive bout of flames stretched another seventy feet before eventually dying off. The dragon dropped her gaze back to the ground and gave the small group of dwarves a sheepish look.

"I'm sorry. I hope we didn't frighten you. We were expecting something else."

"Dare I ask what?" one of the six dwarves asked.

"Shabewts," Galman spat. He returned his axe to its holder and regarded the newcomers. "I realize I am not on the Council and it is not my place to say this, but during the last session was it not suggested that the Council should not travel abroad without armed protection?"

One dwarf, outfitted in black trousers, a gray tunic, and a heavy white robe decorated with pins and badges, approached. He gave the dragon a wary nod before he turned his attention to Selwyn, who instantly dropped to one knee. Harrig and Galman immediately followed suit.

"Brarvur. What are you doing here?"

The elderly dwarf eyed the three of them.

"When news reached me that our chief of security had hastily excused himself from his duties, only to invite his two brothers to join him on an excursion Topside, I had to see for myself what was going on. It was rumored that the dragons were involved."

"Not in the way that you think," Harrig interrupted.

Brarvur waved him off. "Allow me to finish. After we assumed the worst, and then discovered that your daughter was missing, we formed a search party."

The three dwarf brothers nervously eyed one another.

"Then we get word that a dragon was involved," Brarvur continued. "But this dragon wasn't hindering. It was helping."

"She, not *it*," Steve quietly grumbled.

Hush. Don't speak. This is between them.

Fine.

"So why are so many of you Topside?" Selwyn asked.

"If this is about the athe crystal," Steve interjected, before Brarvur could respond, "then you need to be talking with me, not him. I'm the one who talked him into it. I'm the one you should be mad at."

Selwyn gazed at Steve with shock written all over his features.

"I don't think they knew about the athe crystal," Sarah

quietly informed him.

"I'm sure they do now," Selwyn muttered, fixing Steve with another glare.

Brarvur snorted. "An athe crystal? Are you referring to the athe crystal that was reported missing? The one we know Selwyn snuck out of the refinery?"

Selwyn's face paled. "Aye, that'd be the one. Look, I can explain."

"We were on our way to confront you about your thievery," Brarvur explained. "We were going to relieve you of your duties and your command."

Selwyn's mouth opened in surprise.

Galman angrily grunted. "The missing athe crystal? That was you? What in the world did you take that crystal for?"

Selwyn, resigned to his fate, sadly shook his head. "I cannot answer that, brother. I hope you can forgive me."

Brarvur stared at him a moment longer before he shrugged. "I can answer that. He took it because the crystal was part of some type of exchange with the dragon, am I right?"

Selwyn slowly turned to look up at Pryllan. "I didn't tell them anything. I swear."

"I know you didn't," Pryllan assured him.

"A missing athe crystal doesn't interest me," Brarvur stated, matter-of-factly.

Selwyn swallowed nervously. "Er, what does?"

Brarvur pretended he didn't know what Selwyn was talking about. "What? What do you mean? Be specific, Selwyn."

"What are you interested in?"

"What interests me is the fact that you traded that crystal so that your daughter could fulfill her wildest fantasy."

Pryllan's eyes widened with disbelief.

"That's right, dragon," Brarvur confirmed. "We know you gave little Aislinn a ride on your back. We also know you gave the crystal to the human over there."

Steve nodded. "That's right, he did. I'm sorry to say that I can't give it back, if that's what you want. I'll try and work something else out with you, but not that."

Brarvur again waved a hand dismissively. "We have other athe crystals. The loss of one matters not; not when the repercussions are in everyone's favor."

Steve slowly looked at Sarah. He gave her a questioning glance. She placed a hand on his arm and signaled him to be quiet.

"Explain," Selwyn demanded.

"As a direct result of what we witnessed earlier, with young Aislinn's ride on the dragon's back, followed by the dragon placing herself in danger in order to protect one of our underlings, we, the Council of Elders, have elected to commence negotiations at once."

"Negotiations for what?" Selwyn wanted to know. He looked at his brothers, who both shrugged and shook their heads. They didn't have any idea what was going to happen, either.

"We are en route to see the Dragon Lord."

This got Pryllan's attention. She gave the dwarves an alarmed look. "What? Why?"

Brarvur smiled up at the tall emerald green dragon. "Have no fear, dragon. We seek an audience with the Dragon Lord to commence negotiations … for peace."

Steve's eyes widened with disbelief. He looked at Sarah, who was smiling that smug smile of hers which clearly said she wasn't surprised by this turn of events. He looked up at Pryllan, who was staring down at the dwarves in utter shock.

"There has never been an official alliance between dwarves and wyverians."

Brarvur nodded. "Pryllan, is it? Pryllan, I am aware. *We* are aware. That's what makes this excursion so significant. We are going to broker the first truce that has ever existed between our two species. Thanks to you, we have learned that dragons are more trustworthy, more compassionate, and more laudable than we ever thought possible. It's because of you that we make the effort."

Pryllan's head lifted higher. She closed her eyes and went still. Steve waited a few moments before he knocked his knuckles on one of her talons. "Hey, are you okay?"

Pryllan opened her eyes and stared down at the small

group of humans and dwarves. She slowly nodded, then turned to Steve and gave him an incredulous look.

It's gone!

What? What's gone?

The shachar! It's no longer there! It feels like a weight has been lifted from my back.

How? How was it removed?

I do not know. I felt it disappear the moment the subject of peace was brought up by the dwarves.

Does that have something to—

"Perhaps we can figure that out later," Sarah loudly interrupted, casting a stern look up at Pryllan and then at her husband. "Aislinn is fine. She's back with her father. We really need to be going, don't you think?"

Steve nodded. "Right. She's right. Aislinn, how are you feeling?"

Everyone turned to stare at the small dwarf girl as she shyly clung to her father's leg. She looked around at the various faces and tremulously smiled. She tugged on her father's sleeve. Selwyn bent down so that she could whisper something in his ear. After a few moments Selwyn stood up and eyed Steve and Sarah.

"I, er, think everything is back to normal. Aislinn just asked me if we could go home."

Steve gave Sarah a victorious high five. "That is good to hear, Selwyn. Take her home and spend some time with her."

The half dozen Council members bid their farewells and left, heading straight for the heart of the valley. Harrig and Galman each knelt down and were chatting with Aislinn, who was relishing the attention now that the elder Council members had left.

"What will you do now?" Selwyn asked Steve.

"Now that Aislinn and Pryllan's problem is solved, we're back to searching for a fugitive who shouldn't be here. We have to find him as quickly as possible."

Both Harrig and Galman looked up, interested. They each patted the underling's head and crowded close to the humans.

"You search for someone?" Galman asked.

"You interrupted your search for a loved one to help us search for ours?" Harrig asked, amazed. He looked at his two brothers. The fact that each of their faces mirrored his own confirmed they had heard the same thing.

Steve held up a hand. "I hate to burst your bubble, but the person we're looking for is not a loved one. He's a fugitive."

"I'm not familiar with that word," Selwyn said.

"This man is dangerous," Sarah told the dwarves. "He's done deplorable things and must be caught before he does more."

Galman blinked a few times before he pulled his axe free from its holder. "*That* I understood. Selwyn, take my niece home. Send up reinforcements. Harrig, will you help me look?"

Harrig nodded. He pulled his own weapons out. "Where do we search?"

Steve sighed. "That's the part that stinks. We don't know where. We know he was at a small waterfall east of Avin. His tracks were either heading to Donlari or R'Tal. However, we lost the trail, so whether or not he doubled back and headed in the opposite direction is anyone's guess."

"We think there's a good chance he's heading to the castle," Sarah supplied. She gave the dwarves as detailed a description of Melvyn as she could. "He's pompous and arrogant. He's demonstrated he has no qualms about killing in order to get his way."

The three dwarves nodded.

"I will alert the Council," Selwyn vowed. "We will help you search. If this ruffian heads in our direction we will be prepared."

Steve laid a friendly hand on Selwyn's shoulder. "It's appreciated. We could use the help."

"I could request help from the Dragon Lord," Pryllan suggested. "That will give us more eyes in the air."

"Can you ask in such a way that doesn't arouse suspicion? Humans and dragons are not yet allies."

Pryllan gave him an unreadable look before she closed her eyes. After close to two minutes had passed, her eyes finally opened. "Rinbok Intherer has agreed to dispatch two dragons to help search."

Steve groaned aloud. "Only two?"

"I am impressed he agreed to send any at all," Pryllan admitted. "I convinced him it would be advantageous for the wyverians if we were responsible for the capture of this wanted human criminal."

"How did you let him know that Melvyn is a wanted human criminal?" Steve wanted to know.

"I told him that I overheard several other humans mention this."

Steve grinned. "And he bought it?"

Pryllan gave him a disquieting look. "It's the truth, is it not?"

Steve shrugged. "Yeah, I'll have to give you that one. Who are they sending?"

"He has assigned Beyobe and Clareadon with helping us look. They have been tasked with patrolling the valley."

"We will take the forest," Harrig announced. "We will know if any humans venture into these woods."

"It sounds like you've got this area covered," Steve decided. He looked at his wife and took her hand. "We'll head back to R'Tal and see if Melvyn has shown his face anywhere in the city."

Go in peace, Pryllan's calm thought said to husband and wife. **I can see why I chose you to become my rider. I look forward to our next encounter. If you need additional help feel free to let me know. I will come to your aid. In the meantime, Kahvel and I will continue to search for your fugitive.**

Steve glanced up at the large dragon. *That means a lot, Pryllan. You have my thanks. Until we meet again, my friend.*

Sarah took his hand and together they teleported back to R'Tal. Wanting to be certain she didn't accidentally teleport the two of them into a busy room and end up inadvertently spooking an entire castle full of people, Sarah took them straight to the Antechamber.

"Aaaahhh!"

A silver tray, laden with fruits and breads, flew from the arms of a serving girl. Steve and Sarah had appeared just as a light meal was about to be served.

"I've got the tray," Sarah said to Steve as she reached past the terrified serving girl.

Her jhorun had automatically slowed the tumbling items. Sliced jansas, peeled and halved sidah, and chunks of loken appeared to be lazily floating in the air, while several loaves of bread spun upward in a gentle arc. Sarah plucked the tray from the air, righted it, and began snatching various pieces of fruit. With Steve's help, she managed to return everything to the tray before any of the food could reach the ground. She then held the tray out to the girl, who hesitantly accepted it.

"I'm sorry about that," Sarah quietly told the girl. "I didn't think there'd be that many people in here."

The king rose from his desk. Captain Sauer, seated across from the king, also stood.

"Steve. Sarah. Welcome back. Your arrivals and departures do take some getting used to."

Steve snorted. "Ain't that the truth."

Sarah eyed him. She sighed and faced the king. "Please forgive the interruption. I was certain that there wouldn't be anyone in the Antechamber."

"Have there been any new developments with regards to your missing man?"

"We have at least four dragons searching Lake Raehón and the surrounding valley," Steve reported.

"The Kla Guur is checking the forest surrounding the valley," Sarah added.

The king nodded appreciatively. "You've been busy."

"Have your men been able to pick up his trail?" Steve asked.

Captain Sauer shook his head. "We have alerted the constables in every village. I have shared his description, so hopefully it will be just a matter of time before someone sees him."

"Check the taverns," Sarah suggested. "I know he loves his whiskey. I really don't know what the Lentarian equivalent is, but I'm sure he could find something. More often, I've seen him holding a drink in his hand." She looked at her husband and shrugged. "It's a place to start."

"But what if he uses his jhorun against us?" Steve asked.

"If he can make a person forget, there's a good chance he can completely remove any evidence that he was there."

"No one can cover their trail that well," Sauer scoffed. "The more desperate they are, the more likely they are to make a mistake. And when they do, we'll be ready."

"What jhorun is this?" Kri'Calin asked, curious. "What is this about forgetting?"

"We don't know exactly what his jhorun can do," Steve confessed, somewhat uncomfortably, "but we do know it has something to do with short term memory. I think he can make people forget what has recently happened."

Kri'Calin frowned. "How much time is affected?

"Not much. I'd say maybe five seconds."

"Captain, find this man. Apprehend him at all costs. I would suggest you accompany the Nohrin, as they seem to be able to traverse the kingdom much faster."

Sauer nodded. He looked at the two of them and inclined his head toward the Antechamber's exit. "Come. There are nearly a dozen taverns scattered across R'Tal. He could have visited any of them."

"And if we can't find any traces of him there?" Sarah asked. "What then?"

"Then I'd say we broaden our search and check the other villages," Steve answered immediately. Sauer nodded his agreement.

Nearly an hour later, the three of them were exiting the Dented Chalice, a small single-story inn located in the quiet northern section of the city. This suburb, while nowhere as posh as the dwellings found in the elitist eastern district, was where the upper middle class lived. The streets were clean, vendors packed the streets daily, and crime was kept to a minimum.

"Where's the next closest tavern?" Steve wanted to know as he stretched his back.

He looked up at the sun to judge the time of day. It was past midday, but not by much. Perhaps that was why his stomach was grumbling? He pushed aside his stomach's protests and glanced around the area. Villagers were milling about, vendors were thrusting their wares in front of anyone who happened by, and an occasional pair of guards were seen patrolling along the streets.

Sauer pointed to his right. "The Rusty Axe is that way. We should try there next."

The Rusty Axe had seen better days. In fact, Steve was pretty sure it wasn't around in his time as he didn't remember any taverns in this part of the city. Now that he thought about it, this might have been part of the city that burned during the battle with Celestia a few years ago. He ducked his head as he stepped through the tavern's narrow front door and looked around.

The interior was worse.

Chipped and broken furniture, suggesting nightly brawls were common, met his eyes. A small fire was burning, while a plump blonde woman stirred a kettle suspended over it. Steve opened his mouth, about to speak, when Sauer cut him off.

"Are you the owner of this establishment?" Sauer asked, his voice turning firm and grim.

Detecting the authority in his voice, the woman looked up, her eyes widening with surprise. She hastily abandoned the kettle and approached the three of them. She attempted a curtsy.

"Good day, sir. What might I do for you?"

"Are you the owner of this tavern?" Sauer repeated, keeping a neutral expression.

The blonde woman nodded. "I am. Run this place by myself, I do. My good for nuthin' lout of a husband ran off with one of the serving girls. Damn fool." The woman caught sight of Sauer's darkening expression. "That's my problem, not yours, dearie. How can I be of assistance?"

"Have you had any middle-aged patrons, traveling alone, frequent your tavern as of late? Might have been arrogant or belligerent?"

The woman's eyes narrowed. "Describe him."

Excited, Steve cleared his throat. "Uh, let's see. He'd be a little shorter than me, gray hair, thick mustache, walks with a swagger, and probably tried to avoid paying."

The woman nodded grimly. "Aye, I remember him. Sulky."

Sauer shared a look with Steve. "Sulky? This man was sulky?"

"We named him Sulky," the barkeep clarified. "I could tell he was angry and unhappy. He kept disrespecting my girls. He became belligerent when I told him what he owed me. I've recently had several fights in here and the constable told me if it happened again, he'd close my tavern due to public endangerment or somethin' like that. So, I told Sulky he had to leave."

"What'd he say to that?" Sarah wanted to know.

"He ignored me. He started askin' 'bout dwarves."

Steve and Sarah both paled. Together they turned to look at Sauer, who returned their frank stare.

"Dwarves?" Sauer snapped. "What did he want to know about dwarves? What did he say? Think, woman! This is important."

"After I told him I knew nuthin' 'bout no dwarves, I heard him say something 'bout a lock 'cause he wanted a key."

Steve cursed, as Sarah gasped with alarm.

"If he wanted a key, there are several reputable locksmiths in town," Sauer commented, confused by his companions' reaction to this news. "Why bother the dwarves with something so trivial?"

"Because," Steve quietly answered as he nodded his thanks to the tavern owner and headed back outside, "the key Melvyn is looking for is a portal key. He's looking for Maelnar."

"I've heard about him," Sauer admitted. "They call him the Strathos, correct?"

Sarah nodded. "That's right. He's a portal key maker. Well, he's the only portal key maker that I'm aware of. I can't even begin to tell you how many problems he could cause if Melvyn manages to find Maelnar."

"Why?" Sauer wanted to know.

"Wow. Where do I start?" Steve took a deep breath and let it out slowly. "For the sake of argument, let's assume Melvyn finds Maelnar. I don't actually think there's any way he'd be able to force Maelnar to make him a portal key that'd take him back to Idaho. I think he'd probably try to kill him."

"My thoughts exactly," Sarah agreed.

Sauer's eyes hardened. "Why?"

"If Maelnar dies now, then he wouldn't be able to make us a new portal key when we search him out during our first trip to Lentari. If we don't get that second key, then we'd never make it back home, therefore proving to the king and queen that we weren't suitable bodyguards. They'd think we weren't the Nohrin. Trust me, Melvyn can seriously screw up Lentarian history."

"Maelnar has played an important role in quite a few adventures," Sarah added.

Sauer held out his arm. "Please take us back to the Great Hall. The king must be informed."

Steve reached out to lay a hand over Sauer's. Sarah placed hers on top of Steve's. Moments later, they were standing before the king while Sauer hastily informed him about what they had recently learned. Judging from the king's grim expression, he was none too pleased about the possible outcomes, either.

"Requisition as many men as you need. A full kingdom-wide search for this man begins now. I will notify Zevern to see what aid he can offer. This man must be found. Now."

Sauer nodded and swiftly departed. Kri'Calin eyed the two of them.

Before the king could say anything, Steve beat him to it. "Your Majesty, we'll take our leave, too. We'll keep searching. We can cover a lot of ground in a short time."

The king nodded. "I believe you. Go. Inform me if you find him."

Sarah nodded. "We will."

Before Sarah could take Steve's hand, Sauer came rushing back inside with a full squadron of men in hot pursuit.

"Your Majesty! I have news!"

"Please tell me they found him," Sarah softly whispered, more to herself than to anyone else.

The king rose to his feet. "Report, Captain."

"We just received word from several of our informants. Half a dozen vendors have reported burglaries earlier today."

"Burglaries, while regrettable, are not newsworthy right

now," Kri'Calin quickly informed him.

Sauer nodded. "I agree, Your Majesty. However, wait until you hear what was stolen: one sword and two daggers from a blacksmith, one sleeping roll and several sets of garments from a clothier, several pounds of dried meat from a butcher, two…"

"That's enough," the king interrupted. "What of the burglar? What did he look like?"

Sauer smiled. "That's the interesting part, Your Majesty. None of the vendors, and I mean *none* of them, could remember what he looked like, only that when they inventoried their merchandise, they discovered those items missing."

"It's Melvyn," Steve muttered. "It's gotta be."

"Of course, it's him," Sarah chided. "He's preparing for a journey, and it doesn't take a genius to figure out where he's going."

"He's going after the Kla Guur, isn't he?" Steve muttered a curse under his breath. "Do you think he knows how to find them?"

Sarah shrugged. "I'd like to say no, but after all we've been through, would you put it past him?"

"I wish there had been some visual confirmation," Kri'Calin said. He sat back down at his desk. "Something to let us know we are on the right track."

Sauer coughed. "I wasn't finished with my report, Your Majesty."

Intrigued, the king motioned for the captain to continue.

"This Melvyn person may have duped the vendors into thinking that he wasn't there so that they wouldn't know what he looked like, but he wasn't able to affect everyone."

All eyes were focused on the captain.

The king nodded, pleased. "Ah. Someone saw him?"

Sauer nodded. "The children. Melvyn didn't take into consideration that there are always children running about, playing, causing mischief, and so on. He was witnessed by no less than a dozen different children as he collected the supplies he needed for his journey."

"How long ago was this?" Kri'Calin asked.

"Over four hours ago."

Steve sighed heavily, as he thought about trying to catch up with Melvyn on foot or on horseback. He looked over at his wife and raised an eyebrow.

"We can probably overtake him," Sarah told him, answering his unspoken question, "but I do think there might be faster ways to track him down."

"She's already done so much," was Steve's response.

"She's your friend. All you have to do is ask her."

"What about you?"

"What about me? I'll be fine. I thought I'd go check on Luther and Cora. I want to make sure they're okay."

Puzzled, Steve leaned closer to his wife. "Luther has been there now for several years. I'm sure he's fine."

"You didn't hear what the sheriff threatened to do to Luther and Cora in order to get me to play along. He really scared me. I need to make sure they're safe."

Steve nodded. "I'd probably do the same, if the tables were turned. Go. Make sure they're fine and then come back here and wait for me, okay?"

Sarah nodded. "I will."

She vanished.

"I thought for certain your teleporter wife would assist you in tracking down your man," Sauer said, confused.

Steve waved off his concerns. "It's all good. I have another helper."

The king's curiosity was piqued. "Oh? Who?"

"Someone that must remain a secret, I'm afraid."

Kri'Calin raised an eyebrow. "You are an intriguing person, Steve. Very well. Perform your search. He has a four-hour head start. Will that be a problem?"

Steve shook his head. "Nope."

"The search will continue here," the king declared, "in case he was trying to feed us false information."

Steve grunted. "I'll bet he isn't."

"Be that as it may, I want to be certain he is no longer in the city."

Sauer nodded. "Our search will continue."

The king fixed Steve with a stern expression. "If you find

him, let us know."

* * *

"I knew I would see you again, but I didn't think it'd be this soon," the dragon confided.

Steve leaned to the right and gave her neck a friendly pat. "That makes two of us. Do you think we're following the right trail?"

Pryllan bent her neck around until she was looking directly at him. "Do you doubt my abilities?"

"Er, no."

"Then why ask if we are following the correct scent?"

"It's because we've been flying for close to two hours. Is it really possible to follow a trail by air of someone who walked by hours ago?"

"I can follow a trail as long as it is no older than a fortnight."

"Two weeks? You can seriously follow a scent trail that someone left two weeks ago?"

Pryllan nodded. "The trail would be much fainter but no less difficult to detect. I've known other wyverians who could easily double that time. I trust my skills only up to the first fortnight."

Steve whistled with amazement. That was impressive, no matter how he looked at it. Ten minutes later Pryllan banked sharply to her left. Steve sat up.

"What is it?"

"I believe I have located your missing man."

"You have? Awesome! Where is he?"

Steve's body flushed with warmth as the dragon shared her senses with him. Steve closed his eyes and shared Pryllan's eyesight. An area directly below them leapt into focus.

A single person, wearing a heavily loaded pack, was slowly and carefully picking his way through the thick forest. Dragon and rider could see glimpses of the figure's gray hair under his brown leather hood. Then they got a brief look at the man's face as he suddenly turned to look behind him, as though he sensed he was being followed. The man's thick handlebar mustache gave him away.

It was Melvyn.

"That's him," Steve confirmed.

"I thought he'd be a worthier adversary than that."

Steve chuckled. "Why do you say that?"

"Behold. He wheezes as though he has been running. His body mass is higher than most, and he carries more weight than he should."

"Are you saying he's an overweight old fart who shouldn't be out in the woods like this?"

"I'm not familiar with that term," Pryllan admitted.

Steve sent her a mental definition of the word she was having a difficult time with. He felt Pryllan give a grunt of acknowledgement.

"I accept your assessment of the situation."

Steve pointed down at the ground. "Let's go ruin his day, shall we?"

Pryllan circled high overhead as they waited for Melvyn to reach the glade. As soon as he was in the center of the open clearing, Pryllan tucked her wings and dropped from the sky, landing less than twenty feet from the surprised human. Melvyn cursed, dropped the pack, and sprinted for the trees.

Ten seconds later, he came to a halt, clutching his side and gasping for breath. On the ground directly in front of him was a burning line of fire. Three other fire trails were rapidly approaching, each from a different direction. Once the fire lines were less than ten feet from the sheriff, they each stopped. Melvyn took a step toward the northwest. The four fire trails each moved a foot closer. He took a step back. The fire trails moved another foot closer.

"You can come out now, fire thrower!" Melvyn loudly called out. "This is obviously your doing. Come on out and take the credit for it."

"Gladly."

Melvyn turned to look behind him. He smiled. Steve and Pryllan were less than twenty feet away. Melvyn slowly held both arms out in front of him, as though he expected Steve to slap a pair of handcuffs on him. "Congratulations, partner. You got me."

Steve didn't say a word as he slowly approached the sheriff. The four fire trails moved several feet closer and flared up, as though they had found patches of dry grass to feed them. The sheriff's smug smile never faltered.

"I know your type, partner," Melvyn began. "You're a goody two-shoes. You won't hurt me. Just take me in like we each know you're gonna do and … Arrggghh!"

Steve had raised an arm and blasted a small jet of fire straight at the sheriff, burning off both of his bushy gray eyebrows. Melvyn's smile faded away, replaced by a look of uncertainty. He quickly fumbled for something inside his pocket, pulling out a dark blue vial. Steve realized what was happening, just as Melvyn finally managed to work the stopper free of the bottle. The sheriff started to raise the vial to his lips, when two huge scaly forelegs smashed down on the ground on either side of Steve.

The force of the impact knocked both Melvyn and Steve off their feet. The tiny vial of poison flew into the air where Pryllan destroyed it with a well-timed blast of fire.

"You really are a coward," Steve accused, as he quickly rolled to his feet. "After all the crap you've pulled, you're trying to kill yourself?"

Melvyn sighed, as he slowly sat up. "It'd be easier this way. Just finish me off. Right here, right now. If you can't do it, have your dragon pet do it for you."

Pryllan's deep resonating growl was felt by all. She didn't like this person and had no qualms about letting her feelings known.

"If you don't kill me now," Melvyn vowed, "then I promise you I will never stop trying to wreck your future. Your future hangs in the balance as long as I'm alive. I know it. You know it."

Steve ignited his right hand. A chaser formed. He contemplated Melvyn's words. As long as the sheriff lived, he and Sarah would never be safe. They'd never have peace. Wouldn't it be easier to simply end it now? He could do it. This one chaser could end all their troubles. He'd done it before. But could he do it again?

Steve thought back to the only unpleasant memory he

had of Lentari: the unfortunate, ill-timed attack upon Mikal after he and Sarah had first met the prince. Half a dozen thugs had threatened Sarah and tried to kidnap Mikal. He had done the only thing any husband could. He'd attacked the attackers, driving them away from Sarah and the prince, causing several of their deaths. He'd kept fighting even as more of the kidnappers had appeared. He didn't know how many men lost their lives that day. He didn't want to know then and he certainly didn't want to know now. The fact was, when it came to Sarah's safety, he would do whatever was necessary.

Whatever was necessary.

The chaser burned brighter. He looked at the sheriff with piteous eyes. Melvyn was right. It'd be easier this way. The sheriff would get his wish.

Melvyn smiled victoriously. A split second later the chaser poofed out.

"What—what are you doing? Do it! You want to. I know it! I can see it in your eyes! Kill me!"

Steve scoffed. "And give you the easy way out? You don't deserve the satisfaction."

"I'm warning you, fire thrower. Kill me now or spend the rest of your days wondering how I will get my revenge!"

"Please. I've faced wizards, sorceresses, trolls, therons, and malwerns. Do you really think I'm worried about a peon like you? Don't flatter yourself. Besides, do you really think you're going to get that chance?"

Melvyn's face turned purple with rage. "Kill me, you ignorant, stupid son of a b—"

SMACK!

Steve's hand was stinging. It felt as though he had just decked a brick wall. If only he had been wearing his special gauntlets. Then again, he had the satisfaction of seeing the sheriff's look of surprise at the right hook, which knocked him clean off his feet and out cold.

"Come on, Pryllan. Let's head back to the castle. Will you take our geriatric friend here?"

"Geriatric?" Pryllan repeated, confused. "I'm not familiar with that word."

"Fine. How about old dude?"

"That works. And I would be delighted to."

An hour later they were approaching the castle. From their vantage point, and their shared visual abilities, Steve could see groups of soldiers patrolling everywhere. He could see guards going in and out of buildings, searching vendor stalls, and standing guard at every corner. Kri'Calin hadn't been idle. He had to have called in every last soldier enlisted in his army to help search for Melvyn and fortify the city.

Pryllan's voice broke through his concentration. "Where would you like to be taken?"

"How about the dragon cavern?"

"The what?"

"Oh, that's right. It doesn't exist yet. Umm, why don't you land in the northern orchards there? See where there's a patch devoid of any trees?"

"Aye."

"Do you realize that you've probably been seen by now?"

"I know."

"And you're okay with that?"

"Aye."

"Let me rephrase that. Would Rinbok Intherer be okay with that?"

"I am not attacking the city. I am not a threat. He wouldn't care."

"What about the humans?" Steve insisted.

"What about them?"

"Aren't you worried about what they think?"

"No."

It didn't really matter, Steve finally decided. Minutes later, as Pryllan began pumping her wings to slow their descent, Steve watched a flurry of activity near the northern gate. Armed soldiers were massing on the city's side of the gate. He thought he saw the king in their midst. Was Sarah back? Could she have told them where they would most likely land?

They touched down in the clearing that would eventually be turned into a temporary lair for visiting dragons. Steve climbed down Pryllan's back and approached her closed left claw. The dragon slowly opened the claw to reveal Melvyn, hands bound behind his back and a blindfold over his eyes. A few seconds later, Sarah appeared in the clearing, near a row of jansa trees. She rushed forward to embrace Steve.

"You found him a lot quicker than I had expected."

Steve grasped Melvyn by his right arm and pulled him to his feet. "I forgot we were chasing a pathetic old man," Steve said with a grin. "He was wheezing so bad I thought he was having an asthma attack."

"You are gonna rue this day, partner," Melvyn vowed, his face already red with rage. "You'll never be able to have a good night's sleep again. No one crosses me. Do you hear me?"

"Pipe down, idiot," Steve angrily told the ex-sheriff.

Sarah stepped directly in front of Melvyn and held out a hand. Steve pulled Melvyn to a stop.

"There's someone here who wants to talk to you."

"It's the teleporter, ain't it? I can smell her."

"Where is it?" Sarah demanded.

"Where's what?" Melvyn asked, curious in spite of himself.

"Our portal key. We want it back."

"I'm sure you do," Melvyn sneered.

"Give it back," Sarah ordered.

Melvyn gave her an evil laugh. "Would you like to know where I stashed it?"

Sarah closed her eyes. The green crystal key appeared on her open hand. "You hid it in your boot? You could've come up with a better place to hide it than that."

Melvyn was silent as he fumed with rage.

"Getting the key back was never in question," Sarah explained. "All I have to do is close my eyes and I can see it. Better luck next time."

"There *will* be a next time," Melvyn snarled. "Can you hear me?"

"We all can hear you," an authoritative voice declared.

The former sheriff gave a tiny cry of pain as Steve flash-burned the blindfold off his eyes. Melvyn slowly turned to face the king and three squads of armed men. Steve appeared by his side and gave the sputtering sheriff a hearty slap on his back, which caused Melvyn to stumble forward a few steps.

"Kri'Calin, may I present Melvyn, former sheriff of Coeur d'Alene, Idaho, and prior to that, resident of Capily."

"Secure the prisoner," Kri'Calin ordered.

Two men rushed to Melvyn's side. One produced a set of manacles and clapped them on the sheriff's wrists. Two additional guards were called over as Melvyn began struggling against his bonds.

"You should have killed me when you had the chance!" Melvyn screamed, sending flecks of spittle everywhere. "You'll never be safe again, fire thrower! Do you really think they'll be able to hold me here? Hah!"

Steve tore a thin strip of fabric off the bottom of his tunic. He approached Melvyn and cocked a fist, as though he was going to strike him again. The sheriff flinched. In that split second Steve whipped the fabric around the sheriff's head and quickly gagged him.

Melvyn glared angrily at him.

"I don't know exactly what jhorun you have," Steve told him, giving him a patronizing pat on the shoulder, "but I do know it has something to do with short term memory. Best to keep your trap shut, dontcha think?"

Melvyn ceased his struggles and looked away.

Steve looked back at the king. "You ought to tell Zevern that if he wants to redeem himself, he ought to find a way to neutralize Melvyn. I just don't know how."

Melvyn smirked as his defiant eyes flicked over to the king, as if daring him to try and stop him.

"As a matter of fact," the king slowly began, "I've already tasked Zevern with solving this very problem. A solution has already been formulated and is ready to be administered."

Curious, Steve took a few steps closer to the king. "Can you tell me what it is?"

It was Kri'Calin's turn to smile. "You believe our punishment will not be sufficient?"

Steve shook his head. "On the contrary, I want to make sure you aren't taking on more than you can handle by keeping him here. Otherwise, as soon as we figure out how to get home, I'll come back to get him."

"I know you have a low opinion of Zevern, but believe it or not he is quite gifted. Especially with certain spells. He's already written a few new ones in anticipation of meeting Mr. Melvyn here."

"Zevern is going to cast some spells on Melvyn? Color me intrigued! What's he planning on doing?"

"The last I heard," Kri'Calin companionably said, as he turned to walk back to the castle, "Zevern had perfected a spell which will cause someone to detest weapons. He tried it on a few guards. It worked beautifully."

Steve laughed out loud. "Perfect."

"And," the king continued, "earlier today, he finished his most recent spell."

"What does it do?"

"It renders people afraid of the outdoors."

"Nice. In all honesty, what do you plan to do with Melvyn?"

The king sighed. "I have never been a fan of throwing people in the dungeon. There's no doubt in my mind that this man deserves to live out his remaining days clapped in irons. However, I prefer atonement over incarceration. We'll see to it Mr. Melvyn lives out the remainder of his life performing some type of service."

"What about his jhorun?" Steve asked, as he fell into step beside the king. The armed phalanx of guards followed, with Melvyn surrounded on all sides.

"Zevern is working on it as we speak. He assures me he has found a way to make our friend forget he even has a jhorun. What of you? What are your plans now?"

"We're heading back to Idaho. We still have that oh-so-minor problem to figure out, namely how to get home."

"If ever there is anything I can do for you," Kri'Calin told him, laying a friendly hand on his shoulder, "you have but to ask. I am honored to have met you and your lovely wife."

Steve looked at the king and smiled. "You know what? There is something you can do for me. It would be a huge help."

"Of course. I will help in whatever way I can. You have my word."

Steve cleared his throat. "I'm going to hold you to that. Here's what I need…"

Chapter 12 — One for the Books

So, he admitted he had one after all, huh? I'm still curious how the joriis are made. Or if someone creates them for him. Has he let you in on their secret yet?"

Steve shook his head. He and Sarah had bid their farewells to the king and queen and were taking one last look at the castle and its grounds before they would teleport back to Idaho. First, Sarah wanted to go see what the vendors had for sale, so she guided the two of them to a busy street lined with stalls and carts.

"The castle really hasn't changed much from our time," Steve had told Sarah when she asked if they'd like to take a final walk around. "It's not as if we won't be seeing any of this again."

"Much of the city will be different." Sarah pointed toward the closest street, which happened to be packed full of buyers and sellers. "Take that street, for example. It was in a part of the city that burned down during the fight with Celestia. It has vendors now, but in our time, I believe it houses the barracks."

Steve nodded. "That's right. Twin barracks, one on either side of the street if memory serves." He pulled Sarah to a stop. "All of this is fine and dandy, but don't you want to go home now? Oh. You're kidding. Look at all those vendors. You wanted to go shopping, is that it?"

Sarah clutched his hand tighter. "We've gone through so much in the last couple of days. It's been crazy. I know when we get back to Coeur d'Alene the craziness will continue. I just wanted to take a little time for ourselves and, therefore, go on a walk."

Steve shrugged. "It's to be expected. We're finally starting to check things off our To Do list. However, there's still a big one that remains."

"Right. How to get home."

Steve patted his chest. "Thanks to this fully-charged jorii the king gave us we at least have a chance now."

"What did the king say when you asked him if he had extra jorii lying around?" Sarah asked. "He said before that he didn't have any extras. What was his excuse for holding out on you?"

"Just what we surmised," Steve answered. He gently pulled Sarah around and started walking back to the castle. "He had one left, in case of any emergencies that might arise. I told him that our predicament definitely qualified and explained what Luther wanted to do with it. I could tell he was reluctant to part with it but he finally admitted that we needed it more than he did. He did tell me, though, that the next batch of joriis should be ready by early next year."

Sarah hesitated. "Was he worried about not having access to a jorii should he need one?"

"A little. Again, he could tell that we needed it more."

"So there will be more jorii available next year? I don't know about you but I am really curious how those things are made."

Steve chuckled. "What if they aren't made, but are some type of natural phenomena?"

"Like what?" Sarah wanted to know.

"No clue. Just a possible suggestion."

They were nearing the castle. As they stepped foot onto

the drawbridge, they saw a familiar face come rushing toward them. It was Captain Sauer. He looked wildly around before a look of relief appeared on his face as he spotted the two of them.

"There you are! I'm glad I found you."

"We're heading back in," Steve told him, pointing across the drawbridge to the castle. "The king is letting us take the portal back. Why waste Sarah's jhorun if we don't have to?"

"You're getting ready to leave?" Sauer asked, as a note of worry appeared in his voice.

"Yeah. We already told the king we're heading back. We need to get the jorii into Luther's hands and hope that he'll be able to modify the portal to send us back through time."

"Yes, yes, I caught all of that. I need you to hold that thought and come with me."

"Why?" Steve demanded, growing alarmed. "What's the matter?"

"The king needs to speak with the two of you right away."

Steve looked at his wife incredulously. Hadn't they just seen the king less than fifteen minutes ago?

Husband and wife followed the captain as he led them straight to the Great Hall, where Kri'Calin was pacing in front of his throne. The queen was absent. The king's head jerked up as he spied Sauer approaching with Steve and Sarah in tow. He nodded in the direction of the Antechamber. Steve's eyes narrowed. The king wanted a private meeting.

"I'm so glad the captain managed to find you before you two departed," Kri'Calin began as they entered the enchanted chamber. Instead of sitting at his desk, as he was wont to do, he remained standing, staring fixedly at them. Or, more specifically, at Sarah.

"Care to tell us what's going on?" Steve asked.

"Did you perhaps forget to tell me anything about what happened up north?" Kri'Calin asked anxiously.

Steve cocked his head as he stared at the king. Kri'Calin was excited, he decided; antsy. What was on his mind?

"Not that I'm aware of ..." Steve answered.

"Perhaps regarding our dwarf allies and their winged neighbors?"

Steve looked at Sarah. How much did the king know? What did he suspect? More importantly, what should they tell him? There was no point in confessing to anything until he knew what he was being accused of.

"Er, what about them?"

The king gave him a fleeting smile. "When two species forge an alliance for the first time, news of the historic event will undoubtedly filter down to everyone. Myself included."

"Okayyy…" Steve was still unsure where the king was going with this.

"Level with me. Have the wyverians opened dialogue with the dwarves in order to facilitate peace?"

Steve nodded. "You're close. It's the dwarves who are reaching out to the dragons."

The king's eyes widened. "The dwarves are making first contact? Are you sure?"

"That's what they told me," Steve confirmed. "Why? What's the big deal?"

"Do you know what precipitated this monumental gesture from the dwarves?"

"They witnessed several acts of kindness from the dragons," Sarah answered.

Kri'Calin nodded thoughtfully. "Ah, yes. Of course, you're referring to the ride given to a young dwarf child by a green dragon, are you not?"

Steve choked. Sarah gasped with alarm. "How in the world could you possibly know that?"

"I am not without some secrets of my own," Kri'Calin admitted with a smile. "Listen, the reason I ask is that I believe your wyverian friend may be in peril."

That got Steve's attention. He stiffened with alarm. "What? Are you sure?"

"What do you think will happen once the Dragon Lord asks the dwarves what is responsible for this sudden change of heart? Are you not concerned that your dragon friend will tell the Dragon Lord everything that has happened to her?"

Steve confidently shook his head no. "You'd have to understand Pryllan, Your Majesty. She knows full well that she'd get into trouble if her willingness to allow a rider, especially a dwarven rider, would ever become known. To answer your question, no, I'm not worried about Pryllan letting anything slip."

"What about the dwarves?" Kri'Calin insisted. "Can you be certain they will hold their tongues about your involvement?"

Steve was silent as he stared at the king. There was something he was missing here. Why was the king so concerned about what was happening up north?

"Selwyn is there," Steve immediately responded. "He knows what the ramifications would be if our involvement became known. In fact, the other dwarves wouldn't ever say anything derogatory, either. They know what's at stake. Trust me; we can be certain that neither of them will mention our involvement."

"Are you sure?

"Stop beating around the bush and just tell us what's on your mind!" Steve demanded, growing angry. "You clearly have some type of motive for this. Why are you asking us all these questions?"

The king sighed and his shoulders slumped. Whatever he was hoping to hear, clearly hadn't been said. More confused than ever, Steve continued to stare at the king, waiting for an explanation. Steve caught sight of Sauer suppressing a smile.

Sarah finally smiled. She looked into Steve's eyes and winked at him. She slowly turned to the king and cleared her throat. "I think I have it."

"By all means, please share," Steve grumbled.

"Something historic is happening up north," Sarah began. She smiled at the king. "The dwarves are asking for a cessation of hostilities between their two species. I think the king is looking for an excuse to go there. Am I right?"

Steve began to smile. A flush was starting to creep up Kri'Calin's face.

"You don't need our permission to go up there. You're the king. I should think you would have been invited to attend whatever ceremony is taking place. Is it taking place now?"

The king shook his head. "It begins at sunset. Tonight, in the dragon's valley. I may not have been invited, but I also wasn't told to stay away."

"Which, of course, means the same thing as being invited," Steve dryly observed. Sarah swatted his arm. "Rinbok Intherer isn't going to be mad that you'll be there, will he?"

"If the Dragon Lord didn't want people to witness the event, then he shouldn't have let the news slip," Kri'Calin stated matter-of-factly. "Representatives from the Kla Guur, Kla Chanus, and a few other clans will be there. There should be a human presence there. The dwarves are our allies after all."

"I'm surprised Rinbok Intherer agreed to meet with the dwarves out in the open," Steve remarked. "I would have thought he'd prefer to carry out his business affairs in private."

"Where would you suggest they meet?" Sarah teased. "In one of the dwarf cities?"

"Hardy har har. You know what I mean. The Dragon Lord has gone on record quite a few times stating how he doesn't want the dragons' private matters becoming known."

The king shook his head. "You speak as though you've met the Dragon Lord."

"We have. Several times."

Sauer, who had been content to stand idly by, gaped in undisguised wonder.

"You've actually met the Dragon Lord? In person?"

"Is there any other way to meet him?" Steve asked, injecting a healthy dose of sarcasm into his question.

"None of you have met him before?" Sarah asked as she looked at both the king and the captain. "He's really not that bad. He can be a touch irritable at times but overall, he's just a dragon that wants to protect those under his care."

"All the more reason to meet him," Kri'Calin sighed. "If only I could broker such a treaty with the wyverians. That's why I want to go."

Steve automatically glanced around the Antechamber, looking for a window. There weren't any. He looked at his wife. "What time is it?"

"It's not quite sunset, if that's what you're asking."

Steve returned his attention to the king. "If you're set on

going, what are you waiting for? Unless…" He smiled. "You know you won't make it in time, don't you? You need a certain someone to give you a lift, is that it?"

Kri'Calin smiled sheepishly. "I have my portal key for Verdayn but it would still be too long a journey to reach Lake Raehón by sunset. I am asking your wife if she'd be willing to teleport me there so that I can be a witness to this historic event. Sarah, would you do me the honor?"

Steve frowned and automatically shook his head. "I don't think that'd be a good idea for us, Your Majesty."

"Why not?" Kri'Calin inquired.

"We're already walking a fine line with our own future," Sarah answered. "As we mentioned before, we have already met the Dragon Lord. Trust me when I say that we know full well how irritable Rinbok can be. With that being said, could Rinbok's behavior be altered during our first meeting with him years from now?"

"I'm getting a headache," Steve reported.

"The dwarves are also involved," Sarah continued. "The Kla Guur are involved. We know many of them. If we reappear, we run the same risk with them. Anything that can jeopardize our future, or alter it in some unknown fashion, I'm against."

"Hear, hear," Steve agreed.

Captain Sauer was rubbing his temples, too. "I don't see how meeting a dwarf you already know could possibly affect your future."

"Here's a hypothetical situation for you," Steve began. "Let's just say, for the sake of argument, Maelnar will be up there. We aren't supposed to meet him until we search him out many years from now when we first visit Lentari. That was the whole problem. We were stranded here without any way to get home. We didn't realize you were supposed to take your portal key with you when stepping through an active portal. So, we needed to find Maelnar to help us make it home."

"And you convinced him to make you another key?" Kri'Calin guessed.

Steve nodded. "That's right. So, continuing on with this hypothetical situation, let's assume Maelnar will be there.

Let's also say he's in a lousy mood. What if just meeting the two of us puts him in a worse mood and now he doesn't want anything to do with humans? Then, when Sarah and I eventually find him in the future, he remembers us or else steadfastly refuses to do us humans a favor."

"That's a mighty big 'what if'," Sarah observed.

"True," Steve admitted, "but it's possible."

Sauer interjected, "You have no way of knowing if this was supposed to happen this way."

Steve shook his head. "Unfortunately, in this case, I do."

Sarah looked at him. "Do tell."

"I remember hearing, during our first trip here, that the dragon-dwarf alliance happened not long before the hu–" Steve trailed off as he realized he was about to let slip the humans would eventually become allies with the dragons, too. "Ummm, that is to say, before the, uh, hurricane, er, really big storm hit."

"Brilliant save, Sherlock," Sarah quipped.

Thankfully the king was so distraught he didn't notice Steve's slip. Sauer gave him a speculative look but didn't say anything.

"The point I was trying to make," Steve lamely continued, "was that we've already proven that the future has been changed. This alliance wasn't supposed to happen for a number of years."

"But it *was* supposed to happen," Sarah pointed out. "Does it really make that much of a difference *when* it happened?"

Captain Sauer nodded. "I think I see where you're going with this. A wyverian-dwarf alliance was inevitable. Whether it happens in your time, or ours, is irrelevant. It was fated to happen, so it did."

"I guess we really won't know what's been changed until we make it back home," Steve said, looking glum. "I just hope we haven't screwed too many things up."

"With regards to the wyverian-dwarf alliance in the future," Kri'Calin suddenly said, "was the human king of your time present for the proceedings?"

Steve thought for a moment. "I don't know. I don't

remember hearing anything about it. Hon, do you know?"

Sarah shook her head. "I don't know, either. I'm sorry."

"How did you learn of it, anyway?" Steve asked the king. "I don't know how you get your news but clearly it works very well."

"Verdayn's constable," the king answered. "He reported that he had noticed heightened activity in the area. His patrols encountered groups of dwarves traveling north. As you may know, most dwarves prefer to spend their time underground, so seeing large numbers of them above ground will generate a question or two."

Steve nodded. "That's right. I forget the term for it, but it's the exact opposite of claustrophobia. Acrophobia, I think."

"Agoraphobia," Sarah corrected. "It's the fear of open spaces. Acrophobia is the fear of heights."

"As I was saying," Kri'Calin continued, "the soldiers responsible for patrolling the northern district thought there might be a battle brewing between the dwarves and the wyverians again, so when the constable became aware of the activities, he visited the valley to see for himself the increasing number of dwarves massing in the area. He finally found a dwarf willing to talk to him and the dwarf assured him they were there for peaceful purposes only."

Steve didn't think a response was necessary so he elected to do what he usually did: smile and grunt politely.

"The constable inquired further and learned that the Dragon Lord himself would be visiting the valley soon. The dwarves were there to negotiate peace between their two species. The constable deemed this information important enough to forward to me."

Steve gave the king another smile.

"What you might not realize is how rarely the Dragon Lord is seen in public. I have been trying for years to get him to grant me an audience but I have been rebuffed more times than I care to admit. Don't you see? This is my chance! I have an opportunity to speak with the Dragon Lord. I cannot pass it up. Please, you must help me!"

Sarah turned to Steve and pulled out one of her most

effective weapons: a pouting look.

"Oh, for heaven's sake. You're telling me you want to go up there, are you?"

"Why not? We've waited this long, what's another few hours? Besides, we have a chance to witness Lentarian history as it's happening. I don't think we should pass that up. Besides, we really don't have to worry about Rinbok. I mean, he doesn't know our scent, right?"

"That's no excuse to go, dear."

"I know that. I would still recommend avoiding him at all costs. However, if he does happen to pick up our scent then he's just going to chalk it up as another unknown human."

"And the dwarves?" Steve countered. "What about them? You and I both know Maelnar will be up there."

"What about him? He wouldn't know us if we bumped into him, either. He'll just see us as an insignificant couple of humans, too."

"Do you know the dwarf key maker that well?" Kri'Calin asked.

"He's a very good friend of ours," Sarah answered. She took Steve's hand. "It seems like every time we come to Lentari, we inadvertently end up seeing him, as something happens that Maelnar is directly, or indirectly, involved in."

"He's the Lentarian version of R2-D2," Steve chuckled.

The two Lentarians stared at him with blank expressions on their faces.

"Umm, it means that Maelnar always seems to be involved with whatever is going on," Steve translated.

"Didn't she just say that?" Sauer asked as he looked pointedly at Sarah.

Sarah smiled at her husband and patted his arm. She looked back at Captain Sauer.

"On our world it's called being a nerd. It's a label you're assigned when other people realize you enjoy certain things wayyyy too much."

Steve gave her a two-finger salute. "We nerds have way more fun. Besides, you're the one that said 'I do', remember?"

"You weren't this crazy when I married you."

Uncertain what was happening, Kri'Calin and Sauer eyed

each other.

"Does this mean you'll take me up there?" the king asked.

Husband and wife looked at each other before they turned to the king. Sarah curtsied. "Why, I'd be delighted, good sir."

The king smiled. "Thank you. Thank you very much."

"How many people are you planning on taking with you?" Sarah asked.

"Just myself," the king told her as he snatched a few things off his desk. "I wouldn't want to overtax your jhorun by making unnecessary trips."

Sarah was silent for a few moments as she studied him. "The most I've ever teleported was about twenty people, Your Majesty."

"At the same time?"

Sarah smiled. "Yes."

"Incredible. The queen will be overjoyed. When I told her of my plans, I could see that she would like to accompany me. Now you're telling me that she can?"

"That's right," Steve confirmed. "May I also recommend you take a few others with you? Guards, assistants, and so on? That way Sarah and I can blend in with them."

Sarah nodded. "That's a good idea. Gather whoever is going," she told the king, giving the monarch the first set of instructions he was willing to obey in many years. "Be in the portal room in half an hour. Will that work?"

"We'll be ready," the king assured her as he hurried off.

Standing in the middle of the Great Hall, Sarah took Steve's hand and pulled him over to a nearby table to sit down.

"I'll bet this event is what Melvyn was trying to get to," Steve said as he pulled a bench out for Sarah. "Although how he found out about it is beyond me."

Sarah stretched her back and let out a yawn.

"What do you think would have happened had Melvyn been able to get his hands on Maelnar?"

Sarah shuddered. "I don't even want to know. Maelnar plays such an integral role in so many parts of our history that the slightest alteration could severely affect us."

"Do you think he would have forced Maelnar to make

him a key to get back or do you think he'd just kill him?"

Sarah shrugged. "Probably both. Who knows? Either way you look at it, I'm very glad he's out of the picture."

"Me, too," Steve agreed.

* * *

"How long do you want to give him?" Steve whispered as he pulled Sarah aside. "I'm telling you, he looks rather green around the gills, if you catch my meaning."

No one else had felt the ill effects of Sarah's jhorun as she teleported them to the southern tip of Lake Raehón's valley. The king, however, had grasped his stomach and staggered to his knees within moments of arriving. The last thing Sarah wanted to do was to make anyone sick, let alone the king! Sarah hurried over to Ny'Alena, who was crouching by her husband.

"It'll pass, Your Majesty. I'm so sorry. I tried to warn you." She looked at the queen's twinkling eyes. What was going on?

In answer to Sarah's unspoken question, the queen faced her and smiled. "Please forgive Calin. It's very easy for His Majesty to grow queasy. That's why we do not travel on ships, or on horseback for that matter."

"Then how do you travel from village to village?" Steve wanted to know as he joined Sarah.

"We have a special carriage that was built for this reason. It delivers a very smooth ride, smooth enough for Calin to use without becoming nauseated."

Once the king regained his composure, he smiled fleetingly and hurried to the front of the procession. The guards spread out, with three taking the lead, two walking on either side of the royal couple, and three bringing up the rear. Together they emerged from the trees and started across the valley.

"Are you sure this is a smart move?" Steve asked as he nervously looked around. "Dragons can disguise themselves as anything. We could be walking into an ambush."

"With the Dragon Lord nearby? Fear not. We are safe."

"What if Rinbok has his own set of guards? What if they

see us coming and move to intercept us before we can get there? I held off one dragon, but barely."

Surprised, both the king and queen briefly looked back at him. "You held off a dragon?" Kri'Calin asked, amazed. "The longer I know you, the more impressed I become."

"Don't be. It was only for a minute or two. If we hadn't found the dwarf door then we would have become French fries."

"French fries?" the queen repeated. "What is that?"

"Umm, a type of fried food. Deep fried, if you get my meaning."

Ny'Alena smiled complacently. Whether she understood or not, Steve didn't know.

"Besides," the king continued, "we have you! If we meet a dragon, and he or she isn't friendly, then you will be able to protect us."

"I wouldn't bet on it," Steve murmured quietly to himself. He turned to Sarah. "Do you see anything?"

Sarah shaded her eyes as she stared across the valley. She saw no traces of dragons or dwarves.

"This valley is fairly decent in size," Steve observed. "Are you sure we're at the right place?"

"My informant said the south. I assumed the southern tip of the valley."

"What about the southern tip of the lake?" Sarah asked as she looked at the large body of water directly ahead of them. "Could your informant have been referring to the lake instead of the valley?"

Kri'Calin hesitated a few seconds before he shrugged. "It's possible, I suppose."

"Can your stomach handle another jump?" Sarah asked, already knowing he would never admit it if he wasn't.

"Of course," the king quickly answered, although his face drained of color. "I'm ready whenever you are."

Sarah motioned for everyone to huddle close. "Right. Here we go! Everyone take a deep breath."

Lake Raehón's shore stretched beyond view to the west, while the eastern shore curved abruptly to the left and angled north. Flocks of tiny red kytes were flying overhead while a much larger, white species floated lazily on the lake's surface about a hundred feet from the shore.

There were still no signs of any dragon or dwarf.

Steve glanced at the setting sun. It was less than fifteen minutes away. If the king was going to witness the creation of a new dwarf-dragon alliance, then they needed to find out where to go. Quickly.

You could just ask, you know.

Pryllan?

Have you been in telepathic contact with any other dragons while you've been here?

Hah! As a matter of fact, I have.

Who?

Kahvel.

Oh. He doesn't count.

Pryllan, we have the human king here. He wants to watch the dwarves and dragons become allies. Is that allowed?

"What's going on?" Sarah asked. "Why have you gone quiet and why are you smiling?"

Steve winked at her. Sarah's eyebrows shot up. "Oh. Um, carry on."

Were you talking to your mate?

Yes. Apparently, I had some goofy look on my face just now and she was asking me what was going on.

I see. To answer your question, I don't see any objections to the human king's presence. There are already four different dwarf clans represented. I don't think he would mind other bystanders.

Has this event started?

No. Rinbok Intherer has yet to arrive.

Perfect. Where are you, anyway? We are at the southern tip of the lake and can't see anyone around here.

We are northeast of your present location, at the northern most tip of the valley before it returns to the forest.

Steve recognized the location but didn't reveal that fact to the dragon. **If you wish to witness this, you'd best hurry. The Dragon Lord approaches.**

Steve turned to look at his wife. He took her hands.

"Remember the lilacs?"

Sarah nodded. "From when the new…"

Steve's hand appeared over her mouth. "I almost gave that away to Pryllan, too. Don't say it out loud."

Sarah nodded. "Got it."

"And we need to hurry. Rinbok wasn't there yet, but he was approaching as we were finishing."

"He's near the lilacs. Got it." Sarah clapped her hands to get everyone's attention. "One more jump. Everyone ready? Your Majesties, take a deep breath. It's almost over."

Kri'Calin grimaced and screwed his eyes shut. The lake's southern shore was replaced by another shore, one running north to south. The valley's grasslands narrowed to less than half a mile wide. To the east, a faint thin purple line bordered the forest.

Sarah clapped her hands. "I can smell the lilacs! Aren't they wonderful?"

"I think we have a more pressing problem to deal with," Steve quietly told her.

Sarah spun around and went still. Two dozen dragons of various sizes and colors were staring impassively back at them. Steve couldn't see Pryllan or Kahvel anywhere, which wasn't surprising as the two white dragons closest to them were so enormous that they blocked most of the other wyverians from view.

Also immediately apparent were the vast number of dwarves. Steve couldn't recall ever seeing that many of them Topside before. The different clans huddled together. There were the Kla Guur, dressed in black armor. Next to them were a dozen or so Kla Chanus wearing dark brown leather armor. Then Steve could see a group of dwarves with long, flowing, unbraided beards in scaly green armor.

Which dwarves are wearing the dragon scales?

Those are the Kla Luthur.

They're really wearing dragon scales to a dragon peace treaty? Don't you find that insulting?

Those aren't real wyverian scales.

Oh. They look like it.

The Kla Luthur have already explained their attire to

Rinbok Intherer. The style is done to honor the dragons, they claim.

Do you believe them?

We have no reason to believe otherwise.

How about the group of dwarves wearing the chain mail? Those outfits look like they weigh a hundred pounds each. I didn't think dwarves wore metal armor anymore.

Most do not. Those, however, are the Kla Snakkoth. They are a steadfast clan that believes in traditional values. For a dwarf. At one time their ancestors wore those outfits, so they deem it an honor to wear them today. I am surprised to see them here as they prefer living in isolation than seeking out companionship.

I assume they all live nearby?

Some clans had to travel farther than others, but aye, all live fairly close to one another.

One of the two enormous white dragons lowered its head down low to gaze curiously at their small group, as though it was seeing a human for the first time. The dragon sniffed curiously a few times before something coming their way caught its attention. The white dragon gave a warning growl and moved off. The ground had begun shaking as an even larger dragon, this one green with black stripes, approached. Steve grabbed Sarah's hand.

"It's Rinbok!" he hissed at her. "We really shouldn't let him smell us. Come on. We need to hide."

Husband and wife ducked behind several of Kri'Calin's trembling guards as Rinbok's massive face appeared. He lowered his neck down to give the king a cursory sniff.

"Who are you, human? Your scent is unfamiliar."

"I am Kri'Calin, human king. I am honored to meet the noble Dragon Lord, Rinbok Intherer."

"What are you doing here, human king?"

"The dwarves are our allies," the king answered, without batting an eye. "We are here to congratulate them on this significant occasion."

Rinbok Intherer snorted. "Significant, eh?"

Kri'Calin was unrattled. "The strife between dwarf and wyverian has been well documented."

"It has indeed, human king."

"Do you object to my presence here? If so, then I can leave. I wish you to know that I bear no ill will."

"Your presence for these proceedings matters not," was the Dragon Lord's curt response.

Rinbok Intherer stepped in the opposite direction when his head lifted and he sniffed the air. Steve held his breath as he watched the ruler of all wyverians sniff the air a second time. After a few moments, the Dragon Lord moved off.

"Wow, that was close," Sarah whispered in his ear.

"Too close," Steve agreed.

Sarah suddenly giggled.

"What's so funny?" Steve demanded.

"What do we have to be worried about? I told you. Rinbok doesn't know our scent. Not in this time. We're fine."

"Then what'd he pause for? He clearly picked something up."

A commotion sounded behind them. They turned to see a group of nearly three dozen dwarves approach. These were all wearing black. Black armor, black weapons, even black helmets. It meant they were Kla Guur. Steve took one look at the dwarves and ducked back behind the group of guards, pulling Sarah close to him.

"Now what?" Sarah wanted to know.

"Don't you see him? Maelnar is out there! Did we call that or what?"

"Wow, he certainly gets around, doesn't he?" Sarah agreed.

"I still find it hard to believe that we were originally told he was a recluse."

A large group of dwarves, including Maelnar, meandered by. He was looking less gray than in their time. Both husband and wife turned away as Maelnar paid his compliments to Kri'Calin and the queen. Sauer raised an eyebrow. As soon as Maelnar moved off, he quietly approached.

"What was that all about?"

"That was the dwarf we were telling you about. That's Maelnar, the key maker. We're not supposed to meet him for over a hundred years."

"Tell me something. Do you think your future will be affected by what is transpiring here today?"

"I know it is, Sauer," Steve whispered, looking away again as another group of dwarves wandered by.

"How so?" Sauer inquired, curious.

"The dwarves and the dragons aren't supposed to become allies for a few more years," Sarah told him.

"Are you certain?" the captain asked, surprise evident on his face.

"The humans become allies with the dragons not long after they became allies with the dwarves," Steve added, looking up to see if he could spot Pryllan.

"Humans are allies with the dragons?" Sauer exclaimed as his voice jumped several notches higher.

"You weren't supposed to tell him that," Sarah chided.

Steve scowled. "Dammit. You're right. Dude, you have to forget I said that."

"That's not something I can easily forget," Sauer dryly told them. "That's what you almost said in the Great Hall, wasn't it? You cut off in the middle."

Steve sighed. "That's right. Can you do me a favor? Please keep that to yourself, okay? Don't tell the king."

Captain Sauer finally smiled. "Fear not. Your secret, well, this secret, is safe with me."

Sarah gave a grateful sigh. "Thank you."

Sauer wandered off. A commotion drew their attention. Rinbok Intherer stepped out in front of the dragons and thumped his tail several times on the soft grass. Every dragon instantly fell silent. Rinbok eyed the group of Kla Guur and waited. After a few moments Maelnar and a few others broke away from the rest and timidly approached the giant leader of dragons.

Members of the Kla Chanus and the Kla Luthur also broke away from their respective parties and approached Rinbok Intherer. The leader of the Kla Chanus bowed.

"You are dealing with our revered brothers, the Kla Guur," the elderly dwarf announced, as if he needed to remind the Dragon Lord what he was doing. "I humbly ask that myself and several honorable members of the Kla

Chanus be allowed to accompany the Kla Guur."

Rinbok nodded. Whether he was interested or didn't care was unknown, as his large reptilian face remained impassive.

"The Kla Luthur would also like to be included," the spokesman for the dwarves wearing the green dragon scale outfits said, raising his voice to be heard.

Rinbok nodded again. He then looked straight at the final dwarf clan and waited. After a few moments, two of the Kla Snakkoth hesitantly stepped forward, clanging loudly in their metallic armor.

"From this day forward," the Dragon Lord was saying, "no wyverian will attack a dwarf. No wyverian will lie in wait for a dwarf to appear out of their tunnels. No…"

"There's no need for that," one Council member interrupted. He wore the green scale outfit making him a Kla Luthur. Rinbok Intherer, with his jaws still open, stared at the dwarf, flabbergasted he had been interrupted. "We move our entrances all the time. There's no way a dragon could know about all of our entrances."

"And why's that?" Rinbok demanded. "Do you think we dragons haven't figured out how to discover a disguised door?"

"A sealed dwarf door will look just like the surrounding countryside," another dwarf haughtily informed the towering dragon. This one was one of the two Kla Snakkoth. "You couldn't find our doors even if you tried."

Steve eyed Sarah and shook his head. This wasn't going well. Then they heard a loud clang. The other Kla Snakkoth had literally bonked his companion over the head with the flat of his axe. The first Kla Snakkoth dropped to the ground in a noisy heap.

"I apologize for my companion," the dwarf formally began. "We of the Kla Snakkoth stand with our Kla Guur brethren. We look forward to peace."

"By knocking out your own kin?" Rinbok Intherer wryly asked.

"Again, my apologies. I had to shut him up."

"The brotherhood of the dwarves have taken a tremendous step today," Rinbok declared, his voice booming across the valley. "No more lying in wait. No more ambushes. No more wanton destruction of dwarven tunnels."

One of the Kla Guur stepped forward. Surprisingly, it wasn't Maelnar, Steve noted.

"We thank the Dragon Lord for agreeing to these talks," the dwarf began. "There will be no more traps. No more disguises. From this day forward dwarf and wyverian will live together in harmonious peace."

"Traps?" Steve whispered to Sarah. "Disguises? What's that supposed to mean? Can the dwarves actually inflict harm on the dragons?"

"Aye, we can," a voice softly answered.

Steve turned to see Selwyn standing quietly by his side. "Hey there, Selwyn. How's it going?"

"I am well, friend Steve. Miss Sarah, it is a pleasure to see you again."

Sarah smiled warmly at the dwarf. "Hello, Selwyn. We need to stop meeting like this."

Selwyn gave a soft snort.

"What did you say about being able to harm a dragon?"

"As you can imagine, if someone our size is tasked with facing an adversary much larger than ourselves, much *much* larger, then we will find a way to protect ourselves. We have developed some fairly lethal weapons, which we have, I am sorry to say, used on the wyverians."

"Like what?" Steve wanted to know.

"Have you ever heard of a soran stone?"

Steve shook his head. "What is it?"

"It's an artificial stone that is designed to be launched into the air, where it explodes and sends out hundreds of razor-sharp projectiles in all directions."

Sarah gasped aloud. Steve cleared his throat. "And the, uh, disguises? What's that all about?"

Selwyn's head fell. "We have become quite gifted in making solid surfaces look like something else."

Sarah put a hand over her mouth. "Like what?" she whispered.

"For example, making the side of a mountain look like open sky? Or perhaps creating false caves?"

Steve was horrified. "Dude, if a dragon hit something like that while flying at normal speed then it'd … it'd…" He didn't finish. He knew what the results would be. So did Sarah.

Selwyn nodded. "Aye. That's why the Dragon Lord said what he did."

Rinbok Intherer continued to address the dwarves as they talked about what each species would and would not do. There'd be no deliberate provocations from either side. There'd be no verbal taunts. There'd be no spying by the dragons. On and on the list went.

Selwyn, being no taller than Steve's chest, tapped his arm to get his attention. "Do you know that it was little Aislinn's ride which prompted this whole conclave?"

Steve nodded. "I had wondered."

"When you and Aislinn landed with the dragon, you were being watched, which was completely unbeknownst to me."

"We were? By who?"

"Several members of the Council were conducting a private meeting Topside when the dragon landed nearby. Curious, they moved closer and witnessed the entire exchange between Aislinn and Pryllan."

"What happened then?" Sarah asked, enjoying a story that clearly had a happy ending.

"The three members went straight back to the Council and shared what they saw. When it became known that my little princess had run away, and they saw Pryllan fight to protect one of their own, they revisited everything they thought they knew about our winged neighbors. The decision was made to approach the Dragon Lord and see if he was interested in ceasing all hostilities between our two species."

"I'm really glad it worked out so well for you," Steve commented. He turned to check the status of the peace talks. Rinbok was now silent but the dwarves were talking.

"How was the shachar broken?" Selwyn asked as he tapped Steve's arm again. "How was it absolved? I thought it would be exceedingly difficult to break."

"I really don't — "

I am still confused by that, too.

Hello, Pryllan.

Steve.

"What's going on?" Sarah asked.

"Pryllan is echoing Selwyn's confusion."

Selwyn looked around. "I do not see Pryllan around here."

"She's in my head," Steve told him. Then he cursed and slapped a hand over his mouth.

Selwyn sighed. "Allow me to venture a guess. I'm not supposed to know dragons are telepathic?"

Steve scowled, angrier with himself than with anyone else.

Sarah nodded. "Yes, please, Selwyn. Keep that to yourself. Promise me."

Selwyn nodded. "Very well. I promise."

You told the dwarf about our communication?

Sorry. If it means anything, he promised not to tell.

You're not very good at keeping secrets, are you?

Have you been talking to my wife?

Pryllan chuckled. **About the shachar, I still have no idea why it was absolved. I would have thought defending the little underling from the shabewts would have made things worse, not better.**

Could this peace treaty have something to do with it?

How?

Well, based on what I heard the dwarves could do to you dragons, this peace treaty probably saved the life of more than one dragon.

I disagree. Everything I have learned about shachars says that I alone would have to be affected. The child would have had to save my life in order for the life-debt to be absolved.

I think there's something we're missing here.

I would agree. Hmm. It would appear the ceremony is wrapping up.

Steve looked back at the Dragon Lord. He was now standing motionless in a sea of dwarves, as it seemed every dwarf present wanted to thank him personally. To his credit, Rinbok waited patiently for the numerous accolades and introductions to finish. While every dragon became acquainted with each and every dwarf, Kri'Calin began edging surreptitiously closer to Rinbok. When he was within fifty feet, the king stopped and waited for the Dragon Lord to look his way. When Rinbok finally did, the king gave him a formal bow.

Two tiny tendrils of smoke escaped from each nostril as the Dragon Lord watched the human king approach. Steve held his breath. This could end very badly or have even more dire changes for the future of their Lentari.

"Greetings, Dragon Lord."

"Human king," Rinbok returned.

"I want to commend you on taking this huge step in becoming allies with the dwarves."

Since he wasn't asked a question, Rinbok Intherer remained silent.

"Do you think it possible that at some point in time we might be able to open a dialogue to become allies ourselves?"

The Dragon Lord waited a few moments before grunting noncommittally and then moving off.

Ny'Alena appeared by Kri'Calin's side. "How rude! The least he could do is tell you he wasn't interested."

Surprisingly, the king turned to his wife and gave her a victorious smile. "Quite the contrary, my dear. He might not have agreed to the notion right now, but he didn't turn it down, either. That tells me that he'd be open to the idea sometime in the future! Isn't that exciting?"

"It's insulting," the queen disagreed, frowning as she turned to look at the retreating Dragon Lord's backside.

Steve watched as the dwarves started to lose some of their nervousness around their colossal allies. Many of the dwarves were slapping their new friends on whatever body part they could reach, which due to their size, were predominantly the dragon's huge talons. The dragons, on the other hand, looked completely disinterested and were politely tolerating the close proximity of the dwarves only because of Rinbok Intherer's presence.

It was a start, Steve decided. He could tell that it would take some time for each species to completely trust the other, but at least both dragon and dwarf were heading in the right direction. And speaking of heading in the right direction, it was time to head in theirs. Steve took Sarah's hand and approached the king.

"Your Majesties, we need to get you back to the castle now. It's time for us to see if Luther can get us home."

Kri'Calin, completely comfortable mingling amongst the dwarves and the dragons, looked longingly back. One of the dragons had volunteered to light an enormous cooking fire, while another dragon had dropped the carcass of a bolger. Tools were sharpened. A group of dwarves had gone into the nearby forest and returned with a sizeable tree. Within moments, they stripped the bark from the trunk, cut it into planks, and hastily assembled some tables. Instruments were produced. Music began. It had the makings of a full-fledged party and the king clearly wanted to stay.

"Verdayn is not that far away," Captain Sauer announced. "I can send a messenger to the village and have them prepare the portal for return later tonight. Or, er, tomorrow morning if you so prefer. I can have them send a squadron of guards to help secure the area."

Kri'Calin looked over at one of the huge white dragons they had first encountered.

"Leave them be, Captain. There's no one foolish enough to try anything with so many dragons and dwarves around. We are perfectly safe. And I think I will stay a bit longer, if that's alright by you, my dear."

The queen smiled. "Of course, my love. I know how important this is to you."

Steve smiled. "In that case, Your Majesties, we're off. It's been a real pleasure."

Sarah echoed his sentiments and curtsied. Steve turned to Sauer and held out his hand. The captain grasped his forearm instead.

"It's been an honor," Sauer informed him.

"I'm sorry for calling you a sourpuss when we first met."

Sauer cracked a smile. "It wasn't the first time I've heard that and I know it won't be the last. Good journey to you both."

Sarah took her husband's hand and teleported them back to Idaho.

Chapter 13 — Rise of the Gatekeeper

You had me worried," Cecil admitted with a sheepish smile. He and AnnaBelle were sitting on the only loveseat in the large living room. "Based on everything that has happened to us over the last couple of days, I thought for certain we'd need to mount another rescue mission."

"Your vote of confidence is overwhelming," Steve quipped as he strode into the room. He returned Cecil's smile. "Believe it or not, it went much better than I had thought possible."

Steve guided Sarah toward the back of the room and plunked down onto the sofa. Sarah sat beside him and leaned back against the plush cushions, sighing contentedly. They heard footsteps from the floor above and listened as they made their way down the stairs. Luther and Cora, walking hand in hand, appeared and together they joined Steve and Sarah on the couch.

Quinn arrived next, with a book in one hand and a glass of water in the other, and claimed one of the three plush armchairs scattered about the room. Lissa, also holding a thick book in her hand, claimed another. Mina arrived last and claimed the final armchair.

"You're looking much better, Mina," Sarah told her, giving the girl a friendly smile.

Luther's sister smiled shyly at her and tried to sink even lower into the chair.

Steve pulled a small leather pouch from within his pocket and untied the drawstrings. He tipped the pouch over and caught the smoke-colored sphere as it plopped into his hand. His jhorun automatically flowed into the hand holding the powerful talisman as it sought to investigate the foreign object. Steve noticed his hand had turned red and instantly tossed the jorii over to Luther, who neatly caught it with his left hand.

"You have no idea how glad I am to get rid of that thing," Steve told his ancestor as a frown appeared on his face. "Fire thrower plus one jorii equals job security for the local fire department."

Luther's eyes lit up. "You found one!"

"Find one? No, I didn't find one. I guilted the king into giving me his last jorii."

Luther gazed deep into the heart of the smoky sphere. "You can't even begin to imagine how long I've waited to hold a fully charged jorii again."

"Why?" Cora asked, curious.

"Because now I can use my jhorun again."

Steve pointedly looked up at the ceiling directly over his head. "By all means, please use your jhorun again."

Gripping the jorii tightly, Luther slowly stood and headed up the stairs. Cora made a move to rise to her feet, until Sarah caught her arm and pulled her back down onto the couch.

"It'll be best if you leave him alone for just a bit. He's probably going to need peace and quiet so he can concentrate."

Cora nodded. Sarah saw that Quinn had his book open and was slowly skimming through its pages.

"Quinn, can I ask you something?"

The schoolmaster looked up from his book. He placed a slip of paper in the book to mark his spot and closed it. "Of course."

"How familiar are you with Lentarian history?"

Quinn smiled. "It's my area of specialty, milady."

Sarah nudged her husband on the arm. "You ought to call me milady more often."

Steve glanced over at Quinn, who instantly gave him a sheepish smile.

"What would you like to know?" Quinn asked, setting his book down on the closest table.

"When did the dragons and the dwarves forge their alliance?"

"It was about twenty years ago."

"And if it happened earlier than that?" Sarah asked.

Quinn shook his head. "But it didn't. The dragons finally made peace with their land-bound neighbors after one of the dragons found an abandoned soran stone. You see, a soran stone is…" The schoolmaster trailed off as he noticed Sarah's horrified expression. "You know what a soran stone is?"

Steve nodded. "It was recently explained to us."

"Unpleasant business for sure. A dragon was killed in the explosion, which almost instigated another wyverian-dwarf war."

Steve ran his hands through his hair. "I don't think I ever realized how much the dwarves and dragons hated each other. I wonder what dragon it was. I hope it wasn't anyone we knew."

"How would you know him?" Quinn asked. "He was killed several years before you or Sarah ever stepped foot on Lentari."

"We've made some new friends lately," Sarah quietly told him. "Do you know who it was?"

Quinn nodded. "Dragon lore is a hobby of mine. The dragon's name was Caradoc. Did you know him?"

Steve shook his head. "No. It's a cool name, though. I would have remembered if we did. What? What's the matter?"

Once more Sarah had a look of sheer horror on her face and had placed her hands over her mouth. "You don't remember, do you?"

"What? We've met Caradoc?"

Sarah shook her head. "We haven't, no. But we have heard of him."

"We have? How?"

Sarah placed her hand on her husband's. "Caradoc is Pryllan's father. Remember?"

"Oh, man. You're right. I had forgotten about that. Rinbok mentioned the name during the trial, didn't he? Oh, poor Pryllan."

"Why would you ask what would happen if the alliance had been created earlier?" Quinn curiously asked.

"Because it just did," Sarah answered.

"The alliance? That is impossible."

"It just happened," Steve confirmed. "We were witnesses."

Quinn was silent for a few moments. He gave a light cough and held up a finger. "Well, hypothetically speaking, if that is true then Caradoc will more than likely be alive in our time right now."

Steve blinked with surprise. "Would you care to run that by me again?"

Alarmed, Sarah sat up straight. "I think I see where you're going with this."

Steve turned to her. "You do?"

"Think about it, honey," Sarah said with a trace of exasperation in her voice before the schoolmaster could respond. "Since the dragons and dwarves are now allies, way before Caradoc will ever find that nasty stone thing, chances are the dwarves would be certain they don't leave any of their dangerous weapons lying around."

Quinn raised a hand again. "Umm, excuse me? Were you serious about the dragon and dwarves becoming allies? That shouldn't happen for another hundred years by my reckoning."

"Well, it did," Steve confirmed. "Due to recent events, the dwarves approached the dragons and extended their hand in friendship."

Quinn's eyes were as large as saucers. "They didn't!"

Sarah nodded. "Yes, they did."

The two of them proceeded to give their companions a run-down on what had happened. Steve included his interaction with the dwarves as well as his ride with Aislinn, and concluded with their search to find the little girl after she had wandered away.

Quinn smiled. "That really pleases me. The dwarves and dragons do not deserve to be fighting. Good for them. I've heard enough about their skirmishes to know that becoming allies will save a lot of lives."

"I wonder what that's gonna do to the future?" Steve wondered aloud.

"Well, what's the worst that could happen?" Sarah asked. "Pryllan's father would still be alive, right?"

Quinn took a deep drink of water from his glass and hesitated as he stretched out an arm to place the glass back on the table.

"You alright over there, buddy?" Steve called out. "You look a little pale."

"We already know that history has been changed."

"No," Steve disagreed. "Our *future* has been changed."

Quinn tapped the coffee table in front of him. "But for us, this time *is* history for us."

Steve swallowed nervously. "Okay, let's hear it. What did we do this time?"

Quinn slowly stood and began pacing. He started ticking off points on his fingers.

"Let's forget about the possibility of Caradoc being alive back in our time. Off the top of my head, I'd say there are a number of things. First, there's Verdayn. It underwent numerous renovations over the years as a direct result of several parts of the village burning down due to the incessant attacks both the dwarves and the dragons played on one another. If there are no more hostilities, then that would mean no more buildings would be burnt to the ground. What would the end result be? The village might not ever expand into the surrounding hills.

"Second, the ordinance which forbade hunting in the northern section of the valley might never have been issued. If memory serves, in our history, nearly fifty years ago,

Verdayn's constable, fearing for the villagers' lives, issued orders to avoid the north valley at all costs due to rising tensions with the dragons. That ordinance was in effect up until the day of the treaty.

"Third, as a result of how long the hunting ban lasted, several villagers snuck into the valley one night. They were hunting for a white bolger, I believe. Maybe it was gray. It's not important. What is important is that they were discovered by the dragons and were pursued. When several of them tried to hide behind a large boulder, which was consequently destroyed by dragon fire, the dwarves became involved."

"Let me guess," Steve interjected. "They were hiding behind a dwarf door."

Quinn nodded. "Aye. The door was destroyed, the dwarves were outraged, and yet another skirmish started. That was one of the shorter skirmishes, lasting only about three months."

"Three months is considered short?" Sarah reached for her glass of water. "That is eleven weeks and six days too long for my liking."

"And we mustn't forget the terrible battle of Rujin Rock."

Steve glanced at Sarah and saw she was confused as he was. "The battle of what?"

"Rujin Rock," Quinn repeated. "It was unarguably the bloodiest battle ever fought by dwarf and dragon alike. Nearly a thousand dwarves and close to a hundred dragons lost their lives that day."

"Wow. I've never heard that before," Steve admitted. "Did any humans die in that battle?"

Quinn shook his head. "The dwarves, allies they may be to us humans, never once called for aid."

"Why is that?" Cecil wanted to know.

Quinn shrugged. "The reason isn't documented. If I were to venture a guess, then I'd say it was either because the dwarves felt they didn't need the help or else they thought that whatever they were fighting for was personal. One thing was certain, though."

"What's that?" Sarah asked.

"The full scope of how effective dwarfish weapons of

war were became readily known. There were many casualties."

Steve whistled. "Wow. I'm very glad that Pryllan and Kahvel were never involved with that."

"How do you know they weren't?" Quinn countered. "For all you know they both fought in the battle and came out unscathed."

Steve shrugged, conceding the point. Sarah suddenly gasped and reached for her husband's hand. "What if Pryllan was involved in that war?" Sarah asked.

"So, what if she was?" Steve said. "Obviously she survived, if she did."

"Based on everything that we've seen and that's changed since we arrived, I'd say Pryllan would have played a more active role this time around."

Steve's curiosity was kindled. "What do you mean?"

"What do you think would have happened if the Dragon Lord had learned of Pryllan's involvement with the dwarves and she had allowed a dwarf child to ride on her back?"

"He wouldn't have been pleased," Steve speculated. "Not in the slightest."

"Right," Quinn added, picking up Sarah's train of thought. "So, if the Dragon Lord learned about Pryllan's involvement sometime later, but before the battle, what role do you think he would have forced her to take? Think about it. The Dragon Lord is angry. You're in direct violation of his orders and have openly disobeyed him. He'll view it as disrespect. As such, if a war were to happen, he'd make Pryllan take a much more active role. I believe Pryllan was killed in that battle."

"That's preposterous," Steve sputtered. "She clearly survived that war because we're friends with her back in our own time."

"You're still assuming the history we're familiar with is going to happen," Sarah added, coming to Quinn's defense. "Forget about that history. It's, well, ancient history if you'll pardon the pun. We have to consider *this* history now. There's no way of getting around it. We've changed the course of events."

"Let's not be melodramatic," Steve cautioned, eliciting a punch on the arm from his wife. "You have no way of knowing Pryllan was ever involved with that battle."

"Yes, but you've involved your dragon friend more than she's probably ever been," Quinn argued. "Pryllan should have been largely ignored but, thanks to her involvement with you, she's been given more attention than she'll ever want."

Steve groaned. "I'm getting a headache again."

"I can make you some tea," Lissa offered, who up until now had been quietly watching the adults arguing back and forth.

"Tea? Not unless you dump a pound of sugar in it."

Lissa frowned. "Too much sugar isn't good for you."

"Thanks, but I think I'll have to —"

"He'd love some," Sarah smoothly interrupted. "Thank you, Lissa."

The teenage girl slipped out of the room and headed to the kitchen.

"I don't like tea," Steve grumbled. "And she'd better not spike it this time."

"And I don't like a grumpy husband," Sarah responded. She patted his knee. "This will make you feel better."

"I doubt it," Steve muttered crossly. "I'm just not really buying any of these 'would have been' or 'could have been' scenarios."

Quinn looked over at Cora. "Could I possibly borrow a piece of paper and a pencil? I'll bet I could explain it better if I could illustrate what I'm talking about."

Cora quickly left the room, returning moments later with several sheets of paper and both a quill and a pencil. Quinn thanked her and set a few sheets out on the coffee table in front of him. He selected the pencil and drew a straight horizontal line across the paper. He placed the tip of the pencil on the far-left end of the line. Steve rose to his feet and knelt down by the table so he could see what Quinn was drawing. Everyone else crowded around the table, too.

"Can we all agree that the natural flow of time can be thought of in linear terms?"

No one said a thing. A sea of blank faces stared at the schoolmaster. Quinn cleared his throat and tried again. "Let me rephrase that. The passage of time can be represented by this single line. Let's assume that this point," and he tapped the left end of the line, "represents the Lentari of the past, before it was ever visited by anyone who shouldn't have been here. As the time flows forward, notable events happened."

Quinn placed an X on the line.

"Let's say that this represents the creation of the hunting ordinance and this," he placed another X a few inches to the right, "is the small three-month long skirmish I told you about. And this," an X was placed two-thirds of the way along the line, "is the battle of Rujin Rock." He added another X several inches from the right-hand end point. "This will be the point where the dragons and dwarves become friends. Now, time keeps progressing until we reach our time, nearly a hundred twenty years from this first point." Quinn added an X on the far-right end of the line. "Can we agree that this is the history that Lissa and I are familiar with, and to some extent, Steve and Sarah?"

Everyone nodded. Quinn pushed the paper aside and selected a second sheet. He redrew the first line, complete with the Xs he had added, on the top of the page and also added a large number two in the top right corner. Then he drew a line from the farthest X on the left and angled it down a few inches before changing course and drawing another horizontal line straight across the paper.

"This is the second timeline," he began. He added an X on the left end of the line and tapped the mark. "This X signifies when we all arrived here. At that point our timeline has skewed down to this one. This upper timeline is never going to happen now thanks to our presence here." Quinn tapped the new line a few times. "So, what's happened on this line? Let's add what we know." Quinn drew an X immediately to the right of the new timeline's start. "Here's where the events begin changing. This X will represent the dwarf child's ride on Pryllan's back. The result was the creation of the shachar."

"Which you're not supposed to know about," Steve warned with a quiet tone.

"Right. We'll call it 'the debt', alright? Now, from what you told me, several dwarf council members witnessed the young dwarf girl disembarking after her return."

"That's right," Steve agreed.

Quinn placed another X almost immediately to the right of the second X, giving the appearance of three Xs right in a row.

"What's the third X for?" Cecil asked.

"It represents another monumental event," Quinn answered. "At this point the dwarf council has become open minded about the possibility of becoming allies with the dragons."

"Then is the next X for the new alliance?" Steve asked.

In response, Quinn drew another X on the line about half the distance to the right-hand endpoint. Surprisingly, he shook his head no.

"The next X is for the battle of Rujin Rock."

"I thought you said that battle would never happen?" Steve argued. "They're friends now. That battle is history. Er, pardon the pun."

"Not yet it isn't," Quinn disagreed. He tapped the X signifying the battle. "Unless circumstances changed, the battle would still happen since neither side have officially become allies. Now, I realize that until here everything that happens is speculation at best, but I do believe that at this point Pryllan, and possibly Kahvel, were killed."

Steve's eyes widened. "But … but … that can't happen, can it? They're going to become allies!"

"Well, they haven't yet," Quinn corrected. "Remember, I said the dwarves had become open-minded about the possibility of becoming allies. I didn't say that they did."

"But they will eventually," Steve argued.

"Possibly. We don't really know." Quinn placed a few more Xs on the second timeline. "Chances are some of the events from the first line would transfer to the second. The battle of Rujin Rock. The approach of one side to the other to begin peace talks. What I'm saying is if the events of this second timeline were to play out, as I believe they would, then your dragon friend would more than likely be killed. As it turns out, you don't have to worry about that ever happening because I don't think this second timeline will ever happen, either."

"What? Why not?"

Quinn selected another sheet of blank paper and recreated the same two lines at the top of the page. He drew a number three on this sheet's top right corner. Then drew a third timeline below the second. With exaggerated flourish he drew an X near the left of the third timeline. This particular X was not quite on the far left.

Steve eyed the third line and the X. "Explain yourself. What's this one for?"

Quinn smiled and tapped the X on the lowest line.

"At this point the line changes again, erasing any possibility that the second timeline will ever happen."

"What happened then?" Steve wanted to know.

"Aislinn ran away," Sarah guessed.

Quinn smiled. "Not exactly. The sheriff escaped, activated the portal, and fled to Lentari."

"Why does that get its own X?" Steve wanted to know.

"Because at that point the timeline skews again, creating yet another tangent. When someone from the future steps foot into the past, unless they're careful, history will inevitably be changed. And, I think we can all agree, the sheriff was anything but careful."

Several people nodded their heads.

"Thanks to the sheriff," Quinn continued, "Steve and Sarah returned to Lentari. The Lentari of the past."

"So what?" Steve argued. "I had to go back there eventually. I had to fix Pryllan's problem."

Quinn nodded excitedly, as if Steve had just proven his point. "Exactly! However, you really didn't know what to do in order to abolish the, uh, debt, am I right?"

Steve nodded.

"Therefore, once you stepped back on Lentarian soil, without a clear plan on what you were going to do, the timeline changed. Hence, the X."

Everyone was silent as they stared at the third sheet of paper. Quinn coughed a few times and decided to keep going. "I don't think we'll ever really know how much changed when Steve and Sarah were actively searching for Melvyn. From what I remember hearing, Melvyn refused to pay bar tabs and committed a number of burglaries. And that's just what we know about. Who knows what else he did?"

"Just get to the point," Steve demanded. "Why does this require its own timeline? The second one already proves things have changed."

"Hear me out," Quinn pleaded. He bent over the paper and added another X. "I'm almost done. Now. This represents the dwarf child becoming lost and Pryllan's involvement with her rescue. The child placed herself in danger. What was the result? Pryllan came to her aid."

"Which should have, er, fortified the strength of that debt," Steve observed.

"Quite the opposite," Quinn countered. "Because the girl ran off, the dwarves saw that the dragons had yet again proven their trustworthiness. The decision to approach the wyverians to begin peace talks commenced."

Quinn drew an additional X on the third line.

"The alliance was forged here. This alliance guarantees that none of the horrible Xs from the second timeline will happen. What's the result? Pryllan's life was spared."

"By Aislinn's actions," Steve whispered, as he looked at Sarah. "That's why the sha--, er, debt was broken. I'll be damned. Aislinn saved her life after all."

"Are there any more Xs that you can add to the third line?" Cora quietly asked. "Learning about what will and could happen is fascinating!"

Quinn scratched his head. "Well, this line and the first timeline only have one X in common. Since an X from the original timeline appeared on this one, would that mean the same events might appear, too? Albeit in a different order? Well, we can pretty much assume these Xs from the top line here will never happen. There won't be a need to create a ban on hunting. There will never be a three-month long skirmish here, nor will there ever be, thank the wizards, a battle at Rujin Rock."

"I can't believe there's a good chance Pryllan's father will be alive when we make it back," Steve commented. He looked at Sarah and smiled. "I can't wait to meet him!"

Luther appeared in the doorway and slowly ambled into

the room to take his place next to his wife. He slowly looked around the room before he smiled weakly at Cora. "What have I missed?"

"I take it things didn't go well?" Steve inquired.

"I'll tell you all about my news once you tell me yours. Why does everyone look so glum?"

"I think you're mistaking glum for confusion," Steve dryly told him.

Quinn sighed aloud. "Steve is being sarcastic. It's really not that bad."

"It really is," Sarah quietly disagreed.

The schoolmaster quickly filled Luther in on everything he had covered thus far. Steve smirked. Judging by the look on his ancestor's face, Luther was having just as difficult a time as he was in trying to assimilate Quinn's theories.

"Let that sink in for a while," Steve told him, breaking a ten second silence. "Tell us what happened upstairs."

The entire room fell silent as all eyes turned to the gatekeeper. Steve, noting his ancestor's behavior, sighed loudly and slapped a friendly hand on his back.

"Thanks to the jorii, my jhorun is working again," Luther reported, his face grim. "But I was unable to modify the portal to target another time."

"But you could change the destination, right?" Steve pressed.

Luther waved a dismissive hand at him. "Of course."

"So, what happened?" Sarah softly asked him. "You obviously have some bad news to tell us. What is it?"

"My jhorun is complicated," Luther slowly began. "The only way I can explain it is to relate it to visions I see in my head. Sarah, you know what I'm talking about, right?"

Sarah nodded. "I do. If I can create an image of a destination in my mind, and I can hold it there, then my jhorun will take me to wherever I want. I don't know how it works, only what I have to do in order to make it work."

Luther nodded. "Aye. My jhorun is similar. Now, whenever I modify a previously activated portal, an image of the destination will appear in my mind. If I can get the image to move, I can therefore change the portal's destination. Do you understand?"

Sarah nodded, as did everyone else in the room.

"This time I not only wanted to change the destination, but also the time involved. I decided to leave the location alone but tried to imagine the portal depositing the traveler in another time."

"Which time?" Steve wanted to know.

"Still ours," Luther answered, "but five minutes later. I began probing the image. I wanted to see what it would take to change the time. Fifteen minutes of exploration and I believe I found what I was looking for."

Sarah anxiously took her husband's hand in hers.

"When I was studying my vision, I thought about what it would look like several minutes from now. I chose a time that was only five minutes from the present. I then imagined that our time was represented by a line, much like what Quinn explained earlier. I then focused on the sun and I tried to accelerate it until it was flying across the sky."

"Did it work?" Steve asked.

"Let me finish," Luther scolded. "I looked up in the sky and stared at the sun. I concentrated with every fiber of my being. I wanted that sun to move."

"Let me guess," Steve interrupted again. "It didn't."

Sarah smacked his arm. "He asked you to be quiet, so be quiet!"

"Sorry."

"Steve was right. It didn't work. However, what I should mention is that when I tried to adjust the time, I felt as though something was pushing me back. Some force was blocking me. No matter how hard I pushed against the barrier, it refused to buckle. I wasn't strong enough."

Steve frowned. "Wait a moment. You were holding a jorii. Won't that amplify a person's jhorun to wizarding levels? You should have had enough power to do it!"

Luther nodded. "The joriis don't work like that. Away from Lentari, a jorii will allow a Lentarian access to their jhorun. If the user were Lentarian, standing on Lentarian soil, their jhorun would be amplified. It doesn't work both ways. In this situation, the jorii is allowing my jhorun to work once more."

"So, are you saying we should move this operation to Lentari?" Steve asked. "If the jorii is only allowing your jhorun to work, and if you just happened to be on Lentari, do you think your jhorun would be strong enough to change the portal's time frame?"

Luther shook his head. "No. It wouldn't make any difference. My jhorun's nature prevents it from being amplified."

The room fell silent once more.

"What do you mean?" Steve finally said. "You're saying your jhorun can't be amplified? That doesn't make any sense."

Luther was silent as he considered the easiest way to explain his point. "Forgive me, but I will use an analogy from this timeline and this world. Let's say you have a gun."

"Luther!" Cora gasped, horrified.

"I'm not planning on ever buying one, my dear," Luther gently explained to his wife, "I'm using it as reference only. Now, as I was saying, let's say I have a gun. My jhorun is the bullets. As you know, most guns hold six bullets. The bullets have to be the correct caliber in order to work with the gun. Are you with me so far?"

Steve nodded.

Luther held up the jorii. "This jorii amplifies your bullets and now they are much larger than what can fit in the gun. Can you use the bullets now?"

Surprised, Steve nodded. "I get it. No matter how much your jhorun is enhanced, for the type of task it performs, your jhorun will only recognize a certain portion. Is that it?"

Luther nodded. "Precisely."

"What about two gatekeepers?" a quiet voice asked.

Everyone slowly turned to stare at Mina, who was perched daintily on her chair. Her thin frame looked tiny in comparison to the large overstuffed arm chair. Her eyes had settled on her brother's.

"I have nowhere near the experience as you, brother," Mina hesitantly began, "but I have demonstrated that I share your jhorun. Could I help?"

Luther quietly studied his sister for a few moments before

wordlessly rising to his feet. He held out a hand and waited for Mina to take it. He pulled her to her feet and together they ascended the stairs.

"Two gatekeepers," Steve breathed with excitement. "There's still a chance to get home yet!"

Several minutes later, they heard parts of an excited conversation filtering down from the floors above. Steve anxiously looked at his wife. In a flash, both were on their feet and rushing for the stairs, prompting the rest of the group to follow.

"Did you do it?" Steve apprehensively asked. "Were you two successful?"

Luther shook his head no, but he was also smiling. "We were unable to modify the portal's place in time..."

"But we could feel the barrier fluctuate," Mina excitedly finished for him.

"We couldn't modify it, but at least we know it is possible," Luther added. "Mina claims it was my imagination, but I will swear that the sun actually trembled in the sky."

"How are you even able to look at the sun and not be blinded?" Steve asked, frowning.

"This was a vision," Luther explained with a smile. "I was not physically present, so therefore my eyesight was undamaged."

"Then why are you smiling?" Steve wanted to know.

"When I was by myself," Luther slowly explained, as though he was addressing a group of children, "I was unable to touch the time barrier. Now, with Mina, we felt it was possible. The time barrier fluctuated when we pushed at it. Don't you understand? With one gatekeeper it was impossible. With an additional gatekeeper we learned that it *became* possible. We still weren't strong enough to modify it but at least we know we're on the right track."

"The right track?" Steve repeated, incredulous. "How can you say that? You're suggesting you need another gatekeeper when there aren't any more. You said so yourself. You don't have any more family, Luther."

"You're mistaken," Luther softly told him. "I have *you*."

"Me? I'm no gatekeeper. I'm a fire thrower."

"I didn't think I was a gatekeeper, either, until you encouraged me to try," Mina's quiet voice told him. "Thanks to you, I now know I'm a gatekeeper, just like my brother."

Steve held up a hand. "Hold up. The difference here is I already know what my jhorun is. It's not as if I haven't been able to do anything and have always wondered what it could be. No, I'm sorry to say I won't be able to help you there."

"So you were a fire thrower ever since you were born?" Luther casually asked.

"No. I was given my jhorun once we stepped foot on Lentari. You know that. I told you."

"You're part Lentarian," Sarah added. "It stands to reason you might have the family jhorun but don't know it."

"I think I'd know if I was," Steve informed her, growing defensive.

Sarah took a deep breath and refrained from ordering her jhorun to physically knock her stubborn husband across the room. She grasped his hands and pulled him close.

"What they're trying to say is that you'll never know until you try. You are Luther's great-great-grandson. The gatekeeper jhorun seems to pass through to future generations. Are you trying to tell me that it isn't worth your time to try?"

Steve sighed. "Fine. What do I have to do, Luther?"

Sarah headed for the stairs. She hooked her left arm through Cora's, and her right through AnnaBelle's, and pulled the two women along with her. The rest of the group followed them down.

"Clear your mind," Luther began, pulling another chair over to the immense closed doors leading into the master bedroom. He placed a hand on the frame and waited for Steve and Mina to copy him. "There must be no distractions. If a thought appears in your mind, then don't try to block it. Allow it to come. You will find that most thoughts, if left unchecked, will leave just as quickly as they come. Once your mind reaches that state, you should be able to visualize where the portal leads."

"Meaning a vision will appear in my head," Steve guessed.

Luther nodded. "That's right. Once you have the picture, you should get a feeling of being in control. By that, I mean you should now be able to mentally push the image and see it move. Once you're at that state then, and only then, do we address time. What you'll have to do is find a way to have time represented in your vision. You can try a timeline, such as Quinn suggests. In my vision it was the movement of the sun. However you choose to let it form, determine what it'll take to modify time. Accelerate the sun, move an X across a line, whatever works. For this exercise you should use the physical timeline paradigm. Let the line form. That's what you'll give to your jhorun. Your natural jhorun, that is. Once your jhorun has something to reference, you'll more than likely feel the barrier I was referring to before. Whenever you try to push time forward, that force will push back."

"What if Quinn's line analogy doesn't work for me?" Steve asked. "What should I do then?"

"It'll work," Luther assured him. "That's why our first attempt lasted so long. I was trying everything I could think of to get time represented in such a way that I could relate to it. Mister Quinn's illustration allowed me to do just that, only for me, my jhorun latched on to the sun and its movement across the sky. I think you'll just have to see what works best for you. Hopefully it'll be something like Quinn's illustration."

Steve sat back in his chair and closed his eyes, all without breaking contact with the portal. Luther and Mina did the same.

Thirty seconds later Steve heard Luther grunt satisfactorily. "I am ready."

"I'm not," Mina immediately told him. "I'm not there yet."

"Dude, I don't even have a picture yet," Steve complained.

"Fear not, Steve," Luther assured him. "We will wait for you."

A few minutes later, Mina was ready. Scowling, Steve tried to quiet his mind, as he was instructed, but it was a losing battle. Didn't Luther say to not block any errant thoughts but, instead, to allow them to come?

It wasn't working.

The errant thoughts were coming, no doubt about it, but they wouldn't leave him alone. What would happen if this didn't work? What does Aislinn look like in his time? Would Caradoc still be alive? Would Pryllan know that she had died in another time?

"Steve," Luther's voice cut in. "Are you having any luck?"

"None whatsoever."

"Try taking a nap!" Sarah's voice called up from below.

Steve's eyes snapped opened. "A nap? Really?"

When no answer was forthcoming, Steve shrugged. What could it hurt to try? Since both Luther and Mina were now waiting patiently for him to catch up, the least he could do is try his wife's suggestion.

Steve spun his chair around so that he could lean back, rest his head, and still maintain physical contact by wedging his hand in between the chair and the frame. Comfortable, and much more relaxed, Steve felt himself drift off. He briefly wondered what sort of prank Sarah would play on him if he were to actually doze off.

One by one the thoughts bouncing around his head started to disappear. Sighing contentedly, Steve waited to see what would happen next. When the last thought vanished, namely the question about whether or not Pryllan's father would be alive in their time, an image formed. Steve was so surprised he almost opened his eyes.

"I'll be damned," Steve muttered. "I didn't see that one coming."

"Is it working?" Luther's gentle voice asked. "Can you see anything?"

"Yep. I'm looking at the path in the forest, the same one Sarah and I have used a bunch of times."

"Excellent. Just a moment. Mina and I will join you there."

"You will? How?"

"You'll see. We're tuning in now…"

Steve felt another presence in the woods. He couldn't see anyone else. Heck, for that matter, he couldn't see himself. Having never had an out-of-body experience, Steve could only imagine what he was supposed to be feeling. Shock and amazement, he decided, was high on the list.

This is weird, Steve thought to himself.

No more so than seeing someone light their hand on fire, Luther mentally said to him. *Mina, are you here?*

Aye. I am here.

Are we ready to try again?

Aye. I am ready.

Steve, are you ready?

Uh, sure. Let's take a crack at this. What do you need me to do?

Do you remember what I told you about visualizing time? Try to either imagine time as a line, or if that doesn't work, see what you can use as a reference to the passage of time.

Yeah, sure. Easier said than done.

I need you to do that for me now. Once all three of us are in agreement and are in harmony with one another, then we will be facing the same time barrier and collectively we should be able to push against it.

Before, were you and Mina looking at the same image? Steve wanted to know.

No, Mina answered. *Luther pictured the sun. I watched water flowing over the waterfall.*

Steve sighed. *Okay. I'll see what I can come up with. Better give me a minute.*

We'll wait, Luther's voice told him in his mind. *Let us know when you're ready.*

Right. Geez, no pressure. What the hell. I can do this. Give me a moment.

Steve thought back to Quinn's explanation of the timelines. It really was a simple way to describe time, Steve decided. Those lines, with all the Xs he added, had been a clear and precise way to describe just how mucked up their original timeline had become. Battles, skirmishes, alliances … all were nothing but points of time on a long line that stretched off to infinity. Could he imagine that he, along with Luther and Mina, were nothing more than another X on a line that was slowly ticking forward, like the second hand on a watch?

His focus on the mental scene was gently pulled to the side, until he was facing the nearby trees. Steve angrily shook his head. How were trees supposed to help him?

He refocused his attention on the path in the woods.

Once again, his attention was pulled up and to the left until he was looking at a large pine tree that stretched upward for at least a hundred feet.

As he watched the trees gently swaying in the breeze, Steve realized that watching the trees was something that could show the passage of time. It could grow larger, it could shed its needles during the seasons, and it could even be cut down.

I'm looking at a tree, Steve announced. *It's not perfect, but it'll work.*

A tree? You're looking at a tree and not a line? Luther was silent as he considered. *Very well. We may each have different visions but this should still work. Now, we all need to try and accelerate time. Mina, increase the flow the water. Steve, umm, what are you supposed to do? Make the tree grow?*

It was swaying earlier, Steve told him.

That will do. Is it swaying now?

Yes.

Then you must make it sway faster.

Easier said than done. How, exactly?

Try to give the tree a mental push.

I did. Nothing happened.

Did you feel any sort of resistance?

It felt like I was trying to push a brick wall, Steve told him.

Steve felt Luther's excitement.

Well done, Steve!

Well done? The damn thing didn't move. You don't offer congratulations for that.

That resistance you felt is the barrier.

Oh. What now?

Collectively we will all push against our barriers at the same time. In essence you are using my strength and Mina's to move the tree. For Mina, you and I are going to help affect the flow of water. And for me, you...

Yeah, yeah, Steve cut in. *We're moving the sun. We got it. Let's give this a try.*

Very well. Mina, Steve, we're going to focus all our attention, all our energy, on the barrier. Pretend you're standing directly behind the barrier and give it a mental push, as though a door inside your home is closed and all it needs is a push to open it.

My barrier is a tree, not a door, Steve pointed out.

It's the same principle. Go on, give it a try.

Steve focused his attention and thought about the tree. He imagined he was standing directly in front of it and tried giving it a mental push. The tree didn't give him the slightest indication that it had been affected. He cleared his mind and tried again. Nothing.

Switching tactics, Steve pushed his vision of the tree to the side and brought up an image that infuriated him to no end: waiting in line at a restaurant drive-thru. The car ahead of him was, for whatever reason, holding up the line. Steve imagined he was sitting in his truck and for once, was allowed to throw his truck in gear and push the offending vehicle out of the way.

This time there was no denying the time barrier. Something was pushing him back. There was no way the little hybrid car in front of him would keep from being pushed away from the window. In his drive-thru truck scenario, the driver in front of him had thrown his car into reverse and slammed on the gas.

Steve scowled and stamped down on the accelerator. His truck lurched, pushing the small car a few feet forward.

It's working! Luther's excitedly told him. *It's moving!*

Steve concentrated harder. He willed the truck to push the errant vehicle out of the way. He felt the barrier slip a few more notches as the car in his drive-thru scenario was forced another few feet away from the cashier's window. He brought back the image with the tree. It was swaying faster! Not much, but it did look like a healthy breeze was blowing.

Luther's voice spoke again.

On the count of three we are going to all stop pushing. One, two, three!

Steve mentally took his foot off his truck's accelerator just as he allowed the drive-thru scenario to vanish.

Wizards be damned! It's correcting itself!

What?

We should awaken. We must inform the others.

Wait! Inform me first! What the hell just happened?

Luther and Mina's presence faded from his mind. The tree vanished, followed shortly by the entire vision of the forest path. Steve grunted and groggily sat up in his chair. He yawned and rubbed his eyes. He cast a worried look at Luther, who was staring at him.

"Oh, man. Tell me I didn't just dream all of that."

Luther gave him a sad smile. "You didn't, my friend. We were able to modify the time barrier."

"Then why do you look so sad? We did it! We changed the portal's time! This should be a cause for celebration!"

"On the contrary, all we did was adjust the portal's time by no more than ten seconds."

"But we did move it," Steve argued. "I don't care how you look at it. It's good news."

"Did you do it?" Sarah excitedly asked from the ground floor. "Did I hear that right?"

"Sarah," Luther called, "could you bring everyone up here? We have some news."

Less than five minutes later everyone was crowded around the master bedroom doors once more. Steve looked at Luther and indicated the group. "You're the gatekeeper. You understand it better than anyone else. You tell them."

"Very well. We were successful, only —"

Luther trailed off as he was drowned out by Sarah's whoop of joy, Lissa's squeal of excitement, and Quinn's victorious shout.

"Let me finish. It worked, only not by much."

"What do you mean?" Sarah asked, her joy quickly evaporating. "How far were you able to change it?"

"About ten seconds," Steve answered. He frowned at Luther. "I don't care what he says. I think it's a good thing."

"Did you not see how difficult it was to accomplish?" Luther argued. "The three of us could barely change it, and that was only for a few seconds. We need to push it forward by over a hundred years! At the rate we were pushing, we would run out of strength long before we were anywhere close to where we needed it to be."

"So you're saying we need a fourth," Steve guessed. "Is that it?"

"A fourth what? Gatekeeper? You may have noticed that we don't have one. There are no more in Lentari."

In less than sixty seconds the entire group had gone from joyous celebration to utter hopelessness.

Cora gave a quiet cough and cleared her throat. "Perhaps I could help?"

Luther shook his head. He had risen from his chair and was irritably pacing around the top floor.

"You're not Lentarian," he angrily told his wife. "You wouldn't be able to do anything. We need another gatekeeper. Do you understand that? I knew we potentially had two, with myself and Steve. My sister's arrival was an uncalculated surprise, and a most welcome one, but believe me when I say that there are no more."

"There is one you're overlooking," Cora quietly insisted. She was standing, motionless, with her hands clasped together in front of her. Cora watched as her husband came to a halt directly in front of her. Luther took her hands in his.

"Dearest, you must be mistaken. You know of no one from Lentari. The only gatekeepers that exist happen to be in this very room, nowhere else. Do you understand?"

Cora nodded. "Perfectly. There are four gatekeepers in this room."

Confused, Luther looked at Steve, then Mina, and finally back at his wife. "I do not understand."

Sarah's eyes lit up and she clapped her hands excitedly as she bounced up and down. "Oh! Oh! I know!"

Cora smiled warmly at her. She nodded.

"Cora's pregnant!" Sarah announced to the room. She smiled at Luther. "There's your fourth gatekeeper. Cora's baby has Lentarian blood. Your blood, Luther. Just like Steve turned out to be a gatekeeper, so will this baby!"

Luther had sunk back into his chair as he stared at his wife. "Is it true? Are you pregnant?"

Cora nodded happily. "I've had my suspicions, but I wasn't sure until earlier today. I have been waiting for the right opportunity to say something. I guess I couldn't ask for a better time than now."

"The baby's jhorun isn't going to be that strong," Steve

pointed out. "Are you sure this will work?"

"The level of jhorun matters not," Luther answered. "As you yourself pointed out, Steve, your natural jhorun, your gatekeeper jhorun, has been reduced in power due to the amount of Lentarian blood in you. You still have it, but it is very weak. Despite that, you were still able to help modify the portal. The added strength from a fourth gatekeeper will tip the scales in our favor."

Steve spun in his chair until he had wedged his hand up against the door frame.

"Let's find out, shall we?"

Chapter 14 — No Time Like the Present

We had that sun *flying* across the sky," Steve told his wife while the others listened closely. He smiled again as he remembered what had happened in his drive-thru scenario. Thanks to the added strength of a fourth gatekeeper, his truck had morphed into a retro muscle car with well over six hundred horses under the hood. He'd rammed the car that had been holding up the line so hard that he embedded it in the building across the street.

Once the barrier was gone, they were easily able to push the portal's time forward. In fact, it was as if someone hit the fast-forward button on the vision. They collectively watched the sky go dark as the sun set, then in only a matter of minutes it brightened as the new day started. Flexing their mental muscle, they pushed harder and watched the scene flicker between day and night so fast it became a blur.

As before, once they stopped modifying the portal's

time it would slowly revert back to its original preset. Their window of opportunity would only be about five seconds. That meant Steve would have to help get the portal tuned to his own time, and once he released his hold, he'd have less than five seconds to hurry through.

As Luther explained, Sarah brought up a very good point, silencing everyone on the spot.

"How will we know when you guys have hit the correct time on the portal? If you're moving time that fast, couldn't you accidentally exceed the right time and end up going too far forward?"

Steve, Mina, and Cora all looked expectantly at Luther.

"That'll be the difficult part," Luther admitted. "The only thing we can do is slow the passage of time and watch the events transpire, or we could determine how many nights must pass in order to be at the correct time. Then we could count how many days and nights as they pass by."

"That sounds very time consuming," Quinn observed. "May I make a suggestion?"

Steve nodded. "You've got the floor, professor."

"I'm sorry?"

"Forget it. What's on your mind?"

"One of you ought to change the portal's destination. Point the portal at something that you can easily follow through time."

Steve nodded as he looked over at his ancestor. "That could work. What do you think would be the best thing to watch?"

The schoolmaster was ready with an answer. "The portal we all fell in. That way you could theoretically watch us fall in again and since Steve was the last one to go through it, once you see him go in, you'll know you've arrived at the right place. And then…"

"And then Luther would have the power to change the portal back to where it's supposed to be pointing," Steve finished. He grinned at their resident scholar. "Well done, Quinn!"

"Remember the five-second window," Luther said.

"That means we all have to get ourselves through the

portal as quickly as possible," Sarah surmised. "And then get out of the way because Steve will have to jump through in order to make it."

Luther was nodding. "That's right. When do you want us to start?"

Steve looked over at Lissa, then Quinn, and then finally at his wife.

"I'm ready to go home, Luther. You and Cora have a long life ahead of you here. Cecil, that goes for you and AnnaBelle, too. As for us, we belong back in our own time. I'd like to go home. Now, please."

Lissa nodded. "Me, too."

Quinn put a friendly hand on Lissa's shoulder. "I am in total agreement."

Sarah's eyes instantly welled up. She walked over to Cora and embraced her. "That means we have to say goodbye. I hate goodbyes."

Cora's eyes teared up as well. "It warms my heart to know that you and Steve will lead such a wonderful life together. I will cherish all the time that I have spent with you. With both of you." She pulled Steve in for a hug, too. "To think that you are my descendant! I'm willing to wager no one has ever been able to embrace their great-great-grandson before."

Steve hugged her back. "I'll never look at family trees the same way again. Thank you for all you've done, Cora. And you, Luther."

"This has been an experience I will never forget," Luther told him. "Thank you for helping complete my mission. Thank you for giving me hope when I thought there was none. And most importantly, thanks for breaking me out of jail."

Steve snorted. "Anytime. Thank you for being a cool great-great-grandpa."

Luther groaned, shook his head, and punched him on the arm. "You take care of him, Miss Sarah. I sense he's prone to getting into trouble."

Sarah wiped the tears from her eyes. "You have no idea."

Steve looked around the room and noticed that one of their friends was absent. "I was really hoping Rosamund would be here. I wanted to personally thank her for all she's done for Sarah. Do you think we could get word to her before we go? She's done so much that I think she at least deserves a chance to say goodbye."

As if on cue they all heard a wagon approach the house. Luther hurried to a window and watched Rosamund arrive in her buckboard. From the looks of the glossy sheen that was on the horses' coats, Luther guessed Rosamund had them galloping most of the way from town. The tiny owner of the Silver Spike Saloon carefully climbed out of her wagon, followed shortly thereafter by a second person.

"Who is it?" Cora asked, coming to stand next to her husband. She spotted the second person. "Who's that?"

Luther quickly descended the stairs and met Rosamund at the front door. After a few moments, they could hear the three people below start up the stairs.

"Allow me to introduce someone," Luther announced, as they arrived on the top floor. "This is Ruskin. He's been working as a carpenter here in town for the last year. Ruskin is Lentarian and, I believe, from your time as well."

The man was in his mid-thirties, Steve judged. He was short, about the same height as Sarah, and lean. He was wearing thin wire-rimmed glasses and had just pushed them up the bridge of his nose as he shyly looked around the room. Steve could see that he was quiet, timid, and afraid to look anyone in the eye.

"Ruskin, I take it you fell through a portal and ended up here?" Steve asked, using the friendliest tone of voice he could come up with.

Ruskin nodded his head. "Aye."

"How long ago?" Steve asked, curious.

"I've been here for a year and a half," Ruskin quietly told them. "I've been working as a carpenter in the local mill. It is very mundane work. Are you really the fire thrower?" Ruskin quietly asked Steve as he turned to face him.

Steve ignited his right hand in response.

Ruskin quietly sank down on the closest chair and let out a long breath.

"Are you returning back home? Have you found a way?

Will you take me with you? Please? I don't want to stay here anymore."

Steve nodded. He indicated Sarah, Quinn, and Lissa.

"We all are going home. All of us. As cool as this place is, and as nice as the people are, I don't want to stay here. I want to go home, back to my own time. I take it you're ready to leave?"

Ruskin nodded his head.

"I don't like it here. The people are too rude and too easily angered. I miss my shop. I miss my tools. I miss my trees."

"Then this is your lucky day, pal," Steve told him.

"You're getting ready to leave?" Rosamund's indignant response came. "Without saying goodbye first?"

Sarah approached the tiny woman and enveloped her in an embrace. "Steve had literally just asked where you were not ten minutes ago. He said that he really wanted to see you again and thank you for all that you've done for me."

"I don't know what to say to that."

Steve approached. "You don't have to say anything. You took my wife in and kept her safe when she didn't have any place to go. If it wasn't for you, I don't think Sarah would have survived."

"Oh, don't be so dramatic," Sarah scolded her husband. She smiled moments later. "I am thankful for everything you've done. I'll never forget you."

"See that you don't, dear," Rosamund primly told her as she dabbed at her eyes again. "And it was my pleasure."

Steve looked around the room and then eyed Luther. He then smiled at Mina and looked over at Cora.

"Are we ready to do this?"

The two gatekeepers nodded, while the mother of the newest gatekeeper also nodded. Steve pulled four chairs over to the door frame and settled down into one of them, wedging his arm between the chair and the frame like he had done last time. He looked over at Sarah as he leaned back in the chair.

"Once we get the portal on the right time then I'll give you the signal. Wait for us to say something. When we tell you to, activate the portal."

"Understood," Quinn answered.

Lissa nodded. She was ready. She turned to look at Ruskin, who, even though he avoided eye contact, nodded his readiness. Sarah positioned herself near the portal's surface. Lissa, Quinn, and Ruskin joined her. Sarah suddenly cleared her throat.

"You know what? The four of us will have plenty of time to make it through. You're the one that'll be in a rush."

Steve nodded as he shrugged. "That's not... that's... Okay, fine. Good point. You guys get through, then just get out of the way, okay?"

Everyone nodded.

"All right then. Here we go."

The room went silent as Luther, Mina, Steve, and Cora all leaned back in their chairs and closed their eyes.

"I'm ready," Luther instantly reported.

"I'm not," Mina answered, with a frown.

"Nor am I. Cool your jets there, Sparky."

Luther smiled. "Sparky? I will miss your terms of endearment, Steve."

"Mmm-hmm. Cora? How are you doing?"

"I'm ready," Cora's soft voice announced.

"Ah. Now I am ready," Mina told them.

"That was quick," Steve grumbled. "So, I'm the odd man out here? How could Cora have possibly become ready faster than me?"

Sarah opened her mouth to say something, but Steve instantly raised a hand and pointed it right at her, without opening his eyes.

"Nope. Zip it. Don't say a word."

Sarah stifled a laugh.

Steve sighed contentedly as he waited for his mind to clear. One by one, the thoughts disappeared and his mind quieted. After a few seconds of complete silence, the image formed.

Excellent, Luther's thought said. *Are we all here?*

I am here, Mina confirmed.

We're here, Cora's quiet thought announced.

Steve? Are you ready?

I'm ready, Luther. Let's do this.

Very well. Let us proceed. The first thing we need to do is change the portal's destination to that of the interdimensional portal. If you will all just observe, I will take care of this.

The image of the path in the woods went dark, replaced moments later by a familiar wooded scene showing a familiar ring of ferns. Inside the ring was the infamous interdimensional portal, still gently swirling, floating just a few inches off the ground.

There we go, Luther excitedly thought. *I didn't think I'd see that again. Now, let us all do whatever we need to do in order to visualize the time barrier. This image will be different for each person.*

Steve's drive-thru scenario instantly appeared. He eyed the two scenes, choosing to focus his attention on the image of himself sitting behind the wheel of his truck, waiting impatiently for his turn to arrive at the cashier's window.

Now, all together, Luther's voice thought, *we push forward.*

Steve's truck transformed into the retro muscle car and he slammed his foot down on the gas. The huge sports car's engine roared to life and the car surged forward, ramming the much smaller vehicle in front of him. The tiny little hybrid car holding up the line was steadily pushed out of the way. He watched as the hybrid's reverse lights lit up and tried to push back, but thanks to the collective might of all four gatekeepers, Steve's sports car easily moved forward.

He noted with surprise that the image of the horizontal portal was changing. The ferns were starting to grow right before his eyes. The sky darkened, then brightened, then darkened again. The tempo increased until the sky had become a blur of color.

If you will permit me, Luther's voice broke in, *I will control when to slow everything down. For now, I'm guessing we are several months ahead. Please sit back, make yourselves comfortable, and allow the scene to play out.*

The scene stayed the same for close to ten minutes, with the only discernible change being the surrounding ferns and trees. Just as he watched the ferns grow to enormous size, they were then reduced to tiny nubs barely poking up out of the ground. The only thing Steve could think of was maybe some sort of animal might have feasted on the plants. Steve then watched it happen once, then twice, then several more times.

The portal then disappeared, and some type of rock formation appeared in its place.

What's that?

The scene in the woods stabilized.

The portal has been sealed, Luther told them. *It means we have overshot your destination. We should pull the barrier back toward us for a little bit until the portal reappears. Then we can push more slowly until we figure out the best place to stop.*

Agreed. Mister Spock, you have the conn.

He felt Luther's confusion. *What?*

Never mind. You're in control. Do what you have to do.

Very well.

They all felt the scene reverse itself and start moving backwards at an accelerated pace. After a few moments, the mound of rocks disappeared and became the portal once more.

There it is, Steve announced.

We know, Luther dryly told him. *We see it, too. We'll stop it here and start pushing again. Slowly this time.*

The scene froze in place and they all again pushed at the barrier, this time not as hard. The scene began moving forward.

Keep going, Steve told Luther. *We're not there yet. We'll have to keep watching.*

Very well. Moving on.

The scene shifted forward. There were about thirty seconds of silence until they caught another blur. This time Luther reversed the image and then proceeded forward even more slowly. It was Lissa. They watched the girl approach the portal holding some type of plant in her hand. She stumbled forward as she pushed her way through the large ferns, disappearing just after she threw up her hands in surprise. The plant she had been holding ended up being flung away from the portal and out of the scene.

*That was Lissa. We know she went in right before Sarah. We're *close. Go even slower.*

Luther complied, slowing the vision's progress even further. After a few more moments they saw a group of soldiers appear and poke the portal with a large pole. Another few seconds of silence passed before Shardwyn appeared and began inspecting the anomaly. Maelnar showed up moments later. Before he knew it, Steve was watching himself console Sarah. Then he saw himself standing alone, staring, aghast, at the portal and gesturing angrily to someone outside the picture. The scene jumped forward again and Steve was gone.

That's it, Steve confirmed. *If I'm not there, then that means I just went through.*

How far forward do you want to go?

Right about there ought to do, Steve told him. *At the rate it's been progressing I'd say we're three or four days after the point in which I jumped in.*

The scene stabilized and they were once again watching the gently swirling mists within the interdimensional portal.

"We're there," Steve quietly informed the group. "Activate it."

Sarah practically flew forward as she rushed toward the key sticking out of the portal's keyhole. She carefully twisted it one full revolution, pulled the crystal key out, and then stepped back a few paces. Sarah handed the key to Luther and hugged his prone form one last time, before doing the same to Cora. She pulled AnnaBelle in as the portal fuzzed out and became a scene showing the interdimensional portal and the surrounding forest.

"Thank you all so much," Sarah told them as she smiled at Cecil and AnnaBelle. She turned to Cora, who was sitting in her chair with her eyes closed, gave her a fleeting smile, and hurried through the portal.

Lissa and Quinn smiled at their hosts and then they, too, hurried through.

"You'd better get going, Ruskin," Cecil advised the quiet man. "If you're going then you need to get moving."

The shy woodworker hurried through the portal without saying a word.

I owe you all my life, Steve solemnly thought as he stared around the familiar forest. *You've given us our lives back. How do we ever repay you?*

You don't, Luther thought at him. *It's what family does, Steve. Go now. Go home. Be happy.*

Cora, take care of him, Steve instructed, directing his thought toward his great-great-grandmother. *And make sure he spoils you rotten.*

He felt Cora giggle. *Be certain of it, Steve. Give Sarah my love.*

I will. Mina? Be safe. You're in good hands.

Thank you, came Mina's quiet thought.

Luther's voice sounded one last time as he started to reawaken his senses. *Remember, Steve. From the Earth to the Moon.*

What? What does that — ?"

Go! Hurry!

Steve's eyes snapped open. He gave a fleeting smile to those staying behind and bolted through the portal. When he turned to look behind, sadly, the portal wasn't there. All ties to the past were gone.

"Steve?" Sarah's voice called out. "Where are you?"

"I'm over here!" he answered. "I'm—whoa!"

He stumbled forward, flailing his arms. There was nothing in front of him except for the swirling mists of the interdimensional portal.

"Oh, *hell* no. This ain't happening." Steve bunched his legs and tried to jump over the portal.

"Steve?" Sarah pushed her way through the foliage. "Where'd you go?"

She arrived at the base of the portal and stared. He was stretched completely over the swirling mists. The tips of his shoes were digging into the dirt on one side of the portal while his entire weight rested on his fingertips on the opposite side. To Sarah it looked like the 'exhale' yoga position except there was nothing peaceful or serene about the situation.

"Don't just stand there!" Steve shouted. "Help me out of here!"

Quinn and Lissa appeared at Sarah's side.

"What goes on here?" a voice demanded. "No one is allowed here by order of the king. How did you …"

Sarah whirled around. Two soldiers of the king's royal

guards stood less than twenty feet away. "Help him!" Quinn shouted.

Without a blink, one guard leapt forward, wrapped his arms around Steve's waist, and wrenched him sideways. Together they tumbled to the ground a few feet from the portal. Steve landed on his back with the guard resting on his chest.

"Smooth move, my friend. I sure as hell didn't want to go through that thing again."

The guard hastily got to his feet and pulled Steve up with him. "Again? You've been … Wizards be damned! You're the fire thrower!"

The second guard jerked his head over to stare at Sarah. "Lady Sarah! We didn't recognize you in your costume! We were told you had fallen through the portal!"

"I did," Sarah confirmed as she smiled at the two guards. "We all did. We literally just made it back."

The first guard, the one who had prevented Steve from revisiting the past, grinned broadly and slapped his companion on the back. "Good tidings, indeed! We must notify the king immediately!"

Sarah held up a hand. "Stay here. We'll make sure everyone knows we're back. You guys can officially seal that thing up once and for all."

Both guards nodded, pleased. "It would be very much appreciated, Lady Sarah. Standing guard over an anomaly such as this is monotonous."

"No doubt," Steve quipped. "I'll personally see to it the king learns how your quick thinking prevented me from taking a second trip through that damn thing."

The soldier bowed. "You are too kind, Nohrin."

Steve pulled Sarah along as he walked away from the portal, anxious to put as much distance as possible between them and the one-way ticket back to the nineteenth century.

"Should we go to the castle?" Steve asked. "And why didn't you just teleport me away from that portal? I almost went back in!"

"The guard got to you first," Sarah explained. "It all happened so fast. I saw you about to go in, and was ready to push you away, when that guard pulled you away. I'm sorry. It's been a really long day."

Steve wrapped his arm around her as they walked. "No worries. So where do we head first?"

Sarah shook her head. "We're already in Capily. Lissa, Quinn, and Ruskin are all from these parts. We should make sure they get home."

"We seem to be missing the wood carver," Quinn remarked, looking around. "I guess he was anxious to get home. I can't say that I blame him."

"That's gratitude for you," Sarah grumbled, as she held out an arm. "First stop is the constable's office. All those who want to go should grab on."

Steve laid his hand over Sarah's and the others added their hands to the pile. Less than two seconds later, they were standing in front of a building directly facing the western shore. As the four of them gazed quietly at the solemn structure, the front doors opened. Constable Fensham stepped out, looked up, and saw four strangely dressed men and women. When his eyes found the youngest of them, Fensham fell to his knees.

Lissa ran, crying, to her father. She sank to her knees as well and wrapped her arms around him.

"My darling girl!" Fensham exclaimed, as he held her tight. "I thought I would never see you again! How ... what ... when...?"

"We just made it back, father," Lissa sobbed. "You will never believe what we had to go through."

The constable finally looked up at the remaining three members of the group. The woman was dabbing at her eyes with a delicate handkerchief while the two men smiled with approval.

"Father, allow me to present the Nohrin, Steve, and his wife, Lady Sarah. Quinn, like me, fell through the portal and had to be rescued. He used to be my teacher."

Constable Fensham's eyes shot open. "The missing schoolmaster! Mister Quinn, it's so good to see you again! And we have the Nohrin to thank? How splendid! I can't even begin to imagine how much courage it must have taken to do this. How can I ever repay you?"

Steve looked over at Sarah. "Ummm…"

"It was our pleasure," Sarah finally answered. "Lissa is a bright girl. I think the king will be pleased to hear how such a young girl can be so skilled with healing. Don't be too surprised if the king himself decides to oversee the rest of Lissa's education."

The teenage girl gasped with shock. "Do you really think so?"

"He will, if I have anything to say about it," Sarah vowed with a smile.

Fensham looked over at the former schoolmaster. "I'm sorry to say, Mister Quinn, that we have reassigned your quarters. However, there are vacant houses and we can assign one to you. Provided you still plan on resuming your duties at the school?"

Quinn smiled. "I would be delighted. I just need to get word to my parents, to let them know I'm safe."

Fensham nodded and held an arm out to encompass his office. "If you'll follow me, I will see to it that a message is sent."

"We're off to see the king," Sarah told the constable. A split second later her arms were full of teenager. Lissa gave Sarah a fierce hug.

"Thank you for everything, Sarah. You, too, Steve. I won't ever forget what the two of you have done for me. And, I won't ever forget that bath behind the house."

"What was that?" Fensham asked, his brow furrowed.

"What was that?" Sarah repeated, looking up at her husband.

Steve's face flushed red. "Not a damn thing happened, you tease," he reminded the girl. He looked over at his wife. "I swear."

Something collided with Steve and knocked him off his feet, sending him tumbling down onto the ground. It felt as though two steel bands had locked around his chest.

"Mikal!" Sarah exclaimed. "It's so good to see you! What are you doing here?"

The lanky teenager easily rolled to his feet and embraced

Sarah. "I haven't left Capily. As soon as I learned you and Steve had gone through the portal, I have been waiting for you to return."

Steve grunted as he rolled painfully to his feet. "You've been waiting here? For over two weeks?"

"I knew you'd come back," the prince told him, as he wiped his eyes with the back of a hand. "I just knew it."

"It wasn't easy, sport," Steve told him as he gave the affectionate youngster a slap on the back. "There was a time when I actually thought we wouldn't make it back."

"Only one time?" Sarah teased. She placed an arm around Mikal's shoulders as they turned to face Fensham's office. "There were more times than I care to admit."

Fensham and Lissa approached. The constable dropped to a knee and lowered his gaze.

"Your Highness. My apologies. I had completely forgotten you were here. I should have notified you the instant I learned that they had returned."

Mikal waved off the constable's apology. "Think nothing of it, Constable. I am just relieved that they are back safe and sound."

Lissa quietly cleared her throat.

Fensham briefly looked behind him, as if he had forgotten his daughter was there. "Ah. Lissa, come here. Kre'Mikal, this is my daughter, Lissa. Lissa, this is Kre'Mikal."

"Hello," Lissa shyly said, as she curtsied in front of the prince. A blush had formed and was rising steadily up the teenager's face.

Mikal took the girl's hand and raised it to his lips. "Hello. I don't think we've met before. I'm pleased to meet you, Lissa."

"Lissa is one of the people who came back with us," Steve helpfully supplied.

Mikal turned to Fensham. "That's right. You had mentioned your daughter was one of the portal's victims. I am relieved to see that she has returned safely," he formally told the constable. Mikal turned back to Lissa and looked at the hand he was still holding. "I would love to hear what happened when you fell through the portal."

Blushing furiously, Lissa smiled. "I would be delighted to

tell you all about it, Kre'Mikal."

"Please. Call me Mikal."

The three adults stared at one another, and without another word, Mikal and Lissa turned away. Steve cleared his throat loudly enough to cause Mikal to turn around.

"Oh, I see how we rate. A pretty girl bats her eyes at you and —"

"And what?" Sarah demanded. She frowned at her husband. "Would you care to finish that statement?"

"I was going to suggest Mikal should come to R'Tal with us. I'm sure his parents would like him back."

Fensham hurried to his daughter's side. "That's a good idea. Why don't we let the prince return home for a while? The poor lad has been waiting here for so long that I'm sure the Kri'yans have forgotten what their son looks like."

Mikal turned back to Lissa, who was still blushing. He sighed, brought Lissa's hand up to his mouth for another kiss, and let Fensham take his daughter's arm.

"You're right. I should get back home. Lissa, can I see you again? I would very much like to hear about what happened to you on the other side of that portal."

Lissa couldn't stop the smile from spreading across her face. "I would like that."

Sarah turned to Quinn, who had been watching the exchange between the prince and the teenager. She gave him a hug as well. "Good luck, Quinn. I'm sure we'll see each other again."

Quinn gave husband and wife a dramatic bow, complete with a sweep of his arm. "You have my eternal thanks, milady. Steve, I thank my lucky stars you arrived when you did at that griski cave. I shudder to think what would have happened."

Steve gave the schoolmaster's proffered arm a friendly shake. "It's my pleasure, pal. Until we meet again."

Sarah hooked one arm through Mikal's and the other through her husband's and together they walked a few paces away from the constable's office. "Care to tell me about this bath?"

Steve paled. "Nothing happened. I just had to heat some water for Mina."

"Oh. I just assumed Lissa would have been there, based on what she said."

"Um, she was."

Sarah raised an eyebrow. Now Mikal was frowning. "What bath?"

"It was nothing," Steve assured him. Then he frowned. "Why do I have to explain myself to you, sport? You don't even know Lissa. We do. I rescued her."

Sarah chuckled. "No need to get defensive, dear. I don't think Mikal was trying to take your girlfriend away from you."

"Hardy har har. I think she likes me, but that's it."

"Well, do you like her back?" Mikal hesitantly asked.

Dumbfounded, Steve pointed at Sarah. "Mikal, I'm married! To her! Geez, why are you trying to put me in the doghouse?"

"You like her," Sarah guessed. "Don't you? You can admit it."

Mikal's cheeks colored. "Well, she seems nice."

Steve snorted. "Right. Let me guess. I'm willing to bet you're going to be spending more time over here in Capily, aren't you?"

Mikal scuffed the ground. "I don't know. Maybe. Is that a problem?"

"We're not your guardians anymore," Sarah told him, eliciting a smile from the boy. "You don't have to convince us."

Mikal smiled. "Thank you."

"You have to convince your parents."

The prince's smile quickly vanished.

"It's their problem now," Steve happily told him. "They can figure it out."

"Did you really take a bath with her?" Mikal quietly asked.

"Absolutely not! I don't care what you heard, it didn't happen. That little snot is just trying to get me into trouble."

Sarah gave him a sly smile. "Mm-hmm. Alright, let's go see the king."

She envisioned one of her safe zones and teleported them to R'Tal, placing them directly before the open drawbridge leading in to the mighty castle. Several guards, in the process of interrogating a large family, paused as they looked over at them. Steve realized both he and Sarah were still dressed in nineteenth century clothing. Mikal had stepped behind Steve. Husband and wife returned the guard's frank stares, while Mikal remained concealed.

The closest guard approached and dropped his right hand to rest on the hilt of his sword. "State your business, friend. Who are you? What are you doing here?"

Steve smiled and stretched out his right hand as though to shake the guard's hand. He waited a few moments and then ignited it.

"Hi there. My name is Steve. Steve Miller. You might know me as the fire thrower. This lovely lady is Sarah, my wife."

All four guards gasped with shock. "Sir Steve! Lady Sarah! We had heard that you disappeared!"

One guard instantly turned around and bolted inside the castle.

"We did disappear," Steve confirmed. "We just made it back."

"What happened?" a second guard asked, genuinely curious. "Where did you go?"

Mikal stepped out from behind Steve and walked around his former bodyguard. The prince eyed the three guards, who instantly snapped to attention.

"Kre'Mikal. Our apologies. We didn't see you."

"We have business to discuss with my parents. Would you…" Mikal trailed off as a commotion sounded from somewhere within the depths of the castle. It sounded as though a herd of elephants were heading in their direction.

"I think it's about to get super noisy, pal," Steve told the friendly guard. "Why don't you help that poor man and his family out of the way? I think that they'd appreciate it."

The three guards quickly ushered the large family of seven to the side. "Please forgive us, Nohrin. You may pass."

Sarah smiled at them. "Why thank you, good sirs."

They only managed a dozen steps toward the interior of the castle, when a group of soldiers came barreling out of a side door and came to a stop before them. Leading the way was a familiar and very welcome sight. Steve's face split into a grin.

"Rhenyon! It's good to see you, buddy!"

Rhenyon stared at the three of them as though he was seeing them for the first time.

"Wizards be damned! It's true! You're back! Finally!"

Steve shrugged. "Sorry. Uh, due to circumstances that were damn near out of our control, we are just glad to be back. We were shooting for no more than three or four days later, but clearly, we misread the signs."

"Misread the signs?" Rhenyon repeated, puzzled. "What is that supposed to mean?"

The king and queen emerged from within the heart of the castle. Judging by the large number of soldiers scrambling to keep up, the Kri'yans must have dropped what they were doing and hurried outside. Mikal approached his parents as the guards hurriedly reformed their squadrons.

"Son!" Kri'Entu exclaimed, surprised. "I am pleased to see you home!"

The queen embraced her son, and, while still holding Mikal, gently turned him so that she could look at Sarah.

"We are so very relieved," Ny'Callé exclaimed as she released Mikal from her embrace. "We all are. What happened?"

"What happened?" the king echoed at the same time.

Steve pointed toward the castle's interior. "Do you mind if we find a place to sit down? It's been a very long day."

"Of course, of course. We will adjourn to the Antechamber. Commander, you are welcome to join us."

Rhenyon smiled. "Don't mind if I do, Your Majesty."

Once they were all seated Steve looked straight at the king and cleared his throat. "Now would be the time to seal that portal, Your Majesty."

The king nodded. "Consider it done. We were waiting … hoping to hear from you two before we did that. We didn't want to eliminate all chances of your return."

"We didn't use the portal to get back," Sarah told him. "That's what took so long. We couldn't. It was a one-way portal."

"Created by Zevern the Inept," Steve automatically said.

The queen's eyes widened and she covered her mouth, but was unable to prevent the giggle from escaping. The king leaned back in his chair and smirked.

"Zevern the Inept, is it? How odd. I always thought it was Zevern the Magnificent."

"Not even close," Steve assured them. "He really didn't know what he was doing when he created that portal."

"Why did he create it?" Rhenyon asked.

"That was how Luther Miller arrived in our world," Steve answered. "That's how they linked your world to ours."

"What of the villagers that fell through, besides the two of you?" the queen wanted to know. "Were you able to find them?"

"We found four. One elected to stay behind while the other three returned with us."

"And the girl?" the king worriedly asked. "Please tell me the girl isn't the one who remained behind."

"That would be Lissa," Sarah answered. "And no, she wasn't. Steve found her on Lentari."

"What?" Kri'Entu demanded. "I thought the portal was linked to your world."

Steve and Sarah took turns relating the adventure, from the moment each of them went through the portal, discovering they'd traveled back to their home world and also back in time. There were odd discrepancies in each traveler's experience: Melvyn the Lentarian, who was elected sheriff, and held an entire town in fear; Steve's realization that he was meeting his own great-great-grandfather; and the way they worked together to open the two-way portal and straighten out the timeline.

"The trickiest part was making certain we didn't do something in the past that would affect the future—well, the present now. We still don't know what we might have changed," Steve said.

"Seeing dragons and dwarves make an alliance was one of those things," Sarah reminded. "The ceremony was actually attended by Kri'Calin and the queen."

"You met Kri'Calin?" the king breathed. "His rule was

considered one of our kingdom's best. I am envious of your adventures."

The Antechamber's doors opened. Two unusually quiet figures, walking side by side, approached. Maelnar instantly dropped to one knee while Shardwyn snatched his hat off his head and began wringing it between his wrinkled hands.

Kri'Entu raised an eyebrow and looked over at Steve. The king nodded, giving him permission to deal with the somber pair. Steve slowly stood and approached the two figures. "On your feet, my friend."

Maelnar looked up, hopeful. "Words cannot even to begin to describe the anguish I have suffered since you and Sarah fell into that terrible portal," the elderly dwarf began. "I offer my humblest apology. Shardwyn and I have promised to end all grievances between the two of us."

Shardwyn nervously cleared his throat. "Aye. Master Maelnar is quite correct. I haven't spent two weeks as miserably as I have since the time Maelnar bested me at a game of turkin in less than five moves."

"Turkin?" Steve repeated, looking around the room for an idea of what it could be.

"It's like chess," Mikal translated.

"Ah. Got it. Listen, Shardwyn. I promised myself that if I ever got back here, I was personally going to make the two of you bury the hatchet. As it turns out, it looks like our disappearance has done that. Since Sarah and I went through that portal, has either of you raised your voice to the other?"

Surprised, Maelnar looked up at Shardwyn just as the wizard looked down at the dwarf.

"Er, no, Sir Steve," Shardwyn admitted.

Maelnar nodded. "I would concur. We were so worried about what horrors you might face that we didn't give our grievances a passing thought."

"Continue like this and you'll have no problem with me. Will the two of you agree, in front of the king and queen, myself and Sarah, Mikal, and Rhenyon? If so, you will be held to your word. Do you understand?"

Maelnar bowed. "Of course. And I hereby agree."

The wizard bowed low. "As do I."

Maelnar nodded. "I do believe it's time that I returned home to Foronlir."

Shardwyn nodded. "I will accompany you to the portal room, my friend."

Maelnar bowed. "Appreciated, my friend."

Wizard and dwarf walked companionably toward the Antechamber's main door and departed the room.

"They certainly look chummy," Steve observed. "It's starting to freak me out."

"They have become practically inseparable," Kri'Entu agreed, masking the smile that wanted to form.

Steve nodded. "Good. Hon? Are you ready to go home? I think we have earned a vacation."

"A very long vacation," Sarah agreed. "Wait. Wait a minute. What city did Maelnar say he was going back to?"

"Foronlir," Kri'Entu answered.

Steve blinked with surprise. "Didn't he say he was going home? Doesn't he live in Bohragg? I've never heard of Foronlir."

It was the king's turn to be confused. "Foronlir is his home. He's lived there for years."

"Really? What happened to Bohragg?"

"Foronlir is Bohragg's sister city," the queen informed them. "Usually when a dwarf clan grows too large, a second city is built."

"Foronlir is a Kla Guur city?" Steve eyed his wife. "That wasn't there in our time."

The king smiled. "Someday, when you have some time, I would very much like to hear as much as you can remember about what originally happened here. Before your visit to the past. I think it's absolutely fascinating."

"We will," Sarah promised. "Just not today. I'm sorry. I've been away from home for a very long time. I just want to get back to Idaho."

Both Kri'yans nodded. "Understood, Lady Sarah. You've earned your rest. Go now."

So, this is the point in time to which that portal

returned you?

Steve's head snapped up. *Pryllan?*

I have been wondering for a very long time if I had simply imagined our shared experiences. As you might have surmised by now, that was why I agreed to help Kahvel look for you when he reported a human had become lost. I wondered if you were the same human I had befriended all those years ago. It was the first time you met me, but not I you.

Steve smiled. Sarah gently nudged him in his ribs. "What's going on? Is it Pryllan?"

"Yes. Apparently, she's been waiting for us to get back."

"Ask her about her father," Sarah urged.

What about my sire?

"She heard you," Steve whispered.

Of course, I did. We're sharing senses. Surely you haven't forgotten that we sometimes do that?

About your father...

What about him?

Is he, uh, alive?

Ah. Now I understand the source of your confusion. Your return means that you will not have remembered anything that transpired during the last hundred twenty years. Am I correct?

Completely. Something tells me it isn't the same anymore. Just tell me. Is your father still alive?

Aye. I've been chatting with him while waiting for you to discover my presence. He accompanied us on our hunt for the red oskorlisk. You will have no recollection of that. He wants to talk to you.

He was with us when we were hunting the oskorlisk? Not in my original timeline.

I surmised as much. However, as far as I'm concerned, he accompanied us the one and only time we hunted the serpent. In fact, Caradoc was one of the dragons we competed against.

He was? Did we win?

Of course. It's still a bitter point of contention with him. Now that he knows you have returned, he wishes to

converse with you. In person.
Your father wants to talk to me? Oh, that's just great.

Epilogue

"He really was quite nice," Sarah remarked, as she and Steve appeared in front of their manor in Coeur d'Alene. Sarah stifled a yawn as she looked up at the huge house she had come to love so much. Her gaze swiveled over to her gardens, and she sighed wistfully. "I can't even begin to tell you how much I missed my English gardens."

Steve grunted noncommittally.

"I can definitely see where Pryllan gets her inquisitive nature. Caradoc wanted to know everything about our world. And, he wanted to know more about Lentari."

"He wanted to know more about the version of Lentarian history where he was killed," Sarah corrected. "If it wasn't for Pravara, we'd still be there answering questions."

Steve smiled. "I don't know how Pravara knew we needed a diversion, but she did. How she managed to get her grandfather interested in target practice I'll never know, but I am eternally grateful. Holy cow, babe. Is it good to be home or what?"

Exhaustion began to seep in. Sarah stretched her back

and had taken a step toward the stairs leading up to their front door when she paused. She slowly turned her head to look back at their exterior garage.

Steve caught her gaze and stared at the huge building, too. He hooked a thumb at the garage and looked back at his wife. "Weren't there four bays when we left, not six?"

Sarah nodded, her eyes open wide.

"I don't think it's anything to be concerned about," Steve gently told her. "Apparently, for whatever reason, Luther decided to expand the garage. I'm not going to argue. How cool is that?"

Sarah took another look around their property and suddenly clutched Steve's arm. "That's what is different. The garage is sitting farther away from the manor. Look at the driveway!"

Surprised, Steve's mouth fell open. "Since when did it run between the manor and the garage?"

Looking closely, he could see that it wasn't the same building. Luther must have torn down the old garage and rebuilt this larger one, only he had situated it very differently.

"Why would he have angled the driveway to the north?" Steve wondered aloud. "The only thing that way is the Jensen's property. All fifty acres of it."

The Jensens were an old retired couple who had purchased the land adjacent to theirs but had never done anything with it. Steve had tried to persuade the senior citizens to sell him the land, but they had stubbornly refused. Why would the driveway be headed straight toward their property?

Sarah walked over to the garage and peered in. She whistled with amazement and motioned for Steve to come over. "Look! Those last two doors are just for show. There's a little apartment in there."

Husband and wife silently toured the small. but elegantly furnished apartment. Steve eyed his wife. "Why is this here? Who would we put out here?"

"Not us," Sarah corrected. "Luther. What do you want to bet he put Mina out here?"

Steve nodded thoughtfully. "That makes sense. Wow. I wonder what else has changed."

"Besides having an apartment in our garage and our driveway heading in the wrong direction? Who knows!"

"I sure as hell would like to figure that out," Steve commented, as he pulled the door to the apartment closed. "I wonder why this apartment is still here. It would suggest someone has been using it."

Sarah pulled him back toward their house. "Do we have an Idaho history book? I'd love to see what else might have changed with Coeur d'Alene."

Sarah pushed open the front door and headed for the stairs. She ascended to the second level and headed straight for the large room that housed well over two thousand books. Steve was right on her heels.

"I know I've seen an Idaho history book in here before," Steve muttered, approaching the closest shelf, and running his fingers along the many tomes.

Sarah took an opposite wall. "I think you're right. I've seen one, too. However, who knows where it is now? Or even if we still have it? It could be … Hold up! I found it!"

Sarah pulled a large coffee table book from a shelf with similarly sized hardcover books, and headed toward the closest sofa. She placed the book on the small table before her and opened the cover. She gasped with shock as she slowly pulled out an envelope.

"What's that?" Steve wanted to know, sitting down next to her. "What do you have there?"

She showed him. "Let's see what it is."

Sarah carefully opened the yellowing envelope and extracted a thick piece of paper. She opened it and began to read aloud.

My dearest Steve and Sarah,

If you're reading this, I will have to admit that my beloved Cora was right. She believed the two of you would probably have many questions and, as such, go looking for answers. Where, then, would we expect you to find them? Where else but a history book? I purchased this book the instant I saw it on the shelf. I wanted my library to include this invaluable resource. It was Cora's suggestion to place this letter inside.

Allow me to tell you some of what has transpired since you and Sarah returned to your time. As we expected, the sheriff was quickly replaced by a new sheriff. Hank. He has performed admirably and has continued to do so until his retirement last year.

The sheriff's compound up at Jackknife Peak burned to the ground the day you rescued your lovely wife from Bixby's clutches. The city has since decided to turn the entire compound into a wildlife sanctuary. The townsfolk were so thankful that Sheriff Bixby was gone that no one put up a fuss regarding the decision to quietly usurp the sheriff's lands back into the city's and turn it into a park.

Please tell Miss Sarah that her ploy to make people believe the manor was haunted worked! No one wants to venture this far east. Not unless they have to. Do you know what? Cora and I wouldn't have it any other way. For two people who enjoy their privacy, I will say that this arrangement has worked out splendidly.

Sarah sniffed loudly and wiped a tear from her eye.

I should also tell you about Mina. We set up a room for her in the stable. I know what you're thinking. The manor is huge. Why not give her a room? Well, I tried. Cora tried. Mina wouldn't have it. She didn't want to feel as though she were intruding. So, after careful consideration, and an unfortunate misunderstanding of how to light a stove, it was decided to tear down the old stable and build a new one. I remember you telling me that the stable was still standing in your time. I didn't want you or Sarah to be inconvenienced by my decision to put Mina out in the stable so we increased the size to accommodate her quarters while leaving the number of stalls at four.

Once again, I want to extend my thanks for helping me complete my mission. By doing so, you have freed my conscience so that I may devote all my energy to being a good husband and the best father that I can be. Cora gave birth to a strapping son the following summer. I have taught him all about his father's homeland and I hope to someday take him there so he can see for himself what wonders the kingdom of Lentari can hold.

Live well, my friends!

Luther Miller

PS. How many things have been denied one day, only to become realities the next!

Sarah refolded the paper and slid it back into the envelope. "So Rosamund was right. From the sounds of it, Hank made a great sheriff."

Steve was frowning. "What an odd thing to say at the end of his letter."

"What? Why do you say that?"

"It's a famous quote from an H.G. Wells book. *From the Earth to the Moon.* You know what? That was the last thing Luther ever told me."

Sarah stared at him with a confused look on her face. "The last thing he said was the name of a book?"

Steve slowly looked around the library and the many shelves full of books. "What do you want to bet he has a copy of that book somewhere in here? Doesn't it sound like he wants us to find it?"

Sarah got to her feet. "Alright. I'll help you look in exchange for a fifteen-minute back massage."

"Five."

"Fourteen."

"That's not how you negotiate, dear," Steve told her. "You should have said ten."

"Fourteen," Sarah repeated.

Steve scowled. "Ten."

"Thirteen."

"I don't like this game."

"Want me to go back to fifteen?"

Steve threw up his hands in defeat. "Fine. Thirteen."

Sarah smiled victoriously and moved to a mahogany bookcase to begin perusing the titles. After a few minutes, she gave a shout of triumph. She tapped a thick, leatherbound volume on the second shelf from the top and started to pull it out, but the huge book stopped after a few inches. Surprised, Sarah let go of the book and watched as it gently settled back into place on the shelf.

They both heard a loud click and felt the floor start to rumble. After a few seconds, the rumbling stopped. Sarah pointed at a thick shaggy rug in the far-left corner of the room. The rug looked as though it was being pulled down from below. Steve hurried to it and slid the heavy rug off to the side. A dark, five-foot-diameter hole met their eyes. Steve pointed at the opening and stared at Sarah in utter astonishment.

"How many times have I seen that circular stone mosaic thingy on the floor and wondered why it was there?" Steve demanded. "How could we have missed this? I mean, what's directly under this room?"

Sarah thought for a moment. "This is the northeastern section of the house. Directly under us is your office, but your office isn't as big as the library. That's why we never noticed it before."

"What if Luther installed it after we left?"

Sarah shook her head. "You said it yourself. You've seen that design on the floor before. There are so many rugs in here that we usually don't give them any thought."

Steve lit his hands and slowly descended the tight spiral steps. Sarah placed a hand firmly on his back and followed him down. Once they had descended well past the first floor, the stairs abruptly ended in an immense basement. Steve held his lit hands near the wall and waited for Sarah to find the light switch. After a few moments there was a loud click and several of the oldest light bulbs Steve had ever laid eyes on lit up.

For the first time ever, they were standing in the manor's basement. Judging from the amount of dust in the room, the last person to have come down here was probably Luther himself. Three large, old fashioned wardrobes sat silently against one wall. A dozen trunks were stacked against another. They could see several objects covered by dusty tarps. Sitting directly in the middle of the room was a large object that had to be at least fifteen feet long and maybe eight feet wide. It, too, was covered by old, musty blankets.

Steve reached for the closest sheet, which happened to be draped over something that was standing upright. A statue? Steve gave the sheet a good yank and immediately covered his nose. He fanned away the dust in the air and waited as it settled. It was a suit of armor. Steve's eyes glanced around the room and spotted three other suits of armor.

His eyes were drawn to the large object in the middle of the room. He pulled one corner up and then whistled with admiration. It was the ornately carved griffin-dining table that Sarah had admired before. What it was doing down in the basement was beyond him. For that matter, how had they moved something this big down here? There had to be another way into this room, Steve surmised.

Sarah gave a tiny squeal of delight. She had opened one of the wardrobes and discovered Cora had saved her dresses. All of them, judging from the existence of the other two wardrobes. There they were, all hanging in pristine, albeit dusty, condition.

"Thank you, Cora," Sarah softly muttered.

Steve opened one of the trunks. His eyes widened. He gazed at the contents for a few seconds before closing the lid and moving to the next. He repeated his inspection on five other trunks before he was satisfied with what he had seen.

"What's in there?" Sarah wanted to know.

Steve ran a shaky hand through his hair. "Ingots. Gold ingots. I'd say we now know where Luther put his gold."

Sarah gazed with wonder at the trunks lining the wall. "They *all* have gold ingots in them?"

"Each one I checked did," Steve confirmed. "This is gonna be one mother of a weekend project."

Sarah nodded, as she eyed the room and all its treasures. She looked back at Steve, looked up at the floors above them, and smiled.

Sarah walked over to one of the walls and saw that a large picture was covered by a cloth. She carefully pulled the cloth away from the frame. Steve appeared by her side and gently wrapped his arms around her. It was a family portrait. Luther was sitting stiffly at attention in a chair while Cora stood proudly just behind him. Cradling a baby. The placard identified the Miller Family: Luther, Cora, and *Stephen*.

Author's Note

I certainly hoped you liked the two-part 'Portal' mini-series. Honestly, guys, I've never had two books flow so well for me before. As you know, *A Portal for Your Thoughts* was never supposed to be a two-parter. I just couldn't help myself. I kept getting ideas. I'd talk to my wife and together we'd say, "Wouldn't it be cool to do this, or that?"

In this manner chapters were created. Those chapters inspired others and before I knew it, I had hit the hundred-thousand-word mark and I was nowhere close to resolving anything. Therefore, I ended *A Portal for Your Thoughts* at (what I hoped was) a suitable place and began working on its sequel. I've never written anything with a cliffhanger before, so I hope you still don't feel any animosity toward me for doing so. :)

Now that you've finished *Thoughts for a Portal* you may be asking what's next for Lentari. Will I give any hints about what the next book will be about? Well, I suppose I can. Let's just say that a certain renegade wizard has traipsed about long enough without atoning for his actions. It's time to find out who this person really is. Don't miss *Wizard in the Woods* (Tales of Lentari #5).

Thank you very much for continuing to follow along with the adventures of Steve and the gang as they roam about Lentari. Keep an eye on the blog as you never know when I'll ask to see if anyone would like to name a fictitious character. If you haven't done so already, please sign up for the Daily Scroll. It's the only newsletter that I send out, so if you want to make sure you don't ever miss another book launch, or would like to hear about when I start contests, or offer additional insight into Lentari and its characters, please sign up today. You'll be glad that you did!

As always, if you would ever like to help an author, please leave me a review for the book wherever you purchased it.

Wondering what to read next? If you like my books, then

I would suggest checking out the following books:

The Emperor's Edge, by Lindsay Buroker. This is a wonderful series that introduced me to steampunk!

Klondaeg — the Monster Killer, by Steve Thomas. Klondaeg is a fearless monster killer that travels abroad to slay any and all monsters with his dual personality talking battle ax!

The Blue Moon Detective series, by JH Sked. Seriously. How can you go wrong with a witty detective series that features a were-cat, ghost, and a vampire all working together?

The Dragon Blade series, by J.D. Hallowell. I love reading about dragons. This one was very well-written and features a man accidentally bonding with a dragon.

Hemlock and the Wizard's Tower, by B. Throwsnaill. Join Hemlock as she tries to break into the one place everyone says can't be broken into. Merit for president. :)

From a Far Land, by G. David Walker. Follow along with Jason as he has the adventure of a lifetime!

I've personally read each and every single one of these books. They are all indie authors, and all are worthy additions to any library. I keep an active eye on my blog, as well as my Facebook account, so if anyone would like to stop by and say hello, I'll definitely say hello back!

If you'd like to follow the progress on the latest book I'm working on, then I would encourage you to sign up for my newsletter so you'll never miss another book release, or contest, or any other bit of news that I pass along to the readers. You'll even get a free short story for signing up!

The Daily Scroll: http://www.lentari.com/?page_id=1900

I'll see you all back in Lentari!

J.

PS. Keep reading if you'd like to see who's responsible for naming certain characters!

Fan Submissions

Any fan of Lentari is officially an honorary citizen. Trust me. These fans went above and beyond the call of duty and submitted the following names:

Erik Munson — Leanna, Bertol, Torya, Eslac
Toni Trick — Tessler
April Enos — Graylan, Ruskin, Quinn
Gunnar Kristjansson — Gunnar
Derek Pritchard — Breet
Brett Gable — Melvyn, Fensham, Zevern, Merrith
Rachel Gardner — Tyril, Ruan
Duncan Wheatley — Duncan
Kendall Davis — Hattie
Deb Shapiro — Brent
Heather Doyle — Gabriel
Tina Batson — Calin
Claire Jones — Selwyn, Aislinn, Jonquil

Jeffrey M. Poole is a professional writer who writes in both the fantasy and mystery genres. His series are listed below. Jeffrey lives in picturesque Southern Oregon, with his wife, Giliane, and their Welsh Corgi, Kinsey. His interests include archery, astronomy, archaeology, scuba diving, collecting movies, collecting swords, and tinkering with any electronic gadget he can get his hands on.

In March, 2015, Jeffrey became a proud member of SFWA, the Science Fiction & Fantasy Writers of America! Jeffrey encourages readers to connect with him on Facebook (facebook.com/bakkianchronicles). Fans can also follow him online and sign up for his newsletter at authorjmpoole. com. Scan the QR code to get started!

BOOKS BY JEFFREY POOLE

Epic Fantasy
BAKKIAN CHRONICLES
The Prophecy
Insurrection
Amulet of Aria
Disneyland Debacle (short story)
Winter Wonderland (short story)

TALES OF LENTARI
Lost City
Something Wyverian This Way Comes
A Portal for Your Thoughts
Thoughts for A Portal
Wizard in the Woods
Close Encounters of the Magical Kind
The Hunt for Red Oskorlisk (short story)
May the Fang be With You (Pirates trilogy #1)
The Hammer is Strong with This One (Pirates #2)
These are Not the Stones You're Looking For (Pirates #3)
Blast from the Past

DRAGONS OF ANDELA
Harness the Fire
Strike the Spark
*Clear the Water**